Whiter than White

G.G. CARVER

Createspace Edition

CHAPTER ONE

'You can go for your lunch now, Elena.'

Elena raised her eyes to the oversized black-and-silver clock that hung above the main entrance to the bank.

'But it's only eleven o'clock, Dawn.'

Dawn: a first-class, top-of-the-tree mega-bitch and the manager of the bank.

It wasn't just Elena's life she made hell, it was every member of staff.

'Well, Tim's not here to cover, is he? So it's eleven o'clock or not at all.' She spoke like a headmistress scolding a naughty child.

'Oh right,' replied Elena in the tone of a child that *had* been naughty.

'And make sure you're back by twelve.'

With that last verbal slap in the face, Dawn spun her hefty frame around on her heels and marched back to her office.

Elena grabbed her bag from the staffroom, pushed open the large glass door, and left the cool air-conditioned calm of the bank to join the hot noisy hustle and bustle of the High Street. She drifted along with the current of people, heading towards a coffee shop, and managed to grab a small table by the window of the café, much to the annoyance of a middle-aged couple also competing for it.

She placed her slightly spilt latte—from her dash to get the last spot—on the table, along with a blueberry muffin. She took her book and reading glasses from her black patent bag and sat back with a relaxed sigh.

She hadn't got to the bottom of the page when her peace was interrupted.

'Elena? Elena White! Oh my god! Elena White, how are you?'

Elena's head popped up from behind her book, and she glanced around the coffee shop like a meerkat scouting for trouble.

Heading towards her was a beautiful woman with long raven hair, olive skin, and big brown eyes so dark they were almost black. She was immaculately dressed in a black tailored shift dress, holding a clutch bag in one hand and coffee to-go in the other.

It took Elena a few seconds before she remembered who the mystery woman was.

'Jasmine Saunders. Oh my word, I'm sorry I didn't recognise you for a moment. You look fantastic. How are you?'

Jasmine gave her a beaming smile. 'I'm fine, thank you. I almost didn't recognise you with those glasses on.'

Elena self-consciously removed her glasses and placed them beside her book. She felt decidedly plain with her hair tied back and very little makeup on, especially when looking at the glamour puss standing before her.

'There's no mistaking that beautiful red hair of yours. How long has it been? Eleven years since we last saw each other?'

'Yes, I suppose it must be. It's almost eleven years since we left school. Oh my god, where did that go?'

'I know,' replied Jasmine as she slid elegantly into the vacant chair opposite Elena. 'I can't stay long. I've got an appointment at Bo Bo's to have my hair and nails done.'

Bloody hell! Bo Bo's? That would cost a week's wages for me, Elena thought.

'So where are you working at the moment?' Elena asked casually as she stirred her coffee.

'Well, I'm . . . a sort of self-employed personal assistant at the moment. How about you?'

'I work at the bank, in the High Street. It's . . . er . . . it's okay.'

It wasn't okay. It wasn't okay at all. She hated her job, and she hated that she devil bitch, Dawn.

'Listen, honey, I've got to go. I'm already late for my appointment. Give me your number and we'll go for a drink and catch up, yeah?'

'Yes, that sounds lovely.' Elena jotted her number down on a napkin.

'I'm busy all week, but I'm free on Thursday. How's Thursday for you?'

'Thursday's good for me, yep.' Elena tried to emulate Jasmine's confidence.

The truth was any day was fine. Any day, of any week, of any month.

'Okay, honey, I'll ring before Thursday.'

With that, Jasmine leaned over and kissed Elena on both cheeks then strode out of the coffee shop, flicking her glossy black hair over her shoulder as she went, leaving a fragrance of expensive perfume.

She didn't go unnoticed by virtually the whole of the shop, especially the male customers. Jasmine had an air of confidence and beauty that commanded attention.

Elena sat there puzzled. She and Jasmine hadn't been best friends at school. Yes, they knew each other, but they moved in different circles. Jasmine had been the girl all the boys wanted, was always picked first for sports, and always got the lead role in the school play. Elena never got to be in the school play, and she was always one of the last to be picked for sports, and she certainly hadn't been popular with the boys.

But as she sat there reminiscing about those old school days, Elena remembered that Jasmine had been one of the few who hadn't teased her about her red hair, as many so-called friends had. Jasmine had been a beautiful, intelligent, confident girl at school, but she also had a very caring nature. And now she wanted to go for a drink with Elena. *It might be eleven years too late, but I'm finally in with the in crowd.*

Elena sat awkwardly at the bar with her glass of white wine. She hadn't been out for ages, and it felt as if all eyes were on her because she was on her own. She glanced at her watch for the fourth time in five minutes. Seven fifty. Elena checked the text message she had received from Jasmine just to confirm to herself that she wasn't too early or too late, although she already knew what it said:

Hi, honey, let's meet at Transitions in town, say 7:30. Jasmine x.

Elena slipped her phone back into her bag.

She could just about see the entrance to the bar through the growing crowd of people.

Elena noticed the giant doorman open the glass door and bend to give a welcome kiss to the lady entering: Jasmine. She entered the bar, and the doorman turned to admire her rear view. His eyes narrowed, and he puckered his lips as he scanned her from head to toe.

Elena watched as Jasmine floated from one person to another, greeting them with a big smile and kisses to both cheeks. She chatted briefly and then moved on to the next person like a social butterfly.

Elena began to worry that Jasmine had forgotten she was meeting her there.

'Hi, Elena. Sorry I'm late. I couldn't do a thing with my hair tonight.'

Jasmine looked perfect, with a dark blue pencil skirt and crisp white fitted blouse, her hair tied loosely at the back, very business-like, very, very sexy.

'That's okay. I've only just got here myself actually,' Elena said nonchalantly.

'Wow, look at you! Elena, you look fantastic. Your hair's beautiful. Turn around.'

Elena turned around reluctantly to reveal the beautiful mane of autumn and sunset red hair, which flowed down her back in gentle waves, ending with perfect spirals.

'Honey, you look gorgeous. It's so nice to see you again after all this time. Now what are you drinking?'

'I've just got white wine,' said Elena.

'White wine? Maybe on a Monday night after work but not on a Thursday night. It's Friday eve!'

Jasmine sat next to Elena and waved her hand in the air as if she was hailing a cab. 'Barman, we'll have two apple martinis to begin with, please.'

She turned back to face Elena. 'Now tell me everything that's happened in the last eleven years.'

After two Cosmopolitans, a Mojito, and rather lovely Kir Royale, Elena was suitably tipsy. She couldn't remember when she had enjoyed an evening so much. The last time she'd had a drink, it had been a glass of Baileys to toast the New Year in with her mother—nine months ago.

Jasmine was fun to be with. Her confidence was infectious, and in a funny way, it made Elena feel more confident too, although that may have been the last five cocktails. She felt comfortable with Jasmine as though they had been friends for years. Elena didn't feel self-conscious like she usually did with other people.

As the evening progressed, the two friends talked about everything from old school friends to old boyfriends, both of them oblivious to the admiring stares from the male clientele.

'How long have you worked at the bank?' asked Jasmine.

'I've been there nearly two and a half years now.'

'And what's your role there?'

Elena blew out a large puff of air and rolled her eyes. 'General dogsbody at the moment. Before I worked at the bank, I had a job with Whitehouse and Finch, an independent financial services company.' She paused to drink the remainder of her glass. 'It started out great. I would go out to see clients with one of the financial advisers to get some experience of the way things worked. They were paying for all my training and exams, and with each successful exam passed, I got a raise in salary. Once I was fully qualified, there would also be a company car.'

'So what happened? Exams too tough?' asked Jasmine while she hailed the barman yet again.

'No, no. The first exam went really well. The exams weren't the problem. It was my boss's hands on my backside every time he passed me at the photocopier, or the coffee machine, or anytime he felt like it really.'

'What an arsehole,' frowned Jasmine, which turned to a friendly smile as she ordered more drinks from the barman. 'Same again, please, honey.'

She turned back to face Elena, the smile returned to a concerned frown. 'What did you do?'

Elena ran her fingers through her hair and shook her head. 'It was such a good job that I hoped it would just stop if I didn't react to it, but of course, it didn't. It made me ill. I couldn't sleep, I wasn't eating. I'd panic every time he entered the office. Then one day I'd had enough, I couldn't stand it anymore. So I told him, calmly but firmly, that I didn't like it and I wasn't interested. That was the beginning of the end of my career at Whitehouse and Finch.' Elena shrugged. 'Then, eventually, I got a job at the bank with a promise of picking up where I left off once an opportunity became available.'

'So are you training as a financial adviser with the bank?' Jasmine's dark eyebrows rose towards her perfectly styled fringe.

'No. And as long as Dawn, the manager of the bank, has a say in it, I never will. I can't do right from wrong: If I talk to a male customer for too long, I'm flirting. If I talk to a female customer for too long, I'm gossiping.' She paused and gave the barman a kind smile as he placed their drinks down. 'I'm barely keeping my head above water financially. It's crap.'

She reached for her cocktail glass with a heavy sigh. Jasmine placed her elbow on the bar and rested her head on her hand, her big brown eyes narrowed, and her manicured fingers tapped on her full red lips as though she was deep in thought.

'What're you thinking?' Elena was puzzled by her expression.

Jasmine held the cocktail glass to her mouth for a moment before taking a sip then placed the glass back on the bar.

'After a run of failed relationships with men my own age, I wondered what it would be like with an older, more mature man, someone who didn't own an Xbox or a bloody PlayStation.' Elena laughed as Jasmine rolled her eyes. 'So I decided I would ask the all-wise and powerful Google to find me an older man. I registered with a few online dating sites. Some of them were good, some not so good. But there was one site that I seemed to get the most intriguing messages from, called Daddy Daddy Sugar.'

Elena's jaw dropped, and her eyes were wide open. 'You are joking!'

'I know, I know,' said Jasmine, holding her palm up as if she were stopping traffic. 'But I thought, what the hell, I'm just going to go with it and see what happens.'

'And what did happen?' Elena encouraged her to continue.

'I've seen eight men so far, and I've had a brief sexual relationship with two of those.'

'And are you seeing anyone at the moment?' Elena was dying to know more.

'Yes. His name's Marcus, and I've been seeing him for almost a year now.'

'A year? Getting serious.' Jasmine gave a tentative smile.

'When Marcus first contacted me, we exchanged e-mails and we Skyped. Eventually, we arranged to meet. We had dinner together and got on really well. I saw him a few more times, and one day, he said he had to go to Prague on business just for a couple of days and would I like to go with him. So after giving it some thought, I went to Prague. We had a lovely time. Have you ever been?'

'No, I haven't.'

'It's a beautiful city.' Jasmine crossed her tanned legs and brushed her fringe away from her eyes. She moved with the grace and poise of a ballet dancer and had a certain allure about her. 'That's where we first slept together, and on our flight back home, he made me a proposition. He knew that I was still receiving messages from other guys, and he hated that. So he asked me if I would remove myself from the site and see him exclusively whenever he wanted. In return, I get a new apartment, a convertible Mercedes SLK, and a monthly allowance. He takes care of me, and I take care of him.'

Elena hadn't thought she was *that* kind of PA. But then again, she wasn't as surprised as she should have been. Jasmine seemed like a girl who knew what she wanted in life and how to get it.

'Wow! I didn't expect that. Is he married?' Elena was intrigued.

'Yes, he's married to some dry old bag who went off sex years ago. All she's interested in is her beloved poodles and shoes. He can't divorce because she would take half of the business and clean him out, so they lead virtually separate lives.'

'Does she know about you?'

'Now that would be grounds for divorce, so no, she definitely doesn't know about me.' Jasmine paused. 'Do you think I'm just a rich man's plaything?' She stared straight into Elena's eyes and watched her closely.

'No, of course not.' Elena reached out and touched Jasmine's hand, sensing that she was somehow seeking her approval.

'It's not all about sex. Very often, the evening doesn't end with us having sex, and I don't have to do anything I don't want to. These men have their cars, houses, and yachts, private jets even. The one thing they don't have is their youth, but with a beautiful young girl on their arm, they feel thirty years younger. They forget they're fifty-seven, and once again, they're buying flowers and sexy lingerie.'

Elena was shocked at how open Jasmine was being after only a few hours, or maybe it was common knowledge amongst her friends. She certainly wasn't a shy girl.

'Do you love him?' Elena probed.

'I respect him. He's kind and considerate, and we have a great time when we're together. I know this sounds odd, but because love isn't an issue, there's no pressure, none of the insecurities you usually have in a relationship.'

'What do you mean no pressure?' Elena was fascinated by the whole story.

'Oh you know—where is he? Why hasn't he called? Who's he on the phone to?' Jasmine's head tipped from side to side as she spoke. 'None of it was planned, it just happened. So I'm going to go with it and see where it takes me.'

'You're so brave. I wish I had half your confidence.' Elena reached for her drink, and Jasmine leaned forwards and gently tapped her index finger on Elena's nose. 'And that's where my story leads me.'

'What do you mean?'

'Elena, look at you. You can do whatever you want. Life's there for the taking. You just have to take charge. *You* control your own destiny. You need to break out of the daily monotony. You need some excitement. And that's why we're going to register you with Daddy Daddy

Sugar.'

Elena almost spat her drink all over Jasmine. 'Me? Don't be silly.'

'Why not?' Jasmine's hands flew out to the sides.

'Because . . . I . . . I . . .' Jasmine had caught her off guard. She didn't quite know what to say.

Jasmine interrupted before she could think of an excuse. 'Because everything's great at the moment? That's not what you've been telling me tonight.'

'But I'm not like you. You're glamorous, and confident, and I'm just . . . oh, I don't know.' Elena's eyes diverted to the floor.

'Stuck in a rut?' Jasmine peered at her with her head bowed down, as if she were looking over a pair of glasses. 'You don't have the confidence because you live a mundane life.'

'Oh, thanks, mate.' She was slightly offended by Jasmine's bluntness.

'Honey, I'm only telling you what you already know. Working nine to five at a job you hate, told what to do, what to wear, when you can go for a break, just about making ends meet—all that takes its toll. I don't mean to offend. I think you're lovely and you deserve better. And you *can* have better.'

Elena couldn't pretend what Jasmine had just said wasn't true. Her daily life had become pretty mundane. When you did something for long enough, it just became normal after a while. She massaged her temple. How had things got so crap? She'd been on autopilot for what seemed like forever.

Jasmine reached out and took Elena's hand with a warm smile. 'Honey, look at you. Beautiful red hair, ivory skin, a body to die for, and the greenest bloody eyes I've ever seen. You've got everything you'll ever need.'

Elena's lips curved into a smile as her cheeks flushed.

'Okay here's what I think you should do. Say to yourself, "I'm going to step out of my comfort zone for the next two months and try some new things in life. I'm going to try to be more assertive and confident to get *my* way a little more often and not give in to other people's will." If you're not happy with the way things are going, you can just go back to the way things were. But you won't.'

Elena couldn't believe she was actually considering Jasmine's suggestion. It must be the drink. Jasmine sat and watched as Elena mulled things over, pressing her palms together, her index fingers touching her lips, as if she were praying.

'Why don't you come 'round to my place on Sunday, and we'll get you registered and online?'

Elena bit her lip.

'Trust me, it will be fun, and all you have to do is answer some admiring e-mails. You don't have to do anything you don't want to.'

Jasmine waited with an expectant look on her face. Elena took a deep breath, her inhibitions low from the cocktails. 'Oh, sod it! What time on Sunday?'

A big smile spread across Jasmine's face and revealed her perfect white teeth. 'That's my girl. You won't regret it. I've got a workout session with my personnel trainer on Sunday. So if we say six o'clock?'

'Six it is.'

'I'll text you my address later.' Jasmine held up her half-empty cocktail glass. 'To exciting new beginnings!'

Elena raised her glass. 'To new beginnings!'

The two friends walked through the bar arm in arm, heading for their waiting taxi.

Elena walked taller, held her head higher. She felt a surge of inspiration and excitement as if Jasmine had woken her from a deep sleep. Woken her to discover that the world *is* her oyster.

As they exited the bar through the glass doors, Elena felt like the name above the door; she too was at the beginning of her transition.

CHAPTER TWO

Elena pulled up at large black cast-iron gates, which sat between two colossal brick pillars. Beyond the bars, she could see the subtly lit building. *This was it. Grosvenor Court. Wow!*

Elena wound down the car window and pressed number 25 on the intercom.

'Hello?' Jasmine answered in her usual upbeat way.

'Hi, Jasmine, it's Elena,' she shouted at the intercom.

'Hi, honey. I'm on the fifth floor. I'll buzz you in.'

The mighty gates slid open silently. Elena drove in and parked her old red VW Golf between a shiny black Porsche and a convertible BMW. Her car door squeaked as she opened it carefully, making sure it didn't get anywhere near the black Porsche.

'Please don't tow my car away,' she said to herself as she looked around at all the luxury cars.

Elena entered the apartment block through the black double doors. Her solitary footsteps on the glistening white-tiled floor echoed off the contemporary curved timber panels of the impressive lobby. *This place must cost a fortune.*

She entered the elevator, which was mirrored floor to

ceiling, and pressed the fifth-floor button. Elena examined her appearance, feeling very underdressed to be in such a stylish building in her faded jeans and tight black T-shirt. The elevator pinged, and the doors opened onto a plush cream carpet; five high-gloss black doors were embedded in the white walls. A row of square flushed wall lights just above the skirting board gave the space a sultry feel.

She stepped over to number 25, and just as she was about to press the doorbell, Jasmine, wearing a towel on her head and a white fluffy bathrobe that finished just above the knee, opened the door. They said their hellos and exchanged kisses.

'Come in. I've only just got back from my workout with Anton. He has the body of Adonis, but the inclinations of Liberace. What a waste.'

Elena followed Jasmine into the stylish lounge. Two ivory lounge suites, decorated with brown and grey cushions, were positioned in front of the fireplace facing each other, separated by a large glass-topped coffee table. Everything looked very expensive and as if it had just been delivered that very day. The whole place smelled new, mixed with perfume and flowers.

'Make yourself at home. I'll just get changed.'

'Thanks. It's a beautiful place you've got here,' Elena shouted towards the bedroom.

'It's a bit on the small side for me now, so I may be moving to somewhere bigger soon,' Jasmine called back. Elena mouthed *small?* to herself as she looked around the spacious room.

Jasmine returned, dressed casually in grey leggings and a long white T-shirt, her hair tied back in a ponytail. She disappeared into the kitchen and, a moment later, reappeared in the doorway and held up a bottle of red wine in one hand and a bottle of Martini in the other.

'Drink?' She gently shook both bottles.

'I'll just have tea, thanks.' Jasmine pulled a sad face. 'I'm driving.' Elena screwed up her nose.

'Okay, honey. Do you take sugar?'

'No, thanks.'

Elena looked around the room while Jasmine sang to herself in the kitchen. She wandered over to an oblong occasional table below a large black-and-white picture of Paris and the Eiffel Tower. There was an assortment of picture frames of various sizes placed in a cluster on the table between two ornate lamps.

Jasmine glided into the lounge carrying her Apple Mac and a plate filled with an assortment of cheese, crackers, breadsticks, and grapes. 'Nibbles?'

'Oh lovely. Thank you.'

Elena held a silver photo frame with a black-and-white picture of a grey-haired gentleman. 'Is this Marcus?'

Jasmine glanced at the photo as she headed back into the kitchen. 'Yes, that's Marcus.'

'He's very distinguished-looking.' Elena placed the photo back in its original position.

Jasmine returned to the lounge, humming to herself as she carried a glass of red wine and Elena's cup of tea. 'He's a sweetie. Help yourself. Are you sure you won't join me for a teeny-weeny glass of wine?' squeaked Jasmine in a silly voice.

'What are you like?' Elena laughed. 'Only if it's a teeny-weeny one then.'

The two friends chatted for a while as they ate. Elena looked with dread at the laptop sitting there on the coffee table as though it was a snarling dog waiting to pounce.

'Right, down to business.' Jasmine sat next to Elena on the lounge suite, opened the Apple Mac, and placed it on Elena's lap. Her big green eyes sparkled as the screen illuminated her face.

She swallowed hard. 'Jasmine . . .' Hesitancy laced her voice.

'Oh no, you don't, missy.' Jasmine smiled, knowing full well what Elena was about to say. 'It'll be fun, I promise, and if it's not, you don't have to speak to me ever again.'

Elena took a deep breath. 'Okay, where do we start?'

'First of all, I'll show you the website, and then we'll take some photos of you to upload onto the site.'

Elena started to panic. 'Photos? But look at the state of me.'

'Don't worry, your fairy godmother is here.' Jasmine waved a breadstick in the air as if it were a magic wand. 'And by the way, you look absolutely fine.'

'You fruitcake!' Elena tittered.

'So first, let's do your hair and makeup.' Jasmine stood and held out her hand.

Elena placed the laptop on the coffee table, took Jasmine's hand, and followed her into the en suite bathroom. She sat in just her underwear with a towel around her, her back to the mirror, while Jasmine did her makeup and refused to let her see until she was dressed. She felt like a little girl putting on Mummy's makeup to play dressing-up.

Once Jasmine had finished, they moved to the bedroom, and a long fur coat was placed over the full-length mirror to stop Elena from peeking. Jasmine entered her walk-in wardrobe and was swallowed up by a hoard of clothes. She returned with an armful of dresses and placed them on the bed.

'These should fit. You're about the same size as me, although you've got bigger tits.'

'Have I?' Elena glanced down with her hands on her breasts.

'God yeah, look at them! Bitch!' Jasmine smirked. Elena laughed. 'Let's try the green one first. It will go with your eyes. And no peeking in the mirror until I say, okay?'

'Oh no, of course not.' Elena couldn't keep the sarcasm from her voice.

'I mean it, lady!' Jasmine waggled a finger at her.

Seven changes and a teeny-weeny glass of red wine later, Jasmine still couldn't decide which dress Elena should wear.

'One more. Try this one.' Jasmine handed Elena a black cocktail dress.

Elena unzipped it and noticed the label—Christian Dior. *This dress probably cost more than I earn in a month.* She slipped the dress on and turned to Jasmine to zip her up.

'Turn around. Let's have a look.' Elena turned. Jasmine stood back and inspected her from head to toe. 'Honey, you look stunning, absolutely stunning.'

She held out her hand. 'Close your eyes.' She led Elena the few steps to the full-length mirror and removed the coat from it. 'Ready?'

'Yes.'

'Open your eyes.'

Elena looked in the mirror. Her whole body jolted with surprise. Was that really her reflection? She took a step closer to examine the beautiful woman in the mirror. Her full dark red lips and long black lashes accentuated her green eyes. Her red hair cascaded over her shoulders and down her back, highlighting her pearly skin.

The black cocktail dress looked like it had been made to measure; the deep V neckline teasingly gave a sample of her full round breasts and ample cleavage. It hugged her small waist and clung to her perfectly round pert bottom.

'You look fucking gorgeous!' uttered Jasmine with her hand on her cheek.

Elena's eyes filled with tears. She did look gorgeous, elegant, beautiful—sexy.

'Hey, what's wrong?'

'I'm sorry, Jasmine. It's been a long time since I've felt this good.' Elena turned to Jasmine and held both her hands tightly. 'Thank you.'

'Don't be silly. You don't have to thank me. Just don't ruin your bloody makeup, madam!' Jasmine gave her a big hug. 'Look, you're starting me off now.'

She bent down to her bedside cabinet and took out a long black box. 'There's just one thing missing.' She opened the box and took out a delicate gold chain with a single pearl hanging from it.

'Turn around, honey.' Jasmine attached the necklace, which hung beautifully around Elena's neck. The pearl sat just above her cleavage. 'Perfect.' Jasmine nodded.

One hour and twelve photos later, they finally settled on which two pictures to use.

'There you go, all done. Your picture and details are now floating through cyberspace, all over the world.' Jasmine closed the laptop.

'So what happens now?' Elena bit her lip and placed her hand over her mouth.

'Well, in the next day or two, you should get some e-mails, and the way you look in those photos, your inbox is going to be red hot. And that's not the only box that's going to be red hot either!'

'Jasmine!'

'I'm sorry.' She laughed. 'That was very crude of me.' She giggled into her wine glass.

'Jasmine Saunders, you're nothing but trouble.' Elena shook her head.

'Who me?' she said teasingly with a wry smile. 'Why, I don't know what you mean, Elena White.'

Elena drove home with a positive glow about her. Jasmine was lovely, and her self-assured zest for life was infectious. Hopefully, some of it would rub off on her. She was a little apprehensive about Internet dating, but like Jasmine said, she was the one in control—wasn't she?

CHAPTER THREE

BEEP! BEEP! BEEP! BEEP! Elena shot her arm out from under the duvet and pressed frantically at the alarm clock and rolled onto her back.

'Is it really Monday already?' she groaned.

Showered and dressed, she went down stairs for breakfast. Elena sat at the table staring into her cornflakes. She wasn't a morning person at the best of times, and in the cold light of day, the thought of what she had embarked upon last night made her cringe. *What was I thinking?*

She glanced at the time on her phone, which sat on the table next to her now soggy cornflakes. 'Shit, I'm going to be late!'

Elena grabbed her keys and bag and rushed out of the front door, leaving her phone on the table. She drove the usual congested route to work, trying to think of a way to tell Jasmine that she was revoking her two-month life-changing plan, starting with the website.

She arrived at work on time by the skin of her teeth, threw her bag into the staffroom, and headed straight to the banking hall, where she was a customer meet-and-greet for the day.

The morning dragged along with its usual customer problems and complaints. Elena had just finished dealing with a particularly awkward lady when Dawn marched over.

And from one arsehole to another.

'Elena, it's almost eleven. You can go for lunch now.' Dawn nodded towards the large clock above the entrance doors as if the clock itself had ordered that she go for lunch now.

She was about to reply when Dawn interrupted. 'And why have you got your hair down?'

Elena had only been working at the bank a week when Dawn called a meeting suggesting that all the female staff with long hair should wear it tied back, as it looked more professional, but in the rush to get to work that morning, Elena had forgotten.

Dawn sighed impatiently and stood there with her arms folded. She tutted and shook her head.

Elena was about to apologise and go for her usual early lunch when she had a flashback to the previous night with Jasmine and how good she had felt—confident.

She looked Dawn straight in the eyes. 'Firstly, Dawn, I've been having *lunch* at eleven o'clock three to four days a week for months. I don't want lunch at eleven. I want it at lunchtime. I think it's someone else's turn now, don't you?' Elena's eyes were still locked on Dawn's.

Her tone was firm, determined. Dawn opened her mouth to speak, but this time Elena interrupted. 'Secondly, is it company policy that all female staff wear their hair tied back?'

'No, but we all agreed—'

'No, Dawn. *You* agreed,' she interrupted once more.

Dawn's lips pursed tightly. She knew she had no say over hairstyle, and as her hair was short and spiky with pink highlights, she wasn't exactly leading by example.

'Fine, fine. I'll ask Jane to go for lunch now. She's more

of a team player, if you want to play rogue employee.'

'No, Dawn. I just want some fairness.'

Dawn opened her mouth as if to say something but didn't. She gave a small cough to clear her throat and retreated back to her office.

In the past, Elena would have conformed, just to save the earache, but not anymore. A faint smile touched Elena's lips. *Thanks, Jasmine.*

Dawn stayed in her office for the rest of the day like a hibernating cave bear. Elena had one of the best afternoons she'd had in a long time: lunch at one o'clock, no Dawn on her back, friendly customers. Even the drive home was fairly traffic free. Things were looking up, and as she turned the key in her front door and entered the house, she felt like a different person from the one who had left that morning.

She picked up the pile of junk mail and bills and went into the kitchen. Dropping the mail on the kitchen table she spotted her phone next to the bowl of milky mush that was breakfast. *There it is.* Elena made herself a cup of tea and sat at the table. She was about to open the mail when her phone buzzed—four missed calls from Jasmine and one text message. She checked the text first:

Hi, Miss Sexpot, have you looked at your e-mails yet? And why aren't you answering your phone? Call me, or there'll be trouble. Love, your fairy godmother xxx

Elena chuckled to herself. She started to open the mail, but her curiosity got the better of her. She grabbed her phone, logged on to the website, entered her password, and clicked on messages.

'Holy shit!' Elena stared at the phone. *You have twenty-five messages.*

She ran to the hall, grabbed the home phone, and dialled Jasmine's number.

'Hello?'

'Jaz, it's Elena. I've got twenty-five bloody messages!' Elena was half excited, half nervous.

'Oh, you little minx! I told you so.'

'I didn't think I would get anything for a week or two,' she said with self-doubt in her voice.

'Honey, with that body in that dress, you're a walking man-magnet, believe me.'

'What do I do now?' Elena asked, slightly panicked.

'Go through them all, and delete the ones that don't feel right, and send a reply to the ones that do. Remember, you're the one in control. You don't have to reply to any of them if you don't want to.'

'What do I put in the e-mails though?' A hundred different questions flew through Elena's mind.

'Don't worry. You'll be fine. Honey, I've got to go. I'm going to the theatre with Marcus, and I need to get ready.'

'Okay, Jaz. Enjoy your evening.'

'I will, and you enjoy your evening with all those male admirers, you little sex kitten. Call me tomorrow. Bye.'

'Bye, Jasmine.'

Elena decided before she switched on her laptop to go through the messages that she would shake off her working day with a nice hot bath. She had only been lying in the scented bubbles for five minutes when she just had to get out and check her messages. It was driving her mad. She couldn't relax, and her stomach was doing somersaults. Wearing comfy PJs, she flopped down on the couch with her laptop. She nervously logged on to the web site and went to messages.

'Right, let's start at the top.' She clicked on the first message, nibbling her nails as the text appeared on the screen.

Hey Gorgeous

This is Derrick Donaldson here. I'll be picking up my new Ferrari California at the weekend, and I think you would look great in the passenger seat next to me. I would love to take you for a ride. .

in the car, that is!

Get back to me babe.

D.D x.

Elena sat there open-mouthed.

'Oh my god! I've got twenty-four more of these to get through!'

She squirmed as she reread the message just to make sure she hadn't taken it the wrong way.

'Nope, he's a knob. Derrick, you can go and play with yourself in your Ferrari.'

Elena clicked 'delete' extra hard to make sure the message had definitely gone.

'Next.'

Hello Elena,

I do hope you don't think me too presumptuous, but I would be delighted if you could join me for dinner on Sunday evening at seven. I am a man who appreciates the finer things in life, and I have no reserve in telling you that, indeed, you are one of those, finer things.

I await your reply with great anticipation.

Sincerely,

Chauncey Barrington

'Oh god, it gets worse! Who wrote that? Oscar Wilde?' Elena sighed with her head in her hands. 'The finer things in life, eh? You mean my tits more like. Dirty old man. Delete!'

She trawled through the remaining messages one by one—some were downright weird, some were pompous, quite a few were boring.

'Four left to go. Okay, let's try this one.' She opened the message with disinterest.

Hi Elena

My name's Alan Windsor. I'm 49 years old and am the director of a very successful import and export business. This Saturday evening, I have to attend a business presentation with dinner afterwards.

All my fellow colleagues are either married or have partners, and I always feel the odd one out as I have been divorced some ten years now. I would be delighted (and grateful!) if you would join me.

Kind regards,

Alan

Elena was surprised. She thought that was quite nice—not overly friendly but not too formal. She clicked on the link to his profile page, and Alan's picture appeared. He was tanned with dark hair, greying slightly at the sides, clean-shaven with dark eyes. Elena could see that as a younger man, he would have been very handsome, although time hadn't completely taken away his looks, and he was still an attractive man, with a genuine friendly face. She thought there was something very familiar about him.

Elena had a good feeling about this one, and as he had said, it was a business presentation, so there would be other people there to talk to, just in case there were any awkward silences. She checked out his details.

Age: 49

Status: Single

Height: 5'10"

Registered as a member for one month

Hobbies/Interests: Overseas holidays, fine dining, race horses, and boating

Occupation: Director of a large international corporation

Elena decided to be bold and reply. She paused for a moment before typing her message.

Hi Alan

Thank you for the invitation. I would be happy to accompany you on Saturday evening.

I would be grateful if you could send me some details (time, place, dress code).

I look forward to hearing from you.

Regards,
Elena

She hovered the cursor over the 'send' button, wondering if it was the right thing to do, and then she thought, *I haven't been out on a Saturday night for ages,* and clicked send.

Elena went back to her inbox. *You have thirteen messages.*

'What?'

More messages had come through in the time it had taken to read and reply to Alan's message. Elena couldn't face reading any more offers of secret liaisons and weekends away. She was going to take things one step at a time. She had replied to one offer, and that was it for now. She would wait and see how Saturday went. Closing the laptop, Elena felt quite pleased with herself. Today had been a good day.

Elena filled Jasmine in on all the *juicy* details, as she called them, and exchanged several e-mails with Alan throughout the week. He had suggested they meet at seven on Saturday so they could have a drink and a chat for an hour, to get to know a little about each other, before she was in the company of a table full of strangers.

The rest of the week was hassle free. Dawn had turned her vile attention to the pretty new blond girl that had just started at the bank. All Elena was worried about was what to wear for Saturday.

She was going through her wardrobe and drawers, trying to find something suitable. She didn't really have any posh going-out clothes, although Alan had said that the dress in the photo looked fantastic, and whatever she wore, he was sure she would look amazing. Elena held up a gold-and-green maxi dress and was trying to decide if it would be suitable for Saturday when her phone rang.

'Hi, Jaz, how are you?' She threw the dress on the bed.

'Stressed! I'm supposed to be going to Paris tomorrow for a long weekend with Marcus, and I can't find my bloody passport!'

'Well, I'll just have to go in place of you then, won't I?' Elena said mischievously.

'Oh no, you don't, missy. You've got to go and meet Mr Alan Windsor. Are you excited?'

'I am, actually. I'm just going through my wardrobe at the moment, trying to find something to wear.' Elena turned to look at her bed which was piled with clothes and looked like a table at a jumble sale.

'You're going through your wardrobe on a Friday night? Girl, you have got to spend some more time with me.'

'I think you've done quite enough, thank you.'

'Listen, next week, I'm going to be moving into a larger two-bedroom apartment. So next Saturday, I'm having a house—well, apartment—warming party, so we can catch up then.'

'That sounds great. Will Marcus be there?' Elena was curious to meet him.

'Er, no, but you can meet my parents. They're coming down for the weekend. You could bring Mr Windsor, maybe?'

'Jasmine, enjoy Paris. Bring me back a beret or a hunky Frenchman.'

'I will, thank you honey, and you enjoy tomorrow evening. If you get chance, send me a text to let me know you're okay. I'll get all the gossip next week.'

'Okay, I will. Bye, Jasmine.'

Elena looked at the pile of clothes on the bed and puffed away a stray hair from her eyes. 'Bugger it! I'll go out and buy something new tomorrow.'

She spent the rest of the evening giving herself some TLC. She began with a facial, shaved and waxed everywhere, plucked her eyebrows, and painted her nails. When she finally fell into bed, she felt like a shiny new pin.

Elena was woken by a loud banging on her front door. She looked at the clock, her eyes barely open.

Eight o'clock? Who the hell was that on a Saturday? She sighed and dragged herself out of bed, put on her dressing gown, and headed down the stairs. The banging continued. 'Okay! Okay! I'm coming!'

She opened the door to find a skinny young guy with a baseball cap on backwards and more teeth than a donkey. 'Yes?' Elena said impatiently.

'Two parcels for you, love.' He thrust the boxes into Elena's hand. 'Sign here, please.' He handed Elena a crumpled piece of paper and a pen, and she scrawled her name. 'It said on my delivery notes knock hard and wait. They weren't wrong either.' Elena handed back the paper with a scowl. 'Cheers,' said the courier and ran back to his oversized white van.

She placed the two parcels on the kitchen table and made herself a cup of tea as she looked at the boxes suspiciously. She tore open the first one to find a large matte black box. Elena took the lid off and removed the fine white tissue paper embossed with the letter D in gold, and there was Jasmine's black Christian Dior cocktail dress.

'Oh, Jasmine. What a sweetheart!' Elena took the dress out of the box and held it against herself.

There was a card in the box, which read,

I want you to have this dress, Elena, and I don't want any arguments. Besides, after seeing you in it, I could never wear it again. It looks far better on you. Bitch! Love you really. Jasmine. x x

Her attention turned to the other parcel. 'So what's this one then?'

She opened it to find another smaller black-and-gold box. She removed the lid to find a beautiful black lace bra and thong by Bordelle. Jasmine was naughty, but they were gorgeous.

There was another card that read,

Have a good time, honey, and if you can't have a good time, have a naughty one!! x x

Elena sat at her kitchen table, cradling her cup of tea in both hands, and smiled to herself as she admired the beautiful Dior dress and sexy lingerie. For some strange reason, Dawn popped into her head. If it hadn't been for Dawn making her go for all those early lunches, she may never have 0bumped into Jasmine. *Everything happens for a reason,* thought Elena.

'Thank you, Dawn,' Elena said, with her cup of tea in the air in a mock toast to the she-devil.

Her thoughts turned to shoes. Now she had a fabulous dress and lingerie, all that was missing were shoes. She sprang to her feet eager to complete her outfit, having just found her purpose for the day.

CHAPTER FOUR

Elena added another coat of lip gloss and glanced at her watch.

Ten minutes until the taxi gets here.

Alan had offered to send a car for her, but she had declined the offer, not wanting to give her address to a man she had never met.

Elena checked herself over in the mirror. She couldn't deny she looked gorgeous. The dress was a perfect fit as was the new lingerie.

Self-doubt entered Elena's thoughts. Had she gone over the top? Maybe she should have worn something a little less, well, sexy, like her gold-and-green maxi dress.

But she was always playing it safe; that's what she had done her whole life. No, she looked fine as she was. The beep from the waiting taxi interrupted her thoughts. She checked her appearance for the final time, grabbed her clutch bag, and slammed the door behind her.

The taxi pulled up outside Desiderio. Elena looked a puzzled. It wasn't a bar, it was a restaurant.

'Is there another Desiderio?' she asked the taxi driver.

'Not that I know of, darlin'.'

She paid the fare and stood outside the restaurant. *Was this the right place?* Her nerves worked their full potential, and she began to wish she'd stayed in the taxi and gone back home. Too late now.

Elena entered hesitantly to be greeted by a young man dressed in black. 'Good evening, madam. Do you have a reservation for tonight?'

'Er . . . I'm not sure actually,' she said embarrassed. 'I'm supposed to be meeting someone.'

'Do you have a name, madam?' The young maître d' ignored her awkwardness.

'Alan Windsor?'

'Please follow me, madam.' She sighed with relief.

Elena followed him through the opulent restaurant. Chandeliers hung down from the high ceiling above the round dining tables, which were draped in brilliant white perfectly pleated tablecloths. Deep purple tub chairs surrounded the tables, which were laid to perfection and sat on an extravagant purple-and-gold carpet. Golden-speckled panels lined the walls and were broken by intermittent mirrored strips. She definitely wasn't overdressed, not here.

The place was full. She could feel eyes crawling all over her as the maître d' led the way. She held her head high and tried not to stare, although her fellow diners didn't extend her the same courtesy.

All the staff were dressed in black and looked like silhouettes as they drifted by with plates filled with food that looked and smelt exquisite. The buzz of conversation and laughter mixed with the chink of knives and forks on ceramic. Her heart quickened as she spotted Alan. He was sitting at the back of the room, and she was relieved to see he looked just as he did in the photo.

'Elena, lovely to meet you,' he said with a warm smile as he rose up to greet her with a kiss on both cheeks.

'And you, Alan.'

'You look beautiful, and you're wearing the dress.'

'Thank you.' Elena resisted the temptation to heave it over her breasts. She wasn't used to so much flesh being shown.

The maître d' pulled out her chair, and she took her seat at the table. 'Can I get you anything to drink, madam?'

'I'll have an apple martini, please,' she said confidently.

'Sir?' The maître d' turned his attention to Alan.

'I'm fine, thank you, Michael.'

Once Michael had left them, Alan turned to Elena with a nervous smile. 'I have a confession to make, I'm afraid.'

Oh god, I knew it was all going too well. He's probably married, and he wants me to be his dirty little secret.

'The business presentation was cancelled midweek, and I didn't say because I feared you would cancel tonight.'

Phew! Was that it?

'That's why I arranged to meet here. I hope you don't think I've been underhanded.' He leaned forward, his thick dark eyebrows raised.

'Not at all, Alan, it's fine. In fact, I'm relieved, to be honest.'

'Really? Why is that?'

'I'm not sure. Maybe it's being the stranger amongst a group of people that all know each other. Sometimes it can be awkward.' She already felt relaxed enough to be honest with him.

'Well, don't worry yourself. There will be no strangers, just us, and the food here is excellent.'

Elena returned his generous smile. 'It's a beautiful place.' She looked around the room, and now Alan had put her at ease, she was quite excited about the evening ahead.

The waiter came with her drink and gave them both a menu.

'To be honest, I was worried about tonight myself.' He looked up from the menu.

'Worried, why?'

'Well, I work long hours, some days 7:00 a.m. to 1:00

or 2:00 a.m. That's the price of success, I suppose, and not to bore you with too many details, but ultimately, that's what caused the breakdown of my marriage. It's very difficult to maintain any kind of relationship when you're cancelling dinner arrangements four or five times a week.' He placed his elbows on the table with his hands clasped in front of him.

'It's not until I have to go to one of these presentations that I feel . . . well, envious, so I registered with the website. I felt a bit silly really and almost cancelled my membership as soon as I'd registered, but then I saw your photograph, and it didn't seem quite so silly after all.'

He leaned back in his chair. 'Of course, I didn't expect you to reply to my e-mail, but I am thrilled and honoured that you did.'

Elena thought that was very sweet of him to be so honest. He looked every inch the successful, confident businessman, but he was still vulnerable to the same insecurities as everyone else.

'I felt exactly the same when I registered. It was a friend who suggested I join, and I was very unsure, never having done anything like this before, but I'm glad that I did.' Elena's reserve was starting to loosen its grip as the alcohol worked its magic.

The evening was off to a good start. Elena felt relaxed in Alan's company. He had a very familiar way about him as if they had met before, and as the evening progressed, they chatted like old friends. So by the time they had finished their delectable meal, she felt completely at ease with him. She had caught his eyes fixed on her cleavage more than once. He was a man after all.

Alan drank his Kinclaith whisky, and Elena noticed his tanned hands against the crisp white cuff of his shirt. She glanced at his wedding ring finger. There was no band of pale skin to indicate where a ring may have been.

'Elena, will you excuse me? I have to make a quick business call.'

'Of course.' *Great! I can text Jaz.* She waited until Alan was out of sight and quickly took her phone from her clutch bag and held it below the table.

Thank you so much for the gifts, you shouldn't have. All going well so far, he's lovely. How's Paris?

Love, E x x

Elena quickly put her phone back into her bag and took a sip of her drink when she heard her phone buzzing. She looked around to see if the coast was clear. No sign of Alan, she placed the bag on her lap and left her phone inside.

That's great! Now make sure you're in bed by twelve, and I don't mean to sleep either!! Paris is full of annoying French people, and so far, none of them hunky.

Love, Jaz x x

Elena giggled to herself just as Alan returned.

'Sorry about that,' he said as he took his seat. Elena placed her bag back on the table.

'No, it's fine really,' she replied, glad of the opportunity to text Jasmine.

The waiter returned to give them the dessert menus.

'We'll have some more drinks, please.'

'Certainly, sir.' The waiter nodded.

'Elena?'

'Oh no, I'm fine thanks.'

'Come on, one more drink,' said Alan enthusiastically.

'Really, I'm fine, thank you.' She'd already had one drink too many.

'I've got to buy you at least one glass of champagne. This place has the best champagne.' He was very insistent, and before Elena could answer, he ordered for her. 'My usual whisky. And champagne for the lady.'

She felt a little annoyed, but it wasn't going to spoil the evening.

Alan turned his gaze to Elena. He was smiling at her, but it wasn't the same warm smile she had seen all evening. 'Now what would you like to do after we leave here?'

The question took her by surprise, and she didn't know what to say. It made her feel uncomfortable, but before she could answer, they were interrupted.

'Alan, how are you?' Alan looked up at the man towering over him.

'Conrad,' said Alan flatly as he held out his hand.

Elena gazed up at the stranger. He was tall, wearing light grey trousers and a pale blue shirt. His sleeves were rolled back over his thick forearms, and a chunky silver watch clung to his wrist. He had short light brown hair and slight stubble over a strong square jaw. There was an undeniable presence about him. *Breathe, Elena!*

The two men shook hands. 'Sorry to interrupt. I just thought I'd say hello. How's business?'

'Fine, fine. As busy as ever,' mumbled Alan.

'I've got a big shipment coming in from China in a couple of months. Can you handle it for me?' asked Conrad.

'Of course. You know me. Nothing is ever too big.' Alan leaned back in his chair, with his hands behind his head. He didn't make eye contact with Conrad.

'Aren't you going to introduce me?' Conrad looked down at Elena, who gazed up at him from under her long lashes.

'Conrad, this is Elena. Elena, Conrad,' Alan said quickly while he checked his fingernails.

Their eyes met as they greeted each other. He had strong hard hands, not coarse but not soft like Alan's.

'Nice to meet you.'

'And you.' Elena's heart accelerated, and her face attempted to turn the same colour as her hair. *Very nice to meet you.*

Alan cut short the introduction. 'Right, Conrad, I'll be in touch, and we can discuss your shipment further.'

Conrad seemed to take the hint. 'Enjoy your evening.'

He gave Elena a nod, a faint smile appearing on his lips. She couldn't take her eyes off him as he walked back to his table, his pale blue shirt straining against his broad shoulders, and a perfect arse in snug-fitting trousers.

Her gaze wondered back to Alan. The crease in his tanned forehead displayed his annoyance while his fingers tapped the table. The mood of the evening had completely changed, and for the first time, there was an awkward silence between them which was broken by the waiter returning with their drinks.

As he placed the drinks on the table, Elena took the opportunity to glance over Alan's shoulder to Conrad's table. He was sitting with his back to her. Opposite him was a young attractive woman with blond bobbed hair.

'So is Conrad an old friend of yours?' she asked nonchalantly.

'Conrad is a business associate, nothing more.'

She was aware that Alan had been agitated by Conrad's interruption, but she couldn't help herself. She had to know more. 'And what is his business?' She fiddled with her dessert spoon and tried desperately not to seem too interested.

Alan cocked an eyebrow. It was clear he was tired of the questions. 'Conrad has his fingers in many pies. He's what I'd call a player and a man to be avoided.'

His words of warning didn't dampen Elena's interest. She knew she was pushing her luck, but there was one more question she had to ask.

'Is that his wife he's with?' Her eyes pointed towards the couple.

Alan gave an audible sigh and turned to take a look. 'Yes, that's her. Now where were we before we were disturbed? Ah yes, what shall we do next, after this place?'

Oh shit! 'Erm, well . . . it's . . .' Elena looked at her watch. 'It's getting late, Alan.'

'Nonsense! The evening is just beginning.'

Think! Quick, quick! Toilet! 'Would you excuse me for a moment? I have to pop to the ladies.' Elena rose from the table and grabbed her clutch bag.

'Of course.'

She headed for the safety of the bathroom and could feel his eyes on her as she walked away. Elena looked back to the table, and sure enough, there was Alan sitting sideways on his chair. He raised his glass to her with a nod.

I knew it was all going too well.

As she passed Conrad's table, he was deep in conversation with his blonde companion.

She entered the bathroom and looked at herself in the huge mirror which hung over the white granite bench top. Her mind spun round as she tried to think of an excuse for her not to be out too late on a Saturday night of all nights.

I know—christening! I've got to go to a christening at ten in the morning. Yeah, that'll do.

She took several deep breaths and headed back to Alan.

Elena had thought of a new tactic: distraction. She sat down at the table. 'So, Alan, do you get out on your boat much?'

Bingo! Alan's face lit up like a Christmas tree. His boat was his passion, and he talked nonstop for twenty minutes about everything, from life jackets to pirates. And the whole time, Elena stole looks at Conrad. Finally, Alan stopped for breath.

'It's my turn to ask to be excused this time. Have you tried your champagne?'

'I haven't actually.' She reached for the glass and took a sip as Alan paused to watch.

'Mmm, lovely,' she said and took another sip.

Alan grinned. 'I knew you'd like it.'

Now he had gone for a moment, she could finally spy on Conrad. She looked towards his table, but he wasn't there, although his wife was at the table writing something down in what looked like a diary. Elena looked at the empty chair opposite her. The relaxed friendly atmosphere had disappeared and left her feeling uncomfortable.

She told herself not to worry, Alan had been a gentleman all evening, and when he came back, she would thank him and say that maybe they could meet again. Hopefully, the possibility of another meeting would appease him.

She drank more champagne. He was right. It was good. But then again, she didn't really know what bad champagne tasted like.

Alan entered the bathroom to find Conrad standing at a basin.

'We really should stop meeting like this,' Alan said sarcastically. Conrad washed his hands and watched him in the mirror as he stood at the urinal. 'So this shipment from China, more bloody gym equipment I suppose?' Alan continued with his sarcastic tone.

'Well, I don't own a chain of fruit and veg stalls, do I?' Conrad returned the sarcasm as he dried his hands. 'That's a good-looking woman you're with tonight, Alan.'

Alan zipped up his fly and headed for the basin. 'Mm, yes, and she's going be fucked six ways from Sunday tonight.' He spoke with cocky arrogance.

'Really? And she's up for that, is she?'

'She will be with one of these in her champagne.' Alan took out a small silver engraved pillbox from his inside pocket and shook it in front of Conrad's face.

Conrad took his hands out of his pockets. His eyes narrowed. 'You are joking, right?'

Alan saw the expression on his face and broke into a laugh. 'Of course, I'm joking!' He slapped Conrad on the shoulder, realising he had overstepped the mark. 'What sort of a man do you think I am? These are blood pressure tablets.' He chuckled to himself as he ran his hands over his hair and left Conrad in the bathroom.

'I know exactly what sort of man you are,' Conrad mumbled to himself.

Alan returned to the table. His eyes had a predatory look about them. 'Finish your drink, Elena,' he encouraged.

She took a sip from the glass. She felt drowsy, disorientated. 'I think I've had enough now, thank you.' Her eyesight was blurred, and the room started to move around. 'Oh, I'm sorry, Alan. I think I've had a bit too much to drink, and it's . . . suddenly . . . hit . . . hit me.' Elena was struggling to keep her head upright.

Alan called the maître d' over. 'Michael, can you get me a cab? I'm afraid she's had too much to drink. Put the bill on my tab, will you, and I'll settle up in the week.'

'Of course, sir.' Michael hurried off to execute Alan's wishes.

Alan managed to get Elena to her feet. Her arm was around his shoulder, and his arm was wrapped around her waist. 'Come on, Elena. Let's get you home to bed, shall we?' He steadied her swaying body.

'Sorry, Alan,' Elena slurred.

'That's all right. Just walk with me. Come on.' He managed to steer her between the tables of diners who were staring at her once again but this time for a very different reason. He didn't take the obvious route to the exit but went the long way around to avoid Conrad.

Conrad was engaged in conversation when he overheard the lady seated at the table behind him.

'Look at that young woman. How did she let herself get into that state?'

He glanced around to see who the lady was talking about and just caught a glimpse of Alan and the maître d', with Elena in between them, exiting through the black door.

A black cab was waiting for them. Michael opened the rear door and helped Alan get Elena into the back of the cab. She slumped over onto her side.

'Thank you, Michael.' Alan turned towards him and spotted Conrad standing in the doorway. 'Fuck!' Alan mumbled under his breath.

'What's going on, Alan?' Conrad's tone was harsh.

'The girl can't handle her drink.' Alan tried to appear calm.

'Oh really?' Conrad had more than a hint of sarcasm in his voice.

'Piss off, Conrad! She's had too much to drink, and I'm doing the decent thing and taking her home.' Alan regretted losing his cool.

Conrad walked towards him and stopped within inches of him. 'And where is that?' His face was like stone.

'What?'

'Her address, what is it?' demanded Conrad.

'Well, it's . . . erm . . . it's . . .'

'Are we goin' or what? I ain't got all night!' interrupted the impatient cab driver.

Conrad pushed Alan to the side with one arm, got in the cab, and slammed the door. 'Yes, we are. Drive!'

The cab drove off, and Alan stood at the side of the road humiliated. His knuckles were white from his clenched fists, and his face burned with rage. The car disappeared into the traffic.

'Fuck you, Conrad! Fuck you!'

CHAPTER FIVE

Elena's head was buried under a warm duvet. She was exhausted, and her mouth was so dry she could barely swallow. As her senses roused, she realised this wasn't her bed. The blurred memory of Saturday evening slowly sharpened. She pulled the duvet from over her head and froze for a moment at the sight of the strange room.

Where the hell am I?

Elena launched herself up in a panic and threw the duvet back. She was still wearing her underwear. A sigh of relief escaped her as she held her throbbing head while her eyes cast around the room looking for her dress. It was neatly folded on one of two chairs placed opposite the bed, with her shoes underneath the chair, and her clutch bag was on the bedside cabinet, next to a tall glass of water.

'What have I done?' she murmured as she reached for the glass and took a long welcome drink. *What happened last night with Alan? And where the fuck am I?*

She was just about to get off the bed and grab her dress when she heard someone at the door. *Shit!* Diving back under the duvet, she pretended to be asleep.

The door closed. Quiet footsteps entered the room,

and a set of keys were placed down.

Elena lay perfectly still, holding her breath. Another door opened, and she heard the sound of a shower and clothes being thrown on the floor. The cubicle door closed, and she heard the water hitting the glass and shower tray.

This was her chance. It was now or never.

Slowly, Elena pulled the duvet down below her eyes. The bathroom door was slightly open, and from the bed, she could see the reflection of the shower in the bathroom mirror. She sat up tentatively and looked to make sure Alan was in the shower.

Bloody hell! Alan's in good shape! She caught a glimpse of his muscular back.

Elena stretched her neck higher to get a better view. The V-shaped back tapered down to a tight waist, and she could just about see the top of his toned square buttocks. Elena caught herself staring. She slid her legs over the edge of the bed, pushed her hands down on the mattress to raise herself, and glanced back through the door at the image. The figure in the shower turned around. Elena froze once again with her backside raised just off the bed. It wasn't Alan in the shower, it was Conrad.

She looked at her neatly folded dress and turned back to look at the muscular torso in the mirror. Very slowly, she lowered her bottom back onto the bed, swung her legs under the covers, lay down, and pulled the duvet up to just below her eyes. Elena watched as the strong hands glided over the full hard chest and down his defined abs. It felt sleazy watching him, but not that sleazy. She could see less and less as the steam encroached on her viewing pleasure and clouded the mirror.

So what did happen last night? She wasn't quite so worried now but was desperate to know. Alan had warned her about Conrad being a man to avoid, but she was willing to take her chances.

The shower stopped. Elena's head retracted under the

duvet like a tortoise hiding in its shell. She listened hard. The shower door opened and closed. She heard the ruffling of a towel, and then it all went quiet.

Conrad stood at the bottom of the bed, noticing the half-empty glass of water on the bedside cabinet and smiled to himself. 'Good morning. How are you feeling?'

Shit! Did he know I was watching him? I can't stay under here. He obviously knows I'm awake.

Elena popped her head from under the duvet, yawned, and pretended to have just woken not very convincingly. Conrad was still standing at the end of the bed, a small white towel around his waist, and his hands on his hips. Elena's eyes darted everywhere as she tried to get a good look at his magnificent body before she got to his handsome face.

'Morning,' she croaked. 'Where am I?' she asked, looking around the palatial room as if for the first time.

'The Savoy.' Conrad wandered over to the window, looking like a Greek god, and opened the thick floor-to-ceiling curtains to reveal a fantastic view over London.

Elena blinked as the warm morning sunshine spilled into the room, giving her a clear view of his toned body.

The Savoy . . . with Conrad? What's going on? Is it a dream?

Her head spun with confusion. 'How did I end up here? What happened to Alan?'

Conrad took out a pair of dark blue jeans and a black polo shirt from the wardrobe and hung them over his arm. 'How long have you known Alan for?'

What can I say? He contacted me via a sugar daddy website. I met him for the first time last night, and yes, I am a cheap hussy! 'Er, only a short while.'

He headed into the bathroom and pulled the door to but didn't close it.

'You obviously don't know him very well.' His voice resounded like he had a microphone with him. 'He's a very successful businessman, and he's as ruthless in life as he is in business.'

There was a hiss of aftershave being applied, and he came out dressed in the clothes he had taken in and ruffled his damp short brown hair, the black polo shirt pulled tight across his muscular arms. The redolence of his aftershave floated seductively over to her, and she eagerly breathed in his scent. He was a feast for the senses.

'Let's just say, I saved you the displeasure of finding out how ruthless he can be.'

He stood at the bottom of the bed, tucked in his shirt, and tightened the brown belt on his jeans. She couldn't take her eyes off him. He looked like a beefed-up catwalk model.

Conrad felt sorry for Elena. She had been fooled by Alan. He knew only too well that Alan could be very charming, especially with the ladies, but underneath that charm lay a cold predator, who would stop at nothing to get what he wanted. Conrad's only regret was that he hadn't taken his head off last night. As he looked at her in the bed with the duvet pulled up to her chin, he saw a little lost vulnerable girl, and for some strange reason, he felt a primal urge to protect her.

'That doesn't explain how I ended up here with you.'

He sat down on the edge of the bed. He didn't want to scare her, but she had to know about Alan.

'How much did you have to drink last night?'

'Erm, three—no, four drinks, with the glass of champagne Alan ordered for me.'

'And you've drunk alcohol before?'

'Of course.' She frowned, obviously offended.

'Don't you think it's strange that you suddenly passed out after only drinking a small amount?'

She sighed and shook her head. 'That's what I don't understand.' He could see she was getting flustered. 'What the hell is going on?'

Conrad spoke quietly and calmly; he didn't want to panic her. 'Alan spiked your drink last night.'

'What? No!' She looked horrified at the thought.

'He spiked your drink and was about to take you back to his hotel. I'm sure you can guess the rest.'

She sat staring at a spot on the duvet, and a cold shiver ran through her. That couldn't be true, could it?

Deep down, she knew Conrad wasn't lying to her. She didn't know this man, but for some reason, she trusted him.

'I managed to step in before he got you into the taxi, and I brought you back here.'

So he rescued me. Elena tried to piece together what happened while she was out of it. 'How did I get in here?'

'I carried you.'

She could believe that, with those arms. He made Superman look like Mr Bean. Elena looked into his perfect light brown eyes.

'And how did my dress get over there?' She glanced towards the chair.

His eyes narrowed mischievously, and a smile crept into the corner of his mouth. 'I helped you out of your dress, and I was the perfect gentleman,' he said, holding up his hands. 'The light was off, and I had my eyes closed, didn't see a thing.'

Mmm, yeah right. Thank God I'd got decent underwear on! 'So where did you sleep?' This was the question that interested her most.

'I didn't. I sat there.' He pointed to the empty chair opposite the bed. 'And kept an eye on you.'

'What, *all* night?'

'You were completely unconscious. If you'd have been sick, you would have choked.'

She felt incredibly touched by his obvious concern, even though they were strangers.

'You need to eat something. I'll call room service.' He

leant to pick up the phone from the bedside cabinet. He was close enough for her to smell the gorgeous scent of his freshly showered body.

'No, Conrad, thank you. I can't face food at the moment.' She touched his forearm to stop him as he lifted the phone, and it was as if an electric charge shot through her body. Her sense of touch was heightened; his arm was warm and hard. He turned to look at her, their faces no more than a foot apart.

He gazed at her full open lips and deep green eyes, tousled red hair tumbling down over her face. She had panda eyes from the smudged mascara, but it didn't matter. She still looked beautiful. What was it about this girl? Conrad pulled himself away and took a deep breath.

'There're clean towels in the bathroom. I'll have tea and coffee sent to the room,' he said as his self-control returned to its normal level. 'I've got to go out, but I should be back in an hour.'

He grabbed his keys and phone from the desk and was half out of the door when she called him. 'Conrad?' Hesitation rang through her voice. 'Will you . . . walk me out of the hotel when you come back?' His head tipped to one side slightly with a questioning look. 'I don't want to walk through the lobby on my own wearing that dress, looking like a cheap tart the morning after.' She was embarrassed by the situation that fucking prick had put her in.

He could see she was close to tears, and it bothered him. Why? This girl was a total stranger.

'Elena,' he said warmly, 'when I come back, I'll take you wherever you want to go.' He gave her a reassuring smile. 'Use the hotel phone if there's anyone you need to call. Boyfriend? Girlfriend?'

She fought back the tears with a smile. 'No, there's no one . . . no one I need to call.'

'See you in an hour.' He looked pleased with himself as he closed the door.

He'd said her name for the first time. She heard her name dozens of times a day, but this felt different somehow, special.

Elena lay on the bed for a few minutes and let it all sink in. The very thought of the name Daddy Daddy Sugar made her cringe. How could she have been so stupid? As soon as she got home, she was going to remove herself from the website—life-changing plan over. It very nearly had been life-changing but for all the wrong reasons.

She wandered into the bathroom and nearly died of embarrassment. 'Oh Christ!' Staring back in the mirror was a wild red-haired young woman with black eyes and smudged lips. She looked like an extra from *The Rocky Horror Show*.

Right, first, let's sort that out.

She reached to turn on the shower when a knock at the door stopped her. She threw on the fluffy bathrobe and answered the door. A middle-aged man with a bald head and a friendly face stood there with a trolley. 'Room service.' His tone matched his face.

Elena smiled and stood back to let him in; he wheeled in the trolley and placed it next to the desk opposite the window.

'Enjoy, madam.'

'Thank you,' she said appreciatively. He gave her a small bow and closed the door as he left.

Elena lifted the silver cover from the platter, which sat between the tea and coffee pots, and unveiled a selection of fruit, yoghurt, croissants, and jams. She was touched by Conrad's thoughtfulness. It gave her spirits a much-needed lift, but it was short-lived, as she remembered the blond lady he had been with last night—his wife.

Feeling deflated, she placed the cover back over the food. The memory of his pretty companion dissolved her appetite. *That's probably where he was now, downstairs having breakfast with his wife.*

Elena stood under the shower and tried to wash away the memory of Saturday night, recalling how good the week had been. She'd felt so upbeat, and the evening had started off so well. How had it ended in this car crash?

She dragged herself out of the shower and, in a bathrobe, sat on the edge of the bed, looking at the black dress. Elena was postponing putting it on. It was a dress you wore when you felt sexy, confident. It had lost its allure and seemed almost threatening.

There was a knock at the door which broke her melancholy mood. Conrad pushed the door open with a granite shoulder, his hands full of an assortment of shopping bags.

'Sorry, I'm not dressed,' Elena blurted out as she jumped to her feet. 'I . . . I just . . .'

'That's fine,' interrupted Conrad, putting the bags down. 'How are you feeling?'

'I'm okay, thanks.'

'Just not hungry, eh?' He lifted the cover off the platter.

'I'm sorry. It was very kind of you.' Elena suddenly grabbed the dress. 'I'd better go. I've taken far too much of your time already.' Embarrassed and flustered, she bundled her shoes and bag on top of the dress.

'Elena, stop.' He grabbed her gently by the arm. She did as she was told and turned to face him. 'I said that I would take you wherever you wanted to go when I got back. And I will after we've had lunch.'

Just when Elena thought she couldn't get any more mind-fucked. 'Lunch? But I don't have anything suitable to wear.'

'Yes, you do.' He let go of her arm and gestured with an open hand towards the pile of bags he'd left by the bed. 'I took Isabelle with me, checked your dress and shoe size while you were asleep last night, and bought accordingly.'

'Isabelle?' A frown flickered across her brow.

'Yes, the lady I was with last night.'

'You mean your wife?'

'No, Isabelle's my PA.' He laughed.

PA? Hang on—was she a real PA or a Jasmine PA?

'There're four or five pairs of jeans, four pairs of shoes, and four or five different tops. Oh, and a jacket. All Isabelle's choice. I'll give you some privacy. I've got a business meeting with Isabelle, and there's just one other thing I need to collect, so I should be back in about another hour, and then we'll go, okay?'

'Mmm.' She nodded, having lost the power of speech from the shock.

'Okay, I'll see you in an hour." He popped his head around the door as it was about to close. 'Oh, and the cream bag is lingerie, and that's all my choice.' He gave her a brash smile and left her open-mouthed and red-cheeked.

How did he do it? Whenever he was in the room, she just felt better, happier, safe.

She sat down in disbelief and stared at the cluster of bags. No man had ever done something like this for her. A few ex-boyfriends had attempted to buy lingerie, which was only suitable for prostitution purposes. But then again, she hadn't seen what he had bought.

She shook herself back to planet Earth and grabbed the bags. *Oh god, I hope Isabelle's not a Goth.*

Isabelle had good taste, although she wasn't sure about the short leather jacket. She lay the clothes out on the bed—all designer. Not that it mattered to Elena, she wasn't that kind of girl. It wouldn't have bothered her if it was all from a charity shop. What mattered most was that this gorgeous man had saved her from a monster, watched over her like a guardian angel all night, and now he was taking her out to lunch.

Her eyes turned to the lingerie bag, curious to see what he had chosen. He also had good taste: four beautiful bra and thong sets in deep red, sheer black, pale green, and electric blue. Her head was spinning with excitement. She glanced at her watch.

Concentrate, Elena. You've got forty-five minutes.

Elena darted into the bathroom to do her hair. She looked at her flushed face in the mirror.

Everything happened for a reason. She recited this mantra every time things were going wrong, but this time things were going right, very right.

There was a knock at the door, and in walked Conrad with another bag. He stopped dead in his tracks when he saw the seductive vision in front of him in black wedge boots that finished just above the ankle, faded blue skinny jeans that followed every contour of her perfect legs, a tight-fitted grey T-shirt which buttoned up the front, with a collar and two breast pockets. The crowning glory was her magnificent mane of red hair, which was the perfect complement to her flawless skin.

'Wow! Isabelle chose well.'

'So did you.' She hadn't intended to say it out loud, but it just came out.

The corner of his mouth curled slightly. Elena turned away quickly and fiddled with the shopping bags unnecessarily as she felt her face burn.

He took a thick black canvas jacket from the wardrobe and placed it on top of the bag he was holding. 'Don't forget yours,' he said. Elena grabbed the leather jacket from the bed.

Conrad held out his arm. 'Shall we?'

Her ecstatic face answered for her, and she linked her arm through his. Looking around the room at his laptop and paperwork, she wondered how long he was staying there for and if she would be back.

'Isabelle will check out for me. She's my very own Mary Poppins.' He unwittingly answered her question as he opened the door for her.

They stood in silence as the elevator lowered them down, but it wasn't an awkward silence, it was quite reassuring. The doors opened, and they walked arm in arm across the large chessboard-like floor.

Elena couldn't help but look around in wonder at the grandiose lobby. Hotel guests arrived and left, each with their own smartly dressed porter, who carried or wheeled bags and suitcases of all sizes. After the whirlwind morning, she wondered where the day would take her. They went through the revolving door and down the steps.

'Thank you, Steven,' Conrad said to the regally dressed doorman.

'You're more than welcome, sir,' he replied.

There was a row of cars parked, waiting to be claimed by their owners. She tried to guess which one was Conrad's. *Yellow Lamborghini? No, too flashy. Four-wheel-drive Mercedes? Mmm, nah. White Porsche? Maybe. Rolls Royce? Definitely not. Range Rover Sport? Yes, that's the one.*

They passed the other cars and stopped at the black Range Rover. Elena felt very pleased with herself.

'Here we are.' He placed his bag on the floor.

'Lovely,' she said, with her hand on the passenger door handle.

Conrad chuckled and scratched his stubbled jaw. 'Not that,' he said as he looked at the Range Rover. 'This.' He indicated behind him with his thumb.

Elena leaned over to the side to see what his bulk was hiding. 'That? Seriously?' Before her was the most fearsome motorbike she had ever seen: a bright red Ducati.

'Yeah, seriously, and that's why you need the jacket.' He pulled out a crash helmet from the paper bag he was carrying and handed it to a terrified and dumbstruck Elena.

Oh god, no more surprises, please.

'Have you been on a bike before?'

She was shaking her head before he had finished the question. 'No, never.'

'Right, there're a couple of things you need to know. When we turn a corner, the bike will lean over. Lean with it. Don't try to stay upright, okay?'

'Is that it?' she asked while he put on his jacket.

'Oh, and hold on tight. You'll be fine. You'll love it,' he said casually.

Elena gazed at the dormant beast. Conrad folded the paper bag and put it with Elena's clutch bag in the small compartment under the seat. He turned the key and the two-wheeled monster came to life with a powerful roar.

If the devil had a motorbike, this would be it.

He climbed on the bike and put on the black helmet that sat on the handle bars. 'Ready?' He held out his arm for her too use as leverage.

I could tell him maybe next time and catch the bus home? She looked into his mesmerising eyes which were framed by the open visor. *Not a chance.*

'Ready.' She squeezed her head into the snug-fitting black helmet and climbed on the back of the beast, her skinny jeans just about allowing her to straddle the bike.

Tingling vibrations travelled through her bottom and into her tummy as he revved the powerful machine. She placed her hands on his hips with trepidation and braced herself.

'No, no, like this.' He gently grabbed her by the wrists and wrapped her arms around his solid midriff. 'Any problems, just tap, okay?'

'Okay!' she shouted above the roar of the bike.

Elena had always wondered what it would feel like to be shot out of a cannon, and now she was going to find out.

They pulled away from their parking spot. Conrad's legs splayed each side of the bike like two stabilizers. They stopped at the junction, and she thought it wasn't too bad after all. Then suddenly, the red beast turned left onto the strand at what seemed like one hundred miles an hour. Her grip tightened as though she were trying to crush him. Conrad worked up the gears as the bike increased in speed. The intensity of the vibration through her backside increased with it. Her eyes were shut tight, and her leather-clad chest pressed hard against his back as they swayed from left to right. The bike was so powerful it felt as if an invisible force was trying to rip her away from Conrad's torso. Then suddenly, the bike came to a halt. She dared to open her eyes—traffic lights. *Thank God!* She had never been more grateful to be stopped by a red light.

Conrad lifted his mirrored visor. 'Okay?' he shouted.

But before she could answer, the lights changed, and they were propelled through the air at a speed that only seemed suitable for a NASA rocket.

Eventually, her senses adjusted to the assault that had been thrust upon them, and she opened her eyes to see evidence of the city melting away. The rows of buildings and houses dwindled, replaced by trees and hedges. The sudden jolt of the bike left to right had now eased to a smooth, almost fluid motion. It felt as if they were flying through the air in a jet but without the security of the cockpit. She liked it—no, she loved it! Elena knew Conrad had complete control of the machine, and that's not all he had control of.

They pulled onto a gravel drive. The bike crunched its way over towards a picturesque old pub. He parked next to a rustic picket fence and removed the key from the ignition. The red beast fell back into its slumber. She climbed off the bike and was glad of the respite. Her arms and legs were weary from resisting the aggressive force of the Ducati.

Conrad removed his helmet and ran his fingers through his hair. He looked more biker from heaven than biker from hell with his growing stubble. 'How was that? Did you like it?'

Elena removed her helmet and shook her hair free. A big cheesy smile spread across her face like a child that had just ridden her first roller coaster. 'I loved it!' She was hooked and not just on the bike either.

They walked towards the old pub, which was overflowing with character: original six-panelled sash windows sat at each side of the entrance to the old building; tall chimneys reached for the sky as if they were trying to escape the red clay-tiled roof; she could just about see the old brick through the exquisite mass of wisteria. They walked through the sweet smell of an English garden littered with white and red roses.

The interior of the pub was as charming as the exterior. Chunky timber beams bowed under the weight of the low ceiling. It was tastefully decorated and had a nostalgic welcoming feel about it.

'Shall we sit outside? There's a lovely courtyard out the back.' He removed his jacket.

'Yeah, sounds lovely.'

'You grab a table, and I'll get the drinks. What would madam like?'

No more cocktails. Look where that got me. 'Small white wine, please, sir,' she replied playfully.

Conrad watched as she walked out towards the courtyard. He couldn't take his eyes off her pert denim-clad arse. He watched the rise and fall of each round cheek with every step she took.

Standing at the bar with a £20 note screwed up in his fist, his heart pounded, and he felt the sudden rush of blood to his groin. Exhaling slowly, he relaxed his clenched fists. This wasn't in his plan. He thought he had it all worked out. He should have called her a cab and sent her home, but there was something about this girl, and it wasn't just that great arse.

It's just lunch. Then I'll take her home, he thought, not entirely believing himself.

CHAPTER SIX

Elena wandered into the quaint cobbled courtyard, whose walls were lined with hanging baskets that overflowed colour: reds, sunshine yellows, and vibrant blues. She thought how wonderful nature was to have created something so beautiful, so perfect. Conrad entered the courtyard carrying their drinks with his jacket over his arm.

I rest my case. She admired his strong physique as he strode over.

'Shall we sit here?' He placed the drinks on one of the wooden tables that were dotted around the courtyard, each decorated with a single white rose in a small vase.

Elena hung her jacket on the back of the chair and sat down at the table, looking out over rolling fields of bright green and yellow squares like a huge patchwork quilt.

'What have you got?' she asked.

'Orange juice. You don't get second chances on a bike.'

'No, I suppose not. How long have you been riding?'

'Five years now. I've never driven a car that even comes close to giving the adrenalin rush you get from a bike, and once you've experienced it, nothing else compares.'

'I can imagine,' she mumbled into her wine glass.

Elena stared at him with smiling eyes and unwittingly gave her head a shake. 'What?' he asked curiously.

'I got onto a motorbike and rode at warp speed to God knows where, with a man whose full name I don't even know.'

He held out his hand. 'Bailey, Conrad Bailey.'

They shook hands. Elena held on longer than necessary. 'White. Elena White,' she replied, copying his smart introduction.

'Charmed, Ms White.'

Her bright face dimmed. 'Thank you.'

His eyes pinched inquisitively. 'What for?'

'I dread to think where I might be now if you hadn't stepped in.' Her imagination taunted her with vile images.

'Elena, you've already thanked me. It was my pleasure.'

'Do you think I should have gone to the police?'

Conrad let out a sigh and rubbed a large hand over his spiky jaw. 'Anybody could have spiked your drink. Alan could say you passed out and he was taking you home and nothing happened.'

She knew he was right, although she didn't like the thought of Alan getting away with it.

'How did you know he'd spiked my drink?'

'Because . . . I know Alan. He's a narcissistic man, hates to be beaten in any area of life, and doesn't take no for an answer. He has an import-export and haulage business. I have a few gyms spread across the UK, and if I have a completion date that I need to meet for a new gym, Alan never fails. He won't be beaten by rival companies. He has to be the best, the winner, although I'll be taking my business elsewhere from now on.'

Elena held her white wine up to her red lips and paused. 'It is safe to drink this, isn't it?' Her eyes dropped to her wine and back up to Conrad's face. 'Or will I wake up in a hotel with another strange man?' She was trying to lighten the mood.

He took a sip of his drink and placed it gently back on the table. 'Not as long as this heart beats.' There was no humour in his reply. His eyes pierced her very soul, and she absolutely knew he meant what he had said, which almost made her cry. 'Besides, I'm not that strange am I?' He smiled at her with his eyes crossed, which caused Elena to burst out laughing, and lightened the mood once again. 'You must be starving. The roast beef here is fantastic. Shall we order?'

Elena's mouth watered at the thought of roast beef, or was that just the thought of Conrad?

She went with his suggestion, and they enjoyed a traditional roast beef Sunday lunch in picturesque surroundings.

Conrad moved his chair next to Elena's. 'That's my favourite flower.' He pointed to the small vase on the table. 'A pure white rose. Perfect. Every time I see one now, I'll think of you, Elena White.'

A short round man with rosy red cheeks and bushy grey sideburns interrupted the moment. He had come to clear their empty plates. 'All done, folks?' he asked with a melodic tone.

'Yes, thank you,' they answered in unison and glanced at each other with a smirk.

'George, it was as lovely as ever.' Conrad touched the rosy-cheeked man on the shoulder as he bent to pick up their plates.

'It's a pleasure and lovely to see you again, sir.'

He waddled off in his tweed trousers held up with red braces over a checked shirt, and Elena thought he was the perfect complement to the old pub, just what you would expect to find at a place like that.

Conrad sat with his legs stretched out in front of him, arms folded, as he stared out at the open countryside. He tilted his head back to gaze at her profile. Elena turned to look at him.

'What?' She was curious to know his thoughts.

He looked straight ahead again. 'Oh, I'm just admiring the view,' he replied casually. 'The scenery's not bad either.' Elena was in fits of giggles at his schoolboy humour. 'What? That's one of my best lines. Usually works every time.' His face lit up with a huge grin.

She stood up still laughing. 'I'm going to the little girls' room. Oh, and it's worked this time too.'

'You're only saying that to be nice!' he shouted as she walked away with a grin from ear to ear.

Standing in front of the mirror in the ladies', Elena checked her hair and makeup, wishing that the afternoon would never end. It all seemed too good to be true. Yes, she'd had a lucky escape, but if that had caused her meeting with Conrad, then she didn't regret it for a second.

She looked at her watch. Five thirty. The reality of Monday was waiting in the shadows. She shook off the thought and headed back to Conrad and found him wandering into the pub, carrying two large ice cream sundaes.

'I think the alfresco dining is over.' His eyes pointed at the black clouds sailing towards them.

They sat at a small table by the window with a view of the rose garden through which they had entered.

'Mm, this is naughty. Nice though,' she remarked with her spoon full of chocolate ice cream. 'I thought you were Mr Fitness. There must be a lot of calories in one of these.'

'Around five hundred. Don't worry, I'll work it off one way or another.' He raised and lowered his eyebrows like Groucho Marx.

Elena almost choked on her ice cream from another fit of giggles. She was completely at ease with him. He'd restored her faith in humanity with his charm and warmth. He treated people with respect, and she totally and utterly trusted this man who she had known for less than twenty-four hours. *Careful, Elena, careful.*

His phone rang. 'Sorry, do you mind if I take this?'

'No, of course not.'

'Isabelle? No, that's fine . . . Yes, we go ahead as planned. It will add more value to the deal . . . Yes, book the usual place and have my bike sent up for me . . . No, the BMW.'

Elena pretended not to listen as she ate her ice cream, although she was doing the exact opposite.

'I'll get Elena's address and e-mail it to you. Can you make sure she gets the clothes and shoes? Great. What would I do without you? Thank you for all your hard work. I appreciate it . . . Apologise to Mark for me keeping you busy all weekend . . . Speak to you in the morning . . . And you . . . Bye.' He slipped his phone back into his pocket.

'Sorry about that. We're expanding into Scotland with our first gym, and I'm going to view one of our sites in a couple of weeks' time.'

'You don't have to send me the clothes. Take them back.'

'No, they're yours.' He spooned in a mouthful of ice cream.

'Will you thank Isabelle for me?' She was a little jealous of Mary Poppins getting such high praise from Conrad.

He stood his spoon in the ice cream and wiped his mouth with a serviette. 'No, *I* will thank Isabelle. You look lovely.' Elena felt the heat from her no doubt glowing cheeks.

A loud rumble of thunder permeated the walls and announced the arrival of the rain. A few gentle drops tapped the window and gradually got heavier until it looked like there was a waterfall outside.

'That's not good,' he groaned. They peered through the water-speckled window at the deluge outside. 'Not good when you're on a motor bike anyway.'

'Maybe it will blow over?' Elena secretly hoped they'd

be trapped by a monsoon for the week and would have to live on roast beef and ice cream.

'Yeah, maybe.' He didn't look convinced.

The next two hours passed like ten minutes. The time just raced away. She wanted to savour every minute spent with him. There was no break in the weather, and the heavy clouds had brought the darkness earlier than usual. They had the place to themselves, apart from a couple of regulars propped up at the bar.

'Excuse me for a moment.' He rose from his chair and ambled over to the bar.

Elena noticed he made a point of speaking to the two old guys, and within a few seconds, they were all laughing like old friends. How did he do that? There was something about this man that put people at ease.

Yes, the physical attraction was there, and he was gorgeous to say the least, but it took more than just looks and a great body. Most men who had successful careers and great wealth had an air of arrogance and superiority about them. When they had what they wanted, when they wanted, it could poison the soul, but not this man. Elena often judged people by the way they treated others, and so far, it was ten out of ten.

He came back to the table and was chuckling to himself with a large white wine in one hand and a pint of Guinness in the other. She glanced at his drink and diverted her gaze to his handsome face, remembering what he'd said about the bike and second chances. He spotted her observation and decided to explain.

'Alf and Ron, over there—farmers, by the way—tell me this weather is in for the night. It's meant to clear in the morning.' He sat down in his chair and sipped the fluffy white head of his pint.

'Oh.' Elena glanced over to the two old guys. 'So you know them?'

'No, but you can't beat local knowledge.' More

evidence of his geniality. 'So . . .' He pulled out a small key on an overly large key fob and dangled it by his fingertips. 'I got the last room. They've only got three anyway.'

Elena raised her eyebrows, excited on one hand but hesitant on the other. There was nowhere else she would rather be right now, but it was less than twenty-four hours since they'd met, and they were spending the night together? Damn right! *Dirty stop-out!*

'Don't worry, I can sleep on the floor,' he said hastily. 'I'll get you home first thing in the morning.'

Elena knew she would be perfectly safe with him, and once she had given herself permission, she felt like a child on Christmas Eve.

'You don't have to sleep on the floor. We'll sort something out.' *You can sort me out. God, I'm turning into a floozy.*

'You still haven't told me the name of your gym empire?' She tried desperately to redirect her thoughts.

'It's called Superior Fitness.'

'Is it a family business, or did you start from scratch?'

'My brother ran the first gym I opened, and as the business expanded, so did his role.'

'So you and your brother are partners?' She wanted to know everything about him, what made him tick.

'No, he used to work for me.' He took a deep breath and ran his fingers through his hair.

Elena could tell it was a touchy subject. 'Are you a hard taskmaster?' She leaned forward and placed her elbows on the table.

He gave her a mock smile. 'He abused his position, shall we say.'

Conrad sacking his brother? That didn't seem to fit with the man in front of her. He must have done something pretty serious.

'Is he older or younger than you?'

'He's thirty-six, two years older than me.' He wasn't very good at hiding his unease as he brushed away imaginary crumbs from his shirt. 'How about you? Brothers, sisters?'

She suspected it was more than just an innocent question. He was steering her away from the thorny issue of his brother.

'No, just little old me.'

His mood had darkened, just a fraction. It was clear she had wandered into hostile territory. Time to change course.

'Right, Mr Fitness. How often do you hit the gym?' *Every day by the look of him.*

'It depends on work really. I had a workout this morning in the hotel gym, while you were getting your beauty sleep. And may I say it's working so far.' Darkness lifted. She loved the way his eyes traced her face as he spoke. His compliment was repaid with a sweet smile.

'I haven't had a good workout for ages.' She leaned back in her chair and crossed her legs seductively, the white wine wasting no time in weakening her self-restraint.

Conrad swallowed hard and watched her intently. 'What areas do you think you need work on?' A devilish look flashed across his face, he leaned forward with his arms on the table.

'You're the expert, what do you think?' This was so unlike Elena's usual behaviour, but she just couldn't stop herself.

'Well, with most ladies, it's usually the tummy area or thighs. But in your case, I would say your backside needs some attention.' His hand gripped the pint glass tightly.

Elena felt her face flush again. She liked this game. 'Really? And what would you suggest? A hard or a light workout?'

'Definitely hard—the more intense, the better. The backside can be a very stubborn spot for ladies. It tends to need a good going-over.' His face displayed signs of a repressed grin. He liked it too.

'Mm, I think you're right. Mine is desperate for a good

going-over.' *I'm turning into a slut. What is this man doing to me?*

Darkness coupled with the lashing rain and the empty pub seemed to intensify the already charged atmosphere between them. They were in a bubble; no other people, no noise or distractions; just the two of them. She was satisfied from the food, but there was a part of her that was hungrier than ever.

She had never had a one-night stand before, and now she was about to spend the night with a virtual stranger. So far, he'd been the perfect gentleman, so far.

Elena fought to maintain the illusion of calm. Her face burned red hot, and that wasn't the only place either.

'Anything else you would suggest?' She finished her wine.

'I'd probably give your chest some attention also.' Despite his cool exterior, she could see from the rise and fall of his chest that he was almost panting. He gulped down the remainder of his pint. 'You know, being your personal sentry for the night has worn me out.'

'Well, it's what every princess expects. I hope I haven't worn you out too much.'

'No, not yet.' His words almost had the same effect as touch. The only thing keeping her from pouncing on him was the table acting as referee, keeping them apart.

'Well, maybe we should head to our room before you fall asleep on me because I don't think I can carry you up the stairs.' She scrutinized his expression, wanting confirmation that he felt the same.

'Don't you worry, I'm sure you'll keep me *up* a little while longer. Shall we?' He gestured towards the stairs. They both stood a bit too quickly and smirked at each other.

'After you, madam.' He walked behind her towards the crooked oak-panelled door that led to the stairs.

She knew exactly where his eyes were as her heart hammered in her chest as if it was trying to escape. She felt a little dizzy. Was it the wine? Or not enough oxygen for her craving body?

Conrad stood in the doorway and held it open with an outstretched arm. 'Ladies first.' He handed her the key. 'We'll be staying in the penthouse tonight.'

She was close enough to smell his gorgeous cologne as she squeezed past his large chest, which filled the narrow opening. They headed up the dimly lit staircase, each tread squeaking more than the last. She glanced back at him and saw his eyes transfixed on her bottom and swayed her hips as they ascended to the first floor.

Two crooked old doors marked with the numbers 1 and 2 sat on the landing. A TV show emitted loudly from one of the rooms as she apprehensively checked the long key fob. Room 3 would be theirs for the night.

She climbed the last flight. Her mouth was dry and her legs weak with anticipation. Another well-worn door came into view. A tarnished brass number 3 hung in the centre of it.

'This is it.' She fumbled with the key nervously and dropped it on the carpeted floor.

Stopping one step down from the landing, she bent to retrieve it. He was several steps below her, his face level with her protruding backside stretching the denim to its max. His eager hands gently caressed her bottom, and a deep lusty groan rumbled from him.

She gasped unintentionally at the feel of his touch as she rose slowly, clutching the key, her skin hypersensitive even through the denim. It felt so good. She had yearned to feel his touch all afternoon, and now her wish had come true.

His hands became firmer, more aggressive, more demanding. They slipped under her T-shirt and went straight for her shoulders. The firm pressure eroded her inhibitions, with each sensual squeeze sending a surge of lascivious thoughts flashing through her mind. His fingers left a trail of tingling flesh as they headed down to her waistband and pulled impatiently. His breathing was harsh, and even though she couldn't see his face, she could feel his urgency because she felt it too.

Slowly sliding her hands along her thighs to her hips, she unbuttoned her jeans, giving him the green light. Conrad ripped them down like they were on fire. He paused to relish the white round fleshy cheeks divided by red lace.

'Oh fuck,' he groaned, and instinctively, she bent over and dropped to her knees, just a small strip of lace hiding her modesty.

His face was so close she could feel his warm breath. She felt half crazy, desperate for his touch. She arched her back and thrust her bottom back towards him.

He buried his face deep in the hot damp strip of material. The feeling was exquisite, a relief, the sensation almost too much to bear. Clamping his hands on her hips, he thrust his face deeper. A loud gasp escaped Elena through gritted teeth. This was utterly filthy, but she didn't care. Hormones coursed through her body superseding all logical thought. Coming up for air, he slid his hands under her T-shirt and expertly released her bra, freeing her swollen breasts from their captivity. His big hard hands squeezed and groped greedily.

His attention turned to her back, and his hands slid slowly, firmly, from her hips to her neck, forcing her shoulders down towards the floor. She was trapped like a gazelle caught in the claws of a lion, the difference being she wanted to be caught, to be eaten by this king of the beasts.

Thrusting back towards him once more, her bottom high in the air, she waited to be taken with a growing, aching want, a desperate need. He took the hint and returned to the hot fleshy cushion, his expert tongue knowing exactly where to go as it slid gloriously along each edge of the lace barrier, teasing her. The retreating tongue was replaced by a ravenous mouth, gently biting, tasting, hungry for more.

Anyone could have walked up those stairs, but it didn't matter. There was no one else, no staircase, no pub. It had all fallen away, leaving unimaginable lust.

The lion lifted his head and stretched her spread cheeks wider, her soaking lips slipping each side of their red border. Another low groan—no, a growl—came from behind, but the respite was short-lived.

Her exquisite torture began once more. Biting and then sucking her wet lips free, the pressure of his nose stimulating her tight anus, she heard the jingling of his belt being undone. Desperately, she wanted to feel him inside her, to move her position, but she was paralysed by pleasure.

Reaching back and pulling aside her thong with a frantic need for release, she granted him access, which he took full advantage of as his tongue slipped in an out of her soaking wet sex. The skilled tongue circled her throbbing clitoris, teasing it, taunting it. Reaching back with both hands, her face pressed hard into the coarse carpet by his need, she pulled her cheeks open for him. The feeling grew more intense, more ferocious. The exploring lips sucking her clitoris showed no mercy, she could tell from the on-off pressure of his face that he was pleasuring himself at the same time, and it sent her over the edge.

Her whole body bucked and jolted with an explosion of pleasure. In those last blissful moments, she had no control of her body. It had been taken over, possessed by an unseen force. He removed his face as she jumped from the aftershocks of her orgasm.

Conrad had a sheen of sweat, and Elena's excitement smeared across his face; his breathing was ragged. She wobbled to her feet, her whole body weak with pure satisfaction. They didn't speak. He quickly pulled up his jeans, his huge erection poking out, and then he grabbed Elena's face with both hands and kissed her deeply. The tongue that had been inside her and was responsible for that heavenly orgasm was now exploring her mouth. She could taste the bitter sweetness of her own sex, and it turned her on. How could she still be turned on? She had just had the orgasm to end all orgasms.

Her jeans around her ankles and her bra hanging off, they stumbled over and banged into the door, lips still locked. Elena desperately tried to put the key in the door.

'Quickly.' Conrad panted.

The door swung open, and they tumbled into the room. He kicked the door shut and grabbed her by the neck, kissing her as though his life depended on it. Their room was up in the eaves, and the heavy rain rattled on the tiles and lashed hard at the window of the dark room. They kissed deeply, tongues delving into each other's mouth, eager to explore every part of each other.

Pushing his trousers to the floor, he took Elena's hand and placed it on his solid erection, he stopped kissing her long enough to say one word, 'Pull.'

She did as she was commanded and pulled his length with a reverse grip. Instantly, he gave a groan of relief, desperate for release. His hand slid between her cheeks, and he slipped his fingers inside her, his thumb pressing against her tight arse.

God it was dirty, but she loved it. Biting into his lip, Elena tugged harder, desperate to make him climax. She couldn't stand it any longer and sank to her knees to return the favour, after having just experienced what it felt like to be so achingly close.

Gripping his girth, her red lips slid over the hot salty flesh. She felt like a slut, but that was part of the turn-on. For this man, she would do anything. His cock filled her mouth as she sucked and slurped greedily, sliding backwards and forwards over his veiny length. Elena knew he was close and wanted to please him the way he had pleased her.

'Shit, I can't hold on,' he moaned.

'Give it to me.' She pumped away at him with both hands, and he grabbed her hair in his fists and shot hot thick semen into the back of her throat with a roar of relief.

His stiffness subsiding, she held him in her mouth and pulled his softening cock a few more times to make sure she had milked him dry. Elena liked the thought of a little part of him inside of her.

Taking his cock out of her mouth, she looked up to him, his chest rising and falling. He looked down at her. 'You didn't spill a drop, did you?' She shook her head. 'Naughty girl!'

Conrad wobbled over to the bed, his jeans around his ankles, and drained in more ways than one, he fell onto the bed which squeaked even more than the stairs. Elena slipped out of her shoes and jeans and straightened her ravaged underwear. A flash of lightning illuminated the room, briefly giving a quick snapshot of the lion sprawled out on his back, paws above his head, and a look of satisfaction on his face from the feast on which he had just gorged.

Pulling off his shoes and jeans with his black shorts, she could just about see his flaccid penis resting on his soft balls, looking just as spent as its owner. Her eyes adjusted to the dark, and she could see there was a bedside lamp, but the darkness seemed to bring an intimacy that the light would destroy.

Tugging his polo shirt over his head, Elena gently kissed his lips.

'Thank you,' he whispered before drifting into sleep.

She yearned to talk to him about, well, anything really, just to hear his voice. But he had gone a whole night without sleep, and the physical toll of orgasm was more than his body could bear.

Elena fumbled around in the old wardrobe and found a thick blanket and placed it over him, removed her T-shirt and climbed into bed, snuggling next to his warm body.

Sliding her hand over his stomach, she rested her head on his chest.

Elena had never been more content than lying with this lion of a man, but lions were wild animals, they couldn't be tamed, couldn't be trusted, could they?

CHAPTER SEVEN

The morning sun shone brightly through the old sash window, the room seemed much smaller in the daylight with its floral paper and chintzy curtains. The weight of their bodies had caused the soft mattress to buckle, and they lay in the centre of the sunken bed facing each other. A feather-light kiss to the lips woke her.

'Morning. Sleep well?' he asked through sleepy eyes.

'Mmmm,' she croaked, stretching an arm over his shoulder. 'Very well, thank you. It must have been that workout you gave me.' His hand ran down her side and stopped at the hollow before her hips.

'I usually work out first thing in the morning,' he mumbled.

'Really?'

'Yeah, I like to get the blood pumping, you know?'

'Yes, you do like a good pumping, don't you?' *What the hell is happening to me? I can't even face toast first thing in the morning.*

He ran his hand over her leg. She could feel his growing erection. 'Someone's up early, aren't they?' She kissed him on the lips lightly, sucking his bottom lip hard, and felt his full erection push against her leg.

'See what you do to me?' he murmured.

'Well, we can't go for breakfast with that wide awake, can we?' Elena teased. 'Whatever shall we do with it?'

Conrad rolled on top of her and pinned her down by the arms. He licked her slightly open mouth.

'You have such a naughty mouth.'

Kissing her firmly, deeply, their tongues embracing each other, she felt lust eating away at all rational thought, at all reasoning, consuming all other thoughts until nothing else was left.

'I'm not sure if I shouldn't give it a damn good fucking just to teach it a lesson.'

God, I want him.

Like all predators, he went for the throat. The sensation of his warm moist mouth on her neck, sucking and biting, caused her body to break out in a wave of goose bumps from head to toe. He parted her legs with his, and his face moved down to her bare chest for a taste of flesh. His tongue circled her hardening nipples before sucking and licking to the point that they ached. Elena grabbed his hair with both hands to stop her arms flailing about as the heat of desire built. His cock brushed over her vagina, and she raised her knees.

'Then again, I haven't finished with that backside of yours. That needs a damn good fucking too.'

Elena had never ever considered anal. It wasn't something she was interested in, but the feeling of his hot cock nudging between the cheeks of her bottom was undeniably erotic.

She didn't want to wait any longer. Her impatience took over. 'Fuck me . . . please.'

He looked into her eyes for a moment and sat up on his knees. She lay there wide open with no inhibitions. Positioning his cock at the entrance to her sex, he slid the tip between her wet lips and placed his hands each side of her head. It was a tease, and he knew it. He slid deeper, watching her every expression with a determined look carved on his face. She wriggled and bucked, trying to get more of each move he made.

'Greedy girl.'

Reaching and grabbing his hard buttocks, she tried to pull him closer, wanting to feel him deep inside her. Slowly, he lowered himself down. Elena groaned at the exquisite feeling as he stretched her open until every last inch filled her up. Christ it felt so good, thick and hard. Their mouths locked. She could still taste remnants of herself on his forceful lips.

He eased in and out, building the pace steadily. Each stroke built with intensity, a little harder, a little faster until he was ramming into her, his heavy balls slapping against her bottom. They were both grunting like animals, unaware of the noise they were making. Conrad was fucking her hard now, harder than she had ever been fucked before, inching her up the bed with each thrust.

Feeling her orgasm building, her hands grabbing and clutching at the bed, she knocked the lamp off the bedside table, and it smashed on the floor. The bed squeaked like a well-used trampoline, and she could feel him twitching inside her. He lay across her chest and grabbed her backside with both hands, filling her to the hilt.

It was more than she could take. Elena's nails dug into his back as she clung onto him, every muscle a ball of knots as she came closer and closer until she let out a shriek and climaxed around him gloriously. She was still bathing in the glow of post-orgasm heaven when, suddenly, he withdrew with a grunt and shot his hot creamy liquid over her belly, the force so powerful it reached her neck.

He collapsed next to her like he'd been shot with a tranquillizer, groaning into the bruised mattress. Turning onto his side to cuddle her, his arm landed in the sticky pool that lay on her tummy.

'Hmm, sorry. I didn't have time to put it anywhere else,' he puffed, gently tapping his finger on her mouth.

'Naughty boy,' she retorted.

Getting off the bed, he went into the en suite bathroom that was no bigger than a phone box.

'I think you needed that, didn't you?'

'Well, you shouldn't be so damn sexy then, should you?'

Standing in the bathroom doorway with a towel in his hand, she got her first proper look at him naked as he stood there in all his glory, gladiatorial-like, every part of him in proportion. A light dusting of hair covered his chest, his swollen penis now hanging, swung gently as he moved. Using the towel to remove the evidence of his climax, he wiped Elena dry and threw it like a basketball into the bathroom.

His hands on his hips, he glanced at his clothes folded neatly and then back to Elena. 'And how did my clothes get over there?' He had a bogus frown on his face.

Elena tried to stifle the smile that had crept onto her mouth. 'Don't worry, I was the perfect lady. The light was off, and I had my eyes closed. Didn't see a thing.' She held up her palms level with her raised eyebrows.

'Well, that's okay then. Is this a fetish of yours?' he asked with his head bent down, looking at his feet still clad in black socks.

She leaned over the edge of the bed to see what he meant. Looking from his feet up to his face, trying not to laugh, she replied, 'I didn't get that far down.'

'Good answer.' He smirked as he pointed a finger at her. 'Well, in that case, let me take you to breakfast.' He could take her anywhere he wanted, she would gladly follow.

They showered separately, the cubicle was so small Conrad could barely move and banged just about every part of his body as he showered.

As they left their lust nest, Elena took a last look at the pretty room before the door closed. It wasn't the Savoy, but it didn't matter, it would always be their special place.

Conrad closed the door, and they both glanced at the scene of their first sexual encounter then looked at each other mischievously.

He slapped her bottom. 'Quick, my appetite's growing.'

They entered the lounge, George stood behind the bar, cleaning a glass.

'Morning, George.'

'Good morning, sir, miss. Did you, erm . . . sleep well?'

'Like a baby, thanks, George.'

'Would you like breakfast?'

The smell of bacon and toast mingled with the aroma of fresh coffee made Elena's tummy rumble. She'd built up an appetite and was hungrier than she thought.

'Yes, please.' Conrad took out a £50 note from his wallet.

'Oh no, sir. The breakfast is included in the price,' said George, waving his hands at Conrad.

'Er, no. I'm afraid, George, we somehow managed to break the bedside lamp last night. I've cleaned up the mess, but I want to pay for the damage.'

'No, don't you worry about that.' He looked left and right as if checking no one was about. Placing his hands on the bar, he leaned over to them. 'To tell you the truth, I'm more worried about the bed. So long as that's survived, I don't mind.' Elena felt her face turn several shades darker than George's rosy cheeks.

'Er, the bed's fine, George.' Even Conrad was stunned.

'Good man. Now what would you both like?'

They ordered their food and sniggered like two teenagers as they headed for the table they'd sat at the night before. They enjoyed a lovely full English breakfast with coffee and orange juice.

'I don't usually eat this sort of food, but I really did need that.' He looked at his watch.

'Do you need to go?' Elena did. She had to be at work in an hour but didn't want to end her time with him.

'Yeah, we're going to have to make tracks. I've got a

very important meeting today, and I need to catch up with Isabelle for an hour before I go in.'

Elena knew it was utterly stupid, but she hated to hear him say another woman's name, especially one as pretty as Isabelle.

'She must have a very understanding partner, working weekends.' She wanted more info on the potential opposition.

'Yes, Mark's a great guy. He's a student doctor in his final year, so he works a lot of weekends, so she has time off in the week with him.' The information didn't really mean anything, but it made her feel better.

Hearing her phone beeping, she took it out of her pocket to check it. 'Sorry, do you mind?'

'No, not at all,' he said, finishing his coffee. It was a text from Jasmine.

Hi, honey, just on way back from Paris. Sorry, no luck with getting you a hunky Frenchman!

I'm exhausted from all the shopping. Well, not just shopping! Busy all week, but you must come to my house warming on Saturday, and I want all the gossip and every detail. Can't wait!!

Any time after 7.00. It's Fairfield Grange, Grange Road, SW3, number 63.

Love, Jasmine x x

'Do you need to go?' He seemed curious as to why the text had made her smile.

'No, it's a friend of mine. She's moving to somewhere called Fairfield Grange, and she's having a get-together on Saturday.'

'Very nice. It's a new development, quite exclusive. What is it she does?'

'She . . . er . . . she's a PA for a very high-profile businessman. Yes, that's what she does.' *Messed that up completely.*

'What time do you need to be at work?'

'Not until about ten or eleven.'

Dawn would go ape if she rolled in at eleven, but Elena was desperate to get more time with him. She wondered how they were going to leave this. Her nerves kicked in. What if he didn't want to see her again? Of course, he would, wouldn't he?

'What's your number? I'll send you a text, and then you'll have mine.' She watched his face closely to judge his reaction.

'Yeah, okay.'

Yes. He didn't bat an eyelid and gave her his number. Elena sent him a text straight away. His phone beeped, but he didn't check it.

'Ready?'

No, not yet. 'Yep!'

Retrieving their helmets and jackets from behind the bar, they thanked their host and headed to the car park to find the Ducati waiting patiently. Elena was just as nervous the second time around getting on the bike but this time for different reasons. The last twenty-four hours had flown by, and she didn't want them to be over yet.

The bike cut gracefully through the air, charging them forward towards the moment of truth. Would he want to see her again? Elena didn't just hold on, she held him, savouring the last cuddle.

She tried to console herself with the thought of telling Jasmine all about her adventure, but it didn't work. And as if she had clicked her heels together and said 'There's no place like home,' she was there, outside her small terraced house. Climbing off the bike, she was completely lost for words. It was the first time there had been an awkward silence between them.

'Do you want to come in for a while?' She tried to extend their time a little longer.

'I can't. I'm short on time as it is.'

'Conrad—'

He interrupted. 'You don't have to thank me, Elena.

Thank you.'

Actually, she wasn't. She was going to ask if she could see him again.

He leaned over and lightly kissed her. 'I've got to go.'

Desperately trying to think of something, she made a joke that smashed her hopes to a thousand pieces. 'Got to get back to the wife and kids, eh?'

As human beings, we are finely tuned to spot the smallest change in facial expressions, to read a situation instinctively. And there it was, the flicker of his eyes, just a fraction of a second, but she saw it.

'Are you married, Conrad?' Her mouth had overridden her brain.

His short pause answered the question. 'Elena . . . it's complicated.'

'Complicated? You're either married or you're not. Which is it?' She knew the answer but had to hear him say it. 'Well?'

'Yes.'

With a heavy sigh, she dropped her head in her hands. A tempest of emotions raged inside of her. She couldn't believe it. He had seemed so honest, decent. Of all the emotions, anger was the first to raise its ugly head.

'Married? You're fucking married? And what about kids? Do you have any kids?'

'No.'

'You and Alan had a competition, did you? To see who could get me into bed first? Did you have wager on the side?'

'Elena, don't put me in the same bracket as that shit.'

She snapped back, 'Why not? You saw your chance, and you took it. Why didn't you just call me a cab on Sunday morning?' He sat staring at the dials on the bike; his silence only fuelled her anger. 'Why didn't you say?'

'It never seemed the right time,' he said with a look of embarrassment mixed with disappointment.

'What do you mean? Before or after I gave you a blow

job?' Sarcasm rang through her voice.

'No, it wasn't like that. I can explain.'

'I can explain? That's a bit clichéd, isn't it?' she barked. 'I think I can guess—have a little fun on Sunday, drop me off on Monday, your wife and I would be none the wiser.'

'Elena, listen to me.'

She interrupted him once more, rather childishly, with a hand in front of his face. 'Conrad, I don't want to know. I've heard enough. Just go,' she said calmly, anger morphed into sorrow.

Turning her back on him, she walked up the path to her front door, her eyes filled with tears. The second the door latched behind her, they spilled, charging down her pale skin.

She leaned back against the door and ran through the time they spent together. She was so disappointed. She knew he was a charmer, but a liar, a cheat? Why was she so upset after only knowing him for one day? People had one-night stands all the time. What was the big deal? After all, he was just a man. So why did she feel so betrayed?

Elena hadn't heard the bike start. Was he waiting for her? Was he going to knock the door? Her sobbing was replaced with hope.

Sitting on the bike, Conrad looked at the green front door. What was he doing? He didn't want to hurt this girl, quite the opposite, but it wasn't the right time to try and unravel the ball of string his life had become.

One half of him wanted to break down that door and take her with him, but the other half said, 'Don't be stupid. You've got it all worked out. Stick to the plan and don't complicate things unnecessarily.'

Looking at his watch, he knew he had to go. He'd been working on this deal for months, and this meeting was pivotal for his long-term plan. Reluctantly, he started the bike and shoved on his helmet. Putting his arm through the chin strap of Elena's, he paused for a moment and then sped away.

Hearing the roar of the bike fading, her hopes faded with it, the tears returned triumphantly with reinforcements. *I knew it was too good to be true.* She opened the door to look at the vacant space where he had been, and hoping that she would hear the bike bringing him back to her, she lingered there for a moment. *That was it then.*

Elena put on the kettle and noticed the time. Nine twenty. 'Shit!' Deciding she couldn't face work, she called in sick, only to be told that Dawn was on holiday for the week. At least that was one thing that'd gone her way.

Conrad sat in the meeting with Isabelle beside him, his thoughts anywhere but on business, even though this was an extremely important meeting.

What had he done? What must she think of him? He already knew that. She had told him so, but she was wrong. That's not who he was, and the comparison between him and that fucking scum Alan made his stomach turn. He wanted to right the wrong, but knew it was better left alone.

'Conrad, Conrad?' His thoughts were interrupted by Isabelle.

'What was that sorry?'

'Mr Duggan wants to see the proposed Scottish sites and the architect's drawings regarding the new layout.'

'Er, yes, of course. I'm afraid I don't have that information with me today, but I will get it to you via e-mail ASAP.' *Don't fuck this up. It's taken five months to get to this point.*

All he could think of was the way they had parted. She hadn't deserved that, but it was too late to go back now.

Leaving the meeting, Conrad apologised for his lack of concentration and blamed it on him feeling under the weather. Isabelle knew something was wrong and suggested he take the rest of the day off to get himself right while she saw to it that the requested information was sent over.

Getting into the car, he switched his phone on. Conrad saw he had one new message. Checking it, he realised it was the message Elena had sent in the pub. It simply read, *don't forget me. X*

Elena spent the next two days in her PJs, watching old black-and-white movies, curled up on the lounge suite with the curtains closed. She knew it was silly but wanted to let her wounds heal.

Her phone buzzed, and she scrambled under the fluffy blanket to find it.

Oh . . . Jasmine.

Hoping it was Conrad, she disappointed. The text message read,

Hi, honey, are you still okay for Saturday? Hope you are well and having a good week. Can't wait to see you! Love, Jasmine x x

Her hand flopped down with the phone, and she looked at herself sitting in the darkened room surrounded by chocolate wrappers and tissues. Elena wasn't looking forward to explaining the weekend to Jasmine, but she could brush over it in some way. She was, however, looking forward to seeing her friend.

Throwing off the blanket, determined no man was going to ruin her life, she switched off the TV and pulled back the curtains, ran up the stairs, and focused on Saturday. She decided the first step to putting Conrad behind her was to buy a new dress for the occasion. Saturday night was going to pull her through the week.

Dressed in something other than pyjamas, Elena grabbed her car keys and slammed the door behind her.

Returning to work with the motivation that Dawn wasn't there, she found it helped keep busy, although she still checked her phone every half an hour just in case *someone* called.

Before she knew it, it was Friday. Elena went home to prepare for Saturday night, hanging out her new mint green dress and feeling pleased with herself that she'd managed to get a bargain in the end-of-season sale.

A dark cloud came over her, and she wondered what Conrad was doing right now. She longed to see him. The thought had been there all week, but shoving it to the back of her mind, she'd kept busy and not allowed herself to dwell on the what-ifs.

Surrendering to her thoughts, Elena wished she hadn't been so aggressive with him. Maybe he did have an explanation. But whatever it was, he had taken his opportunity to leave. He had not contacted her. What could she think but what she already knew?

Determined to enjoy her weekend, Elena booked herself a taxi to Jasmine's. She planned on letting her hair down tomorrow, and after spending the evening with a bottle of wine, she decided to have an early night. Tomorrow was a new day, a new start after all.

CHAPTER EIGHT

Elena was woken by a loud knocking at the front door. Lifting her heavy head off the pillow, she looked at the bedside clock through a veil of red hair. Seven fifty.

What, two Saturdays on the run? Really? She wobbled downstairs in a zombie-like state and wondered what Jasmine had sent this time.

She opened the door to find a small fat man with no hat, no hair, and no teeth and four boxes on her doorstep. 'Sign there please, darlin',' he whistled and handed her a crumpled piece of paper. She scribbled her name before handing him back the delivery note with a grumpy 'thank you.'

Carrying the boxes into the kitchen, she hoped it wasn't an omen. Last Saturday had started in exactly the same way. With a hot cup of tea in her hand, she stretched, trying to shake off last night's slumber.

'Oh no.' She opened the first box. It was the clothes that Conrad had bought for her.

Elena ripped open every box and searched through them. She wasn't bothered about the clothes. She was looking for a note, a card, a message of some kind, but there was nothing. Besides, he hadn't even sent them;

Mary Poppins had.

She'd been trying to put last weekend behind her all week, and then this had landed, throwing her out of kilter. Elena couldn't bear to look at them. She stuffed the clothes into a plastic bag and threw them under the stairs. They'd be going to the charity shop first thing Monday morning. Feeling the gloom slowly creeping over her, she jumped to her feet, intent on enjoying her evening with Jasmine and threw her anguish under the stairs with the unwanted clothes.

Dressed, she headed out to buy a card and flowers, leaving her emotions on the kitchen table together with her cold tea.

Standing at the door of 63 Fairfield Grange, Elena felt slightly nervous. She could hear the distorted noise of conversation and laughter through the black door. Checking herself, she pressed the buzzer. The door opened, and there stood Jasmine with her arms held out towards Elena.

'Hello, gorgeous.' She wrapped her arms around Elena and kissed her on the cheek. 'Welcome to my humble abode.'

'Thank you. I've got you a little something.' She gave the flowers to Jasmine, together with a small silver bag which contained a card, chocolates, and wine.

'Oh, honey, you shouldn't have, you silly sausage. You didn't have to do that. Come in. I'll introduce you to everyone.'

They walked through a spacious hallway which led into a huge open-plan lounge and kitchen. Everything was white, with the exception of the dark hardwood flooring in the lounge. All Jasmine's furniture was in place, which made it look like a bigger version of her old apartment.

The kitchen looked like a florist's, with bouquet after bouquet lined up around the black granite worktop. Elena felt embarrassed by her meagre bunch of roses.

Alive with the hum of people enjoying themselves, the apartment was full to the brim. Jasmine led Elena around by the hand to meet all her friends one by one. With so many different names, she had forgotten the last one with the introduction of every new one.

'Just Mum and Dad left. Jack, have you seen my parents?' she shouted above the noise to a skinny blond guy standing in the kitchen.

'Try the bedroom!' he shouted back, his hand over his mouth to stop the nachos he'd just eaten from escaping.

They entered a modest-sized bedroom where an elegantly dressed lady, wearing a slim black skirt just below the knee and a cream cashmere sweater, was unpacking a Louis Vuitton suitcase.

'Mum, I'd like you to meet my very good friend, Elena White. Elena, this is my mother, Katherine.'

She turned to face them with a warm friendly smile and took Elena's hand and kissed her on both cheeks.

'Very nice to meet you, Mrs Saunders.'

'And you, dear. Please call me Katherine. Elena's such a pretty name. It goes well with your pretty face.'

'Thank you.'

Elena felt at ease in her company. She had blond hair with a touch of grey that finished just below the jaw line, a long fringe gracefully swept to one side of her attractive face, flinty blue eyes, perfect lips, and a slim figure. The V-neck of her sweater showed a hint of cleavage, and she had an air of wealth about her.

'We were at school together,' said Elena.

'Oh lovely, and what do you think of her new apartment?'

'It's fantastic. I'm green with envy, actually,' she whispered, pretending Jasmine couldn't hear.

'Yes, so am I. She does get some very good perks with her work.'

What? She doesn't know, does she?

Jasmine hastily changed the course of the conversation.

'Mum, do you really need to do that now?' Jasmine sighed, shaking her head at her mother putting clothes away.

'Mum's staying the night, and we're having a girly day tomorrow shopping.'

'It will only take a minute. You know I won't relax until it's done.'

'Do you know where Dad has disappeared to?'

'Where do you think he is?'

Jasmine gave a loud puff. 'He's a nightmare with those stinky things. Don't be too long, Mum.'

'No, I won't.'

Once again, Jasmine led Elena around by the hand like it was her first day at big school. Back in the lounge, she could see that the two French doors that led to the balcony were open.

'Yep, there he is.'

As they approached the balcony, Elena saw a man wearing black trousers and a light grey shirt, his back to them, leaning on the railings, surrounded by a haze of cigar smoke.

'Dad, I'd like you to meet my friend, Elena. Elena, this is my dad.'

He turned to face them, and Elena's heart stopped beating. The shock took her breath away.

Alan Windsor! No, no, no!

Puffing a large plume of smoke over his shoulder, he leaned forward with a slimy grin and kissed her on the cheek. Elena recoiled slightly.

'Lovely to meet you. I'm Alan.' His tone was overly friendly. 'How do you two know one another?'

'We were at school together, Dad,' Jasmine answered for her. Then one of her guests called for her attention, asking how to use the built-in coffee machine. 'I won't be a moment.' Elena turned in a panic to see Jasmine swallowed up by the crowd.

'So you know my daughter?' His voice made her stomach turn.

She folded her arms and ignored the question. 'I thought your name was Windsor?'

'Windsor, Saunders, does it matter? Sometimes I use Windsor for business purposes. I have a reputation, shall we say, that can follow me around.'

He sucked hard on the fat cigar, the tip glowing bright red, red for danger. He didn't bother to turn his head and puffed the smoke right into Elena's face making her cough.

'Oh, dear, you okay? Not *choking*, are you?' He had a smug look on his face. 'How's my friend Conrad?'

'You bastard, I know what you did that night.' He didn't flinch.

'What are you talking about?' The cigar waggled in her face as he spoke.

'If you weren't Jasmine's dad, I'd call the police and have you locked up right now.'

'I doubt that, darling. Me, a wealthy businessman with an unblemished past, and you, a cheap tart who advertises herself on the Internet? Wake up.'

She felt like spitting in his face. 'Fuck you, Alan!'

'Anytime, baby. Just name the place.' He grinned. 'Does Jasmine know that's what you do?'

Before she could answer, they were joined by his wife Katherine. 'I knew you'd be out here. I thought you were cutting back on those things.' She stood close by his side.

'Aren't I allowed to treat myself every now and again?'

She put her arm through his and snuggled up to him. 'You have been introduced to Elena, haven't you?'

'Yes, we've met, haven't we?' His eyes ran up and down her, and although she was fully clothed, she felt naked, vulnerable.

'Isn't she a pretty thing? Beautiful hair.'

Elena gritted her teeth and squeezed a smile out.

'Yes, there's a lucky man out there tonight, I'll bet.'

'Alan.' Katherine frowned and tapped him lightly on the arm. 'You'll have to excuse my husband. He gets a bit carried away sometimes.'

Elena was astounded at how brazen Alan was. He hadn't batted an eyelid when he saw her. His arrogance and confidence was sickening. She had to get away. 'Would you excuse me for a moment?'

'Of course, dear,' answered Katherine while Alan did his very best to intimidate her with his unwavering glare.

Elena found the bathroom and locked the door, panic setting in. Fucking hell, *Alan was Jasmine's dad. How did that happen? What a mess! What—a—mess!*

She paced around the small space like a caged animal. Racking her brain, she ran through all her options. It was too early to go, she'd only just got there, but as soon as a respectable time had passed, she would call a cab and get the hell out of there. In the meantime, she would just steer clear of him, maybe find someone to chat to, although she wasn't in a very talkative mood.

As Elena left the bathroom, she was grabbed by Jasmine, who led her into the master bedroom and closed the door. 'Right, while we've got five minutes, how did last Saturday go?'

Jasmine not now, please. 'Er . . . it was . . . okay.'

'Okay? You seemed to be having a great time when you texted me. Wasn't he what you expected?'

'No, not at all what I expected.' *Please let this conversation be over.* Elena's eyes kept dropping to the floor, unable to maintain eye contact while they were having this conversation.

'So you won't be seeing him again then?'

'I hope not, but you never know. We may bump into each other.' *I can't believe I just said that.*

'Well, look at it this way, at least it wasn't a bad experience, and now you can move on to the next one.'

It wasn't a bad experience? It couldn't have been any worse, and it wasn't getting much better either. Elena wrestled a smile onto her face.

'And guess what?' Jasmine said wide-eyed. She tottered

around the king-sized bed in ridiculously high heels. 'I got you something from Paris.' She reached down and handed Elena a small pyramid-shaped gold bag with ribbon handles.

'Jasmine, I think you've given me more than enough.'

'Don't be silly. Go on.' She nodded. 'Open it.'

Elena opened the bag with a counterfeit smile. Inside, the gift bag was a black beret and a bottle of Chanel No. 5. 'Thank you, Jaz. That's really lovely of you. I've never had Chanel before.' She placed the bag down and wrapped her arms around Jasmine, fighting back the tears as the enormity of the situation began to overwhelm her.

'You're very welcome.' Jasmine took the perfume from the bag and opened the box. 'Try it.' Elena raised her chin, and Jasmine sprayed it onto her neck. 'It's lovely, isn't it? I wish I'd got myself a bottle now.'

'Have this one then.' Elena really didn't want any presents. She wanted to go home.

'No, honey, that's for you. Come on, we're being a bit rude, aren't we, hiding in here?'

They went back to the lounge, and the hostess disappeared to mingle with her guests. Elena glanced at the balcony and saw he wasn't there. Her anxiety rose another notch as she looked discretely around the room, trying to see between the moving bodies. She caught a glimpse of his greying black hair through the crowd, heading straight for her, with a glass of whisky in one hand and a glass of champagne in the other.

'There you go.' He held out a glass with the smile of a total bastard. 'You like champagne, don't you?'

'I don't think so,' she snarled, declining his offer.

'So where is he?'

'Who?'

'That big dumb fuck Conrad.' He flung his head back, and the whisky disappeared in one go.

The look on her face gave it away. 'Dumped you, has he?' he sniggered. 'Yes, he'll have another one with him tonight, maybe two.'

Her skin crawled being in the presence of pure evil. He frightened her, and he knew it.

Jasmine came up behind and gave him a cuddle. 'And here's my princess.' She kissed him affectionately on the cheek.

'And what are you two talking about then?'

'We were just saying there's a lack of chivalry with most young men these days.' He really was a twisted son of a bitch.

'Ignore my dad. He lives in a time gone by.'

Yeah, the fucking Stone Age.

Alan sniffed the air with puckered lips. 'Mmm, someone smells nice.'

'That will be Elena. She's got new perfume. Have a smell.'

Elena's breathing stopped. Alan leaned in, his nose touched her neck as he filled his lungs with her sweet smell. It only lasted five seconds but felt like five minutes.

'Good enough to eat,' he murmured as he moved his head away slowly, staring straight into her eyes.

They were joined by Jasmine's mother, and Elena wondered how the hell an animal like Alan could have such a lovely wife and daughter. They chatted for a while, with Elena doing her best to appear her usual self. Alan never took his eyes off her, and she could tell he was revelling in the fact that he was making her squirm.

'What are you doing next weekend Elena?' asked Katherine.

'I'm not sure.' The question caught her off guard. *What now?*

'It's Alan's birthday, and we're all going out on his beloved boat. We would love you to join us. It has five bedrooms, so there's plenty of room.'

'Yes, that would be great,' Jasmine butted in like an impatient child.

'I wouldn't want to intrude. It's family time, isn't it?'

'Nonsense!' roared Alan. 'I'd love to have you.' His sick innuendo made her feel physically ill. She didn't know how long she could keep up the pretence.

Katherine touched her affectionately on the hand. 'Well, the invitation is there if you want it, dear.'

'Elena White, where's your drink? We've got to get rid of all this booze one way or another, you know.' Jasmine was having a whale of a time, the absolute opposite of Elena.

'I . . . I drank it.'

'Dad, here's your chance to be chivalrous. Would you get Elena a very large drink?'

'With pleasure.' Alan sauntered off towards the small off-licence that sat on the worktop.

Fuck! This is a living nightmare. What next?

The evening that she had looked forward to all week dragged on. She didn't want to be the first to go, and no one was showing signs of leaving. Alan was circling the room like a great white shark, watching her every move. Jasmine was in her element, fluttering from one guest to another.

Elena managed to get her attention, and Jasmine danced her way over to her. 'Jaz, I'm going call a cab soon. I've had a mad week, and I'm a bit drained to be honest.'

'No, not yet. It's not even twelve. Stay a little longer, please, please.' She had her palms pressed together, begging like a spoilt child.

'Okay, a little while longer, but I don't want to leave it too late. You know what it's like trying to get a cab on Saturday night.' Jasmine had been so sweet to her, she couldn't say no.

Five minutes later, still in spoilt little girl mode, Jasmine skipped over to Elena and was joined by her mother. 'You know Mum's staying tonight?'

'Yes,' Elena replied hesitantly, terrified by what might come next.

'Well, Dad's going home, so he can drop you off on the

way, and you can stay late, so you don't have to worry about getting a cab.' She clapped her hands excitedly.

Jesus, will this ever end? 'No, it's fine really. I'll get a cab.'

Katherine interjected, 'No, you don't, young lady. We're not letting you get a cab on your own at this time of night. You never know who's in the driving seat.' The irony was sickening.

'And Dad's in the Bentley, so you'll go home in style.'

Yeah . . . or unconscious.

Locking herself in the bathroom once again, she paced the white-tiled floor trying to think of a way out, but every way she turned, there he was, one step ahead. A nervous wreck, she took her phone out and decided to try her last option: Conrad. She asked him via text message if he had any suggestions to get Alan to back off, explaining that he was at the same party. Elena had plenty of dirt on him, but nothing she could use without hurting Jasmine and destroying her relationship with her father, who she clearly adored. Her finger was shaking as she pressed send, and she sat on the edge of the bath hopefully.

Five minutes passed. No reply. She wanted to stay in the bathroom but, knowing that was ridiculous, plucked up the courage and slipped back into the lounge. A group of people were saying their goodbyes and leaving, which made things worse. Her hiding places were dwindling, leaving her vulnerable. Elena checked her phone once more. Nothing.

Twelve forty. Nearly everyone had left, apart from a handful of people. The skinny blond guy was still in the kitchen, now munching through a large slice of chocolate cake.

Jasmine bounced over, not showing any signs of fatigue despite the time. 'Dad's going to take you home now, honey. He's just going to have one last cigar.'

Okay, as soon as I get out that lift, I'm going to do a runner and call a taxi.

'I've got Dad's keys. I'll come down with you. I wanted

a chat anyway.'

No! 'No, stay here. What about your guests?'

'I want a break from this rabble anyway,' Jasmine joked.

Trapped, with no way out of this one, Elena trembled with fear. She looked to the balcony where all she could see was the intermittent red glow of a cigar, indicating where its owner was.

Jasmine jangled the car keys. 'Ready?' Katherine kissed her goodbye and reminded her of the nightmare invitation.

Elena's heart raced as she walked to the front door like a prisoner going to the gallows. Jasmine opened the door and jumped out of her skin. Filling the exit was a tall muscular square-jawed man—Conrad.

'Sorry, I'm late. Traffic was terrible. You must be Jasmine.' He held his hand out. 'I'm Conrad, Elena's friend.' Jasmine was rendered speechless and simply shook his hand. For the first time all evening, Elena could breathe. The relief was overwhelming.

'All right, sweetheart?' He kissed her gently on the cheek, and she tried to blink away the tears. He had come for her. Married or not, she didn't care. All that mattered was he was here right now.

Conrad didn't wait to be invited in and went straight through to the lounge. Jasmine turned to Elena, looking like she had just seen an apparition, and whispered, 'He's gorgeous.'

She noticed Elena's watery eyes. 'Are you okay, honey?'

'Yeah. I've just had a bit too much to drink, you know. I really love you, mate.' She mimicked a drunken slur, although not a single drink had touched her lips all night.

Elena hurried back to the lounge to find Conrad. 'Where is he?' She knew his calm composure was just a front. 'Conrad, wait. Listen, he's Jasmine's dad.' She didn't want to tell him but had no choice.

'What?' He looked totally baffled.

Elena didn't want to explain things there. She was

desperate to leave. 'Just take me home, please. Please?'

She had both her hands on his chest, and he could see she was terrified as her teary eyes pleaded with him. He was surprised at his own feelings. To say he hated seeing her like this was an understatement. His iron jaw clamped shut, and a dormant rage was awakened deep inside him.

Jasmine cut in. 'Can I get you a drink, Conrad?' His face instantly returned to its usual friendly state. 'I'd love a coffee, thanks. Two sugars, please.'

She hurried off to make the coffee, and he noticed the haze of smoke drifting in from the balcony.

'Go and give Jasmine a hand.'

'Conrad, no, please.'

'Don't worry, I'm just going talk with him. Then we'll go, I promise.' He kissed her reassuringly on the forehead.

Conrad stepped out onto the balcony. Alan had his back to him and puffed smoke into the air. He felt like grabbing his legs and throwing him over.

'That'll kill you one day.' Alan jumped to attention and spun around.

'What the hell are you doing here?' His blasé attitude evaporated with the cigar smoke.

'That's not a very nice welcome, is it? This is becoming a bit of a habit.'

'What is?' Alan barked, stuffing the cigar back into his mouth.

'Having to rescue innocent women from you.'

'Fuck off, Conrad! What are you, a saint? How much do you know about that slag in there?'

Conrad took a step closer to Alan, who arched his back over the railings trying to get more distance between them. He took the burning cigar from Alan's mouth.

'You know, I could just put this out in your fucking eye.' He held it close to Alan's face before crushing it in his fist and dropping it over the edge. 'If you ever speak about her in that way again, so help me God, I will fucking tear you in half.' Alan didn't say a word and swallowed hard, almost cantilevered over the railings.

'Coffee,' Jasmine came out singing.

'Thank you.' Conrad stepped back, his temperament seamlessly returned to normal.

'That was quick, Dad. Have you smoked that cigar already?'

'Mmm.' He nodded with raised eyebrows.

'Me and my manners, have you been introduced?

'No, we haven't actually,' Conrad said enthusiastically.

'Conrad, this is my dad, Alan.'

They shook hands. Conrad increased the pressure until he felt the bones in Alan's hand buckle. 'Nice to meet you,' said Conrad as he watched Alan's face redden before finally releasing his grip.

'Dad, Conrad's going to take Elena home, so you can stay a little longer if you want to.'

'Oh, that's very kind of you.'

Conrad finished his coffee and thanked Jasmine as she took the cup from him. He looked back into the lounge to see Elena watching them, a bag of nerves, her feet together and her arms close by her sides, rubbing her thumbs over her fingers in an agitated state. Just the look of her in that childlike state melted him and enraged him at the same time, with the thought that Alan had made her feel like that.

'Jasmine, it's been a pleasure. Sorry, it's been short and sweet, but I'm sure we'll meet again.'

'Yes, I hope so,' she gushed, obviously taken with him.

'Alan.' He nodded sternly.

'Conrad,' Alan replied as he rubbed his hand.

He walked back into the lounge and took Elena by the hand. 'Come on, sweetheart,' he whispered.

She clung to his arm with her other hand. All that was missing was the red cape and the power of flight. Elena felt as if nothing in the world could touch her.

'Good night, every one,' Conrad shouted with his hand

in the air as they left.

There were a lot of questions that needed to be answered by both sides.

Elena climbed into the safety of Conrad's Range Rover, escaping the cool night air. As a single tear rolled down her cheek, she fought hard to hold back the flood that was threatening and wiped her eyes quickly while he put on his seatbelt.

'I'm sorry,' said Conrad. Elena was puzzled. 'I think I've got some explaining to do.'

She nodded. 'We both have.'

Relaxing in the comfort of the cream leather seats, she felt a wave of serenity flow over her. She had been on edge all evening and was exhausted. The serenity only lasted a short while, as it was overshadowed by dread. What would he think of her when she told him how she had met Alan? Too tired to think about it, she turned to look at Conrad as he drove her away from the house of horrors.

Alan stood on the balcony alone while the laughter and conversation continued behind him. He lit his last cigar. Sucking deeply on it, he tipped his head back and blew smoke into the clear night sky. 'He's fucking done it again, the bastard!' He'd watched them get into the car from the balcony and didn't take his eyes off the red lights until they were out of view. 'That bitch needs to be taught a few lessons, I think.'

CHAPTER NINE

The gentle motion of the car stopping broke Elena from her sleep. Her eyes took a second to adjust to the bright light. She wasn't at home.

'Where are we?' She looked around, still confused.

'My place.' She was surprised and relieved in equal measures. She didn't want to spend the night alone.

They were obviously in the garage, which was bigger than her whole house. It was a very orderly space with a row of high-performance cars perfectly spaced alongside one another, all in showroom condition. A cluster of mountain bikes were hanging on the white brick walls, which highlighted various equipment: kayaks, skis, golf clubs, diving gear; all had their own section of wall. Her old friend, the red Ducati, sat alongside several of its brothers, which all looked just as menacing.

Conrad opened her door and helped her out of the car. 'Let's get you inside.'

They walked up a small flight of stairs to the only door in the garage. He typed a six-digit code into the futuristic-looking box that was mounted on the wall next to the door, and she heard the precise click of the lock opening, allowing them entry. They walked through the door into a floor-to-ceiling glass corridor, which lit instantly the moment they stepped in. The wide glass panels were divided vertically by chunky timber posts. Large grey flagstones paved their way.

Elena couldn't see through the glass. The darkness outside and the light within turned the corridor into a mirrored walkway. They stopped at another substantial-looking door. Conrad punched in the magic code, and they were granted entry.

The modern glass corridor was replaced by a more traditional small reception room, which held three very wide white six-panelled doors.

Conrad led her through the middle one into an enormous kitchen full of beautiful antique white units with veined marble worktops on a rich dark hardwood floor. A large black-panelled island housed the sink in the centre, and a matching marble-topped table cantilevered from the island and was surrounded by six black padded leather chesterfield-style stools, all lit from above by an elegant chandelier.

At the opposite end of the kitchen was a lounge area with a large cream rug which was home to a square hardwood coffee table that sat in front of a huge Georgian white fireplace. A black leather lounge suite faced it, flanked by two bronze armchairs dotted with small black squares, each with two sage-green cushions. On the opposite wall were two glazed French doors leading to an orangery, with a row of mullioned windows on each side of them.

'Please take a seat.' Conrad motioned towards the black stools.

'Thanks. You have a beautiful home.' She didn't quite know what to say. The last time she'd seen him, she was screaming at him like a madwoman.

'Thank you. Drink?'

'Tea, please. I couldn't face anything stronger.'

Elena sat with her arms resting on the cool marble

table top. Was it a dream? One minute, she'd been trapped in Jasmine's apartment, and the next, she was in Conrad's home, and he was making her a cup of tea. He slid the steaming cup in front of her. The coffee machine rumbled as it delivered its master's coffee.

The silence was awkward. She sat, and he stood, both sipping their drinks. Elena decided to break it. 'I suppose you're wondering why I was having dinner with my friend's married father?'

He paused as he held the cup to his lips. 'I suppose you're wondering where my wife is?'

She was, but as he had come to her rescue once again, she felt obliged to explain first. He listened intently as Elena told him the story of how she had bumped into Jasmine and, although she now regretted it, had joined the website to break some of the monotony of her daily life, stressing that Jasmine was in no way to blame. She had been a very good friend to her, and it was a cruel coincidence that Alan was her father. He had told her his name was Windsor, not Saunders, and far from being embarrassed at the revelation, he had taunted and terrified her all evening.

When she spoke of Alan, Conrad's face remained calm, except for his throbbing jaw muscle which gave away his true feelings. She went on to tell him that she was no longer registered with the website and had no intention of ever doing so with any other.

'Did he threaten you in any way or touch you?'

What? No questions about the website? 'No, not directly.' She wanted to say, 'Okay, your turn,' desperate to know where his wife was.

'Look, it's late now. You can stay in the guest room tonight, and we'll talk in the morning.'

Guest room. Christ, was his wife upstairs right now? 'Oh okay. Thank you.' Elena felt like she was in the way, like an annoying relative that had turned up unannounced. She declined his offer of something to eat, and he showed her to her room.

They climbed the grand staircase, with its white balustrades supporting the dark hardwood handrail that swept around and up, leading them to a spacious landing. Conrad stopped at the first door they came to, entered the room, and flicked a switch that turned on two bedside lamps lighting the sumptuous room.

She was confused. He had taken her to the safety of his home, but now he seemed distant as if he regretted bringing her there. Having dozed in his car, her batteries had recharged, and she didn't want to sleep despite the late hour. There were so many things she wanted to say, to know.

'The en suite's through there. I'll be in the end room on the right if you need anything. Try to get some sleep. I'll see you in the morning. Good night.' He quietly closed the door.

Sleep? How could she sleep after the night she'd had? Elena undressed and reluctantly got into bed and lay there, reliving the evening. Why did things have to be so complicated? How could she face Jasmine now?

Her mind was spinning with questions she didn't have answers to. She wanted it all to stop and go back to her old life. Yes, it was mundane, but compared to this, it was virtually stress free.

Why had he taken her home with him and put her in the spare room? But then again, she had accused him of taking advantage and had virtually said he was no better than Alan. To a man like Conrad, that was the highest insult. And yet when she had asked for help, he had dropped everything on a Saturday night and come to her rescue once again.

Elena threw back the duvet, went into the en suite bathroom, and put on the white bathrobe that sat neatly in its own built-in shelving unit. She crept along to Conrad's room and stood in front of the imposing door that blocked her access to him. Her stomach rolled and her heart rate rocketed. She felt like she was going into a very important job interview, and she was about to open the door to see if the position was taken.

She summoned up her courage, took a deep breath, and opened the door, not bothering to knock. Her eyes had already adjusted to the darkness, and she could see his silhouette lit by the full moon, which observed them silently through the window.

Elena found him sitting on the edge of the bed, deep in thought. Quickly, she looked to the other side of the bed. It was empty. *Thank you, God.*

'Conrad, I know it's late and that the last time I saw you, I said some nasty things, but I just wanted to say I am truly sorry for that. I know you would never take advantage of anyone, and I can't bear to lie on my own in that room, knowing you're just thirty feet away in here.' She had to stop talking as she had used up all her oxygen in one go.

There was a silence that lasted longer than Elena felt comfortable with. 'I'm sorry. I shouldn't have barged in like that.' She turned to leave.

'Wait, Elena, please'

This last week had killed him. He hadn't been himself, constantly checking his phone for the slim chance that she might get in touch, even though he knew it would be best for him to stay away. But when the text message came through, it had been all the excuse he needed. Leaving his friends Tom and Alex stranded in the restaurant, he had driven like his life depended on it to get to this girl he barely knew but was somehow drawn to in a way that unnerved him.

Considering himself to be a good judge of character, he knew that the dating site was as she had explained—a silly, or even desperate, mistake. Elena had a good heart and a kind soul, which, in this day and age, was hard to find as he knew only too well. But what about his plans? This girl could completely turn everything on its head. Right now, he didn't care. That was a matter for another day.

Conrad stood in front of her in just his shorts. The shadow cast by the moonlight rolled over his wide shoulders and emphasized his full round chest.

'Stay with me tonight?'

There were still unanswered questions, but she couldn't resist him. He stepped towards her. His hands cupped her face, and he gave her a soft kiss which slowly increased in pressure. He pulled the robe from her shoulders, Elena undid the belt and let it fall to the floor, along with all her doubts.

His one hand clutched at her fleshy cheeks, while the other grabbed the back of her hair and gently but firmly pulled her head back. He feasted on her pale flesh like a ravenous animal, his coarse stubble grazing her neck. His breathing was deep and even.

She knew that he wanted her just as much as she wanted him, and that was a very powerful aphrodisiac. He could have her. She wanted nothing more, and she submitted to his raw lust. His erection strained against the tight white shorts and her hand tugged at them, demanding access. Her feet left the ground as he lifted her effortlessly in his powerful arms and placed her on his soft welcoming bed. Elena lay on her back, and Conrad supported his weight on his forearms as he lay on top of her, clamping her legs together.

'You've put a spell on me, haven't you?' he whispered in a low husky voice.

'Have I?'

'Elena White, I'm bewitched by you.' His words reinforced her decision to enter his room and his bed.

Velvet kisses trailed from her forehead down to her neck. He gently bit at the junction between her ear and jaw before, nibbling and sucking her lobes. His guttural groans were amplified by the closeness of his mouth, making her whole body prickle with anticipation. Raising her arms above her head, he and ran his tongue down her skin, biting and sucking on its journey over her rib cage and down her side, making her writhe. Her impulse was to spread her legs and let his mouth ease her aching want. His warm breath stroked her skin as he hovered over the small triangle of red hair. Conrad's wicked tongue ran along the crease of her skin each side of her sex, whose access was restricted by her legs, trapped in the vice-like grip of his muscular thighs. She was desperate to free herself from the confinement.

Her carnal need rising fast; Elena could feel the dampness between her legs. She was more than ready and yearned to feel him inside her. She grabbed his head with both hands and pulled him back up. Conrad's body skimmed over hers like a warm blanket that she never wanted to come out from under. His confined manhood butted impatiently at her wet entrance while his tongue patrolled the perimeter of her open mouth.

'Don't tease me,' Elena begged.

'Who said I'm teasing *you?*'

She wanted to scream, 'Give it to me, give it to me hard!' And the only thing stopping her was his uncontrollable tongue that had taken possession of her mouth. It could have any part of her body it so desired with pleasure, her pleasure.

He rolled onto his back and spun her around with ease, so she was now on top. Leaning over him, her hair made a marquee around their faces, blocking out the voyeuristic moon.

Conrad's hands grabbed her backside. His fingers sank into her flesh and stretched her wet opening to the limit where pain met pleasure, a sharp gasp hissed from her lips.

'Do you want it?' he asked.

'No, I need it,' Elena replied breathlessly.

He threw his arms flat out on each side of him. 'It's all yours. Enjoy.' His eyes were locked on her face, watching intently.

She pulled down his shorts impatiently, leaving them

over his upper thighs, and placed her hands on his chest. She reached underneath herself and positioned his swollen cock between her soaking lips and pushed her bottom backwards. His blunt instrument parted her hot wet flesh, and she inched down his hard length. It was tight. Her urge was to push down harder, make it fit. She eased herself down some more, teasing herself. It felt so good. Conrad had his eyes closed and was biting his lip. It seemed his attempt to tease her had backfired. She moved faster, greasing him with each stroke until she was rocking backwards and forwards. Elena wanted to taunt him some more, but it was driving her crazy too. Any ideas of playing games soon disappeared; there was only one thing her body craved. She slapped her backside against his skin and could feel his cock pulsating and twitching, threatening to explode at any moment. She paused, full to the brim, to savour the moment, knowing she wouldn't last much longer either. Slowing the pace, she began to slide up and down his length slowly, feeling every undulation and contour of his long thick cock, but her self-control abandoned her, and she rode him fast and deep, grinding her clitoris along his shaft as she came down, the feeling growing more intense with each stroke.

Conrad's body was bouncing hard on the bed as Elena rose and dropped her weight down on his length. Her orgasm refused to wait any longer.

'I can't hold on,' Conrad blurted. His face had a look of agony, and knowing he was about to come was all it took for Elena's body to concede.

'Come with me,' she gasped.

He put his hands on her shoulders and pushed her down onto his thick erection, detonating the explosion. They both screamed at the relief of letting go, and she felt his cock pumping inside her. Elena threw her head back and bucked as the intensity ripped through her body, her nails dug into his chest, almost piercing the skin. She collapsed on top of him in breathless elation. A sheen of sweat covered their bodies.

'Oh, that was so good,' she panted, her hair fanned across his chest.

'I aim to please.'

Elena wanted to stay there, she felt more comfortable there than on any bed she'd ever slept on, but she had to attend to her needs.

She rolled off him, and his depleted penis slapped onto his abs as it sprang free of her. She lay at his side. His warm sticky liquid slipped lazily down between the cheeks of her bottom. Too tired and satisfied to move, her fulfilled lust allowed rational thought to return. She would never have had unprotected sex with a man she hardly knew, but Conrad had a power over her that dissolved all rational thought, and since she was on the pill, not for contraceptive purposes but for other medical reasons, at least she was protected in that way.

She wobbled to the en suite like a newborn foal. Returning from the bathroom, she climbed into bed and lay facing him.

'I think we should get some sleep before the sun comes up, don't you?'

Elena nodded with her eyes half open. Now I'm ready for sleep.

She turned over and snuggled her back into his hot body, hot in more ways than one. His arm reached over and held her close. She was cocooned inside of his protective shell.

Elena didn't care about the unanswered questions. Her body had just experienced sexual extravagance, and she melted into him as the overbearing need for sleep took over, and she drifted off happy, content, safe.

CHAPTER TEN

Elena opened her eyes to find the daylight had chased away the darkness. She was lying on her side and stretched out a leg behind her, searching for him. Finding no contact, she turned over to find she was alone in the middle of Conrad's bed, which was more like an island it was so large.

Big mullioned windows lined the walls and allowed the outside world in. Two enormous glass lamps with deep purple shades sat on equally large bedside cabinets; opulent curtains stood guard each side of the windows and continued the deep purple theme.

The white robe she had discarded was now folded neatly on a purple wing-backed chair. She slipped it back on, knotting the belt around her waist, and was dwarfed by the window.

She could see a formal garden with striped lawn and a perfectly square box privet which encased a display of white standard roses. She smiled to herself, remembering their night together at the pub. Elena looked around the room and noticed another door in the far corner; she opened it to find a long walk-in wardrobe. Instantly,

Conrad's aroma captivated her senses like a potent drug, drawing her in.

To the left side was an open unit containing a row of clothes, all compartmentalised. Suits hung in colour-coordinated rows: blacks, blues, greys; his shirts also. Then came the more casual clothes: jeans, T-shirts, sweatshirts, jackets. He was a man who liked order and efficiency. The opposite side contained a range of fitted units. Elena opened a drawer to take a peek. She knew it was naughty but wanted some insight into the man she knew very little about.

The first drawer contained an assortment of cufflinks and folded neck ties. The next had at least ten pairs of sunglasses, each in their own concave holder. Moving across to a deep wide drawer, she found it divided into square sections, each containing an expensive time piece that sparkled under the bright lights. She was about to close the drawer when something caught her eye. Sitting alongside one of the watches was a gold ring. She picked it up, and it reminded her that everything wasn't as simple as she had hoped. It was his wedding ring, there was an inscription on the inside: *Forever and always, my love, Olivia x*

She put it back and closed the drawer, not wanting to snoop anymore, the gold ring having a powerful effect on her.

She took one of his black T-shirts off a hanger, left the dressing room, and closed the door.

Elena ambled into the kitchen wearing Conrad's black T-shirt.

'Hello? Conrad?'

She heard some noise coming from the orangery and walked through to find the French doors wide open. She stepped outside, her eyes fixed on the huge expanse of a beautiful garden and countryside that sat before her.

'You'll catch your death of cold like that, young lady.' The strange voice made her scream as she spun around. 'I'm sorry, luv. I didn't mean to scare you like that. I'm Jim

. . . the gardener.'

He looked like an old salty sea dog, with grey wiry hair, his beard a mirror image of his head. He had a weathered face and kind eyes. He wore old jeans worn at the knees and a dark green shirt rolled up at the sleeves to his elbows. His grey hair was sprouting over the top button of his shirt like flowers themselves.

Elena pulled the T-shirt down to her knees. 'Sorry, I wasn't expecting anyone else to be here,' she said red-faced.

'I'm nearly done, so I'll leave you in peace now.'

'Has Conrad gone out?'

'No, he'll be having his usual morning swim. I'm sure he was a fish in a previous life, you know.' He chuckled to himself.

'Oh yes, of course.' *Where the bloody hell is the pool?*

She didn't like to ask the gardener for fear of what he might think of her, having never been there before and wandering around almost naked. *Tart.*

Being a man of advanced years, he spotted her awkwardness. 'If you go through the door that leads back to the old stables. . .'

'Stables?'

'Well, garage then, or Bat Cave, as I like to call it, but it used to be the stables. Anyway, the room before the fancy glass corridor, the door on the left leads to the pool.'

Slightly embarrassed, she thanked him.

Following Jim's instructions, she opened the door on the left and walked down the sloping corridor. She knew she was on the right track from the smell of chlorine. At the end of the corridor was a white door with a small square vision panel. Through the steamed-up glass, she could just about see Conrad's body slicing through the water. She opened the door slightly and peered through the crack in the door. Jim was right; he was like a fish charging towards one end of the pool and then the other, forcing the water out of his way as he went, leaving a wake behind him like a powerful speedboat.

He came to a stop at the end of the pool farthest from Elena and removed his goggles to look up at the large clock that hung on the wall. He sprang out of the pool in his painted-on trunks, water running down over his well-defined body. Elena felt her tummy flutter at the sight of him. He ran his fingers through his hair and wiped his face with a towel.

There were two equally spaced doors on the wall at the end of the pool; Conrad went through the right-hand one. She waited for him for a few moments, but when he didn't come back, she decided to investigate.

Elena hurried around the pool and entered through the right-hand door into a tiled area with a slatted wooden bench on each side, and three coat hooks above them. Opposite the door, there was a wall of vertical strips of natural timber, each one a different shade of brown. A timber handle was the only giveaway to the door that was camouflaged in the wall.

Opening the door, the heat from the sauna hit her, restricting her breathing for a moment, the dry heat almost scorching her nose. The aromatic fragrance of warm cedar filled the air. Conrad lay on a slatted raised timber bench with his head on a curved slatted pillow. An identical bench jutted out below him.

'Come in,' he said, not bothering to raise his head, his legs splayed. The black trunks left little to the imagination. 'You've met Jim then?' His eyes were half-open, and he looked relaxed, sleepy even. 'Did you sleep well?'

'Very well, thank you.' She took the chance to ogle his body close up while he had his eyes closed. *Those trunks are obscenely tight.*

'You won't need that in here,' he said, referring to the T-shirt she was wearing.

He was right. The material was already sticking to her from humidity. She was naked underneath and felt slightly self-conscious as she peeled it off her damp skin, standing there completely naked, although he had seen her in more compromising ways.

Elena sat down on the bench below him. The hot timber stung her bottom, and she gave a sharp intake of breath as her skin acclimatised to the searing heat. The benches were perfectly positioned for her face to be level with his black-clad crotch. Her eyes ran along his flared muscular thighs and up to the heavy pouch which separated them. She couldn't help but stare.

'Are you hungry?' he asked lazily.

'A little.' *Not for food.*

'We'll just have twenty minutes and then get some breakfast.'

He raised his arms above his head and parted his legs. He was completely spread out before her.

She felt the sweat begin, beads formed on her top lip then on her forehead. Before she knew it, her whole body was ringing wet. Was it the heat or the view? She couldn't take her eyes off his bulging crotch. It had an allure, a magnetism that kept drawing her eyes back to it. Her heart began to pound, even though she was sitting still.

Conrad sat up and caught her staring. He grabbed the ladle next to him and filled it with water from the bucket behind his wooden pillow and poured in onto the hot rocks. The water hissed violently like a thousand snakes as it instantly vaporized. He returned to his lying position, and the wave of heat hit her. It was almost too much to bear. There was no way of escaping it, except through the door, and as long as he was lying there in those trunks, she wasn't going anywhere. Her body shined from the moisture pouring out of her.

'It's not very fair really, is it?' he croaked.

'What's not?'

'Me lying here in these trunks and you with nothing on at all.'

He's going to take them off. 'You can take them off if you like.' *No, he's going to make me take them off.*

He didn't have to ask twice. Conrad lay there, his eyes still closed; Elena knelt on the bench and slid her fingers under the tight waistband on each side of his hips and pulled at the stretchy material, lowering them slightly, revealing his pubic hair. She tucked her fingers in deeper to get a better grip, and she tugged down harder. Conrad lay sprawled out. He didn't bother to raise his hips to help her. She got them down just far enough to see the base of his penis. Her mouth drooled. She knew he was teasing her, and it was working.

Her patience thinning, she pulled desperately at the black trunks, which had now become her sworn enemy from their lack of cooperation. Elena grabbed them at the back of his hips this time, determined to rip them off him, but they put up a good fight. Using her upper-body weight, she wrenched them over his backside, so they were now stretched across the top of his thighs just covering the head of his penis. She took a second to admire the view, now teasing herself. Elena had never thought of herself as someone who was visually aroused. Porn certainly didn't do anything for her, but this live peep show certainly did.

His thick shaft lay dormant on its fleshy bed, the waistband of the trunks just covering the bulbous head. Elena could wait no more. She wanted her eyes to feast on the full view and tore the offending material straight off and threw them triumphantly in the corner.

By now, *every* part of her body was soaking wet. Almost breathless from the combination of heat and anticipation, she ran the tip of her tongue along his soft length. He didn't move or make a sound. She did it again, this time running all of her tongue along him like she was licking a melting ice cream. His body didn't move, but his manhood did. She watched as the blood pumped through the thick veins bringing the monster to life. Another wet lick along the salty shaft and the beast rose from his bed and was thickening rapidly. Still no movement from Conrad.

Elena's eager tongue tasted the underside of the beast,

causing it to rise and topple over, crashing down like a felled oak tree bouncing onto his hard abs. Her body had now gone through that chemical process that turned a perfectly level-headed woman into a salacious deviant.

She placed her hands on his hips. Her dripping tongue dipped down the inside of his spread thighs and over his balls, which hung heavily between his legs. She lifted them with her tongue as she made her way to the tip of his penis. Wrapping her fingers around his thickness, Elena pulled back the tight skin, freeing the head, swollen to almost bursting point.

Conrad had managed to remain still, although his jaw was clenched and his fingers dug into the timber bench. Slowly, she slid her eager lips over his length. His skin was red hot as Elena filled her mouth with as much as she could take. Pulling back, her mouth was dripping, hungry for him. Catching her breath, she slid down once more, feeling his thick veins on her tongue as she gorged on him. Elena grabbed the base of his cast-iron cock and pulled while he was in her gluttonous mouth as she tried to stuff more in.

Now that her tongue had a taste, it was her pussy's turn. The bench groaned under the weight of both of them as she climbed up and straddled him. Her legs effortlessly slid over his thighs, their skin like silk from the moisture. She reached underneath to position him and, without hesitation, dropped straight down onto his erection. Elena had no control over the guttural groan that escaped, feeling the swollen heat of him inside of her. She wasted no time and rocked herself backwards and forwards on him, tormenting her clitoris with the on-off pressure. Conrad sucked in the hot air as his face contorted, blowing his cool exterior to pieces.

Her hands struggled to maintain traction on his slippery carved chest as she selfishly rode him for her own pleasure. Each rhythmic rise and fall edged her closer to the finishing line. Her hands wanted to play now, but her greedy mouth also wanted another turn, and her pussy certainly wasn't waiting patiently. She didn't know which one to appease.

Her hand got to go first. Gripping the shaft tightly, she jerked up and down, watching his cock waggle side to side, his slippery shaft lubricated from her joy ride. Her impatient mouth became terribly envious and barged in, cutting her hands' playtime short by swallowing the solid erection, sucking and licking, claiming it for its own.

But it was something to be shared, and now it was her pussy's turn. Placing it back where it belonged, she rode half of his dick up and down teasingly. Conrad's chest and biceps twitched. She knew he couldn't keep this up much longer. Suddenly, he shot up, forcing her all the way down on his whole length, causing her to scream with the sweet stinging stretch. He lifted her with ease, and she threw her legs around his waist, and he held her by the cheeks of her bottom.

Conrad stood on the lower bench and bounced her up and down on his cock. It was so deep like this. Her clitoris had prime position this way and had no shame exploiting the fact.

'Yes, yes, yes,' she chanted, her mind not her own, the finishing line now in sight.

'Fuck, this feels good,' he breathed, clamping his mouth on hers, their heightened senses taking the kiss to another level beyond pleasure. She felt his cock deliver its load into her as her orgasm shot through her body like a thunderbolt, so intense, causing her to bite down hard on his bottom lip, almost drawing blood, the feeling impossible to describe.

She was a slave for this man and would gladly do anything for him. His thrusts subsided in speed as they both puffed into each other's faces. Conrad sat down with Elena still on top of him. Panting like a race horse, he held her tightly against his hot chest while they regained their senses.

'Air, I need air!' Elena panted.

He lifted her off him and shoved the door open. The rush of cool air as they left the furnace filled their lungs like it was their first breath. The heat-and-energy-sapping orgasm had left her feeling fragile. The coolness of the air subsided, and they could feel the heat radiating from their skin.

Conrad took her hand and led her back to the pool and across to the opposite door into a large wet room. He turned on the shower, and they were blasted with warm water which felt cold to their overheated bodies. As the water washed over them, he kissed her tenderly, which was a welcome contrast to their animalistic lovemaking.

'Breakfast?' he asked.

'I was wondering what a girl had to do around here to get a bacon sandwich.'

'Oh, that'll make your eyes water.'

She laughed, holding on to him under the shower, and noticed small arcs in his skin each side of his chest. 'What's that?'

'That is from the she-wolf I slept with last night.'

'Oops, sorry.' She looked up into his handsome face as the soothing liquid cascaded over his shoulders and pooled at the joining of their chests.

'Scarred for life now. Branded like cattle,' he joked.

Well, Mr Bailey, you've certainly left your mark on me.

CHAPTER ELEVEN

Elena sat at the marble-topped table in the kitchen wearing another one of Conrad's T-shirts and a pair of his black boxer shorts. She felt refreshed from the sauna and nourished from the sex. She had retrieved her mobile from the bedroom, and it beeped as Conrad walked in.

'And what would madam like for breakfast?' he asked with his arms spread apart, leaning on the table.

She thought about making a suggestive remark but decided to answer accordingly, knowing he would probably act upon it. She needed a little recuperation time. Only a little though.

'Madam loves yoghurt in the mornings.' She played along with the game.

'Very good, and would madam care to try one of my special omelettes?'

'I *only* eat omelettes of the special kind.'

He smiled at her reply with a nod. 'Tea? Coffee?' He walked to the fridge and disappeared behind the large stainless steel door.

'Tea, please.'

'Strawberry yoghurt, okay?'

'Yes, thank you.' She liked being waited on.

He returned with her yoghurt and a spoon on a small white plate and placed it on the table in front of her. Elena rested her head in her hands, watching him moving about the kitchen, collecting the equipment and ingredients to make the omelettes. He was quite graceful in his faded jeans and grey T-shirt, which he filled every inch of. His short hair was ruffled, and with his stubble and black flip-flops, he looked like he'd spent the morning surfing.

She quickly checked her phone. It was a text message from Jasmine, and the unwelcome memory of last night returned, curbing her appetite. Plus, there was the matter of Conrad's wife. Was she away? On holiday maybe? Did he take his wedding ring off when she wasn't around? He certainly hadn't denied he had a wife, but he also hadn't offered any explanation either. How was she going to get onto the subject? There were questions she was desperate to know the answers to.

'There you go.' He placed a tall glass of orange juice next to her. 'Do you need to be somewhere today?'

Elena anticipated his thoughts. 'No, not really. Jasmine has just sent me a message, no doubt checking to see if I'm okay.'

His light-hearted mood cooled at the mention of Jasmine's name. It seemed he too was anxious about explaining things.

'I think we've got some talking to do after breakfast.' A serious expression came across his face. She didn't like that face; she liked the happy face.

'Yes, we have.' Elena was relieved he wasn't shying away from the situation and relaxed as she spooned the cool smooth yoghurt into her mouth. 'Do you mind if I reply to her? I don't want her worrying.'

'Of course not,' he said as he chopped an onion, 'although it's a little ironic.' He was referring to Alan. That wasn't going to go away. What the hell was she going to do?

Elena put it to the back of her mind; it was a problem to be dealt with another day. She read Jasmine's text message.

Good morning, you dark horse. Did you stay at Conrad's last night, I wonder? Where did you find him? Was he on the website? I must know more! Thank you for coming last night and for my lovely gifts. Have a fabulous day whatever you're doing. Don't leave me in suspense too long! Oh, by the way, you left your beret and smelly here. Love, Jaz. x x

Elena replied with a short message, saying she couldn't talk now but would call her tonight for a chat. That would give her the rest of the day to come up with a story of how she met Conrad. Finishing her yoghurt she returned her attention to more important things.

'Is there anything you'd like me to do?'

'Plenty.' He turned to face her, holding a red pepper in one hand and a knife in the other. 'But let's get breakfast out the way first, shall we?' His silly humour made her smile.

'No, really, is there anything you want me to do?'

'No, just sit there and look pretty.' He hurried over and took away her plate and empty yoghurt pot and returned with a cup of tea for her and a coffee for himself. 'Are you ready?' he asked as he plated their food.

Elena nodded enthusiastically. Conrad carried the plates high in the air and placed them onto the table with his arms held out proudly. She clapped her hands joining in with the foolery. Elena sliced into the hot golden brown semicircle. It smelled delicious.

'So what's the special bit?' She held a forkful to her mouth.

'Is it burnt?' he asked.

'No, it's fine.'

'Well, there you go then. That's pretty special for me.' He winked at her and filled his mouth.

She shook her head laughing and devoured her food. Elena was enjoying every second spent with this man.

'Mmm, that's lovely.'

'Thank you. You don't have to sound so surprised. I'm no Michelin chef, but I am good with eggs. I eat a lot of eggs and chicken. It's all good protein, good for the muscles.'

'So does that mean I'm going have big biceps after this then?'

'You've got to work out as well. You quite like a good work out, don't you?' His voice echoed into his emptied coffee cup.

'Don't be naughty and eat your food.'

'Yes, Mother.' He flashed her a cheeky grin.

'Am I keeping you from anything?' *Please say no.*

'You can keep me from anything you want to, sweetheart.' Such a simple statement. Why did it have such a profound effect on her?

'Conrad . . . where's your wife?' It wasn't great timing, but she was desperate to know. When would be a good time? He placed his knife and fork down with a sigh. She was nervous at the thought of what he might say.

'We separated eighteen months ago.'

'So the marriage is over then?' She jumped in a bit too soon.

He nodded. 'Yeah, it's over.' His mood noticeably lowered.

Had she left him for another man? Surely not. Or had he been caught with another woman?

'What happened?'

Conrad leant on his elbows with a troubled face. 'Everything was going great. The business was really taking off. I'd just bought this place. All the hard work had paid off. She'd stood by me and believed in me every step of the way, even when I didn't believe in myself. A year after we'd moved in and all the renovation work was done, we decided to start a family. It had always been our plan. She was desperate for a baby as was I. After six months and no pregnancy, we decided to seek help. I had tests, and they came back fine, but Olivia's weren't so good.'

She heard him say his wife's name for the first time. It made her painfully real. Elena hadn't even seen a photo of her, and up until now, it was like she had been a fictional character.

'We tried fertility drugs, artificial insemination, and the last resort was IVF. The doctors said our chances were near impossible.' He hadn't made eye contact with Elena. It was as if he was talking to himself.

'I came home one day, and she was standing right over there.' He pointed to the Georgian fireplace, his eyes were wide open like it was playing out before him. 'I could see she'd been crying, so I panicked and darted over to her. She sat me down and knelt in front of me, put her hands on my face. They were really cold—she always had cold hands—and she said, "I'm pregnant."'

Elena could see he was in the moment, reliving it, and it was just coincidence that she was there.

'We both cried like babies.' He smiled to himself and rested his head on his hand. 'We were so excited. Of all the things I had achieved, nothing compared to that moment. The pregnancy went well, and we were completely submerged in it. We spent weekends looking at prams and baby clothes. We'd sit in bed going through baby name books, making lists.'

So far, it sounded like a fairy tale. What could have happened to destroy it all?

'She went for her twenty-week scan, and we decided to find out the baby's sex.' Conrad fiddled with his fingers, his face reddened. 'A boy. Olivia was over the moon. She'd always wanted a little boy.' The words caught in his throat.

'We began work on the nursery which is opposite our—my room. She was in her element, I'd never seen her so happy.' He paused for what seemed like minutes, and Elena was on the verge of telling him it was okay and he didn't need to explain when he continued. 'I got back from work on Friday, fifteenth of October at 6:30 p.m., a wet horrible grey day. She was over there,' he nodded towards the fire place, 'on all fours, right where she'd told me. I carried her to the car, and she kept asking me if . . . if everything was going to be all right.'

The emotion in his voice was taking hold. He bit down on his lip as the tears rose.

'The staff were brilliant, couldn't have asked for more, but they couldn't find his heartbeat.'

Hot tears trickled slowly down his face onto the cold marble.

'He'd gone. She was seven months.'

Elena searched desperately for something to say. What could she say? Sorry? Instead, she remained silent. Reaching out, she held his hand tightly with both of hers.

'Ethan. We named him Ethan.'

He conceded to the grief. His tears washed over Elena's hands. She too fought back the emotion.

'They wrapped him up in a blue blanket, and we spent a couple of hours holding him, just looking at him. He . . . he was perfect. All the money I made, I could do just about whatever I wanted.' He shook his head. 'But I couldn't help, couldn't help my little boy.' Conrad's face hardened as he lifted his head. 'Couldn't do a fucking thing! Not a thing!' He took a deep breath and wiped his face with his hands.

'When they came to take him, I swear to god, a piece of my soul went with him.' He got off the stool and walked over to the fridge and poured himself a glass of water. 'Everything had been great up to that point, and then it all came crashing down. They told her she wouldn't be able to carry another child. Olivia felt like it was her fault. It didn't matter what I said.' He drank his water and leaned back on the worktop.

Elena watched him guiltily. She felt responsible for his torment, for making him tell her the story. She wanted to do or say something, but felt it wasn't her place. His grief was too personal for her to interrupt.

'Then the drinking started. I'd stay at work late to avoid an argument and come home to find her passed out with an empty bottle of vodka. We tried for a while, but in the end, it had left us different people. The damage was unrepairable.'

Elena felt awful after all the things she had accused him of when he'd taken her home on the bike that morning, especially the comment about him getting back to his wife and kids. But now she knew why he'd been so reluctant to explain.

'I'll take you home now if you like.'

Conrad looked washed-out. It must have taken a great deal to have confided in her. It was obviously still raw. He could have told her anything and saved himself the mental anguish. Elena felt privileged, honoured, that he had shared it with her. She climbed off her chair and went over to him. She leaned back on the worktop and curled her arm around his.

'I don't want to go home if that's okay with you.'

He looked down at her with gratitude in his red eyes. 'Haven't you got anything better to do than hang around with a misery guts like me?'

'There's nowhere else I'd rather be.' He kissed her on the head. 'I'm sorry for all the things I said last Monday.'

'Don't apologise.' He lifted his arm over her head and placed it reassuringly around her shoulders. 'I should have said something, but it's not an easy thing to pop into a conversation. Right, you go and get dressed, and I'll clean up this mess you've made. Then I'll show you the gardens, yeah?'

She sensed he wanted to change the subject. 'Deal.'

'Go on then.'

'Okay, bossy, I'm going.' She hurried away to retrieve her dress from the guest room while Conrad cleared the debris from their half-eaten breakfast.

Elena slipped the dress over her head, leaving his boxer shorts on. She liked having something of his next to her skin. She went into the en suite, relieved to know about his wife, but saddened by the circumstances. What sort of woman was she? Attractive no doubt. How long had they been together? Where did they meet? Elena had developed a fascination about their relationship, and although he said they were separated, he hadn't mentioned divorce, which left her feeling uneasy. He had probably told her more than he'd intended, so it was unfair to expect him to trawl through any more painful memories.

She checked her appearance in the mirror. Her hair had coiled and crimped from the heat of the sauna. It looked quite nice, she thought. Her face still had a warm pink glow, although that wasn't just from the sauna. Happy with her reflection, she left the room and headed back to Conrad.

Her hand glided down the silky handrail, and four steps down, she stopped and turned to look at the nursery door. Would it be an invasion of his privacy if she were to take a look? Elena couldn't resist and crept along to it. She turned the handle and winced at the high-pitched squeak as she opened the door just enough to squeeze her head through.

'Oh, look at this,' she whispered to herself, seeing the beautiful but, under the circumstances, heartbreaking room.

Traditional white bedroom furniture sat against light coffee-coloured walls, pale blue curtains quietly hung each side of the windows. A matching blue armchair was positioned in the corner next to the window. A cream rabbit with big floppy ears waited patiently to be played with. Collections of cuddly animals were placed around the room, and three white picture frames hung on the wall between the windows displaying the alphabet. Seeing it brought the story to life, made it all real. The white cot sat in the centre of the room. A pale blue blanket was draped over the slatted side and embroidered with the name 'Ethan.'

A solitary tear made its way down her face as she closed the door on Conrad's lost dream. Elena composed herself before descending down the stairs. She could hear Conrad talking to someone; he sounded agitated. She entered the kitchen. He was in the orangery on the phone. Elena held back out of sight and listened in.

'We've already been through all this . . . No, I'm going ahead as planned . . . I think you know the answer to that . . . No, but that's none of your business, is it?' He was trying to speak quietly, but the acoustics in the large room enhanced the volume. 'Don't worry, I'm sure you'll do all right out of it.' He exhaled loudly. 'I know . . . I'm sorry, I shouldn't have said that . . . Listen, Isabelle will keep you informed . . . because I think it's best that way . . . There's nothing to talk about . . . Look, I've got to go.' He ended the conversation abruptly, not bothering to say goodbye.

Who was that—a business associate, his brother? There was certainly some bad history there. Or maybe his wife? She waited a moment before bouncing in.

'Okay, I'm ready.' He spun around to face her with a Mona Lisa smile.

A red fleece jacket hung over his arm. 'Here, put this on.' He wrapped it around her shoulders, and she filled her lungs with his scent that wafted from the soft jacket. 'The wind's picking up a bit.' He didn't quiet seem his usual self. Was it the phone call?

'Thank you, kind sir.' Elena nodded, holding on to the fleece like a comfort blanket. 'So you're going to show me your green fingers, are you?'

He opened the French doors, and they stepped outside. 'Well, you've seen just about every other part of me. Shall we?'

She coiled her arm around his, and they walked across the old stone terrace into the fresh clean morning air.

It was a bright but overcast day, and a light breeze hinted at the arrival of autumn. She listened to him intently as they wandered the grounds. He struck her as a man who didn't take things for granted and spoke very highly of Jim and his team as he told her about all the hard work they had done in transforming and maintaining the gardens.

'I expected you to be a city boy with a high-tech pad full of gadgets.'

'Really? Well, there's a lot about me you don't know.'

'That sounds ominous. You haven't got a torture chamber in your basement, do you, full of whips and shackles?'

He looked down at her with a menacing but playful stare. 'You know, I've been wondering what to do with that basement for quite some time now. Good idea, thanks.'

They came to an octagonal summer house, nestled comfortably amongst trees and shrubs and perched on an elevated spot overlooking the house and gardens.

'Did you grow up in the countryside then?'

'No.' He didn't elaborate.

'So you are a city boy then?'

He freed his arm from Elena's grasp to open the double doors. 'You should have been a reporter. You're very inquisitive.'

He took her hand, and they sat on the comfy cushions of the wicker sofa, overlooking the landscape. Was she annoying him with her questions? Breakfast had given her some insight but hadn't satisfied her appetite for information about this man. Her arm returned to its coiled position, and she rested her head on his hard shoulder.

'What about you? City girl?'

There he goes again. Why is he so guarded? 'I'm a slave to it really. It's where the work is. Even if you do manage to get away from it, it seems to draw you back. Do you prefer it out here?'

'I like the city. It's vibrant, alive, but it's a two-headed beast. It dazzles you with its bright lights and its fast pace but then slowly eats away at your decency, your manners. People bump into one another and don't bother to apologise, push to get on the tube before everyone else, fight over parking spaces. Please and thank you? They become invalid. If you spend too long there, it tarnishes you. I like to get away from it, polish myself back to normal.'

His words rang true with her. It was a rat race. And some days she wondered if it was all worthwhile.

'It's a lovely house.'

Conrad nodded his agreement as they admired the handsome building.

'A bit big for just you though.' She regretted saying it the second the words left her lips.

'It was never meant for just me.'

'Conrad, I'm so sorry, I never meant to—'

He quickly interrupted her. 'No, it's okay.' He placed his hand on hers and stared straight at the house. 'You're right though. It's way too big for me now.'

There was an awkward silence between them. Elena knew that the effects of their conversation at breakfast were still lingering.

'Is there . . . anything you want to talk about, Conrad?'

'Yes, tell me some more about you.'

That's not what she meant, but she had pushed the subject as far as it was going to go, for now anyway.

'There's not much to tell really.'

'Were you a spoilt little girl?'

'Not exactly, my dad left when I was five, and I never saw or heard from him again. I've only got a vague memory of him. A few years later, Mum remarried and, a few more years after that, got divorced.'

'Oh . . . sorry, I shouldn't have made that assumption.'

'No, it's fine.'

'Did you miss not having him around?'

'I know it's a silly thing to say, but I missed him most

on parents' evening at school. All the other kids were there with mums and dads, but it was always just me and Mum. That's when I felt it most, and with my red hair as well, it was a bit of a nightmare some days.'

'You've got beautiful hair.'

She looked up into his gaze. 'Thank you. If kids find a weak spot or a difference, sometimes they exploit it, and unfortunately for me, I was the only redhead.'

'Yeah, kids sure know how to be hurtful.'

Elena wondered what Conrad would have been like at school. The male version of Jasmine probably, she thought.

'I bet you had all the girls chasing you, Mr Popular.'

'Hmm.' The corner of his mouth kinked, almost the beginning of a smile.

Okay, not giving anything away then.

There was a distant look in his eye as if he was troubled by something.

Elena's phone interrupted the conversation. 'I'm sorry.' She fumbled in the jacket pocket which was down by her knees.

'Trust technology to spoil the peace.'

She checked her phone. 'Oh, speak of the devil, it's my mum. Do you mind?'

'Of course not. Please take the call.'

'Hello, Mum. I was just talking about you . . . Yes, it was all good.' She rolled her eyes at Conrad and stepped outside.

He watched her chatting away, wandering backwards and forwards, the green hem of her dress just peeking below his red fleece, which looked like a blanket hanging over her shoulders. The light breeze blew her hair across her face; the deep golden red worked in perfect harmony with her beautiful skin. She tucked the stray hairs behind her ear and turned to face him silently mouthing 'sorry.'

She was lovely and unknowingly had turned things

upside down for him. He had never been so indecisive about things. Was it all getting a bit too complicated? A melancholy mood slipped over him as his problems seemed to conspire against him. Maybe he was overthinking things and just needed to relax. Conrad got up and dismissed the gloom that was threatening to spoil the day.

'Okay, I'll call in on Wednesday, and don't forget to make an appointment with the doctor . . . Good . . . Okay . . . Bye, Mum, bye.'

'Everything all right?' he asked, closing the doors to the summer house.

'Yeah, fine.'

'Are you close to your mother?'

'I wouldn't say close. It was hard for her being a single parent, and there wasn't a lot of money to go round, and I suppose those pressures did affect our relationship, but we get on fine.'

He lay his arm across her shoulders. 'Come on. Let's go and get some lunch, and as you're not dressed for the bike, we'll take the car. Plus, we don't want to get stranded by the weather again now, do we? Unless you want to stay here for lunch and have more eggs?'

'As good as your special omelette was, I think a drive out sounds lovely.'

'Agreed.'

They retraced their steps back towards the house. Elena loved the feel of his arm around her. It felt safe, it felt right, and it dared her to hope for more.

'You know, you look like little Red Riding Hood with my jacket on like that.'

'Are you the Big Bad Wolf then, coming to eat me?'

'Ms White, do you think about nothing else?' he tutted and rolled his eyes jokingly. 'You're incorrigible.'

'What? Oh no, it's your mind that's in the gutter, Mr Bailey.'

She slapped him playfully on the chest. That was more like it. He was back to his normal self. They re-entered the house via the orangery.

'I know a lovely pub not far from here actually. We could eat there, and if you're not bored with me by then, we can come back here, and I'll show you my stamp collection, if you like.' He looked at her over his shoulder as he locked the doors and gave her a cheeky wink.

'Now I am excited.' She was very excited and was looking forward to spending the rest of the day with him and maybe the night.

'Well, this is all very fucking nice, isn't it?'

A harsh voice rang out from the lounge end of the kitchen. Elena looked in that direction and could see a hand draped over the wing-backed chair that sat in front of the fireplace. Her head shot back towards Conrad who had stopped in his tracks, a look of horror on his face. 'Oh shit,' His hand passed over his forehead.

It wasn't going to be the quiet Sunday afternoon they had planned after all.

CHAPTER TWELVE

Conrad marched into the kitchen. 'What the hell are you doing here?'

A slim blond woman stood holding on to the chair.

'What am I doing here? It's my fucking house! What's she doing here?'

Elena had wondered what his wife was like, and now she was getting first-hand experience.

'Olivia, you've got no right turning up and barging in like this.'

'You said there was no one here.' She jabbed at him with her finger.

'It's got nothing to do with you if anyone is here or not.'

She didn't have any makeup on, and despite her red puffy eyes, Elena could see she was a very attractive woman. She let go her grip on the chair and wandered unsteadily towards Conrad.

'No wonder you wanted to get me out. Now you've got your own shagging pad.'

'Olivia, have you been drinking?' She wasn't listening.

'You're a fucking hypocrite. The minute I'm gone, you

get some slut in.'

'Olivia, enough!'

Elena wanted the ground to open up and swallow her. Yes, they were separated, but she was still his wife and wearing his ring. This was their marital home. Elena was an intruder, trespassing where she shouldn't have been.

'Are you crazy? You've driven all the way here blind drunk. You're going to get yourself killed.'

'Oh, you'd love that, wouldn't you, eh? That would make life so much simpler for you, wouldn't it . . . if I were dead?' She spat out the words ferociously.

'Don't talk like that.'

'Well, it's true!' she screamed, fists clenched tightly at her sides.

'Olivia, calm down.' Conrad's voice was low and soothing.

She held her head up towards the ceiling, her eyes closed, and swayed gently from side to side. Her breathing was broken by violent sobs. Suddenly, her eyes opened, and she glared at Elena with an unpredictable stare.

'What the fuck are you still doing here? Go on, piss off! He's a married man, you tart.'

Olivia's chest rose and fell. She was panting hard, face blazed red. Teeth gritted, she made a charge at Elena, but unsteady on her feet, she stumbled and fell. Conrad jumped to stop her and caught her in his arms before she hit the floor. He held her and lifted her onto her feet as she clung to him, out poured a flood of emotion. Her head was buried in his chest, muffling her cries.

Conrad rested his head on top of his wife's, his arms wrapped around her. 'Shhh, it's all right, it's okay.' He had his back to Elena. She couldn't see his wife's petite frame behind his bulk.

'Can we go back? We can. Let's just go back to the way it was,' she whispered between sobs. 'Please, please, I can't live without you. It was all my fault. I know, and I'm sorry. I'm so sorry. Don't leave please,' she begged and pleaded as if it was for her life, and despite the shouting and the insults, Elena found it impossible not to feel sorry for her. If he was her husband, she would fight tooth and nail for him.

Elena knotted her fingers and stared at the floor. It was an intimate moment she had no right witnessing, and slowly, she stepped backwards, edging out of the kitchen, leaving them embracing each other, his wife continuing with her pleas to give her another chance.

She didn't know where to go and didn't even know where she was to call a taxi. She headed for the room that suited her most: the guest room. After all, that was just what she was, an unwelcome guest, in the way.

Elena stood at the top of the stairs and leaned over the handrail, she could hear voices but not what they were saying. She opened the door and went to sit in isolation. So far, the day had been an extreme of emotions. She had felt so welcome in his company, but now she just wanted to go.

Although she sat alone in the bedroom, the fracas had followed her, taunting and reminding her of her predicament. Elena sat on the edge of the bed with her knees tight together, her shoulders slightly hunched, and her hands clasping each other. Her whole body was tense, still braced from the attempted attack. She got up and looked out of the window to see if there was a landmark she recognised or any way of directing a cab to her. The empty fields and trees weren't giving away any clues. She was stranded.

Elena didn't really want to go, but she couldn't stay while his wife was there. Maybe a friend or someone would come and take her home. Then they could enjoy the rest of the afternoon together.

She gnawed away at her nails, knowing that was highly unlikely. Why had he told his wife he was on his own at the house? If they'd been separated for a few months, then okay, but after a year and a half? Wasn't it time to move on for both of them? Or was that just wishful thinking?

Elena sat there for fifteen minutes, which felt like two hours, running through all the different scenarios, letting her imagination run wild with a barrage of what-ifs.

She heard the creaky floorboards outside the door, someone was coming. Elena shot up off the bed, her heart pounding. She braced herself for another confrontation.

The handle turned, and Conrad popped his head around the door. A sigh of relief left Elena's lips.

'Here you are. I was beginning to think you were trying to walk home.' He came in and closed the door behind him.

'Has she gone?'

Conrad shook his head. Her hopes were dashed.

'So lunch is on hold then?' She wasn't completely giving in.

'Elena . . .' He broke eye contact, choosing to look at the carpet instead. 'I . . . erm . . .'

'You want me to go.' She helped him along with the words.

'I can't send her home in a taxi in that state. I'm going to have to take her myself. I'm sorry. I didn't know she was going to turn up. She hasn't been here for weeks.'

Weeks? 'It's okay, I understand.' Elena gave her best performance.

'I'm so sorry, Elena. Olivia didn't mean what she said.'

Oh yes, she did.

'Come downstairs. She's spark out on the sofa in the drawing room.'

Elena headed back down the stairs with Conrad behind her. The welcoming feel of the house had been changed to one of intimidation. She went back into the kitchen and sat at the table where they had breakfast. He made her a cup of tea and said the taxi should be there within the hour.

Conrad, sipping his coffee, kept his distance and leaned against the worktop. The embarrassment of the situation had starved them both of conversation. Time passed unbearably slowly, and Elena feared his wife's angry return at any moment and looked nervously towards the closed door every few minutes. She hung on to her empty teacup, pretending to drink from it, not knowing what else to do, while Conrad tided, moving things around unnecessarily.

'Have you got a busy week coming up?' It was the only thing that sprang to mind, just to break the silence.

'I have. I've got to go to Scotland towards the end of the week for a couple of days.'

'Oh yeah, the new gym. Is it all going as planned?'

'Well, I wouldn't say as planned. How about you?'

'Nothing exciting. Just work as usual.'

The trivial conversation was halted by a knock at the door. She jumped off the stool and straightened her dress.

'Right, that's me then.'

Her impending exit seemed to intensify the awkwardness between them.

'Yeah. Have you got everything?'

'I think so.'

They walked in silence to the front door. Elena was desperately hoping he would say something, anything that would give her some hope. Would she see him again, or was this it?

They stood at the front door, and Elena had decided that rather than torture herself, she was going to ask him. She hesitated as he reached over her shoulder to open the door.

Ask him!

The door opened, and she was surprised to see a middle-aged taxi driver standing on the stone steps, his round face stretching the arms of his tinted glasses and his belly testing the breaking point of his belt.

'Good afternoon, sir, miss.' He had parked the silver Mercedes parallel with the steps.

A dirty white Porsche was parked half on the grass as though it had been abandoned. It must have belonged to Conrad's wife.

The driver went back to the car and held open the rear door within earshot of them both.

Oh great! Elena decided she didn't want to make a fool of herself in front of an audience.

'I'd better give you this back.' She slipped her shoulders out of his jacket.

He pulled it back over her. 'No, keep it on. You'll be cold.'

She grabbed his hand as he straightened the collar of the jacket and squeezed it tenderly. Conrad looked down into her eyes apologetically. She felt the tears threatening and snapped her head away, not wanting him to see her upset.

'Okay, Mr Driver, ready when you are.' She tried to sound as carefree as possible and hurried down the steps.

Just as she was about to get into the car, Conrad called her. 'Elena.'

She turned, gripping the car door with hope. He paused. *Yes?*

'Conrad! Conrad?' His wife's call destroyed the moment of opportunity.

He glanced quickly into the house and back to Elena. 'I'm sorry.' It was all he said, and it felt like a knife in her heart. His image became blurred as tears of disappointment clouded her eyes.

'I'm sorry too,' she whispered, fighting to keep the emotion from her voice. Elena got into the car, and the driver closed the door.

She could see Conrad in her peripheral vision. His wife had joined him and was beckoning him in. The door slammed shut just as the car pulled away.

They moved steadily down the long winding drive. Trees lined their way like a guard of honour, paying their last respects to their brief time together. The car came to the end of the drive and left through the inconspicuous entrance. That was it—she had left his company and his domain.

The taxi built up speed, taking her further away from him. As the wheels rolled over the tarmac, so the tears rolled down her face. A mixture of emotions trampled over her. The few steps to the taxi had been extremely humiliating. She felt like a reject from a reality TV show who was not through to the next round.

Elena dried her wet face with her hands and noticed the eyes of the driver watching her in the rear-view mirror. He reached into the glove box and handed her a packet of tissues over his shoulder. 'There you go, darlin'.'

'Thank you,' she murmured.

'I've got a daughter about your age. She was the same a few weeks ago, came home all upset, as her boyfriend didn't want to see her no more, although, between you and me, I was glad. He was a bit of a shit, excuse my language. Then again, no man's ever good enough for a father's daughter. I bet your dad's the same?'

Elena nodded to him in the mirror with a painted-on smile. She knew he meant well, and he had a paternal tone to his voice, but she just wanted to be left alone. As she'd told Conrad, she never really gave her dad a lot of thought, but the taxi driver had reminded her of another gaping hole in her life. Wouldn't it be nice to go and have a cuddle from her dad, and he would tell her it was all going to be all right, to spend time with the one man who would move heaven and earth to keep his little girl happy and would feel her pain greater than she herself, never letting her down?

For Elena, that was just another fantasy. She certainly didn't have that kind of relationship with her mother, who had come to hate men over the years. Sometimes, Elena felt that her mother resented her for not being able to do more with her life. She was always going on about lost chances and it being too late for her now.

'I hope I haven't offended you,' asked the driver

'No, not at all.'

'Just tell me to shut up. I can waffle on a bit sometimes.

For what it's worth, I think the man's a bloody fool. If I was thirty years younger, you'd be tellin' me to bugger off!' He nodded, his greying bushy eyebrows made an appearance above the rim of his glasses, causing his brow to crease below his receding hair line.

Elena chuckled, and she noticed his ID card on the dashboard with a mug shot. His name was Alan, Alan Rickets. That was another nightmare she didn't know what to do about, and Jasmine would be expecting a call with all the juicy details. But there was nothing to tell; now all the juices had dried up. She decided to text her, saying she was busy and would call her tomorrow.

'I'll put some music on and leave you alone now.'

Elena gave him a smile that said, 'That would be nice.'

She looked out the window at the countryside racing past. It had started to rain, and the grey sky had drained all the vibrancy from the trees and fields and mirrored her mood. Perfect spherical beads of water peppered the windows, obscuring the view. He turned on the radio and selected an easy-listening station. The music was uncannily suited to her situation like a higher force was sending her subliminal messages of support through the radio, letting her know it would all be okay. It would, wouldn't it?

What was Conrad doing right now? Probably taking his wife home, or had she replaced Elena as his dining companion? Then maybe back to the house to spend the night? No doubt Olivia would cash in on the emotional side of things.

It was unfair to think that. They had both been through a very tough time, which would either make or break a relationship. Guiltily, she hoped it was the latter.

Elena tried to put things out of her mind, but the radio kept dragging the situation back into her thoughts with songs of love and loss. It was back to reality before she knew it as the car pulled up outside her house.

'You wait there, me darlin'.' He got out, opened the boot and rushed around, and opened Elena's door, holding a large green golfing umbrella. 'There you go.'

'Oh, thank you. You're very kind.' He escorted Elena to her front door, shielding her from the rain.

'How much do I owe you?'

'It's already taken care of. It's on Mr Bailey's account.'

'You know Conrad?'

'Well, I don't know him personally, but I've driven him more than a few times now.'

'I bet you're used to this then, taking home the ladies?'

'In the five years I've been driving Mr Bailey, other than his wife, you're the first one, me darlin'.'

His welcome words made her eyes well up again.

'I know you probably think I'm a silly old bugger, but I've had my share of heartache, and in a few weeks, you'll wonder what all the fuss was about. Now you take care.'

'Thank you.' She rubbed his arm but really wanted to give him a hug for his kind words of comfort. He ran back to the car, and Elena called to him before he got in.

'Alan?' His head popped up above the roof of the car. 'Your daughter's a very lucky girl.'

A broad smile raised his glasses, and he disappeared into his car and drove off into the rain.

She closed the door behind her. The house was painfully quiet. It had the same depressing feeling as when you got back from holiday and were reminded that your time away had been pure fantasy. The house was dark from the inclement weather.

Elena went into the kitchen, turned on the lights, and did what all English people do in a crisis: made herself a cup of tea despite wanting to drink a couple of bottles of wine. She had got just enough milk for one cup and sat down with her hot drink and placed her phone on the table, knowing every time it rang or beeped, she would involuntarily think it *may* be Conrad. Its inevitable silence only tormented her, so she sent Jasmine a brief text and switched it off then wondered if she had done the right thing. *What if he did call?* The phone was already playing tricks on her, so she put it in a drawer and slammed it shut.

The last two weeks had been a real roller coaster since she met Jasmine. It certainly hadn't been boring, although she wasn't sure if it had been an improvement either.

Rain lashed against the kitchen window. It was a real stay-in day; it was the *on-your-own* part she didn't like.

The washing machine seemed to be glaring at her, reminding her subtly that she hadn't washed her work uniform. It really was back to reality.

Maybe she could take another sickie. No, that would just be running away from things, but if Dawn was going to continue with her reign of terror, she'd better be careful. All Elena needed was an excuse to vent her anger.

She took off his fleece and hung it on the back of the chair and wished that it was filled with his physique. She went through the cupboards to see what else she needed other than milk, and there was a box of eggs staring at her, reminding her of him.

Was this what it was going to be like? Everywhere she looked, there he was?

Elena decided she could last until tomorrow, so long as she didn't want anything more extravagant than beans on toast. The rest of the day was spent on autopilot, preparing for the week ahead. She made a shopping list, which was something she never did, trying to fool her brain by keeping it occupied.

Collapsing on the sofa after finally finishing her chores and not having any milk for tea, she decided the wine was a good substitute after all. Elena sat and stared at the TV for an hour as it played out its drama in front of her while her own personal drama played out in her mind. She felt cheated, mislead almost, and the mixture of wine and worry had taken its toll. She hit the 'off' button on the remote and travelled through the house, switching off all the lights, carrying her last glass of wine.

Entering the kitchen, she paused. Her eyes focused on the drawer that contained her phone. She opened it and took out the phone, contemplating whether or not to switch it on. Fearing disappointment, she decided to delay the pain until tomorrow and placed it back on its bed of old receipts, pens, elastic bands, and used batteries.

She finished her wine and left the glass watching over the drawer.

Elena climbed the stairs with a light head from the Pinot Grigio and a heavy heart from the day's events. She abandoned her clothes on the floor, slipped on her nightie, and sat on the edge of the bed to set the alarm for work, hoping that tomorrow would be a nice easy day and that Dawn would leave her alone.

Like that was going to happen.

Lying on the bed, she pulled the duvet over her and switched off the bedside lamp, wishing it was that easy to switch off her brain for the night.

What if, once he'd taken his wife home, he had tried to ring her? Or maybe he had sent message after message, trying to contact her.

Elena tried to fight it, telling herself to get some sleep. It could wait until the morning.

She lay there for a few minutes as straight as a plank, peering into the abyss of the ceiling. 'Bugger it!'

She threw off the duvet, sprang out of bed and ran down the stairs like there was a ticking bomb under her bed, and headed straight to the kitchen drawer, knocking over the empty wine glass in her haste. She snatched her phone from the drawer and switched it on. It seemed to take forever for the screen to light up.

Please, just one message, please.

When the phone was finally ready, it said she had two messages.

Yes!

She pressed the keys, hastily opening her messages. Her excitement turned to disappointment. It was Jasmine.

Busy, are we? Well, I wouldn't want to interrupt. You go, girl.

Enjoy! I'm sure you will. J. x

Elena half-heartedly opened the second message.

Hi, honey. I'll be in town tomorrow. Maybe we could meet for a coffee around one? Call me. x x

She threw the phone on the side next to the toppled wine glass.

I knew it.

Clutching the worktop, she refused to cry any more. Elena didn't want for a lot, she wasn't a greedy person, but god she yearned for him.

'Everything happens for a reason,' she muttered to herself as she ascended the stairs once more for a very restless night.

CHAPTER THIRTEEN

The annoying beep from the alarm clock woke Elena. It took all the will power she had to drag herself out of bed, and the first thing she saw was Conrad's black boxer shorts lying under her discarded dress. She gave a heavy sigh, knowing that the rest of the day would be full of little reminders.

She dressed and made her way downstairs and into the kitchen. Conrad's jacket was there to greet her, hanging on the back of the chair.

'Morning.' She tapped it on the shoulder as she grabbed the kettle. 'Sleep well? No, neither did I . . . What's that? Your wife kept you up all night? Oh, I bet she did.' The innocent kettle bore the brunt of her frustration as she slammed it down onto its base.

She had planned on ignoring her phone today but gave in to its suggestion. Maybe he'd called during the night. Duped by the sleek white messenger once again, she was determined not to show it her disappointment and calmly put it back on the worktop.

Elena opened the cupboard and took out the bread. 'We've only got crusts left, I'm afraid.' Her silent guest didn't comment.

She popped the bread into the toaster and poured the hot water over the tea bag and slipped into a trance, looking at the red reminder hanging there, which was completely oblivious of all the trouble it was causing. The smoke alarm rudely interrupted her reverie, and the toaster spat out the two crusts that were now a lovely shade of black.

'Oh shit!' She took them out and threw them into the bin, burning her fingers slightly. Elena grabbed a tea towel and waved it in the air like she was stranded on a desert island trying to signal a passing plane.

Finally, the high-pitched beeping stopped. She turned to her tea and opened the fridge to get the milk, forgetting she'd had the last drop the night before.

'And there's no milk! Of course, there isn't.' Elena slammed the fridge door.

'It's all your bloody fault!'

She grabbed the jacket and threw it into the cupboard under the stairs with the rest of her Conrad memento collection.

'It looks like it's a supermodel breakfast then.'

She poured herself a glass of water and took a sip. No longer having a reason to linger at home, Elena grabbed her keys and headed out the door for work earlier than usual.

She was feeling quite pleased with herself, managing to get a parking space close to work. Elena walked towards the bank and tried to psych herself up, huffing and puffing like a boxer getting ready for a big fight. She got to the main entrance door and paused.

You can do this, come on.

She pressed the buzzer. The place was empty. Dawn usually had people running about like headless chickens the minute they stepped through the door.

Jenny came trotting over. She was Dawn's right-hand woman and physically the opposite, with long spindly legs that ran up to her armpits, jet-black bobbed hair that hugged her jaw, and a fringe, which was more like a theatre curtain, that threatened to drop over her eyes at any moment. She released the security lock and let Elena in.

'Morning, Jenny.'

She didn't return the greeting and hurriedly secured the door. 'Have you heard the news?' Jenny usually kept her distance from everyone as she was the bearer of Dawn's bad news, but she was bursting with excitement.

'What news?'

'Dawn's gone.' Jenny clapped her hands in a tizzy, hopping from one foot to another.

'What do you mean Dawn's gone?'

'Apparently, head office rang her late Friday afternoon and told her she was moving to another branch as of Monday.'

'Why?'

'Well, you know Victoria?' Elena looked puzzled. 'The new pretty blond girl?'

'Sorry, yes.'

'Well, Dawn had it in for her, but Victoria was having none of it and complained to head office. It turns out she's the niece of Chris Turnhill,' the regional manager, a big sloth-like man that moved slowly and talked even slower and had a look of an imposter who was expecting to be found out at any moment.

'Thank fuck that bitch has gone!'

Elena was surprised at Jenny's crude comment, as she had always seemed so prim and proper, although she didn't really know her, as she had always been at Dawn's side like a faithful Labrador.

'So who's taken over from Dawn?'

'That's the best part.' Jenny's excitement was bubbling again. 'Everyone's in the staffroom.'

Elena followed Jenny, who was half running and half walking like she was in an egg-and-spoon race. They came to the staffroom door, and Jenny bent down to Elena's level.

'Wait till you see him. He's fucking gorgeous!'

What the hell had got into her?

They entered the staffroom, and everyone turned when they heard the squeak of the hinges to see who had come to join the celebration.

'Simon, this is Elena, and that's everybody now.' Jenny was acting all girly and demure, quite the opposite of two minutes earlier.

'Hi, Elena, my name's Simon Baker, and I'll be taking over as the new manager.'

Jenny was right. He was hot. His dark grey suit complimented his tall slender frame and his piercing blue eyes, and with his blond hair swept back, it gave him a clean-cut corporate look.

Maybe things were looking up?

'Okay, guys, now we're all here, I know there's been a lot of speculation and gossip flying around regarding Dawn, and I'm asking you not to focus on that. The branch has been failing to hit targets for some time now, and I've been brought in to turn it around. So let's move on and get things back on track. If you can all carry on with your usual roles, I will try to get 'round to seeing you all at some point today. If anyone has any questions whatsoever, just come and see me. Thank you.'

He was very authoritative, and his eyes wandered in Elena's direction more than a few times as he made his way to his office, smiling at the two ladies as he passed.

Jenny elbowed Elena in the ribs. 'I've got a question for him: my place or yours? So what do you think? Gorgeous, isn't he?'

'Well, he's certainly easier on the eye than Dawn, that's for sure.'

'Right. I'm off to make the love god a coffee and see if there's anything else he wants . . . like me bent over the desk.'

She bolted through the door, her frankness making

Elena a little uncomfortable. While Dawn had reigned, Jenny had barely spoken about anything other than work.

The room was full of the hum of gossip as everybody dispersed to start work. Elena resumed her role as a customer meet-and-greet, and the morning was as busy as ever, keeping her thoughts of Conrad at bay, but as soon as she had a minute to herself, her mind wandered back to him. She took a toilet break and used the opportunity to check her phone. Nothing new.

Elena sent Jasmine a text message, agreeing to meet her at the coffee shop at one. Despite the obvious problems Alan had created, she was looking forward to seeing her and felt there was a special bond between them. She had decided to tell Jasmine the truth about Conrad. He was married. What other explanation was there?

Elena returned to her post. Simon came strutting over with Jenny trailing behind. He had removed his jacket, and his shirt sleeves were rolled up to the elbow, exposing tanned forearms covered in golden blond hairs.

'Elena, everything okay?' He stood closer to her than was normal, he smelt divine, masculine.

'Yeah, fine.'

'Good, I know you're going for lunch shortly, but when you come back, can you come to my office? There're a few things I want to run through with you, okay?' He had a trancelike stare and perfect white teeth. She couldn't help studying his face as he spoke to her.

'Okay.'

'Great.'

He walked towards his office, and Jenny hung back, nodding at his backside. She blew out a lusty lungful of air while making groping gestures with her hands before scurrying off to catch up with him. *That girl needs a man.*

What was there to run through? Probably all the bad reports Dawn had given her. Still, ding-dong, the witch was dead.

One o'clock. Elena grabbed her bag and coat from the

staffroom. The days were getting cooler now. She hurried along, wanting to make the most of her time with Jasmine.

She got to the coffee shop and could see her sitting at a table with her mother, surrounded by shopping bags. Elena was glad that Katherine was there, as it would impede Jasmine's relentless questions about Conrad.

Entering the café, the aroma of fresh coffee and chocolate muffins seduced her senses.

'Hi, honey.' Jasmine looked glamorous as always, as did her mother.

Elena squeezed her way through between the cramped tables, apologising as she passed. 'Hello, ladies. Nice to see you again, Mrs Saunders.' She hung her coat on the back of her chair and set her bag down amongst the collection around the table.

'And you, dear. Please call me Katherine. Now you girls sit there, and I'll get the drinks. Elena, tea, coffee?

'Latte, please, Mrs—er, Katherine.'

'I'll have a mocha, please, Mum.'

'Right, I'll only be a moment.' She joined the growing queue.

'You don't mind me bringing Mum along, do you?'

'No, I think she's lovely.'

'We had such a nice time yesterday that she decided to stay one more day. Dad's picking her up later.' Elena panicked at the mention of Alan and questioned Jasmine's definition of 'later.'

'Oh, is your dad joining us?' she asked, hoping for a no.

'No, he's got some business to take care of, so he won't be over until this evening, and then we're all going out for dinner.'

Thank Christ for that.

'Okay, missy, spill the beans, and make it quick. They're just serving my mother.'

'Well, there's not much to tell really. The short answer is he's a married man.'

'Really? He didn't look that sort.'

'No, he didn't.'

'Are you going to see him again?'

Elena shook her head. She couldn't bring herself to say 'no.'

'So when did you meet him?'

'I . . . er . . . I met him at the gym.' Elena was willing Jasmine's mother to return. She wasn't in the mood to talk about Conrad.

'I didn't know you went to the gym. But I could certainly tell he does.' Jasmine reached over the table and gave Elena's forearm a gentle squeeze. 'I'm sorry. You must be gutted. He was yummy. Well, it seems it's true what they say: all the good-looking ones are married or gay.'

Jasmine peered over her shoulder to see where her mother was and turned back to Elena. 'Have you been getting any interest from DDS?'

'DDS?'

'Daddy Daddy Sugar.' Jasmine whispered it and had another quick glance at her mother. 'Shh, here's Mum. You'll have to come over this week, and we can have a good old chat, just me and you. How about Wednesday night?'

'Yeah, that'll be nice.'

Katherine came back to the table with a young man following her, carrying a tray full of coffee and cakes. She took her seat and directed him. 'Just there's fine, and can you take the tray away with you?'

He looked bewildered and slightly intimidated as he waited while Katherine put the contents of the tray on the table. 'Chocolate éclair, lemon meringue, and a vanilla slice—take your pick, girls.'

Katherine looked to the nervous young man. 'Thank you, dear.' She gave him the signal, and he did as he was told and, without saying a word, took the tray and went back behind the counter.

'What a nice young man.'

'Mother, you're becoming a sex pest, harassing all these young boys everywhere we go.'

Surely, there can't be two in the family.

'The chance would be a fine thing.' She dropped two sugar cubes into her tea.

'I'm not going to fit into any of these new clothes at this rate, Mother.'

'Nonsense, there's nothing to you both. Elena, which one, dear?'

'May I have the lemon meringue?'

Katherine slid the plate over to Elena. 'Of course, you may.'

'Thank you.'

Jasmine reached for the éclair. 'I hope you know Mum that this is going to cost me two hours in the gym.' Katherine flopped her hand at Jasmine, playfully dismissing her comment.

'How's your morning been, Elena?'

'Pretty good for a Monday. We've got a new manager, and he's a big improvement on the last one.'

Jasmine raised her eyebrows suggestively from behind her cup.

'Well, this little madam has dragged me around every clothes store and shoe shop there is.'

Jasmine's eyes and mouth were wide open in fake shock. 'Don't you believe it, Elena. Who do most of these bags belong to, Mother dear?'

Katherine couldn't keep up the act and chuckled to herself. 'Well, since I was there, I thought it would be a shame not to buy something.'

Elena was envious of Jasmine. They were obviously very close. She had never been shopping with her mother, except to buy groceries. It all seemed perfect, except for Alan, who she was still worried might just turn up. Every time the café door opened, she had the urge to turn around just to make sure it wasn't him. That feeling of unease spoilt their meeting. Elena had clicked with Jasmine right from the start and loved being in her company but wasn't sure how it would all work out.

'We were supposed to be looking for something for Dad's birthday. What about a nice ring?'

'Now you know your father and jewellery don't go together. He doesn't even wear his wedding ring.'

Yeah, I can vouch for that one.

'You all right, honey? You're very quiet today.'

'Yes, I'm fine, thank you, just a little tired.'

Elena knew she wasn't her usual self, but it hadn't been a usual weekend. She wanted to relax and enjoy her break with the two ladies, but the circumstances didn't allow for that. Would she ever feel at ease in Jasmine's company again?

Katherine accurately sliced her cake in half with the delicate silver fork. 'You do look run-down. You need to relax, dear, and I have the perfect solution.' She paused and took a sip of her Earl Grey, gently placing the cup back with its partner. 'A weekend with us and *Martha.*' She spoke confidently like a doctor prescribing medicine that would cure the ailment.

'*Martha?* Who's *Martha?*'

Jasmine's eyes lit up. '*Martha* is Dad's pride and joy—his boat.'

Shit, I'd forgotten about that.

Katherine ran her hand through her fading blond fringe. 'We're going to have a party on Saturday evening with a few friends. Then Sunday, we're cruising to a fantastic restaurant called Riverside Retreat. Have you heard of it?'

'Er, no, I haven't.' *Riverside Misery more like.*

'Then we'll spend the rest of the day on *Martha.* How does that sound?'

Elena was struggling to find the energy to lie convincingly and played nervously with her earlobe. 'It sounds great, but I've arranged to see my mother on Sunday, I'm afraid.'

'Elena, you must come, please. Dad will be so disappointed. He thinks you're lovely.'

Yeah, I know. She wasn't good at thinking on her feet whilst under pressure.

'Well, I tell you what, Jasmine will pick you up on Saturday, come and spend the night with us, and then on Sunday morning, we'll get a car to take you straight to your mother's, or wherever you want to go.' She was used to getting her own way and a hard lady to dissuade. 'All you'll need, dear, is an overnight bag. We'll take care of the rest, okay?'

An overnight bag and a shotgun. 'Well, I . . .'

'That's settled then. Don't worry, dear, you're not imposing. Alan loves nothing better than showing people around Martha. It will be our pleasure.'

It's not the boat he wants to show me.

Elena was too exhausted to argue and hadn't got the imagination to come up with a good excuse. One way or another, she wasn't getting on a boat with that maniac with nowhere to run or swim.

Jasmine wiggled in her chair, raised and dropped her shoulders with an excited grin on her face. 'Honey, I forgot to bring your beret and perfume.' She wrinkled her nose. 'Sorry.'

'That's fine, I'm not going to France this week anyway.'

Katherine's brow creased, not being privy to their joke. She encouraged Elena to eat her untouched lemon meringue, but despite only having had a glass of water for breakfast, she wasn't hungry. The stress had consumed her appetite. It seemed as though their whole meeting had been an act so far for Elena, so she continued with the pretence and forced herself to eat the bittersweet dessert.

Mother and daughter chatted happily about their plans for the rest of the afternoon, which included more shopping then cocktails before dinner with the monster.

Elena caught Jasmine observing her and knew she had spotted something was wrong. Elena tried to join in the conversation but had little to say. She was relieved to see from the café clock that it was almost time to get back to work and wondered what Simon wanted to see her about.

They said their goodbyes with kisses all 'round. Elena looked back as she opened the door to leave. Jasmine had a worried look on her face and made the okay sign with her hand as Katherine checked her makeup in her compact mirror. Elena nodded with a faint smile, giving her a thumbs-up. The door closed behind her. She breathed a sigh of relief and had left earlier than necessary. The lunch break had been strained to say the least. At least at the bank, she knew where she stood. There were no secrets or embarrassing situations, just protocol.

She approached Simon's newly acquired office with trepidation and could see Jenny through the glass panel leaning over Simon who was sitting at his desk. Before she had chance to knock, he looked up and beckoned her in.

'Elena, have a seat, please.' He held out his hand towards the plump black leather chair sitting in front of his desk.

It was only the second time she had ever been in the office. When Dawn had been there, she had treated it like a bear's cave, somewhere you never entered voluntarily.

'Jenny, would you mind leaving us for a while?'

'Certainly, Mr Baker.' She spoke in a very submissive manner, and Elena thought she saw her almost curtsey as she left.

'Elena White, you've been with the bank for two years now.' He was reading from a file on his desk. 'Previous experience was with Whitehouse and Finch as a trainee financial adviser. So what happened there?'

His questioning made her feel like she was being interviewed for the job all over again. 'Well . . . the position was no longer available.' She felt defensive. *What's does that have to do with anything?*

'How did you find the role—demanding, rewarding,

enjoyable?'

He forgot degrading. He sat perfectly still and didn't take his eyes off her, which was slightly perturbing. 'Enjoyable and demanding at times, but I like a challenge.' *Where is this going?*

He leaned back in his chair and put his fingers together. 'As you know, Martin is our financial adviser, but we need some new blood. Things have gone a bit stale at this branch, so what I am proposing is to start with you working alongside Martin for a week or two, to get to grips with the way things work. If you're happy to continue, and are coping with the demands of the role, I'll nominate you for the position. Is that something you would be interested pursuing?'

'Yes, that sounds great. Thank you.'

Elena's long-term plan had always been to get qualified, gain some experience with the bank, and then branch out on her own. This was an opportunity she was going to grab with both hands.

'Obviously, it will alter your pay structure.'

'So long as it's going in the right direction.' She pointed to the ceiling.

He laughed. 'Yes, it's good when it goes that way, isn't it?'

Unintentionally, she inspected his hands. No wedding ring.

'How do you think you'll find it working with Martin?'

'Fine. He's a nice guy, and he knows his stuff.'

He had worked for the bank for thirty years and was like a walking textbook, but his weakness was dealing with the customers. He just didn't have any people skills and tended to hide away in his corner, only coming out for coffee. So far, he'd got away with it, but he wouldn't be very happy with Elena's intrusion.

'Okay. I'll see Martin shortly to explain the plan, and we'll start the ball rolling tomorrow. Have you got any questions for me?'

Yes, can you sort Jenny out? She's freaking me out. 'No, I don't think so.'

'Well, if you do, my door is always open.' He got up from his chair and towered over Elena, giving her the signal that the meeting was over. Elena stood, and he offered his hand. 'I'm very much looking forward to working with you, Elena.' His long fingers encased her hand. His gaze was intense, and she had to look away.

'Me too.' She turned to leave slightly flushed and noticed his reflection in the vision panel. He was checking her out. Elena closed the door and, once she was out of sight, did a little dance.

Yes!

A hot new boss and a promising new career with more money—it was just the boost she needed. No more customer complaints about the same things day after day. Finally, she had some goals to work towards, and a small part of her life was back on track.

Simon headed across the banking hall towards Martin's office like the Pied Piper, with Jenny running along close behind him in a hypnotic state.

All things considered, the day had gone better than expected. The fact that the she-devil had gone was more than enough; everything else was a bonus.

Driving home, Elena decided she couldn't be bothered to cook and would treat herself to a Chinese and maybe a glass or two of wine in celebration. She stopped at the convenience store for a few basics, not wanting another supermodel breakfast. She came to the gift isle and reluctantly thought of Alan's birthday. She was going to have to get him a card and gift for Jasmine's sake.

She found a card on special for fifty pence, with an amateurish drawing of a pair of football boots and some golf clubs, but she didn't want to offend Jasmine, so she opted for a contemporary card with a simple birthday greeting, then grabbed a bottle of whisky and a sparkly gift bag. As she waited to pay, Elena contemplated half-emptying the whisky bottle and filling it up with cat's piss, but as she didn't have a cat, she wasn't sure how to get her hands on half a litre of tomcat piss. On eBay maybe?

She managed to get a parking space outside her home, which was a first. The house was in darkness as she stumbled through the front door, carrying the shopping bags, which she dumped in the kitchen. Elena turned on the lights and went through the kitchen drawers, looking for the Chinese takeaway menu. Finally finding it in the bread bin, she rang her order through to the Green Chopstick. The abrupt Chinese man on the end of the phone shouted it would be a least forty minutes, so she used the time to shower and get into her comfy pyjamas and rabbit slippers.

After restocking the cupboards and giving the fridge a purpose once more, she opened the wine just to make sure it was okay before the food arrived. A glass and a half later, she decided it was fit for purpose. There was a knock at the front door, and Elena slopped along, completely unashamed of her attire, and opened the door to retrieve her food. She paid the young skinny guy who only spoke in grunts and who fished around for so long in his pockets for her change that she thought he was hoping she would tell him keep it. But because of his rudeness, Elena stood in her bunny slippers patiently with her hand held out.

With her plate piled high—she always ordered too much—and armed with knife, fork, and glass of wine, she sat in front of the magic box, watching one of the endless soaps, although after the week she'd had, it looked pretty tame.

Surprised at how hungry she was, Elena carried her empty plate back into the kitchen. Faced with the debris from the takeaway and shopping, she had a sudden feeling of loneliness. It had never crossed her mind before, but the sight of the kitchen littered with takeaway rubbish looked sad.

Jasmine was no doubt eating in a Michelin-starred restaurant with her parents. And Conrad—well, he'd be curled up on the sofa with his wife snuggling into his chest in front of an open fire. Here was Elena in the kitchen with damp hair from the shower, pink fluffy pyjamas, and white bunny slippers. She felt pathetic, unattractive, and an overwhelming feeling of loneliness descended over her. The house felt awful, dead. She'd never actually noticed it before.

The phone was on the table next to the Green Chopstick menu. She desperately wanted to call Conrad, to hear his voice, but what would she say? 'Hi, how are you? Did you manage to get rid of your fucked-up wife, or is she still there?'

She dropped down onto the kitchen chair with a humph. That was unfair. She was angry with herself for feeling that way and snatched the empty wine glass from the table to refill it but then stopped herself. No, that's how her mother had coped, and she wasn't going to go down that line. The remainder of the wine bottle was poured down the sink, removing the temptation. Elena tidied the kitchen, returning it to its normal state, and decided to try to be more positive, starting with tomorrow and her new role.

She shuffled back into the lounge with a cup of tea, doing her best to ignore the loneliness following her, and watched trash TV for a while before saying good night to another day.

CHAPTER FOURTEEN

Elena woke before the alarm clock had the satisfaction of startling her from her sleep. She felt good and jumped out of bed determined to face the day. She zipped through her morning routine and left the house ahead of schedule, and managed to park in the same spot she'd found the day before. *Perfect.*

Elena charged towards the bank, feeling like a new woman, driven. She remembered what Jasmine had said, *'You're the one in control.'* She was determined not to feel sorry for herself any longer and to tackle things head on.

She stood at the entrance to the bank and rang the bell. Jenny came to let her in. She usually looked the same every day: trousers, jacket, minimal makeup, and sensible shoes. Not today. The jacket had gone, leaving a fitted blouse with one too many buttons undone, revealing a glimpse of red lacy bra. Suit trousers were now replaced with a tight skirt that finished several inches above the knee. Her sensible shoes had been cast aside for a pair of killer heels.

God knows how she was going to cope in those all day.

Finally, she had full *it's-Saturday-night-let's-party* makeup going on.

'Morning, Jenny. You look nice.'

'Oh thanks. My suit's in the wash so I threw this on instead.' This made Elena smile.

'Is Simon in yet?'

Jenny grabbed Elena by the shoulder in a swoon. 'Oh god, is he in yet? I wish he was *in*,' she said breathlessly. 'Sorry.' She shook herself. 'I had a bit of a moment there. I've just taken him a coffee. He's in his office.'

'Thanks, Jenny.'

'Elena . . . does his girlfriend work for the bank?' She was obviously fishing to see if he had a partner.

'I don't know if he has a girlfriend.' Elena was in a playful mood and decided to tease her. 'Actually, I think he's gay.'

Jenny gave a loud gasp, a look of shock and horror on her face. Elena felt horrible like she'd just told a three-year-old there was no Santa. Jenny kicked off her killer heels, picked them up, and traipsed over to the staffroom.

Heading to Simon's office, she smiled to herself and thought she would put Jenny out of her misery later. Elena knocked on the door before popping her head in.

'Morning.'

Simon had an apprehensive look on his face. 'I thought it was Jenny again. Come in, Elena.'

She took a seat in the comfy leather chair.

'She's a bit full-on, if you know what I mean.'

'I may have just got you some respite.' He tilted his head, and his eyes flickered with curiosity. 'I told her you might be gay.'

It was just a joke, but it was a risky thing to say, especially to your new boss. *What if he was gay?*

He stared at her intently, shaking his head. His perfect cheek bones raised as a sexy smile graced his face.

'Thank you, and for that little gift, you must let me buy you lunch tomorrow.'

Wow! She hadn't expected that. 'Er . . . sounds great. Thank you.'

'I'm sure my boyfriend won't mind.' They both laughed.

Did we just have a moment?

'Right. On to business, you'll be working alongside Martin from now on. I'm sending him out today to call on some of our best clients. We need to re-establish our relationship with these people, and I have a good feeling you'll be able to help Martin with that part. If you have any problems whatsoever, please let me know straight away. I intend to take this branch right to the very top, and I will need everyone on board to do that.'

Elena had no doubt he would. He seemed a very determined man.

'I've got a few meetings today, so I'll be out from twelve till three, but come and see me before you go, and let me know how you get on.'

'Yes, of course.'

'Have a good day.'

'Thank you. You too.'

Elena left Simon's office buzzing with excitement. He had eased her nerves, and she felt under his wing, and lunch tomorrow—now that was exciting. But strangely, Elena felt guilty. What would Conrad think? Well, the nonexistent calls and texts told her what he thought.

She marched over to Martin's office full of confidence. He was surprisingly welcoming. Simon's visits to each member of staff had obviously worked.

Elena couldn't remember the last time she had enjoyed work so much. It felt great to be out of the branch meeting clients. Although she was only at the very beginning of her new career, she felt important, not in an egotistical way, but she had a feeling of self-worth as if she mattered.

As agreed, she called in on Simon to give him a progress report on the day's proceedings.

'So how did it go with Martin today?'

'Great. In fact, better than expected. We've managed to secure a second meeting with most of the clients we've seen today.' He put down his pen and leant forward, resting on his desk. 'Martin and I will be making proposed plans tailored individually to the client so we can secure more investment.'

'I'm impressed.' He paused and gazed at Elena for a while. She wasn't sure if it flattered her or made her uncomfortable. 'I think you're going to do very well here, Elena, very well indeed.'

His eyes sparkled like diamonds under the spotlights of his office. He had a voracious look on his face, which unnerved her somewhat. The room temperature seemed to rise a few degrees. The atmosphere was tangible and was punctured by Jenny's uncouth entrance.

'Simon, can I get you a drink before—oh, sorry. I didn't know you had someone with you.'

Elena noticed she had flat shoes on and smirked to herself. 'I was just going, Jenny. Thanks, Simon.'

'Not at all, and don't forget lunch is on me tomorrow.'

Jenny's face turned to stone. If Simon hadn't been there, Elena was sure Jenny would have pounced.

Time to make a hasty retreat. 'See you tomorrow,' Elena called as she hurried away, wanting to put some distance between her and Jenny, who was so red she looked like she might burst into flames.

Elena drove home riding the waves of contentment. Still in a can-do mood, she decided to call Jasmine to confirm she would be visiting tomorrow as planned and to tell her she wouldn't be risking her safety with Captain Birdseye on Saturday. She hadn't decided what excuse she would give but was sure it wasn't going to happen.

Watered and fed, Elena lay on the sofa and opted for the radio, not wanting reality TV to spoil her positive mood. She dialled Jasmine's number.

'Hello?'

'Hi, Jaz. How are you?'

'I'm fabulous, thank you. And how is Ms White this

evening?' Even down the phone, Jasmine was a ray of sunshine.

'Well, Ms Saunders, as I am the new financial adviser, in training, I am very happy, thank you.'

'Did you get promoted?'

'Yes.' Elena was so excited her voice went into a high-pitched squeak.

'Oh, well done. That's great, honey. When do you start?'

'I started today, and it went very well. I really enjoyed it, actually, which is a nice change.'

'It's funny you should call. We were just talking about you.'

'Were you now? I hope you're leaving out all the bad stuff. Who's we?' Probably Marcus.

'My lovely daddy. He's been asking all about you.'

Elena sat bolt upright; the ray of sunshine had suddenly clouded over. 'There's no bad stuff to tell with you, honey. We all had a bit too much to drink last night, so Mum and Dad stayed with me, and I can't get rid of the buggers now.' Jasmine tittered down the phone.

Elena's blood ran cold, and she paced the floor. What the hell did he want to know? *Don't panic, they're just having an innocent conversation. It's nothing to worry about. I'm the one in control.*

'Are you still okay for tomorrow?'

Shit! What if they're still at Jasmine's tomorrow? 'We can leave it for another time if you've got your parents staying.' Elena bit her nails. Despite telling herself to calm down, it seemed her heart hadn't got the message; it was beating so hard it was almost audible.

'No, they're bloody going tonight. I've had enough. I'm only joking. Dad's got an important appointment tomorrow, which really means he's playing golf with his friends. So it will be just you and me, sweetie.'

'Okay.' Elena breathed a silent sigh of relief. *Now's my chance to tell her. It will be easier over the phone.*

'While we're on the subject of your father, I'm afraid I can't make the weekend.'

'Oh no! Why not?'

'Er . . . my mum's not too good at the moment, so I said I'd spend some time with her, cheer her up a bit with some mother-and-daughter time.' Now she really was stretching the truth.

'Aw, okay, honey . . . Elena can't make your birthday, I'm afraid, Dad.'

She bit on her knuckle involuntarily and listened hard. She could hear a muffled voice in the background but couldn't tell what was being said.

'He said he's very disappointed, but we will arrange for you to spend the weekend on *Martha* in a few weeks. How does that sound?'

I'm going have to sink that fuckin' boat. 'Yeah, that would be nice.'

'I've got to go. Dad wants to get going, and my mother's still doing her hair, bless her.'

'Okay, say hello to them for me.' *And give your dad a kick in the balls.*

'See you tomorrow about seven, yeah?'

'Look forward to it. Bye, Jaz.'

'Bye, honey.'

There, that hadn't been so bad after all. Her heart was still pounding. They were going home right now, so he wouldn't be there tomorrow, and she had got herself out of Saturday. *That had hopefully sprung a leak in his precious boat.* She quite liked this taking-control lark. As corny as it was, she felt empowered. It was all change from here on.

Once again, Elena beat the alarm, and as she had prepared everything for work the night before with a German-like efficiency, right down to the toothpaste on her brush, she had time to spare and took a little longer to get ready, her lunch date with Simon in mind.

Ready to leave, she made sure she had a full arsenal of

makeup with her, including perfume. Elena checked her appearance in the hall mirror. She hadn't done a Jenny on herself but was happy with her enhanced look.

Let's go get 'em.

Car keys at the ready, she left the house, excited about what the day would bring.

Elena stood outside the bank and pressed the buzzer for the third time.

Where was everyone?

She checked her watch. It was early but not that early. Finally, Jenny came and let her in, dressed in her usual attire.

'Morning, Jenny.'

Elena's chirpy mood was met with a scowl, seems her lunch date with the boss really had rattled her cage. She headed for the staffroom.

'Simon wants to see you in his office right away.' Jenny's tone was a bit sharp for Elena's liking. She turned to acknowledge her, but she already had her back to her and was strutting away.

Oh, get over it.

Elena did as she was told and went straight to his office. The door was open. Before she went in, Elena ruffled her hair. He was at his desk, looking through a pile of papers.

'Good morning.' She sang her greeting, which was met with an ice-cold stare.

'Close the door.' His voice was harsh and unwelcoming. Something was wrong.

'You got the last part right, but there's nothing good about it.'

Had Jenny complained? Or had she said something she shouldn't have to one of the clients yesterday?

Elena didn't bother to take a seat as one hadn't been offered. She still had her black coat on and clasped her bag.

'When I arrived here this morning, I was met with a

nice surprise. I found these pasted all over the windows.' He threw a handful of A4-sized papers which landed at her feet.

He's not so charming today.

She was completely confused and very anxious. Elena bent to pick up one of the sheets of paper and turned it over. Her newly found confidence and can-do attitude was stolen from her that very moment.

'The staff were busily going through the bundle that had been stuffed into the letterbox.'

Elena was shaking. She felt sick as she looked at a printout of her profile page from Daddy Daddy Sugar, complete with sexy photo.

Oh god, no, would this ever end? 'Simon, this is a mistake. It's not what it seems.'

'Is that you?' He jumped out of his chair and leaned on his desk with one hand, his other held one of the offending pages at arm's length.

Ashamed, her head held low, she nodded reluctantly.

'Great, just great! I've come to this branch, which is on its knees, with the aim of raising it right to the top, and what do I find? Some cheap hooker to whom I almost gave access to the finances of some very wealthy people.' He was shouting at her. His face was bright red. A vein in his forehead throbbed, indicating his rage.

'Simon, how dare you?' The cool, calm, collected Simon had turned into an unreasonable maniac.

'Oh sorry, yes. You're right. Not cheap at all by the look of this website.' His sarcasm was scathing. 'How. Dare. You.' He jabbed his finger at her with each word like a spear.

'I have worked tirelessly to get to the position I'm in, and I am damned if some . . . *floozy* is going to ruin it.'

She had emotionally imploded and hadn't got the strength to fight. What was the point? He wasn't going to listen to anything Elena had to say. All he was worried about was himself. He had torn strips off her without giving her the slightest chance to explain.

'You should be thanking me. I managed to get all of these before any of the customers got to see them.' He hadn't finished venting his anger. 'You can imagine if the press got hold of this. The staff have all been warned that if this does leak, there will be hell to pay.'

'Thank you,' she whimpered, her head still held down in shame.

'I haven't done it to save your reputation.' He spat the words out at her with bitter resentment. 'Frankly, I couldn't give a shit! Now get your things. You're suspended, pending an investigation, but you can take it from me, you will not be returning to this bank. Now get out!'

Elena left his office. All the staff suddenly jumped into action. She didn't bother to pick up her things; there was nothing of any importance. She just wanted to get away from the judgmental stares.

Exiting the bank, Elena gulped down the cool air. She felt like she was about to pass out. Humiliation and embarrassment crashed down on her.

Alan! The bastard! Was this his retaliation for her cancelling Saturday?

She walked back towards her car in a state of shock, gazing at the pavement. One of the malicious pieces of paper fluttered across the ground. Elena made a grab for it but just missed. She chased after it, dodging between the oncoming people. Every time she got close, the wind teasingly kept it just out of reach. Panic set in.

An elderly gentleman ahead had noticed her trying to catch the dancing paper. He managed to trap it with his foot and picked it up. Elena rushed over. His friendly face turned to one of disgust as she snatched it from him before he could look at it.

'Sorry, I didn't mean—'

He walked on, not bothering to listen to her apology.

Elena sat in her car. It still hadn't sunk in.

It had to be Alan. Who else could it be? What a fucking vile man. Who was next on the list, the neighbours? What was he going to get from this?

She held the paper in her hands. How she regretted ever signing up with that website. That one tiny mistake had created a wave of problems that threatened to drown her.

She didn't know what to do or where to begin. Her thoughts turned to money. She had some savings but not enough to pay the rent for more than a few weeks.

Simon had shown his true colours. He seemed like a really nice guy, but it just went to show you never could tell. He had only helped reinforce how highly she regarded Conrad. If there was ever a time when she needed him, it was now. He'd know what to do.

The reality was that Elena knew what she must do, but was desperately trying to think of alternatives. She could go to the police, but what proof did she have? Plus, she didn't want any more embarrassment either. Where would it stop? Or would it keep happening every time she was climbing back up? Would he kick her back down again?

There was only one way. He had forced her hand. She would have to tell Jasmine everything. Elena knew it would destroy their friendship. She had become so close with her. Jasmine was like the sister she never had. Then there was Katherine, a lovely gentle lady. It would destroy her to find out about her husband's double life, and Jaz adored her father.

What was she to do? Live in fear and poverty, while they lived the high life, eating in five-star hotels, laughing and joking without a care in the world, while Elena kept his other life a secret for him and suffered in silence? Maybe she should arrange to meet him, tell him enough is enough.

After the way he'd behaved at Jasmine's apartment, she knew that wouldn't work. He was the sort of man that got a kick out of seeing people suffer. Conrad had warned her he doesn't give in and won't be beaten.

What a fucking mess.

Elena started the car and drove towards home. She'd got some serious thinking to do.

CHAPTER FIFTEEN

Elena paused outside the open elevator holding a silver party bag with Alan's card and whisky inside. Jasmine would be waiting. Her stomach churned. She hadn't eaten a thing since breakfast with all the worry. She still hadn't decided what to do. If she let things carry on as they were, that would be a signal to Alan that he could walk all over her and get away with it. No, like it or not, she had to tell her tonight.

Elena stepped in exhausted by all the worry. As the elevator went up a level, so did her anxiety. It stopped, delivering her to Jasmine's floor.

Taking several deep breaths, with great trepidation, she knocked on the door. *Here we go.* The thought sprang to mind that he might be there to twist the knife. In a moment of panic, she wanted to run away, but it was too late. Jasmine opened the door.

'Hi, Jaz.'

'Hello, honey, come in.'

The lights in the hallway weren't on, but Elena could see Jasmine was in her pyjamas. She followed her into the open-plan lounge. An assortment of candles placed around the room danced their flickering light romantically across the walls.

'I got something for your dad.' She played along with the pretence and handed the sparkly bag to Jasmine.

'Thank you, honey. That's lovely of you. Can I get you a drink?'

'I'll have a tea, please, Jaz.'

She wasn't her usual bubbly self. Her hair was clipped up, and she had no makeup on. Even in the dimly lit room, Elena could see she looked pale.

Her nervousness heightened. Did she know? Something was definitely wrong.

'How's the new job going?' *No, she doesn't know.*

'It's er . . . it's going well.' *It's going well, all right. In fact, it's gone altogether.*

The hesitation was agony. Elena said to herself, as soon as they were both seated, she was going to tell her; no more waiting.

Jasmine carried their drinks over to the lounge. She had a large glass of red wine. They sat in opposite ends of the lounge suite, facing each other. Jasmine curled her legs under her and caressed the wine glass with both hands while soft music played in the background.

'Jaz, I'm not interrupting anything, am I?'

'No, you're not.' Her voice lacked its usual enthusiasm.

'Are you okay, Jaz?'

'I'm not, actually. I'm . . . I'm pregnant.' Her eyes brimmed with tears as her chin trembled.

This was a Jasmine she didn't think existed. Elena got up and sat next to her. 'Oh, Jaz.' She clutched Jasmine's hand with both of hers. 'I don't know what to say. How do you feel about it?'

Jasmine dabbed the tears from her eyes with her fingers. 'I always thought if it ever happened, I'd get rid of it, but that's easy to say when it's not real. I don't want a baby yet. I'm not ready and certainly not with a man who's thirty years older than me.' She freed her hand from

Elena's and rubbed her temple, shaking her head.

'Have you told Marcus?'

'No.' Jasmine reached for her wine and drank half the glass in one go.

'What do you think he'll say?'

'Oh, I don't know. Depending on what I decide to do, he may never know. I don't understand it. I've always been so careful. I'm on the pill for god's sake.'

'Have you seen a doctor yet?' Elena really didn't know what to say, and she certainly couldn't drop the bombshell about her dad being a sadistic stalker.

'No, I only found out today after doing seven tests—all positive.' She dropped her head in her hands. 'What am I going to do, Elena?'

'You have to do what your heart tells you, Jaz.'

Her head shot up from its cradle. 'That's just it. My heart's telling me there's a miracle happening inside of me—a human being, a child with a beating heart, is growing inside me right now.' She placed her hands on her tummy. 'But my head's saying, "How can you be a mother? Get rid of it. You're way too selfish a person."'

'No, you're not.'

'Yes, I am. I don't want to be big and fat and not fit any of my clothes. And what about Marcus? I'm meant to be his sexy mistress, the one that makes him feel good, gives him the attention he needs, not moans about backache and piles.' She reached for the wine glass again. 'This is so fucked up!'

'Is there anyone you can talk to? What about your mother?' Jasmine didn't need someone to talk to. She needed someone to listen.

'What would I tell her—I had a one-night stand or I've been sleeping with a man that's older than my dad? They've always wanted grandchildren but not like this.'

'Well, there you go.'

'No, Elena. I don't want people gushing over me all excited and looking at things through rose-tinted glasses. I want someone to back me up, tell me I don't want a kid with all the sleepless nights and nappies. Plus, you can't go shopping for the day with a screaming child. There isn't anyone to talk to. You're the only one who knows about Marcus. Everyone else thinks I work for his telecommunications company, and the car and apartment are perks. Most of my life's a fucking lie. I'm constantly telling stories about where I'm going or why I can't meet my friends. You're the only person I can be myself with, and it's such a relief to not have to pretend. I don't know what I'd do if I didn't have you.'

Elena was touched by her words and felt honoured that Jasmine held her in such high regard. She had seen another side to Jasmine; her easy lifestyle had come at a high price. Everyone that came into contact with her saw an outgoing confident girl, but now the curtain was pulled back, it was a different picture.

'I've been running away from real life for years, living this fantasy, this double life.' Jasmine wandered into the kitchen and came back with an open bottle of red wine. 'I need some advice.' She sat down and poured the contents of the bottle into her glass.

'You won't find any answers in the bottom of that bottle, I can tell you that.'

Jasmine nodded, still tempted by the red seducer. 'Yeah, I know. I want you to say you'll come with me to the clinic and tell me it will be over in a couple of hours, and then I can get back to normal, forget all about it.'

Her tearstained face implored Elena to give her consent.

'Jaz, it has to be your decision. I can't tell you what you think you want to hear.'

Elena thought how conflicting life could be. Conrad and his wife had been through hell and back for their baby, only for it to be taken away from them, and here was Jasmine with no intention of having a child, and yet it had been thrust upon her. It made Elena question her philosophy of everything happening for a reason.

'Don't be so hard on yourself. It's a shock to the system, yes, but try to stay calm. Spend the weekend with your parents then make a decision on Monday. Give yourself a few days to clear your head, and things will seem less daunting, I'm sure.'

'Yeah, thank you.'

'Does Marcus have any children?'

'No, he doesn't.'

'Well, you might be pleasantly surprised. He could be over the moon about it.'

'Yes, I know. That's another thing I'm worried about. I don't think I want that sort of relationship with him. I like things the way they are. I've got freedom.'

'But wouldn't you like to settle down one day?'

'I will settle, just not for less.' That was the spoilt little girl talking.

'What are you afraid of, Jaz?'

Jasmine looked around at the apartment. 'If I tell him and he wants nothing more to do with me, and I lose this place and the car, then I'll have to go crawling back to Mum and Dad. I love them to bits, but I couldn't live with them again.'

'What if you don't have the baby?'

'Well, things would carry on as normal, and I'd have to live with another scar on my soul, wouldn't I?' Jasmine stared at the candle on the coffee table, hypnotised by its dancing flame for a moment.

She snapped herself out of it with a shake of her head. 'Are you hungry? I haven't eaten all day.'

Elena smiled. 'Me neither.'

'Come on. I'll make us something to eat.'

The two friends went into the kitchen. Elena carried her cold tea and put it on the worktop and was glad to see Jasmine tip the contents of the wine glass down the sink. She touched Jasmine on the shoulder. 'Come here.' She said holding her arms open.

The two friends hugged, and Jasmine's emotion poured out. Elena also wept silently, partly for Jasmine but mostly because of her own problems. Unlike Jasmine, she didn't have anyone to confide in. They embraced in the flickering light of the candles: one of them confessing their burden, the other suffering silently for her friend. Elena worried that ultimately, her secret would destroy their friendship.

The next morning, Elena was woken not by the alarm, which was also now redundant, but by someone knocking on the door. She checked the time through one eye, still trying to hang on to sleep. Seven ten. She pulled the duvet over her head, deciding to ignore whoever it was, probably the postman or a courier. They were certainly persistent. The knocking became louder.

'Bloody hell! All right!' She got out of bed in a strop, threw on her pink dressing gown, slipped her feet into the bunny slippers, and stomped down the stairs, revving herself up to give the phantom knocker a bollocking.

She flung the door open, a stern look stamped on her face to find Conrad standing there.

'Morning, sleepyhead.'

Oh shit, look at the state of me!

He looked good in his dark blue jeans, faded denim shirt, and black leather jacket. He was clean-shaven, and his hair was immaculately styled.

'Morning.' Elena tried subtly to tame her wild hair, but it wasn't playing by the rules.

'Can I come in?'

'Oh sorry. Yes, of course.' She was in a daze and couldn't quite believe he was standing there.

Elena opened the door for him, and Conrad stepped into the hallway. He smelt gorgeous. He had an addictive aroma that made her want to sniff incessantly like a dog in the park.

'Have you ever tried haggis?' he asked.

'What?' *Has he been drinking?*

'I thought we might try some tonight.'

Elena was completely confused. 'Conrad, have I missed an e-mail or a text message? What are you taking about?'

'Scotland. I'm going there for a few days, and you're coming with me.'

Have I been in a coma for the last week?

'Where's the kitchen?'

Elena was still trying to fathom out what was going on. 'Er, it's straight ahead.'

He went into the kitchen, and Elena stood in the hallway with her eyes closed, cringing because she hadn't tidied up after herself, and there were cups and plates strewn all over the kitchen side. He grabbed the kettle and filled it with water then turned to Elena. 'Sorry I haven't been in touch. I've had a bit of thinking to do this week.'

She was awake now but still confused. 'What, about your wife?'

'Don't worry about that, it's all sorted.'

There he goes again, avoiding my questions.

'Now tea or coffee?' He clicked the kettle on.

'Tea. Conrad?' He looked over his shoulder at her. 'I'm not a plaything you can pick up and put down whenever you want.' *Did I really just say that?* If he'd have walked out after hearing that, Elena would have dived at his feet to keep him there.

Conrad turned to face her and put the cup he was holding down. 'No, Elena, you're not, and I don't want you thinking that's how I see you. It couldn't be further from the truth.'

He looked straight at her with honest eyes. She knew he was telling the truth, and those few words stirred her emotions. She was so pleased he was there; the relief was almost overwhelming.

Elena looked down at herself trying to divert the tears. 'Sorry, I look a mess.'

'You look fine. You've just got up, haven't you? That's the way everyone looks in the morning. If you'd have been at my house a couple of hours ago, you would have found me in my pink dressing gown and bunny slippers.' He made her laugh. She didn't think she'd be doing that so soon. He made everything seem right and lifted her mood like no one else.

Conrad washed out another cup in the sink. 'What about work? Do you have some holidays you can take?'

'I'm on one big holiday from now on.' She pulled out a chair and sat at the table.

'What do you mean?'

Elena hadn't intended to mention it, but it was too late now. 'I've been suspended. There's going to be an inquiry, and I was told that I *will* be fired.'

He dried his hands and sat at the table opposite her. 'Why?'

She got up and took the crumpled up printout from the drawer and gave it to Conrad. 'Because I made one small mistake, which has had a knock-on effect that is slowly destroying my life.' He examined the paper, his brows knitted. 'I'm so embarrassed, I can imagine what you must be thinking.' She flopped back down on her chair, feeling ashamed of herself.

'Elena, if I thought you were that sort of girl, I wouldn't be here. We all make mistakes. It's part of life. Nobody is whiter than white. Don't apologise for it. You don't have to, sweetheart.'

The reassuring words were desperately needed. *He's going to make me cry.*

'Now tell me what happened.'

'I got to work yesterday, and I was told Simon wanted to see me.'

'Who's Simon?'

'He's the new manager, Simon Baker. When I got to his office, he'd got a pile of these on his desk.' She pointed to the paper in Conrad's hands. 'Someone had pasted them all over the windows of the bank and shoved a load through the letter box. Well . . . not someone—Alan.'

Conrad lent back in his chair and folded his arms across his broad chest, stretching the leather tight across his arms.

'Simon completely humiliated me, calling me a cheap hooker and a floozy. He threw a handful of those in my face. I was so embarrassed.' This time she couldn't control her emotions, and two tears raced each other down her red cheeks. 'He didn't even give me a chance to explain, just threw me out like a piece of rubbish. Everyone was talking about me when I left.'

Conrad's jaw set, and he stared at the table for a few moments, his eyes focused. He pulled back his leather cuff and checked his watch.

'Sorry, Conrad. I'm a mess at the moment. I don't think I'd be very good company.'

He stood and leaned over the table. His face still had a look of concern. 'Forget about it for now. I'll sort it. Besides, I need someone to carry the bags. Now get up those stairs and get dressed.'

She smiled through the tears, and he kissed her on the forehead. 'Come on, lassie, we'll be late,' he joked with a Scottish accent.

She got up and shuffled along into the hall. 'Elena, don't worry, I'll be paying Alan a visit when we get back, okay?'

She nodded and ran upstairs to get ready.

Conrad sat down and leaned on the table with his hand on his chin. The truth was he hadn't intended on taking her with him. It could just make things more difficult. He'd been undecided all week, and then when he was on his way to the airport, the colour of the autumn leaves had reminded him of her beautiful hair. He used the excuse that it was nature's way of giving her consent and diverted his route straight to her.

He was glad that he had. Knowing she'd been upset and seeing those tears roll down her face for no fault of her own made him furious. She was a kind gentle soul who had been taken advantage of and trampled on by bullies. If there was one thing Conrad couldn't stand, it was a bully.

Elena came downstairs dressed in tight faded jeans and a fitted black V-neck jumper, with a white towel wrapped around her head. Conrad had washed the dishes and tided the kitchen, and there was a cup of tea and two pieces of toast on the table waiting for her. He had hung his leather jacket on the back of the kitchen chair and had his shirt sleeves rolled up, holding a tea towel.

'Conrad, you didn't have to do that. Thank you.' *Oh god, that means he's been in the cupboards.*

'All part of the service. In fact, if the gym business goes under, this is my next plan—mobile maid.'

Elena giggled, taking a bite of her toast.

'What you laughing at? I think I'd be in high demand.'

'Yeah, if you did it naked.' She raised an eyebrow, her face hidden behind her teacup.

He placed the tea towel over his shoulder and put his hands on his hips. 'If we hadn't got a plane to catch, I could strip off and vacuum the stairs.'

Elena blushed. 'You and stairs are a dangerous combination.'

His hazel eyes raked over her from top to bottom. 'Mmm, don't get me started, we haven't got time. Now eat your toast, drink your tea, then go and pack a bag.' She happily followed her orders.

Elena pulled out a small suitcase from under her bed and blew off the layer of dust. 'What do I need to take?' she shouted down to him.

'You won't need a lot. Bring something comfortable—track pants.'

Track pants? Was that his fetish? She made the small suitcase carry far more than it was intended for. A girl can never have too many clothes.

She was so excited. Her problems didn't seem that big now. That was the effect he had. Screw Alan and work.

The house could burn down. She didn't care. All that mattered was he was there right now.

She bumped the crammed suitcase down the stairs. Conrad was waiting by the front door.

'Shall I take that for you?'

'Oh, just one minute.'

Elena disappeared under the stairs, grabbed the clothes he had bought her, and stuffed them into the suitcase. They had served their time in isolation and been punished enough.

'Okay, ready,' she said excitedly

'Hmm. Is the turban a new look you're trying out?'

Elena reached up and felt the damp towel on her head. 'Damn! Have I got time to dry it?'

'I'll put the case in the car. You dry your hair.'

Finally, they closed the door to Elena's house and drove away in Conrad's Range Rover.

'So is this a progress check to make sure everything's going to plan with the new gym you're opening?'

'Yeah, something like that. It's all a bit boring really.'

He's not exactly an open book. 'Why did you want me to bring track pants?

'The weather's meant to be good for the next few days. I thought we might go for a hike or something—blow the cobwebs away.' Conrad glanced at his watch. 'Do you fancy a coffee?'

'Have we got time?'

'Yeah.'

Elena thought it strange. *Don't they sell coffee at the airport?*

The Range Rover seemed to charge along a little faster for the next twenty minutes, and they pulled up at the bottom of the High Street where Elena used to work. He unclipped his belt and opened the door.

'You stay here, and I'll get the coffees. Latte?'

'Yes, please. Conrad?' He got out and peered at her through the half-open door. 'You are just going for coffee, aren't you?'

'Yeah, of course. Why? Do you want something to eat?'

'No, thanks. Don't be long.'

'I'll be five minutes.'

He walked briskly in the opposite direction from where the car was facing. Elena didn't quite believe he was just going for coffee. She turned on the radio to ease her nerves.

Conrad pulled open the glass door and entered the bank. It was a busy morning. He stood for a moment, having a good look around, when a tall dark-headed lady sauntered over to him.

'Good morning, sir. My name's Jenny. Is there anything I can help you with?' She stood closer than was necessary, with her head held to one side, batting her false eyelashes at him.

'Yes, I think you can. I'm looking for Simon Baker's office. Is he in today?'

'Yes, Mr Baker's in. Do you have an appointment?'

'No, I don't, but'—he leaned in and stared into her eyes—'we're old friends. I haven't seen him for years, and we've been talking via e-mail. I thought it would be a nice surprise if I just turned up to say hello.'

Jenny's face mirrored Conrad's enthusiasm. 'Oh, that's so lovely. His office is just over there, the door on the left. It's got his name on it.'

He smiled. 'Thank you, Jenny. You've been very helpful.'

'If there's anything else I can do for you, just let me know,' she gushed.

'I will.'

Conrad strode over to his office and walked straight in, not bothering to knock. Simon's head jumped up from his paperwork, startled by the sudden intrusion.

'Can I help you?' he asked sarcastically.

'No.' Conrad's eyes searched the ceiling for cameras.

He walked over to the desk and picked up his aluminium name tag. 'Simon Baker?'

'What the hell is this? What do you want? I'm very busy.'

Conrad took a seat. The puffy leather chair groaned under his weight. 'It's about a friend of mine, Elena White.'

Simon rolled his eyes and shook his head. 'And who are you? Her pimp?'

Conrad's jaw set hard. He gripped the timber arms of the chair and squeezed until it creaked under the pressure. He imagined him talking to Elena like that.

'Let's get one thing straight. If you speak to me like that again, I'm going bounce your head off that desk like a basketball.'

Simon's cocky attitude vanished. He glanced at the phone on his desk.

'Your hand won't get within five inches of that before I break it off. Have I got your attention?'

Simon nodded and swallowed hard.

'That was Elena on the website, but if you'd bothered to look a little deeper you'd have seen she hadn't even been registered for a week before she removed herself. She made a silly mistake, and instead of letting her explain, you humiliated and embarrassed her.'

'We can't have girls like that working here.'

Conrad's patience was all but gone. 'Didn't you listen to what I just said? Wasn't it Einstein who said, "Condemnation without investigation is the height of ignorance"? That makes you one big fuckwit.'

'I don't think this is any of your business.' He had a condescending tone to his voice that grated on Conrad's nerves.

'You're nothing but a schoolyard bully. You didn't give her a chance, just trampled over her, and made her feel cheap. Let me tell you what's going to happen next. You're going to have your little investigation into the matter, and you will find her at no fault at all. She's not coming back. That's not what this is about. It's about righting a wrong. Her name will be cleared of any wrongdoing and make sure everyone knows.'

Simon was starring open-mouthed in a daze like a rabbit caught in headlights.

'Are you fucking listening to me?'

Conrad got out of the chair and leant on the desk with his fists clenched, still holding the name tag. He put his face right in front of Simon's, who was now paying full attention, tiny beads of sweat forming on his forehead.

'If you don't do as I say, you're going find out what it's like to be bullied. And I don't take lunch money, I take teeth. Do you understand?'

He nodded.

'Don't make me come back here because I will. And if you're not here, I'll wait a day, a week, a year. You will not shake me off. All clear?'

'Mm.' He nodded again, his face ashen.

Conrad stood upright. 'Not very nice, is it, to be intimidated?' He tossed the name tag at him, hitting him in the face. 'Have a nice day.' Conrad flung the door open and walked casually across the banking hall.

Jenny was floating around and called to him just as he was leaving.

'Sir, excuse me.' She came running over. 'How did it go? Was he surprised to see you?'

Conrad stood outside holding the door open. 'Oh yeah, he was surprised, all right. Thanks for your help.'

'No problem. Anytime!' Jenny shouted as he walked away.

Elena was fidgeting with nerves when Conrad got back carrying two coffees in a cardboard holder.

'Sorry it took so long.' He climbed in the car. 'There was a queue.'

She looked at him suspiciously but thought it best not

to ask.

They drove on heading for the airport. Conrad was pleased he had dealt with Baker. He wouldn't have enjoyed his weekend with the thought of that smug prick eating away at him. Just one more King Shit to deal with.

CHAPTER SIXTEEN

They sat opposite each other in cream leather swivel chairs with a highly polished mahogany table separating them. Elena looked around the chartered plane and took in her surroundings with a big smile on her face. The walls of the aircraft were punctured by a row of portholes, giving a glimpse of the busy airport and its various machinery, which rushed around serving its winged masters.

'I've never been to Scotland before,' said Elena.

'Haven't you? When the weather's good, it's a beautiful place. You'll like it.'

A tall slim blond lady entered the cabin from behind a cream curtain. She had long tanned legs under a light grey skirt with a navy jacket, she wore a small blue hat that balanced on her head, defying the laws of gravity.

'Good morning, Mr Bailey. It's nice to see you again.'

'Hello, Jane. This is Elena White.'

She turned her perfect dazzling smile on Elena. 'Ms White.' She was very pretty with sun-kissed skin and full red lips. Elena couldn't help but feel threatened by her. 'Can I get you any drinks?'

'Elena?' asked Conrad.

'Can I have an orange juice, please?' Elena felt like a little girl sitting in the large chair with the blond goddess towering over her.

'And I'll have a glass of water, please, Jane.'

'Certainly.' Jane sashayed off, much to Elena's relief.

'Jane's a pretty girl.' She watched his reaction closely.

'Yeah, she's lovely.' He was flicking through the onboard magazine.

How lovely?

'When we arrive, we'll get settled in. Tomorrow I've got a bit of business to do. Then we can do whatever we like.'

'Shouldn't Isabelle be with you?'

'Usually, yes, but I've given her a long weekend off. She's been working really hard just lately.'

Working hard, eh? Elena was unreasonably jealous at the mention of other women.

The blond temptress returned with their drinks and informed them that their flight time would be one hour and ten minutes, and they would be taxiing for takeoff in five minutes.

'I'm surprised you don't have your own plane.' She sipped her cool refreshing drink.

'It costs a fortune to have one of these sitting on the tarmac waiting. I think it's an ego thing really. It's a pointless waste of money. You could feed a whole third-world country with what it costs for one of these, and I can charter a plane at any time anywhere. Besides, this way, I get a free toothbrush and a pair of socks.'

'Don't forget the eye mask,' added Elena.

'Ah yes, the eye mask. We won't need it on the plane, but maybe we can use it later.'

'Maybe,' she said coyly.

He raised an eyebrow provocatively, and if it hadn't been for the fact the blond bombshell might reappear at any moment, she would have pounced on him. Forget the

Mile High Club. He had taken her beyond the heights of ecstasy, and Elena was looking forward to another joyride on Air Conrad. He made her feel a full spectrum of emotions, from lust to desperation.

They moved along the runway, and Elena sank into her chair with the force of the acceleration. As the wheels lost contact with the ground, her tummy did somersaults. She wasn't sure if it was the pull of gravity or the delicious thought of spending a few days alone with him. Whatever the next few days where going to bring, she was determined to enjoy them.

The plane touched down in Glasgow airport, and a silver four-wheel-drive Mercedes was waiting for them. Conrad threw their bags in the back of the car, and they sped off.

'Is this where your new gym is?'

'Yeah, and there's another in Edinburgh I'm trying to get hold of.'

'So we're staying in Glasgow then?'

'No, we will be staying on the banks of Loch Lomond. It's about a forty-five-minute drive.'

'Sounds lovely. I'm all excited now.' He smiled at her as they navigated the busy roads.

The big Mercedes tore along under Conrad's command. Suburbia had to relinquish its grip and give way to nature as they entered a world where more predictable wild animals reside. Dense forests lined their route. Colossal mountains looked down upon them graciously, allowing them to pass.

They hadn't spoken for a while. It seemed somehow disrespectful amongst such majestic surroundings. Loch Lomond cut through the land and was equally as impressive as its towering neighbours. The water's surface was perfectly flat and calm and acted as a giant mirror for the vain sky.

'Not far now,' Conrad broke their self-imposed ban.

'What do you think?'

'It feels like we're in Canada, not just a few hours from London. It's beautiful.'

'Yeah, it is, isn't it? When I get into the open countryside, I feel like I can breathe a bit easier, if you know what I mean.'

'Yes, I think I do.' He had the same effect on her.

They turned off the road down a long driveway towards the loch. Through the trees, Elena caught snapshots of a grey stone building. The gravel drive snaked between the trees and brought them to open ground in front of a magnificent stone castle that stood on high ground with a breathtaking view over the loch.

They climbed out of the car. 'Will this do?' He asked with both hands spread out.

'Wow, it's a fairy-tale setting.'

'We'll be staying right there.' He pointed to three sash windows at the top of a cylindrical tower.

Elena thought it looked more like a French château with its high-pitched roof, long windows, and turrets. She grinned with excitement. Conrad carried their bags, and they entered through the arched doorway.

Although it was a bright day, the reception was comfortably dark and gave the space an intimate cosy feel. A roaring fire kept two leather chesterfield sofas suitably warm, and thick heavy curtains kept the daylight at bay. An array of lamps and wall lights created a welcoming atmosphere.

'Welcome back, Mr Bailey,' said the lady behind the reception desk.

'Hello, Veronica. Nice to see you again.'

'It's a pleasure to see you too.'

She matched Conrad for height and had blond hair that just tickled her shoulders. Her ocean blue eyes sat behind delicately framed glasses, and her skin had a sunny glow to it. Or was that just the effect he had on her?

'Did you have a good journey?'

'Yes, we did, thank you. This is Elena. Elena, this is Ms Fix-It, Veronica.'

She giggled at his joke. She obviously had a thing for Conrad. 'Very nice to meet you, Elena.'

'And you.' Elena clung to his arm like a baby orangutan. *He's mine, got it?*

'There're the keys to your usual room. Do you need a hand with your bags, Mr Bailey?'

She had a mild sexy Scottish accent that slightly annoyed Elena. *Stop talking now, please.*

'No, I'll be fine, thanks, Vee.'

'If there's anything you need, just let me know.'

Not giving up, is she? He won't need anything from you, thank you, missy.

They stood and waited for the lift. Elena glanced over her shoulder, and Veronica's eyes shot towards the ceiling. *I knew she was checking him out. Cheek!*

The old lift was worryingly noisy as it strained to raise them to their floor. A short walk and Conrad turned the key to their room door, allowing Elena to enter first. Unlike the reception, it was bright and airy. A large four-poster bed dominated the room, which had direct views over the rugged landscape. Period yellow covered the walls; a suede sofa sat alongside a sage green armchair admiring the scenery. There was a relaxed comfortable feel to the room.

Elena stood at the window. 'Look at the view. It's perfect.'

'I was just thinking the same thing.' His tone was suggestive, and she turned to look at him. 'You know, I wish we'd taken the stairs.' He had a mischievous look about him.

'And why is that?'

'Because I'd have got to watch that gorgeous backside of yours swaying from side to side.'

'And how many other woman's backsides have you brought here?'

'Yours is the first one.'

'Oh really?' Elena's eyebrows rose questioningly, but she saw he wasn't joking. 'Not even your wife?'

'No. She's not really the outdoors type, not enough shops here for her.'

'Well, I don't want shops.' Elena walked slowly towards him, holding his gaze.

'What do you want then?'

'All I want is your undivided attention.' She stood in front of him with her head tilted back, looking up at him, and slipped his leather jacket off his broad shoulders. 'Do you think you can manage that?' She pulled the jacket free of his arms and threw it on the sofa.

'It's good fishing here. Don't you fancy casting a line out? It's very relaxing.' Elena shook her head slowly, concentrating on unbuttoning his shirt. 'What about a walk in the woods? Get some fresh air?' He was teasing her with his silly questions.

'No, thank you.'

She removed his shirt, and it was a test of her willpower not to attack his glorious body with her voracious mouth. His intoxicating essence heightened her senses. She unbuckled his black leather belt. He stood perfectly still and seemed unaffected by her actions. Elena was not unaffected. Her heart rate quickened, and her breathing became tremulous with anticipation as she dropped to her knees and untied the laces to his boots.

'Shoes,' she commanded, and he kicked them off.

'You're very bossy today. I don't know what's got into you.'

'Nothing . . . yet,' she mumbled quietly to herself.

The top button of his jeans stubbornly refused her access, and she was about to ask Ms Fix-It for a pair of pliers when it suddenly decided to play ball.

'Now I know this one will tempt you. There's a very good farming museum a short drive from here.'

The rest of the buttons had no qualms about allowing

her in, and Elena pulled down his jeans.

'We could probably spend most of the day there if you fancied it?'

He looked down at her sitting on her haunches, admiring his body lasciviously as he stood there in bulging white briefs. The outline of his manhood was clearly visible.

'It seems you're hell-bent on something different altogether.' He stepped out of the crumpled denim that lay at his feet.

Elena stood and led him to the bed. 'Lie face down.'

Conrad did as he was told and lay under the canopy of the four-poster bed with his arms raised above his head. He obviously liked this game, teasing her with his almost naked body. It was time to turn the tables.

She slipped off her shoes and sat on his legs as her eager hands started their journey at his waist. They slowly but firmly glided over his toned torso. He gave an involuntary groan into the bed as she pushed down with her weight along his defined back, reaching his stone shoulders. Her hands met at his neck and proceeded to his head, massaging and squeezing his scalp, squashing his face into the soft bed.

'Oh, that feels so good.' The words drifted out on his breath. Tables turned.

Sitting on his bottom, Elena removed her jumper and bra, releasing her heavy breasts. She bent over him, and her now hard tingling nipples danced over his smooth skin. She ran her tongue slowly around his ear and gently sucked his lobe, moaning quietly, urging on his arousal. His breathing was audible, and she was rising and lowering with each breath he took as she lay on his torso. Her skin on his was so sensual she wanted to writhe all over him. Elena's teeth grazed his neck, and goose bumps signalled his body's ecstasy. She moved down his beautifully carved back, biting, tasting, squeezing.

His legs were together, and she sat on his calves,

massaging his muscular thighs right up to his toned buttocks that filled his white briefs. Another groan left his lips as she clawed her nails along his thighs, leaving a trail of pink flesh. Her tummy clenched with a feral desire for him as she grabbed a handful of arse meat, desperate to tear away the white barrier.

Elena climbed off him and quickly removed her jeans and damp thong. Conrad spread his legs, and Elena climbed back onto the bed and crouched between his thighs, the bright day allowing her to get a good look at every inch of him. Her eyes were drawn to his swollen pouch forced down between his legs, stretching the material, making it transparent.

She wanted him desperately but would tease him a bit longer. Her hands stroked the insides of his thighs, and she made sure they just brushed his dick. His heavy balls hung out of each side of his gaping briefs, and Elena's slid her hand under the barrier, once again grabbing a handful of toned flesh. It was as much of a test of her restraint as Conrad's.

He spread his legs wider, and her wandering hands moved down between his cheeks, brushing the ultra-soft skin of his balls. Groans of gratification oozed from him as he lay there enjoying the attention.

Elena was finding it increasingly hard to deny her body's own demands and slid her hand under his erection, only intending to gently caress it, but she couldn't help but pull at it. It was a natural reaction like putting food in your mouth and chewing. The second her hand felt its heat, her fingers locked around the thick girth, and she tugged at his cock through his briefs. Her other hand grabbed his backside for more leverage, and she was yanking so hard the whole bed was rocking. Conrad raised his hips slightly allowing her hand a deeper stroke.

'Don't stop,' he blurted into the vibrating bed.

'Not yet, Mr Bailey. I want some. You'll have to hold on. Can you do that?' Her hand went all the way down to his pubic bone and right to the head of his rock-hard dick.

'You're not making it easy.' She was enjoying watching him struggle to repress his orgasm.

Elena's thighs were wet from her body's carnal yearning. The sight of his naked body had turned her into a salacious cave woman, desperate for her own gratification, and as vulgar as it sounded, she was hungry for cock. Elena turned around, straddled his upper back, and pulled down his briefs as far as his thighs allowed, her head dropped between his legs, and she sucked one of his balls into her mouth.

'Oh my god! That's not fair!'

It danced around her mouth as her tongue chased after it. She sucked hard and could feel the tautness of his body. He was getting to the point of no return.

Her need for oxygen forced her to rise. Taking a few quick gulps, she went down for more. Between her mouth and her pussy, it was difficult to tell which was wetter as her tongue soaked his shaft with saliva.

Conrad began to turn over, so Elena lifted her weight off him, allowing him to roll onto his back.

'Mmm,' a low rumble came from him as she sat back down on his chest with her backside just out of reach of his carnivorous mouth.

He closed his legs together, allowing her to get his underwear out of the way. His hands grabbed her bottom urgently, and he lifted her onto his face. Elena shot bolt upright with the sensational feeling. She sat on his face with all her weight and brazenly writhed as his tongue pressed all the right buttons and unashamedly lapped at her clitoris with only one aim: to make her orgasm. His big hands clamped onto her breasts, pulling her down onto his face as he nuzzled into her soaking wet flesh, spreading her wide open, exposing her weak spot.

He went in for the kill, sucking at her clit. The pressure of his powerful suction was too much as she watched his cock flapping around like a flag in the wind. Selfishly, she ignored it while it waved in front of her for attention, concentrating on her own needs first.

'Don't stop, please don't stop!'

Her orgasm built as the Conrad roller coaster climbed up and up. *Suck, lick, suck, lick.* Up and up it climbed until she reach the top, the tipping point of zero gravity, before plunging full force into climax, twitching and shuddering as the shockwave ran through her. Conrad ignored her body's surrender. His own desire burned like an inferno.

Elena collapsed on his stomach completely spent, her face lay beside his erection. Despite her exhaustion, his penis didn't divert its expectant gaze. Her body rose and fell as Conrad panted like he had just run a one-hundred-metre sprint. His skin burned with desire. Time to douse the fire.

Lying with her head flat on his groin and her bottom inches from his sticky face, she firmly stroked her hand up and down with a steady rhythm, holding his erection vertically, not wanting to be shot at point-blank range. He still had a firm grip on her hips and was no doubt taking advantage of the front-row seat. His buttocks clenched, he raised his pelvis with a mighty growl. Elena didn't take her eyes off his engorged dick, wanting to watch his climax. She slowed her strokes and could feel a throbbing pulse warning her of the impending explosion. Another loud groan emitted from him, and then the first burst, like a powerful firework, shot its display high into the air, the thick creamy juice landing on her cheek. Then another, not as powerful as the first but equal in quantity, covered her hand and lubricated her slow deliberate strokes. *Bang!*—one more eruption of hot sticky semen, this time landing on his tight balls.

Elena slid her hand all the way to the head of his deflating penis, squeezing out the last drop. With her senses returning back to sane, she was embarrassed at having her bottom spread, hovering right next to his face.

'Of all the places I've been, that's got to be one of the

best sights my eyes have ever had the pleasure of seeing.' She threw her leg over his head and turned to face him, with sperm running down her red cheek. 'You're very naughty.'

Elena wiped his thick cream from her face and onto his chest with her hand. 'Thank you, Mr Bailey.'

'No, thank you. I really needed that.' He lay with his hands above his head, his lazy eyes half open.

'I know.' She smiled, holding up her wet hand.

'It's actually very good for the skin, full of vitamins and minerals.'

'Only a man could think of something like that.'

She went to the bathroom, trying to cover her bottom with her hand, despite two minutes earlier having been sat on his face. Elena returned with a washed face and hands, carrying a towel for Conrad, and placed it over the flooded area.

She lay down beside him and kissed his tacky lips. It was the first kiss they had shared that day. Elena had been waiting for a moment, but there hadn't been the opportunity. Now she had him all to herself and could pounce whenever she wanted.

'I really needed that too.'

'I know.' He circled his damp face with his finger.

'Apparently, it's very good for the skin.' Elena managed to keep a straight face repeating his comment.

Conrad laughed out loud. 'You are awful, but I do like you,' he said in a camp voice, sending her into girlish giggles.

Elena was so happy and contented despite all that had happened recently. When he was around, she was recklessly carefree. She wished at that moment, lying with her skin next to his, that time wouldn't find them, and they could stay locked in that room, just the two of them. No work or ex-wives to worry about, just able to enjoy what really mattered in life and not get caught in the insane rat race. Elena lay with her head resting on her hand, admiring his handsome face.

He glanced at her with a concerned look and then down at his feet, which still had socks on. 'This really is a fetish for you, isn't it?'

She laughed. 'No, I've told you, it's that thing.' Elena pointed towards the white towel, hiding the great provocateur. 'I never get that far down.'

'Well, I'm afraid that's a violation of the rules and must be punished.'

'Really? And what will be my punishment?'

'I'm not sure, but it could involve swallowing copious amounts of vitamin and mineral juice.'

Elena burst into laughter. 'Will it now? Well, we'll have to see about that, won't we?' She kissed him on the forehead and ran her fingers through his hair.

'I think we need to replace some of that burned energy. Fancy a quick shower and a spot of lunch?'

'Sounds perfect,' she purred. *Just like him.*

CHAPTER SEVENTEEN

The impressive bathroom had a large shower and a free-standing roll-top bath. As agreed, they opted for the shower. There was ample room for them both in the oblong cubicle which nestled in its own recess.

Elena stepped into the hot rain, which was a perfect complement to her serene mood, heating her sensitive skin. She wiped the steamed-up glass to see Conrad bent over, taking his socks off; he looked up, catching her watching him, and shook his head in fake annoyance, throwing them over his shoulder.

He opened the shower door, and the cool air rushed in biting at her skin. Stepping in, he closed the door, sealing their heated chamber. The powerful jet of water soothed their satisfied bodies with rivulets of therapeutic liquid, each bead playing its part encasing them with hot steam.

'That feels good.' He wrapped his arms around her and kissed her lips tenderly as water bounced off their shoulders and splashed their faces.

'*That* feels good,' Elena whispered into his mouth. 'Can we stay in here for the rest of the day?'

'We'll go all wrinkly.' He kissed her on the nose.

'I'd still want you if you were wrinkly.' She kissed his chest, unable to reach his nose.

A smile tugged at the corners of his mouth, and he reached for the complimentary shower gel. He filled his palm with the creamy liquid. Its sweet fragrance mixed with the rising steam and filled the cubicle with an intoxicating smell of strawberries and guava. Elena turned her back to him, and his hands glided effortlessly over her, aided by the silky cream. As he rubbed her shoulders, her knees decided they were no longer required, and she almost collapsed in a soapy heap.

'Is that nice?'

'Oooh yes.'

Her head was flopping backwards and forwards as her body gave way to the seductive pressure. The five-fingered culprits conquered her shoulders and navigated down her chest, stopping to grope her tender breasts, pinching the nipples, coaxing them to harden. They then swept over her tummy and back up to her shoulders.

'It's quite serious, you know?'

'What is?'

'Breaking the no-socks-in-bed rule.'

She smiled to herself as his thumbs slid along the nape of her neck. 'Is it?'

'Oh yes. You've violated rule 12.3, and that brings harsh consequences, I'm afraid.' His body was pressed against hers, channelling a stream of water between them. 'Every wrongdoing has to be punished.' He had a devious tone to his voice, and his teeth sank into her neck, biting almost too hard, causing her knees to throw another hissy fit.

'And what is to be my punishment?'

'Well, it will certainly be harsh, having committed such a serious breach of the rules.'

He added more creamy liquid to his hands which headed straight for her bottom and groped the fleshy rump. A roving finger circled her tight anus suggestively, waking her sleeping pussy. His mouth and hands were an attack on the senses, but it felt so good. The vibration between her cheeks increased. Elena arched her back, pushing out her bottom, increasing the pressure.

The other five-fingered partner in crime crept around to her tingling vagina, which, after being eaten for lunch, was now preparing dessert. The naughty fingers slipped each side of the hot plump triangle and teased with their slippery fondle.

A third party decided it wanted to join the fun and nudged her thigh, not wanting to be left out. Hot water thrashed down on her, adding to the sensuousness, and she began to feel self-control diminishing rapidly.

'The problem is, it may not be punishment enough.' He spoke softly into her ear as his right hand parted her lips and slowly circled the highly sensitive perimeter of her pulsating clitoris.

How did he get her there so quickly? She had that crazy, wild, dirty urge that only he had managed to rouse.

'You may actually like it.' He tormented her with his words, and the tip of his vibrating soapy finger penetrated her bottom, causing a sharp intake of breath.

It felt so naughty, filthy. What would his cock feel like sliding inside her like that? Would it fit? Elena couldn't believe she was contemplating such a thing, but she was drunk on pleasure, and the feeling was like nothing she had ever experienced.

His hand continued to vibrate at high speed, shaking the cheeks of her butt, while his rock-hard erection slapped her leg, the other hand still tormenting her clit. Elena couldn't believe she was nearing orgasm so soon. The relentless attack continued on both sides while he bit and sucked at her exposed neck.

'Your tight arse needs loosening up before I can give it a good fucking.' His filthy talk pushed her to the edge.

'I think I should bend you over, tie your wrists to your ankles, you can suck my cock first, make it nice and wet, before I slide every inch in and fuck you raw.'

The violent strokes increased in speed. Her mind and body were no longer her own.

'You'd like that, wouldn't you?'

'Mmm yes.' She wanted it, to grab his thick cock and stuff it between her round cheeks.

Elena felt like a dirty slut but didn't care. The feelings had a power she was unable to resist. Each slap of his hot dick against her thigh was like a countdown to her orgasm.

Five. His mouth feasted on her neck. Four. He teased her with filthy suggestions. Three. His hard cock landed heavy blows on her thigh. Two. Her clit was being rubbed into a frenzy. One. His fingers were stimulating her arse in a way she had never known existed.

Lift off!

Elena screamed out as intense pleasure soared her high into the sky in an almost out-of-body experience. She jerked and jolted with the glorious aftershocks of orgasm, the feeling lingered like the after-burn of a rocket.

Conrad's sigh carried his satisfaction at completing his mission with flying colours; he removed those responsible for her meltdown. Elena turned and cuddled into his chest. He held on to her under the persistent shower, her legs not quite up to the task.

'Now can we have lunch, woman?'

She fought the exhaustion and managed a modest smile. 'What about Mr Impatient down there?'

'Oh, he can wait.'

'Aren't you frustrated?'

'Yes, but I'm sure you'll help me with that later.'

Later? I'm not sure my body can take much more.

They left their room of depravity holding hands and decided to risk the old lift, which complained all the way down, but managed to get them to the ground floor safely.

Elena sailed past the reception desk, now arm in arm with Conrad, with a smug look on her face, having had literally more than her fill of him. She glanced at Veronica, who was on the phone and gave them a pleasant smile as they passed.

Conrad opened Elena's door first and helped her into the high four-wheel drive. He climbed in and started the engine.

'So what do you fancy for lunch? English, Italian, Indian, or traditional Scottish?'

'What's traditional Scottish?'

'Well, there's haggis, of course, Cullen skink, which is a fish soup made with potatoes and onions. It's very nice. And the venison here is the finest I've ever eaten. But the tastiest of them all is a Clootie dumpling with clotted cream and a dram of whisky.'

'And you, Mr Fitness, have tried that?'

'Yes, I have, and like most foods that are bad for you, it's addictively tasty.'

'A bit like you then.'

He turned to her with a frown. 'So I'm a bit like a dumpling? You do flatter me.'

'No, you know what I mean.' She laughed. 'I can't imagine you eating something like that.'

'Believe me, I'm as susceptible to sugary fat-filled food as anyone, but I have great powers of resistance, well, with most things anyway.' His eyebrow cocked slightly.

'Mr Bailey, are you suggesting I am something to be resisted?'

He studied her from top to bottom. 'That backside in those tight jeans . . .' He gazed out of the windscreen, closed his eyes, and shook his head. 'Let's go, or we'll never get off of this car park.' He turned the car around, and they drove down the long drive.

Elena loved the fact she made him feel that way. It gave her a feeling of superiority over Jane, the glamorous air hostess, and Ms Fix-It, with her roving eyes.

'Has the lady made a decision on lunch?'

'I will eat whatever you wish.'

Conrad cleared his throat. 'Like I said, later.' He winked with a smile, making her chuckle.

She loved his playful side. He made her feel like a teenager, all hormones and blushes.

'I'll tell you where we'll go—Old Jock's place.'

'That has got to be another joke.'

'No, he's a moaning old bugger, and the place is nothing special, but the food's great, and he's got one of the best spots on the loch.'

'Jock's it is then,' Elena agreed. She'd have been happy with a cheese sandwich in the park so long as he was with her.

They hit the main road and raced to Jock's place.

'Whenever I come up here, I usually have one of my bikes sent up. It's a biker's paradise here when it's dry.'

'I'd like to go out on the bike again with you sometime.'

He looked across at her with a surprised but pleased look in his eyes. 'I'd love to take you out on the bike again.'

Twenty minutes later, they turned onto a bumpy gravel drive that threw them from side to side as the car carried them to a white stone building with a slate roof. There was no sign indicating it was a restaurant, and only a couple of other cars occupied the parking spaces. Conrad was right. It had a tremendous view.

He jumped out and came around to Elena's side to help her out. 'Careful, the tight old sod never got around to getting it tarmacked.'

They hobbled over to the entrance and paused to admire the view. The autumn colours were beginning to take hold: browns and reds mixed with vibrant greens and yellows to create a natural masterpiece. Clumps of trees lined the shoreline, and from their elevated position, they looked like sprigs of broccoli. A cool breeze rippled the water and tickled their faces.

'Shall we go in?' he asked, wrapping his arm around her

shoulder as she shuddered.

'Yeah.'

Conrad pushed open the creaky old door, and they walked through a narrow corridor to another old door, just as creaky as the first, which led them to a big square room, where the welcome smell of hot food filled their nostrils.

It was very old-fashioned but spotlessly clean. Green carpet with a kaleidoscope-like pattern covered the floor. Paintings of famous Scottish landmarks adorned the walls, and large picture windows took advantage of the glorious views. Finally, a well-stocked bar ran almost the length of the room, only stopping to allow the kitchen door a spot on the wall.

Two elderly couples sat at either end of the room, both stopping to inspect the two strangers who dared to enter. An old tap bell sat on the bar, and Conrad dropped his hand on the old brass trinket, which rang out like a new one. They heard a mumbling voice coming from the kitchen door, and then suddenly, it swung open, and a wiry old man with wild snow white hair came storming out with his green checked shirt rolled up at the sleeves under a white apron.

'Naebody rings that bell but the bloody English!' He had a thick Scots accent and leaned on the bar with his hands spread and a stern look on his face.

'Hello, Jock. How are you?'

He gave a single nod as his greeting. 'Are ye eatin' or drinkin'?'

'We were hoping to get some lunch if we're not too late?'

Jock hissed through his teeth and looked at his watch. 'Lunch, man? Where ye been? Lyin' in bed, I suppose?'

Elena was amazed at how rude this man was, but Conrad seemed to have an affection for him.

'We'll take a seat. Give us five minutes and we'll order.'

They sat at a table by the window, between the two couples. 'Don't worry. He's a pussy cat really.'

'I suppose you'll be wanting a drink as well?' he shouted from the bar.

Conrad held back a smile. 'Elena?'

'Tea, please.'

'Tea and a coffee, please, Jock.'

'Bloody tea and coffee,' they heard him mumble as he went back through the kitchen door.

'We'd better look at the menu before he comes back.' Conrad laughed.

They decided to skip the starter, not wanting to upset their host anymore. A few moments later, Jock returned, carrying a tray with pots of tea and coffee, milk, and sugar. He placed them on the table, took out his notepad and pencil, and gave them a nod.

'Elena, are you ready to order?' asked Conrad.

'Yes, can I have the roast loin of venison, please?' He scribbled it down with a look of concentration on his face and the tip of his tongue poking out.

'Good choice,' he said, pointing the pencil at Elena, who was a little frightened of him. 'How do ye like your meat?'

She glanced at Conrad, who raised an eyebrow suggestively. 'Oh . . . er . . . well done, please.' Jock stared at her for a second through squinty eyes. *Shit, should I have said medium.*

'Are ye Scottish?'

'No.' She thought it an odd question but was relieved it wasn't a telling-off.

'Yeah, ye are. Somewhere in your family, there's a Scot. You don't get red hair like that from English descent, no way.' He turned from a stunned Elena to Conrad. 'Go on, lad.'

'Roast shoulder of lamb for me, please.' He scribbled away on his notepad. 'On your own today, Jock?'

'No, my wee lad is wie me.'

'Can we have some water as well, please, Jock?'

'Water? You want water? That's for flushing the toilet,

man. Whisky. Whisky is what ye drink this time of the day.' He shook his head in disgust, putting his pad and pencil into the apron.

Elena sat there with both her hands covering her nose and mouth.

'Well, I'm driving, so it's going have to be water today, I'm afraid.'

'Right.' He stormed off, mumbling to himself as he went.

Elena laughed with her hands still over her face, and Conrad chuckled to himself.

'However did you find this place?'

'I came here for the weekend a while ago on the bike. I saw the drive and wondered where it went, and that's how I found it.'

'I'm surprised you can tolerate such rude behaviour.'

'He's rude—yes, offensive—yep, but he has a heart of gold.'

Conrad opened his mouth to continue but paused for a moment and fiddled with his fork. 'It wasn't long after we lost the baby, Olivia and I weren't getting on, so I decided to come here with the bike, clear my head, get away from things. I came across this place, came in for a drink. The place was empty. Jock was about to close and was his usual self, and I was looking for an excuse to let off some steam. I lost my temper with him, started screaming and shouting. He locked the door, took a bottle of whisky off the shelf and two glasses. He said I could either tell him all about it or have the bottle smashed over my head.' Conrad laughed to himself.

'He and his wife had lost a baby girl some years before, and he knew that look in my eyes. I don't know how, but he did. So we sat at that table over there, and I let it all out, cried like a baby.' He was staring out the window, leaning on his elbow with his hand on his chin.

'He was the first person I'd sat down and talked with. I told him things I'd never told anyone, and he told me things he'd never told anyone. I got drunk and slept it off here, and every time I come here, we both act like nothing ever happened.'

Elena placed her hands on his, bringing him back into the room.

'Right. Tomorrow,' he sat upright and inhaled deeply, 'I've got to go into Glasgow, so you can either come with me or spend some time in the hotel spa, have a nice massage and a facial, a little pampering.'

'I want to come with you, if that's okay.' Elena didn't hesitate. She loved being in his company.

'Yeah, of course. I shouldn't be too long. It's more of a courtesy visit really. There're just a few details I need to check up on. Then we could go into the city if you like, have a look around.'

'That sounds nice. So you're not going to be happy until you're the king of the fitness world, eh?'

Conrad played with his ear and ran his fingers through his hair. 'Mm maybe.'

She sensed his reluctance to talk about his business. Why was that? Was it modesty, or did he have something to hide?

'Because you've never been to Scotland before, I'm going to get you a souvenir.'

'Like what?'

He contemplated the question for a moment before answering. 'Tartan lingerie.'

'There was I thinking fridge magnet or mug.'

'No, no.' He frowned. 'That's no fun.'

'So it's not a gift for me, more for you really?'

He sat back in his chair and folded his arms. 'Let's call it a joint gift. Then we both get something from it.'

'Mr Bailey, do you think of nothing else?'

'Well, if you hadn't accosted me in the shower, we would have been here an hour ago, Ms White.'

A big smile spread across Elena's face as she shook her head.

'Yes.' He nodded. 'You are very naughty.'

'Am I now?' The bright sunshine glistened on the loch and drew Elena's attention. 'It's so beautiful here,'

'Yeah, it is. Developers have been after this place for years, but he won't sell. He loves it too much.'

'Has he been here long?'

'Thirty years. He used to be a chef at one of the five-star hotels in Glasgow. He spent ten years there, had a blazing row with the restaurant manager, walked out, and bought this place. There's more to him than meets the eye. Speak of the devil.'

Jock came hurrying along red-faced, carrying their food.

'Venison for the lady, and lamb for ye. Anythin' else ye want? Oh, I forgot your bloody water.' Off he stomped.

Elena's food sat in the centre of the plate and was perfectly constructed. The delicious smell made her mouth water. She filled her fork with venison, drizzled with game and blueberry sauce, and braised cabbage. Her sense of taste was heightened by her hunger, and the food was exquisite. Elena gave out a moan as she tasted the culinary perfection. Conrad groaned back in agreement, with a mouth full of food, nodding his head.

'That's good.' Elena paused just long enough to get the words out.

Jock returned with a bottle of Highland Spring Water and two glasses.

'All right?' he barked.

They both turned to him, nodding. 'Mmm.'

'Good.' He left them to enjoy their feast.

Conrad swallowed a mouthful of lamb. 'Do you think I'm strange bringing you here?'

'Why?'

'Because it's not exactly glitz and glamour, is it? But I like it here. It's unpretentious, real. Don't get me wrong, I like glitz and glamour, but here you can be yourself.' Elena didn't say a word. She didn't want to interrupt. It wasn't often he gave an insight into himself. 'Nobody's prancing around in designer clothes, all look at me. It brings you back to reality, which is easy to lose sight of.'

It would have been easy to get the wrong impression of Conrad: successful businessman, big house in the country, flashy cars. But underneath all that, he was an ordinary decent man, and she found that endearing.

'Told you the food was good, though, didn't I?'

The window of insight was closed once again.

'It's gorgeous. Can't we stick him in the boot and take him with us?'

'I don't think he would go without a fight. I'm slightly worried about your sudden interest in Jock.'

'You should be. Women love a man who can cook.' She winked at Conrad as she took the food from her fork, making him smile.

'I bet he can't do a special omelette like I can.'

'That's true. You're safe for now then.'

'Phew! You had me worried there.'

Was he always this jovial?

They finished their meal and half the bottle of water.

Jock came, on cue, to take away their empty plates. 'How was that?' His cool blue eyes watched Conrad closely.

'Jock, you have surpassed yourself. It was superb, thank you.'

Elena joined in on the praise, telling him it was the best meal she'd had in a long time, which seemed to please him, as his eyes creased at the corners while his mouth attempted a smile.

'We were just admiring the view.'

'Aye, it's an ever-changing picture: lush greens in the summer; browns, reds, and golds in the autumn; in winter, it looks like a wonderland with the snow and frost; and new life in the spring. It never looks the same. In thirty years, I've never got sick of looking at it.' His eyes spanned the panoramic view with an admiring look, like a father watching his child.

'Still getting offers, Jock?'

'Aye, those bloody developers, they're a pain in the arse!'

Conrad laughed.

'They'll have to carry me out in a wooden box before they get their hands on this place. I suppose you'll be wanting dessert?'

'If it's not too much trouble?'

'Well, all right. I'll be back in a wee while.'

Conrad watched the old man fondly as he walked back to the kitchen.

He persuaded Elena that she couldn't leave Scotland without trying a Clootie dumpling. Conrad had a coffee, and Elena had a glass of lemon and lime despite Jock trying to convince her to have a shot of whisky.

They sat for a while, taking in the scenery before Conrad went to the bar to pay. She sat at the table and admired her other favourite view, still unable to believe they were spending the weekend together.

Conrad had his back to her, and the two men chatted out of earshot. Jock was nodding and shaking his head; his usual gnarled look had softened. He leaned to one side, looking around Conrad's shoulder, and peered at her briefly.

The two unlikely friends looked like David and Goliath and shook hands warmly. Conrad encased Jock's hand with both of his, and the old man tapped him on the arm affectionately.

Conrad walked back to the table with a concerned look about him while Jock busied himself behind the bar.

'Everything okay?' She was fishing for info.

'Yeah, fine.' She wasn't going to get any more.

An unconvincing smile appeared on his face. He held his hand out for her. 'Ready?'

They passed the bar where Jock was drying already dry glasses.

'Nice to meet you, Jock.'

He gave her a nod. 'And ye, darlin'.'

Conrad looked back as he held the door open for Elena. 'Look after yourself, old man.'

'Aye. Lovely to see ye again. Good luck, lad.'

Good luck? With what? Me? He probably meant the new gym.

They made it to the car without twisting an ankle in a pot hole. Conrad opened Elena's door and helped her into the car. He took one last look at the old building before he climbed in and, without hesitation, drove them away, not quite the same man as when they'd arrived.

CHAPTER EIGHTEEN

Conrad was unusually quiet as they travelled along the main road. He switched on the radio which softened the prolonged silence.

'Where are you taking me now then, Mr Bailey?' She coaxed the chatty Conrad back.

'I'm not sure what to do with you actually. Well, I am, but I don't think you'd let me.' He flashed a sexy grin at her.

That's better. 'You never know your luck.' Elena patted him on the leg. She loved their suggestive teasing. It was exciting.

He checked his watch. 'I have an idea. We might just have enough time.'

The car roared into action and followed the road which clung to the side of the loch, not daring to leave its side.

'Are you going to tell me where we're going or keep me in suspense?'

'We're going on a little trip.'

Elena frowned at him, trying to guess what he had in mind, but didn't really care. She was happy sitting next to this near perfect man cruising through the wild Scottish countryside. What more could a girl ask for?

They parked outside a neat dormer bungalow overlooking a vast body of water. A big white porch with a pitched roof held a commanding position in the centre of the house, which had a big sprawling lawn that stretched towards the loch, giving way to the shale shoreline. A long timber jetty reached its arm out into the cool calm water and had the important job of holding a great white boat that sat elegantly in the water like a giant swan. Her name tattooed on her bow simply read, *Beauty.*

'If you wait here for a minute, I'll ask this nice man if he'll take us out on his boat.'

She watched him confidently approach the house. He knocked on the door. A middle-aged man, with more hair on his face than on his head, answered, and within two minutes, he was smiling and laughing. What was Conrad's secret? Money exchanged hands, and Conrad returned with a pleased look on his face and beckoned her out of the car. Elena got out, and he wrapped his arms around her and kissed her on the head.

'He's going to take us out.'

'Did you use your powers of persuasion?'

'And the power of cold hard cash.'

'Oh yes, that's always a good one. Weren't you embarrassed asking a complete stranger to take us out on his boat?'

'Even I'm not that brazen. He does boat charters, usually at the weekend. I've been past here loads of times on the bike, but I've never been out with him.'

Their captain for the evening came, taking strides that were far too big for his stature. He wore a thick knitted blue roll-neck jumper, old faded jeans, and a woolly hat that sat on the rim of his dark glasses, with a bobble on the top like a beacon. With a big bushy salt-and-pepper beard covering most of his face, only a small amount of flesh was exposed to the air.

He shook hands with Elena and introduced himself as

Doug, then led them to the impressive vessel. They boarded onto the main deck, and Doug led them up a steep set of stairs to the elevated fly bridge. Everything was white, except the controls. The air was cooling, and Elena was a little chilly.

Doug fired up the boat, pressed a few buttons, and disappeared below deck, returning with two large thick blue blankets. 'There you go, folks. They should keep you nice and warm.'

They thanked him, and Conrad cocooned Elena in the warm blanket. She snuggled back in her chair next to Conrad, wiggling her bum.

Doug looked back towards the house and sounded the horn, shaking his head. A skinny young man came darting out, putting on his coat as he ran. He untied the boat and bellowed 'all clear,' and the elegant white swan drifted away.

'You picked a good day for it,' said Doug as he scratched his head under the woolly hat. The loch was like glass. The boat drifted through and gently rippled the calm surface. 'What can I get you to drink? We've got a fully stocked bar on board.'

Elena thought that a glass of wine would probably be a suitable thing to ask for, but what she really wanted all wrapped up in her cosy blanket was a hot chocolate.

Conrad looked down at her and curled his arm around her shoulder. 'I think this is a hot chocolate moment, don't you?'

No way! A big smile ran across her face. *Did I say near perfect man? Correction, perfect.*

Doug called down to the skinny young man who was now hiding on the lower deck. 'Three hot chocks, Callum, and be quick about it.'

Elena was so happy, so relaxed. It was bliss. The loch dominated silently with its size and beauty, and they had it all to themselves. The sky began to turn a fiery orange colour, signalling that the sun was required elsewhere in the world. Beauty sailed them towards the silhouetted mountains, which looked down on them from the shadows.

Callum came up the stairs, carrying a small tray with their drinks, staring at them wide-eyed, being extra careful not to spill them. Elena and Conrad thanked him, and he gave the third drink to the captain, who obviously agreed it *was* a hot chocolate moment.

The water was now the colour of molten lava, reflecting the sky's furnace red.

'Have you ever seen anything like it?' said Conrad. The only red glow she usually got to see was brake lights stuck in traffic.

Conrad's eyes mirrored the fiery glow. She felt privileged to be witnessing such a wondrous sight next to an equally wondrous man. Elena thought how true his comments about the city now seemed and understood what he meant. The city was an antagonist, and if you didn't play by the rules, it just rolled over you. But here, she felt nurtured, at ease. The calm stillness was a breeding ground for serenity. She sipped her hot drink; the cool air filled her lungs and stung her nose.

'I think I could live somewhere like this.'

Conrad looked taken aback. 'Really?'

'Don't sound so surprised. I'm a simple girl at heart.'

He stared at her with a curious look on his face.

'What?' She wished she could read his mind.

'Nothing. You're lovely, aren't you?' He squeezed her and rested his head on hers.

Conrad's words were so genuine, her heart melted, and she felt the sting of emotion in her eyes. He had such a powerful effect on her, exciting and unnerving at the same time.

They sat in silence for a while as the daylight made its dramatic exit. Doug quietly took them back to dry land, and after shaking his hand and thanking him for his hospitality, they drove back to the hotel under the cover of darkness.

The fresh air had stimulated their appetite, and they dined in the hotel restaurant before returning to their room. Conrad turned on the lights to find the bed had been turned down and two chocolates wrapped in gold foil had been placed on the white pillows.

He kicked off his shoes and lay on the bed. Elena unwrapped the complimentary sweets and lay next to him resting on her elbow. She popped one of the chocolates into his mouth. 'Thank you. That was a lovely meal.' She watched him intently as he sucked on the chocolate.

'Yeah, it's satisfied my appetite . . . for food anyway.' The corners of his mouth curled slightly.

'You are insatiable, aren't you? Haven't you had your fill?' She ran her hands over his chest.

'This, from a woman who, after having her wicked way with me, was still not satisfied and then assaulted me in the shower. Are you misbehaving again?'

Elena nodded provocatively. *Playtime.* She pulled his shirt out of his jeans and scratched her nails across his abdomen, causing him to jump as his muscles tensed involuntarily.

'Do I need to repay the favour?' She leaned on his chest, her face inches from his, and her hand slipped just inside his jeans and slowly massaged his pubic hair.

'I should say you don't have to do anything you don't want to, but after working me up in the shower, I'm not going to sleep unless you finish what we started.'

'Well, really, Mr Bailey, what kind of girl do you think I am?' Her hand had eased under the tight waistband, and she teased the base of his penis with a feather-light touch.

His jaw clenched, and his eyes had a need about them. 'I don't care how you do it—hand, mouth, pussy, or that succulent arse of yours—just make that thing go to sleep.' He nodded towards the lump in his jeans.

It wasn't spontaneous, but it was such a turn-on for her to be asked to service him.

'Take your clothes off and I'll see what I can do.'

Elena casually got off the bed and looked in her suitcase then disappeared into the bathroom. She could hear his clothes being tossed onto the floor, and after a few moments, Elena came out wearing the green lingerie he had bought for her that had been locked away under the stairs. She switched off all the lights leaving one lamp on. He was naked, his erection curved across his abs, and the sight of him waiting to be pleasured made her hot. She stood at the foot of the bed, her hair draped over her shoulders.

'You like?' She did a pirouette.

'I must say I've got good taste, haven't I?' His eyes examined her body provocatively.

'Are you referring to me or the lingerie?'

'Both.'

She climbed onto the bed on all fours, sinking into the soft mattress, releasing the smell of freshly laundered linen. 'What was it you said? You want me to finish what we started?'

Elena ran her finger slowly along his shaft, causing his erection to twitch and jump. 'Either by hand.' She griped his hot thick meat and resisted the strong urge to pull.

'Mouth.' Reluctantly, she removed her hand and ran her wet tongue around the hard dome head. His whole body tensed as her tongue flicked and teased.

'Pussy.' She straddled him, grinding her lace-covered vagina up and down his length.

He tried to grab her hips, but she pushed his eager hands away. 'No, no. Not until I say so. This is my show.'

She bent down and kissed his chin. 'What was the last one . . . my succulent arse?' Her hand slapped hard on her bottom, the tingly sting giving her a thrill.

Elena moved herself up and sat over his abs, she leaned down over his face and circled his mouth with her moist tongue. He didn't react. Her lips lightly skimmed over his forehead, down to his jaw, over the coarse spiky stubble, to his luscious mouth. His bottom lip was ripe so she took a bite pulling at it with her teeth, making him grunt like an animal caught in a trap. Hungry for flesh, she made her way over his vulnerable neck, licking all the way to his ear. She dug her teeth in, denying herself the urge to bite down on his juicy lobe. She felt wild with lust, he was like the full moon to a werewolf and she had transformed.

'Take my bra off.'

He didn't need to be told twice. The lace bra flew through the air and joined Conrad's clothes on the floor. Her bountiful globes dangled over his face, and she swayed them gently, her puckered nipples brushing his nose.

'Suck.'

Elena was in charge, and like a good boy, he did as he was told, heading straight for her nipples, soaking and stretching the pink buttons with his rapacious mouth.

Her wet nipples tightened as the air cooled them. His hands tried their luck again, only to be met with a slap. She loved being in control, even though it was only for as long as he allowed it.

Kissing him deeply, her tongue swept his mouth while she wiggled her hips back until she could feel the heat of his erection. Sitting upright, she reaching behind and gripped his cock. She couldn't resist sliding her hand along the steel like rod. It felt so satisfying.

Elena pushed her bottom backwards, and his hard dick sat between her cheeks. She placed her hands on his equally hard chest and began to rise and lower her backside, gripping him with her buttocks.

His cock pushed hard against her crevice, and she quickened the pace, masturbating his big dick with her bottom. It felt filthy. She felt filthy.

'Do you want to shoot it between my cheeks?'

He didn't say a word. His body did the talking, eyes shut tight and fists clenched.

'I'll take that as a yes.'

Conrad pushed his head back into the pillow and raised his hips, increasing the friction. Up and down, up and down, she pumped his meat with her willing bottom and dug her nails into his chest, fighting the urge to slide down his length and douse her own carnal lust.

'Not yet, Mr Bailey.' There was a low rumble of frustration from him.

She moved further down to sit on his lower legs, dragging her lace-covered crotch over his erection, teasing herself. His cock sprang free, waggling in the air. Her hands rested on his hips; Elena gaped at the appendage that held so much power over her self-control. Desire coursed through every inch of her body. She moved her face closer to the engorged tormentor and licked her lips, lubricating its entrance. Kissing the red hot tip, Elena looked up to see Conrad grabbing his hair, teeth clenched.

That's what I like to see, desperation.

She eased her mouth down, keeping it tight. His girth forced her lips to spread and filled her mouth, leaving little room for her squirming tongue. Elena went as low as she could go, her lips clamped tight. She sucked in air through her nose, her mouth stuffed full of cock. She pulled back, leaving a trail of saliva, and stopped with the head of his penis still in her mouth. Her tongue ran around it like an excited puppy that wants to play. Conrad was watching. He grabbed his dick and pulled himself into her mouth. She knew it was driving him crazy, and she loved it.

His strokes were short and fast. Elena held her mouth open, with her dripping tongue hanging out as he vigorously pulled himself off. She gave his cock a lick and waited open-mouthed. His breathing was heavy, and she knew he was close. Selfishly, she pulled away and grasped his jerking hand.

'I said not yet.' She wanted some.

Elena squatted over him and pulled her knickers to one side, clutched his dick, and flicked it between her swollen pussy. Her own desire had taken over. The feeling was so addictive and such a turn-on.

His thick cock in her hand, she beat away at her clit in a frenzied attack, the fat head slicing between her welcoming lips. She was enjoying it too much. Her thighs burned from supporting her weight. She rested her knees on the bed and put her hands back on his chest. Elena stretched her knickers a little more across her spread cheeks, tearing them. She wiggled him into position and, with a feeling of exquisite relief, skewered herself all the way down his length. Conrad's hands couldn't resist her swaying breasts. He squeezed them roughly like ripe fruit, tugging at her nipples. They were both desperate for orgasm.

Elena bounced up and down, almost lifting off him then slamming back down, rocking his body, each stroke edging her closer. He grabbed her face and pulled her to him, kissing her madly, passionately. He put his arms around her back and hooked his hands on her shoulders, his fingers embedded into her skin as he pulled her down onto him with all his force. The feeling grew more intense, and she knew it wouldn't take much longer. She wanted to climax with him.

'Grab my arse.' Elena knew that would tip him over the edge.

He obeyed her command and grabbed both cheeks, pulling her wide open until it stung, ramming harder, faster. Her soaking pussy consumed his cock, taking every inch. A low rumble from his throat gave her the signal. This was it.

'Come for me,' she encouraged him, knowing his orgasm would trigger hers, and held on to his hair, arched her back, and flicked her tongue over his lips.

His face contorted, introducing the impending explosion. A gush of semen poured into her as he roared out. Elena's whole body locked as the intense orgasm ricocheted through her, the walls of her pussy super sensitive to his manhood, which continued to slam into her, determined to empty every drop from his balls.

Elena collapsed like a rag doll, burnt out from the glorious but debilitating orgasm. They both panted in unison, drained. She could barely lift her head. Conrad was still clutching her bottom with a relaxed grip, reflecting his body's fatigue.

'Now will you sleep?' Elena whimpered.

He chuckled, rocking her gently on his chest. 'Yeah, I am rather tired all of a sudden. Must have been that hot chocolate we had on the boat.'

'Hmm, you think so?' She removed his exhausted manhood with a wince and went to the bathroom.

Elena checked herself in the mirror. Her face emitted a red self-satisfied glow, and her mauled breasts were equally as flushed. Too tired to try and calm her erratic hair and having refreshed herself, she returned to the bedroom. Conrad was lying in the bed with the sheets pulled back on her side. His eyes were closed, and his chest rose and fell rhythmically.

'Conrad, are you asleep?'

'Mmm.' He was just drifting to a place she couldn't go.

She sat on the bed satisfying her eyes' cravings and running her fingers tenderly through his hair.

'Thank you for today. I've had a wonderful time.' Elena kissed him softly. 'I hope you have too.'

Her whisper was barely audible. She lay next to him, pulled the covers over her, and gazed upon his handsome face, waiting for sleep to claim her until the morning.

CHAPTER NINETEEN

Bright sunshine reflected off the window, putting the bed under a spotlight which woke Elena. She was in the same position as when she fell asleep. Her eyes lazily opened to find an empty pillow facing her, which startled her for a moment.

'Conrad?' She sprang up, throwing the covers off. 'Conrad?' Her eyes darted to the wardrobe, and the welcome sight of his suitcase calmed her blind panic.

Elena flopped back on the bed, her galloping heart slowing to a trot, and the hypnotic allure of sleep returned. She rolled onto Conrad's cold side of the bed and buried her head in his pillow, inhaling the addictive scent. His phone vibrated on the bedside table and stopped her sniffing frenzy.

Would it be really wrong if I took a peek to see who it was? It was probably just Mary Poppins calling to make sure the gym thing was all fine.

She tried to pay no attention to the phone then suddenly snatched it from the table and illuminated the screen, two messages from wifey. Her heart sank.

I knew it was all going too well.

Trying not to overreact, she told herself he was here with her, and they were in Scotland. There was no way she could interrupt them this time. Elena pressed the messages icon. She wanted to know what it said. There were a lot more than two messages from his wife, although the others had been read.

Her finger hovered over the first message when she heard the key in the door. *Shit!*

She threw herself back on the bed and put his phone under the pillow. Her hair had fanned over her face. He quietly opened the door. Elena spied him through the camouflage of red locks in his grey track pants that hugged his bum and a tight white T-shirt. *Yummy.*

He placed the keys down, went to the fridge and took out a bottle of water, then sat in the window, kicked off his trainers, and put his feet up on the opposite chair, sipping the water.

Shit, shit, shit! What if his phone rings? She waited awhile, her anguish growing each minute as she held the ticking time bomb. *Surely, he'll go for a shower any minute?* Instead, he sat there, taking in the view, deep in thought.

There was nothing for it. She was going to have to fake waking up. There was a good reason why she'd never got any parts in school plays. She couldn't risk waiting any longer. *Here we go.*

Elena stretched her arms out wide like a cat in front of a hot fire and groaned. 'Oh dear.' She gave a yawn, which was far too long. 'Is that the time?' She didn't have a watch on, and there was no clock in the room. 'My, that was a lovely sleep. Oh, you're already up.' *Oh God.*

Conrad had a knowing smile on his face. 'Morning.'

And the award goes to . . . not fucking you, Elena!

'Did you sleep well?' He screwed the top back on the bottle.

'Very, thank you.' She piled the pillows on top of each other to muffle any possible ring. 'Where have you been?'

'It's such a nice morning I thought I'd go for a quick

run. Are you sure you want to come with me today? You don't fancy the spa?'

Now she was paranoid that he didn't want her to go with him, especially as his wife was constantly texting. 'I can stay here if you want me to.' Elena put the ball in his court.

'No, I thought I would give you the option.'

He came over to the bed, and she had no control over her eyes whatsoever, and like kids in a sweet shop, they went straight for the goodies, his wavering packet filled with mouthwatering treats.

Conrad leaned over her. 'Hungry?' *Caught!*

'Erm . . . a little.'

He kissed her on the lips. She was unnerved he might notice his phone was missing. Having just displayed her appalling acting skills, there was no chance she'd be able to pull off the I-don't-know-how-that-got-there act.

'I'm going for a shower. Is it safe?'

'Yes, if you're quick.'

Elena watched him swagger into the bathroom and took her chance, moving with ninja-like speed, leaving the phone as she'd found it. The second her hand released it, his head popped around the door frame.

'I'm going to get breakfast sent to the room. Have a look at the menu and see what you fancy.'

He flashed his eyebrows at her suggestively. His phone called for its master. Conrad came out shirtless like Hercules sent down from Olympus.

'I'd better get that in case there's a problem with Glasgow.'

She cringed in case he noticed she had been snooping and watched his face closely.

'It's nothing.'

The telltale phone went into the bathroom with him. Elena flicked through the menu and tried to push the doubts from her mind.

Conrad came out of the bathroom wearing the complimentary bathrobe. Elena was relaxing in the chair by the window wearing his denim shirt.

'What do you think?' It was his turn to do a pirouette; the robe was undone and flared out as he spun, giving her a flash of his white briefs with red piping around the crotch, highlighting the danger zone.

'I think I've got very good taste,' she said, trying not to giggle.

He pointed a finger at her. 'I can't argue with that. So what do you fancy? Sausage?'

Elena gave in to the giggles. 'You are terrible, aren't you?'

'What? You do jump the gun with your filthy mind. I was going to say sausage, egg, bacon, or something lighter?'

She gazed at him admiringly. 'I think I will go for the light option: tea, toast, and yoghurt.'

'Very good, madam. I'll call it down straight away.' He took a bow.

Elena swanned over to the bathroom. 'Have it waiting for me when I get out of the shower, will you, my good man.'

He waited until she was in the bathroom. 'What about the breakfast?' he called.

'Naughty!' her voice echoed from the shower cubicle.

Sure enough, breakfast was waiting when she came out of the shower in her matching robe. Conrad had poured her tea and buttered her toast, which lay out on the table waiting for her, next to his cereal, fruit, and coffee.

'Breakfast is served, madam.' He pulled out her chair.

It was a bright clear morning and a surreal spot for breakfast. He didn't pay any attention to the view. His eyes were fixed on Elena, and she felt slightly self-conscious as she crunched through her toast.

'You have a strange pull, Elena White, and I don't

know what it is.' A menacing look had developed on his face.

'You'll have to try and figure it out then, won't you?'

The piercing gaze didn't divert. He sat with his legs crossed, holding the coffee cup. Elena tried to think of something to say, but his burning stare scrambled her brain.

'So we're off to Glasgow today then?' *Bloody hell, is that the best you can come up with?*

'You have a very sexy mouth.' He disregarded her silly question.

She reached apprehensively for her tea, took a sip, and held the cup over her mouth, trying to hide the provocative opening.

The lazy robe hung carelessly from his shoulders and didn't dare try to cover his powerful chest, which sat above a stack of flesh bricks. He uncrossed his legs. The white briefs bulged hammock-like, holding his most potent muscle. Elena wanted to have a good look, but his undeviating stare didn't allow her the opportunity. Her mouth was dry with nervous anticipation of where his dark mood was taking him. Conrad placed his empty cup on the table, folded his arms, and spread his thighs, giving way to the bulky white pouch which took centre stage.

He reached out his hand and lowered the cup from her mouth, restoring his view. 'That's better,' he purred.

Unintentionally, she licked her lips, which left them with a shiny gloss. Once again, she felt like a prey locked in his salacious glare, waiting for him to strike.

Elena tried to continue breakfast with some normality next to an unpredictable half-naked love god, whose bursting white underwear burned into her peripheral vision like a laser and made her tummy tighten with expectation. She decided to eat her yoghurt before it went off from the intense heat at the table.

'They've forgotten to give me a spoon for the yoghurt.' Elena scoured the table.

Conrad got up. 'Just a minute.' He peeled the top off and took it away. He probably had some camping gadget that had a spoon tucked away. The break from the intensity was a relief, and Elena's attention returned to the other side of the glass. Her admiration was disturbed by his return.

'There you go.'

She turned to him, and he was standing robe-less, with his balls hanging over the top of his briefs and his soft penis smothered in yoghurt.

Her mouth wasn't waiting for her brain's go-ahead and dropped open. She blinked up at him and saw he wouldn't take 'no' for an answer. Elena tucked the stray damp hairs behind her ears and licked the tip of his penis which was about to drip. Her tongue did a good job and didn't stop until every drop was cleaned away. Conrad took hold of his manhood and plunged it into the plastic pot, causing it to overspill onto his fingers. Her keen tongue was quick off the mark, and she licked and sucked his digits clean.

Desire had now kicked in, and she eagerly awaited her next feeding and opened wide, taking his member into her willing mouth. With one smooth pull of her lips, she stripped the sticky coating and went back for more. He pulled away and dipped his penis once more. A flush of heat rose from her envious vagina to her face, burning her hard nipples on the way that had come out to see what all the fuss was about.

He undid her belt and opened the gown, exposing her plump breasts. Her whole body quivered as she waited, her mouth open like a baby bird hungry for nourishment. His dick slapped heavy on her tongue, and she swallowed him, his hot flesh and the cool yoghurt a fine combination in her mouth. This time he let her feast, and she could feel the blood pumping through his veins like a fireman's hose. The swelling girth claimed the space for its own. Her eyes ran along his shaft and up the hard landscape of his awesome physique to his face, which had a look of determination carved on it. She would be swallowing more than yoghurt.

Her slurping mouth ran to and fro, trying to get as much as possible. He pulled his now solid erection out and held it in a tight grip, and the remainder of her breakfast was poured over the voluminous head. His stomach sucked in and out, trying to calm his body's urges.

Her hands clambered to get a grip, but he grabbed her wrists and placed both her hands on his hard butt.

'Mouth only,' he ordered, and she happily obeyed, although her hungry pussy wasn't pleased as it salivated jealously, waiting for its turn.

His dripping cock knocked on the door of her mouth and was welcomed in. Elena moved her head quickly backwards and forwards in short bursts, concentrating on the head, his bottom clenched, giving notice of the build-up as her tongue tickled and tormented to its best ability.

Elena pulled away, her aching jaw needed rest. He glistened with a coating of saliva and the remnants of pink yoghurt. Having rested long enough, she opened wide, taking in the head of his dick. Her tongue rubbed it like a genie's lamp, waiting for the reward to burst from the spout.

Conrad grabbed the back of her hair and knotted it around his fist until it was tight against her head. She slipped her fingers into the crack of his bottom to make sure she had a good grip. She had a feeling it was going to be a bumpy ride. He pushed her head, forcing her mouth onto him, and watched as his length slowly disappeared. He tightened his grip a little more.

Her head was pulled to and fro, deeper and deeper, abusing her mouth, making her swallow more each time. He yanked harder, still jolting her head backwards and forwards, her scalp stretched tight, stinging with the force.

A steady pace had gathered now, and he stood in the window, fucking her mouth hard. Elena's clitoris desperately called for her soothing fingers to ease its swollen torment, but she was hanging on for dear life and struggling to breathe.

There was no chance of him stopping. His length hit the back of her throat. He held her head still and moved his hips backwards and forwards, tensing his buttocks and trapping her fingers. His heavy balls slapped under her chin as he fucked her full force now.

The pace slowed slightly, and he pulled all the way out, allowing her enough time to gulp down some air before he re-entered, sliding in as much as she could take.

'Suck!' he spat. She was a captive slave to his will and obediently complied.

His free hand grabbed a handful of breast and rolled the tender nipple between his fingers while he forced her head further down. In a sudden frenzy, his hips rocked, and he snapped her head up and down, his cock filling her mouth with warm cream mixed with the taste of strawberry, each deep thrust depositing another load into her expectant mouth. Elena squeezed his firm butt while she quaffed it down in one go as her body screamed for attention.

He untangled his fist from her hair and exhaled as he withdrew from her mouth. His hand slid down his abating erection and forced the blood to rush to the head until it was at bursting point. A thick white trickle of sperm oozed out. Elena looked up at him, knowing what he wanted, and didn't take her eyes off his as she licked it away greedily, still in a haze of sexual tension.

Conrad got down on his knees, his face level with hers, and roughly parted her damp thighs. She was so turned on after having strawberry cock and cream for breakfast and had almost climaxed from being rocked around on her chair.

He stared into her eyes while his fingers expertly stretched her open and a lone finger touched the red button that could detonate a nuclear explosion through her body.

'You are very wet, Ms White.'

The finger circled the perimeter, winding up the tension. Just a few firm flicks and she'd be there. The rotating finger delved deeper, sending exquisite waves of pleasure flowing through her, promising release, but stopping just at the moment of no return.

'Are you frustrated, Elena?'

She nodded. Her chest heaved in and out, willing him to tip her over the edge.

He kissed her, his tongue curiously sampled his own flavour, and she wanted his mouth to stay locked on hers and feel her sweet climax. Just a little more pressure and she would shatter into a million pieces. He removed his lips and hand simultaneously.

'I think you'll keep for later.'

'What?'

Her eyes fluttered as she fought the overpowering sexual need. She was high on it, under the influence of his expert touch. He stood and dropped his depleted penis back into its hammock.

'I want you horny like a dog on heat for later.'

You sod! Elena's thighs rubbed together, trying to give some stimulation to her disgruntled pussy.

'Come on. We don't want to be late now, do we?'

Elena eyed the bathroom. She *had* to sort herself out. Conrad watched her closely.

'Ms White, I don't want you finishing things off either, thank you. That's my job.'

Her face flushed with embarrassment that he had read her so accurately.

'I don't do that actually,' she quipped, giving another display of her poor acting skills.

Conrad looked at her with his head down and his eyebrows raised.

'I don't!' She fumbled awkwardly in her dressing gown pocket.

He graciously turned his attention to his clothes with a

smirk and busied himself with getting dressed while Elena stood in a state of sexual unrest, her desire slowly, very slowly, subsiding.

After finally regaining possession of her body and mind, Elena applied the final touches to her makeup. She watched Conrad in the mirror, collecting his wallet and phone. He looked his usual catwalk-model self in light blue jeans with a white V-neck T-shirt and a grey jacket that tapered in at the waist, highlighting his athletic physique. He tied a light grey scarf around his neck, which completed his ensemble.

'Do I look okay?' Elena was worried she didn't match his high standard of appearance.

He looked up from tying the laces of his brown leather shoes. 'You look better than okay. Turn around.'

She tottered around in her brown ankle boots, black leggings, and a casual knitted sweater, with light brown and cream vertical darts and a large round neck. A crimson flood of hair stretched down her back, reaching for her delectable bottom which was covered by the large band of her sweater.

'You look . . . fantastic. I don't think it's safe to leave the room with you looking like that.'

He had a way of reassuring her. Elena's doubts floated away on his words, leaving her excited at the day ahead. He took her hand, and they left the half-eaten toast and empty yoghurt pot on the table. In actual fact, it was far more than just her hand he had taken.

CHAPTER TWENTY

'This is it.'

They had parked outside what looked like an abandoned warehouse. It was a large dirty building with a flat roof. Bands of windows spanned horizontally on each of the four floors, interrupting the brickwork. They left the safety of the car, and she could hear the clanking of iron like a great forge making industrial tools and chains.

'Don't look so worried.' He spotted her unease.

'You want to buy this?' She looked around at the broken glass, crude graffiti-stained walls, each doorway and recess a collecting point for litter.

'This whole area is earmarked for redevelopment—houses, apartments, and shops—over the next five to ten years.'

It was a vision Elena couldn't quite see. 'You're the expert.'

'Let's go inside. We're on the third floor.'

He led the way and held open the solid metal door for her. They entered the foreboding building and went up a bare timber staircase that doglegged around and around to their desired floor. The walls were stained from the army of hands that had used the walls to steady themselves. The paint to the hand rail was worn away from years of palms slowly eroding it.

The third floor had a brown flaky half-glazed door. Conrad peered between the thin strips of wire that crisscrossed the glass. The clanking had increased in volume as they ascended, and loud grunts and groans emanated from behind the door. She felt like they were about to enter some kind of zoo enclosure.

'There's the big man. Come on.'

They entered, and instantly, the smell of sweat and humidity hit her. It was surprisingly busy for the time of day and not at all what she'd been expecting: Large metal benches matching the wear and tear of the staircase were scattered around the room, the ones on the perimeter had frameless mirrors watching over them. Bars, pulleys, chains, and racks full of great cast-iron weights littered the floor's thread-bare carpet which was half-covered with rubber matting. It was more like a dungeon than a gym.

'Just wait here a minute.'

Conrad sneaked over to the men who had their backs to him; one, short and stocky had a bar across his shoulders with so much weight on it that it was bending. His black friend was twice the size and kept a close eye on his partner, calling out encouragement as he squatted down with a grunt. Conrad waited until the screaming powerhouse had slammed the bar back on the rack with a great clang.

Elena stood self-consciously, feeling completely overdressed, as she wasn't wearing washed-out or torn gym clothing. A few of the men had spotted her standing with her arms folded, trying to do her best chameleon impression. They elbowed each other and nodded towards her like Neanderthal man spotting a woolly mammoth for dinner. She willed him to come back to her side.

Conrad poked the black guy in the ribs. He turned his giant head with the look of a bull about to charge, which changed to a toothy grin the instant he saw Conrad. The two men hugged each other. The black guy was taller than Conrad and twice as wide. They laughed and chatted for a while; his friend looked across to Elena and turned back to Conrad nodding.

What was he saying about her?

They walked towards her, his friend getting larger with each step.

'Elena, this is Sheldon, the rogue who's ripping me off for this dump.'

Sheldon chuckled in a deep booming voice and held out a dinner-plate-sized hand. 'Nice to meet you, Elena.' Her petite hand disappeared into his raspy grasp.

'You too, Sheldon.'

'What's a good-looking girl like you doing with a loser like this?'

'Hey, you're never too big to take a fall, remember that.' Conrad interjected.

Sheldon set free her hand and bellowed even louder, 'I suppose he's told you all about how he almost beat me at the national judo championships?' He playfully shoved Conrad, who was shaking his head.

'No, he hasn't actually.' Elena looked at him. There was another anecdote she didn't know about him. He rolled his eyes, dismissing the story.

'No? Well, that's a first.'

'Never mind that. I'm going to show Elena around if that's okay, big man?'

'That's fine with me, brother. Help yourself.' Sheldon returned to keep an eye on his friend.

They went to the opposite end of the gym where a row of beaten-up punch bags hung from the joists. Conrad ran through his plans to turn it from a hard-core gym to one that would cater to everyone, from pensioners to young mums, with four floors devoted to every aspect of fitness. He spoke with real enthusiasm, but Elena noticed a hint of regret in his eyes as he looked around imagining his vision.

'You fought that guy?'

'Yeah, it was quite a few years ago now.'

'You never mentioned you do judo.'

'I don't anymore, but when I was younger, it was a good way of releasing pressure.'

Pressure from what? 'So are you a deadly black belt?'

'I am a black belt, although I'm not sure about the deadly part.'

'Well, I can confirm there are definitely some parts of you that are lethal.'

He was about to answer her suggestive comment when his phone beeped, stopping his reply. 'Ah, saved by the bell.' He took out the phone and looked at it in a quandary before putting it back in his pocket.

Something wasn't right. He was a closed book, and everything she knew she'd had to drag out of him, or had found out by accident. Elena had already tried Google, but there was nothing, not even a photo. He didn't chase the limelight, that was for sure. She was going to have to do some digging, but where to start?

Sheldon handed Elena her tea, and they sat in the makeshift office, which consisted of a fridge full of energy drinks, a kettle, a radio, and an old table. The walls were covered in pictures of overly muscled men that looked more deformed than aesthetic. She was happy to be away from the glare of the testosterone-fuelled men, and the two friends reminisced about their history and how they had gone from being rivals to good friends, but she didn't get any more insight into Mr Secretive. Finally, they said their goodbyes and hugged once more, slapping each other's backs with manly affection. Sheldon kissed Elena delicately on the cheek like she was made of bone china.

'Take care, big man.'

'You too, brother, and you do know I'll be taking you up on that offer?'

'I know you will!' shouted Conrad as he left.

Elena's brow furrowed. She felt completely out of the loop and somewhat annoyed at being excluded from these little conversations. He took her hand as they walked down the stairs.

'What offer was Sheldon talking about?' She decided to be cheeky and just ask.

'I said he could come and stay with me sometime. That's all.'

She felt stupid for being so paranoid about him. It was none of her business after all.

They left the eerie building and drove into the city. Glasgow was like any other metropolis: old and new architecture stood shoulder to shoulder, busy roads crammed with people trying to get from A to B. Observing the usual city chaos through the glass made her feel strangely tranquil, knowing that for a few days she had been taken out of that game.

Elena strolled around the city shops at a leisurely pace with Conrad, while everyone else hurried around them. It was the complete opposite of the tranquil loch; the air was thick from the heat and pollution of cars and buses. An eclectic collection of noises surrounded them.

The urban chaos didn't bother her. She was in a cocoon of contentment. She held her head high, proud to have him by her side, pretending not to notice the envious glances from females of all ages, plus the odd male.

They wandered in and out of various stores window-shopping and stopped to watch the street performers that entertained the gathered crowds before they had a relaxed lunch in a cosy Italian restaurant. They sat at a table by the window and enjoyed the free entertainment, people watching, while the pint-sized waiters paraded like peacocks in their red waistcoats.

'Is there anything you need?' Conrad insisted on buying her something and ignored her objections.

'No. Well, there is one thing.'

'And what's that?'

'I could do with a new kettle. Mine's knackered.'

Two tiny dimples appeared in his cheeks as a broad smile lit up his face. She loved being the cause of that beaming smile, and even though it wasn't their most intimate conversation, she felt a real connection at that moment that was difficult to explain.

'A new kettle it is then. Anything else? Whips, handcuffs, sex toys?' Another burst of sunshine made her glow from the inside out. 'I'd like to see that collection.' He leaned on his crossed forearms, his eyes poring over her face.

Elena copied his action and leaned closer to him. 'If you're good and start playing by the rules, I may let you see it.'

Conrad's eyes ignited with interest. 'What do you mean play by the rules?'

'You can't leave a girl on the edge. Frustration is a terrible thing.'

'Yes, I am sorry about that. It was naughty of me. Are you still frustrated, Ms White?' The formal name-calling was a sure sign of his arousal, and the glint in his eyes confirmed that.

'A little.' Elena's head rested on her hand, and her index finger slipped between her plump red lips.

'Only a little, Ms White?' His eyebrows rose slightly as he posed the question.

She reached for his hand and slid her fingers up and down his thumb. 'I don't want to build my hopes up just to be disappointed again, do I?'

He was putty in her hands, and she got a big kick from knowing that she had such an effect on him.

'There's one thing I hate, and that's to disappoint, especially a lady.'

'Don't worry yourself, it can easily be rectified . . . one way or another.'

His hand brushed over his prickly stubble, and a look of resolve etched itself onto his face. Conrad raised his head in the air and caught the attention of a passing waiter.

After paying the bill, they left the restaurant not quite so relaxed as they'd entered. They hurried across the busy road, dodging traffic. He pulled her along by the hand into a large department store.

'Where are we going?' she asked, trying to keep up the pace.

'To get you something you need.'

The escalator transported them to ladies' wear, and he steered her full steam ahead through the maze of clothing racks until they stopped at a section of party dresses and evening wear.

'Pick a dress.'

He held his arms out to the assortment of clothes. She didn't know where to begin and was puzzled by the urgency of it all.

'You pick one for me.' She was curious to see what his taste would be.

Conrad stood straight. His handsome face looked left to right like a sailor checking the horizon. He chose an electric blue bandage dress with a scoop neck.

'Wow, that was quick.' *It would have taken me a least an hour.*

'I'm a man who knows what he likes.'

It wasn't something she would be brave enough to wear usually, but she'd have worn a potato sack if he had asked.

'Try it on.'

'Can I?' This was a first: a man choosing a beautiful dress then encouraging her to try it on.

'Of course.'

Elena grabbed her size, and they went to the changing rooms.

A rotund middle-aged lady with brown curly hair stood humming away to herself cheerily, hanging clothes on a long rail. She was wearing silver-rimmed glasses that sat so far down her nose they served no purpose. A matching silver chain harnessed them to her neck.

'Good afternoon, young lady. May my girlfriend try this on?

Girlfriend, I like the sound of that.

The shop assistant looked over her glasses and blushed like a schoolgirl as Conrad worked his undeniable charm on her. 'Good afternoon to you too, sir.' She fluffed her fingers through her hair, and her brown curls bounced eagerly. 'Of course, she may. Would you like to take a seat, sir?' She gestured to a wrinkled brown leather sofa that looked like it had given rest to many weary male shoppers.

'Thank you.' Conrad added his name to that long list and sank into the worn sofa.

The assistant pointed the way to a double line of cubicles, each screened with a grey curtain. Her red checks had now cooled to a warm pink.

Elena chose the centre changing cubicle, pulled the curtain, and hung the dress on the coat hook. She took off her shoes and pulled her sweater over her head, which left her hair tangled over her face like a frizzy spider's web. Suddenly, the curtain flew back. Conrad stepped in and pulled the curtain sealing them in. For a brief moment, Elena panicked and wondered what was wrong. He brushed her hair away and kissed her passionately, slowly, deeply, until she didn't care that they were in the ladies' changing rooms.

His hands covered as much ground as possible and grabbed at her flesh. He spun her around and spread her legs with his foot, Elena placed her hands at shoulder height on each side of the mirror, and he firmly patted her down like a suspect being searched. Sparks began to fly in her tummy, and it seemed that she was only ever a hair's breadth away from relinquishment.

His big hard hands breached the waistband of her leggings and helped themselves to her inner thighs and up to her knickers. They bullied the innocent fabric for getting in the way and pulled and stretched, trying to get to the heat. Losing patience, the audacious hands pulled the leggings down, along with her knickers, closing her wide stance. Conrad moved her hair to one side, and his teeth bit into her neck, setting every nerve ending in her body on fire, while he unbuttoned his jeans, followed by a hot slap to her thigh as his erection sprang free.

Next door, they heard the curtain pull, and the buzz of a long zip being undone. Elena's head shot up and puffed hair out of her face. She watched Conrad in the mirror with his finger held to his lips. The lady next door was undressing, but that didn't deter him. His hand sailed over the crease in her bottom and under to her primed sex.

He crudely inserted a finger, checking her readiness. Boy was she ready, it was hours since breakfast but she was fast approaching where he had left her. The urge was there like an itch that *had* to be scratched.

She watched him in the mirror as he leaned back and perused her body with a sleazy gaze. The soft skin of his hard cock burned into her thigh. He held her hip with one hand, and his other hand pushed down on her upper back, bending her enough to gain entry. He then pulled the cups of her bra down letting her breasts spill over.

'Excuse me? Hello?' a high-pitched voice rang out from next door.

'Can I help you, madam?' The assistant had now arrived.

Conrad continued, fully intent on fucking her even with two strangers inches away, with only a laminated partition and a flimsy curtain separating them.

'Have you got this in a size 18? This one's a bit tight,' asked the mystery shopper.

Conrad leaned over her. 'I like it tight.' His warm breath tickled her ear.

'Certainly, madam. I'll just have a look for you.'

He opened her from behind and pulled her apart until he heard the sharp intake of breath.

She watched his image in the mirror as he bent his

knees and lowered himself. His hand gripped her tightly as he positioned his penis at the entrance to her sex, sending vibrations through her body. She screwed her mouth up, fighting to keep the wails of pleasure locked inside. Holding her hips firmly, his cock eased into her taut opening.

'Size 18, madam.'

'Thank you. If this doesn't fit, I will be worried.' The voices reminded them they weren't alone.

'It's a lovely colour next to your hair,' the conversation continued next door.

Elena's unbridled need made her completely uninhibited, and she sat her weight on his cock. It was tight, and she wiggled him inside her.

He pulled up his T-shirt and tucked it under itself to get a better view then grabbed her upper arms, pulling her shoulders back, forcing her breasts to jut out proud. He took a moment to watch them bumping into each other as he positioned her. He wasn't all the way in, and she wanted more; she wanted it all.

They heard the screech of the curtain rings from next door and listened to the soft fading footsteps. He'd got the all-clear, and the onslaught began as he thrust his hips hard while he pulled back on her arms. If she wanted it all, she was going to get it.

He delved deeper each time as her juices eased his way. The temperature rose in the enclosed space as their bodies raced towards the prize. As he rammed his girth all the way in and almost lifted her off her feet, the force so great that she cried out with untamed lust. Her belly tightened, and he slapped hard against her bottom, sending ripples of immense sensation coursing through her.

The force of his stroke was unyielding. Her breasts jumped high in the air with each pounding. Elena watched him as he worked her body with masterly skill, raw need and determination stamped on his face.

The smell of sex filled the air. The feel of her leggings

binding her legs, bra pulled down, with her full boobs clashing against each other, his fingers digging into her arms as he fucked her in the changing room, where anyone could have heard them—all these factors combined to make an obscene situation that made her want to scream with ecstasy.

'Harder!' she demanded, and he obliged as her toes lost contact with the floor. His fat cock sliced into her like a great piston on a steam engine.

The sensation sharpened and focused. Elena bit down on her lip, holding in her screams, and she gladly yielded to the fervent, dynamic feelings that transported her to a place you were only allowed to occupy for a brief, beautiful, ecstatic moment. She returned back to this world, her strength drained. She was held up by his arms and cock alone as the echo of her climax ebbed away. Conrad threw his head back, eyes closed, face tight. His erection pulsed, buried deep, while he came silently, tightening his grip further still. Her feet came back down to earth, and she was released from his grasp to stand alone on her trembling legs, the imprint of his fingers embossed into her skin. They heard the assistant's melody getting louder as she approached.

'Is everything okay, madam? How's the fit?'

Elena straightened her clothes. 'It was a bit tight actually,' she answered wide-eyed in mild panic, not referring to the dress.

'Shall I get you the next size up?'

'Er, no, thank you.' She pulled her sweater back on while Conrad removed his scarf, his face glistening with sweat.

'Okay. If you need anything, just ask.'

Elena thanked her and waited a short while before popping her head through the curtain to see if the coast was clear. 'You're a very bad man.'

He buttoned up his jeans, with his T-shirt still rolled up displaying his six-pack. 'What? I just gave you something you needed.'

She frowned playfully.

'You mean you really *did* want a kettle?' He spoke a bit too loudly.

She popped her head in and out, taking a quick peek through the curtain. Elena giggled, holding both her hands over her mouth. 'Shhh, Conrad! That lady's going to find us.'

'Well, it's a bit late now for a threesome.' He flapped his jacket, trying to get some air circulating, while Elena held her hand on her forehead like she was taking her temperature.

'You're going to get me arrested.'

He stopped his flapping and gazed thoughtfully out of the corner of his eye. 'I must admit, I would like to see you in handcuffs. Nothing else, just handcuffs.'

'Don't you ever stop, Mr Bailey?' She bent over to put on her shoes.

'It's what you do to me.' The jovial tone had gone from his voice.

She stood upright with only one shoe on and looked deep into his sincere eyes. His simple words burned through everything and touched her heart like a beautiful love song. The ludicrous location was witness to a powerful moment. Elena pulled herself to his face with the lapels of his jacket and thanked him with her lips.

They managed to sneak out unnoticed, and Conrad insisted on buying the dress despite Elena pleading for him not to and the fact she hadn't even tried it on.

'I need a sit-down.' She had the legs of a marathon runner that had just crossed the finishing line.

'Yeah, me too. That was a bit of a thigh burner.'

'It's not my thighs that are burning, Mr Bailey.' She put on her annoyed teacher voice.

'Good, like I said, I hate to disappoint.'

He held her hand, and they rode the escalator to the top-floor café. Conrad found them a table while Elena visited the toilet. She returned to find him sitting at a table with his jacket hanging on the back of the chair.

'I got you a latte. Thought you could do with a caffeine boost.'

The chair scraped on the tiles as she pulled it out. 'An ice pack would probably been more appropriate.' She sat down gingerly.

'I won't be a moment,' he said.

She watched his fine figure as he walked to the toilets then had a quick look around to see if any other females were watching him. Why was she so possessive of him when they were out? Did she not feel good enough for him despite his frequent compliments?

His jacket pocket buzzed. She looked towards the toilet door, and then her paranoia overruled her common sense. Elena slipped her hand into his pocket and checked the phone: *one new message from wifey.* A sudden shock of worry hit her. Elena found herself wishing she had ignored it. The door to the toilets swung open as she dropped the phone back into his pocket.

He's with me, not his wife. Right now, he's here with me.

Conrad sat down, tore open the packet of sugar, and sprinkled its contents into the white fluffy cloud that sat on top of his coffee.

'You can try this on for me later if you like.' He shook the paper bag holding the dress.

'Conrad, you shouldn't have. You've done more than enough. Besides, I don't think I could get away with wearing something like that. I'm not sure where I'd wear it.'

The spoon tinkled in his cup as he mixed the brown and white together. 'I'll take you somewhere you can wear it. And anything would look good on you, sweetheart. You doubt yourself too much.'

He was like the warm sun on her back in winter, carrying the promise of brighter days ahead.

'Not everyone has your confidence. I wish I had.'

Elena decided to be bold and test how far confidence would get her. 'There is one other thing I'd like, more than anything in this store.'

'You're not going to say an iron, are you?'

She stared at her glass cup as she turned it around nervously. 'No, I'd like to know more about you, your past, what you were like as a kid . . . everything really.'

Her eyes dared to raise and found him staring into the past. He ran his fingers through her hair which hung down each side of her face.

'There's not much to tell.'

Elena sensed he was stalling and didn't want to pressure him. She was about to change the subject when he interrupted her.

'I grew up on a council estate, never knew my dad. I'd like to say my mother did her best, but that would be stretching the truth. There wasn't a lot of money to go around. Well, not unless it was for cigarettes and booze, that is. I wore my brother's hand-me-down clothes, and we existed on a diet of fried food.'

It was obviously something he didn't like to talk about. She felt honoured that he was confiding in her at last.

'Things got worse when I went to high school. I'd always been overweight, and when I hit teenage years, the weight just seemed to pile on. That's when the bullying started. Cony, they called me, Fat Cony.' He licked his lips and fidgeted on his seat. The sting of the taunts long gone obviously still smarted.

Elena didn't speak for fear of him breaking into a joke and changing the subject like he had a habit of doing. Instead, she sat still, trying to read his body language and every facial expression, intrigued to see what had made him the man he is.

'Because of my weight, I wasn't very good at sports, so school for me was about getting through the day. We had an introduction to judo one week. I was so nervous, but my weight gave me an advantage, and no one couldn't get the better of me. I really enjoyed it, but the following week, we went back to the usual football, and that was it. I left school with no qualifications, no job, but relieved to not have to wake up each morning dreading the day ahead. Sorry, I'm going on, aren't I?'

'Conrad, you're not going on. I want to know everything about you.' She squeezed his hand, encouraging him to continue.

'I don't want to destroy your illusion and you to be disappointed in me.'

She had never seen him like this. He was exposed, vulnerable even. It was the first time she'd seen a chink in the armour, and the very thought that he might think that made her eyes fill with tears.

'Disappointed? My god, Conrad. You're the most honourable, decent man I have ever met. You leave everyone in your shadow. Disappointment doesn't even exist when it comes to you.'

'Oh, you've got a silver tongue, you have.' She knew he'd do this: steer the conversation away with a few jokes.

'I want to know the rest, please.'

He gave out a long sigh and rubbed his temple. 'Okay . . . erm . . . I joined a judo club, run by a guy called Roger Bullas, who had white hair and a white beard . . . Huh, he looked like Kenny Rogers. He took me under his wing and was good to me, like a father. With his guidance, I went from strength to strength. I'd found something I was good at. It was Roger who suggested I join a gym to increase my strength, which would help my judo. So I joined a tatty old gym, a bit like Sheldon's place, and I loved it. My strength went up, and the weight went down. Eventually, I managed to get a job there. I'd turn up early to work out before opening up. Then when I'd finished work, I would do another session. The more I saw the results, the more I wanted to do. I started advising people on their training and diet. I loved it, absolutely loved it, and to cut a long story, it led to me getting a loan and opening my own gym.

And here I am.'

Elena hadn't expected that story, but if anything, it made her feel closer to him. She knew what it was like to be bullied, to be the odd one out. Conrad still was the odd one out but for all the right reasons.

'You should be really proud of yourself. You've achieved so much.'

'I don't talk about it much because it's a negative part of my life, and I like to focus on the positive side like right now.' She was touched and really felt a connection to him.

'Do you still see your mother?'

He shook his head. 'She died of lung cancer six years ago.'

His story explained the desperate need for him to be the parent he'd never had. Elena was so satisfied, not just with the sex, which was the best she had ever had, but because he had touched her body, and soul, in places nobody had even come close.

CHAPTER TWENTY-ONE

'Good morning.' Conrad peeled back the covers and kissed her on the cheek. 'Come on, sleepyhead. We've got breakfast at seven. You need to get dressed.'

'What time is it?' she uttered throatily.

'It's six thirty.' He sat on the edge of the bed, and she rolled into his thigh as the bed sank under his weight.

'What? I didn't hear the fire alarm.' She couldn't believe anyone would voluntarily get up so early on a Saturday.

The bed shook from his chesty laugh. 'No, there's no fire, sweetheart. We're going out.'

'Where're we going?' Elena's eyes refused point-blank to open.

'On an adventure.'

That coaxed one of her eyes to open a fraction. 'Adventure? What sort of adventure?' Her curiosity had surpassed her desire for sleep.

'Did you bring your track pants?'

'Yes . . .'

'Well, get dressed and I'll tell you over breakfast.' The bed sprang back into shape as it was relieved of his weight, and her head bounced on the mattress.

She dragged herself out of bed. The shower had no pity whatsoever and thrashed her with water until she was fully awake.

Elena, dressed in light grey track suit bottom, white T-shirt, and sky blue fleece jacket, felt wholly inappropriate as they entered the stylish dining room, which thankfully was almost empty. They sat at a pretty table by the window overlooking the gardens. Conrad advised her to eat a good breakfast for their day ahead, which really got her wondering what he'd got in store.

'Now will you tell me where we're going?'

'Yes, today we are going on a forest adventure.'

She wasn't any wiser and was concerned at what that might mean.

'Climbing, absciling, zip wires—it's great fun.' He forked in another load of muscle-fuelling scrambled egg.

She had good reason to be concerned. 'Can't we just go to the shops again?'

'Don't look so worried. You'll love it, and it's the perfect day for it.'

The bright sunshine backed him up, proudly displaying its power as warm rays filtered through the glass. Elena was dubious, but as long as she was spending the day with him, that was all that mattered.

'Tomorrow we're going to spend the day here, starting with a long lie-in before breakfast in bed. Then you're going to the spa for the works: facial, massage, nails, etc. The rest of the afternoon will be spent in bed, where I'll give you the works.'

Oh yes, that was more like it. 'Can we skip today's activities and go straight to tomorrow's?'

'I am very tempted,' he said, grinning from ear to ear as he buttered his toast. 'I promise you'll enjoy it.'

With the thought of tomorrow, she was keen to get today over and done with and ate all her breakfast like a good girl.

After a short drive, they followed the signs for Mad Mac's Outdoor Adventure. The name didn't exactly inspire confidence. They drove along a single dirt track through the dense forest and came to a clearing. There were a lot more cars than she'd expected. Conrad added another to the long line.

He maintained his unblemished record as a true gentleman and helped her out of the car. 'Madam, your trees await.'

Elena swung her legs to the side to get out and sat hesitantly as she listened to screams of delight—or was that terror?—mixed with the birdsong.

'Mad Mac's? Really?' She cocked her head to one side and tried to be annoyed.

Conrad clutched both her hands, leaned into the car and kissed the tip of her nose, and kept his face right next to hers. 'I like your angry face. It's very sexy.'

'This isn't a sexy face.'

'Isn't it?'

'No, this is my at-this-time-on-a-Saturday-I'm-usually-still-in-my-slippers-drinking-my-third-cup-of-tea face.'

His eyes creased at the corners, giving away his lovely smile. She couldn't be this close to him and not kiss those lips.

'Whatever face it is, it's working. Come on, gorgeous.' Once again, his charm won her over, and she stepped out of the car.

They rustled their way over to book in at the log cabin, which tried not to be noticed in a comfy spot, settled amongst the bushes. Elena stretched her neck up to the band of blue ribbon beyond the foliage. The timber giants did their best to stop the sun's rays from touching the earth. Bright gold-speckled patterns decorated the leaf-carpeted ground. Enormous wooden poles as high as the trees towered over them and were bound together by various ropes, cables, and nets. It was like a large playground for monkeys.

An unwelcome thought came to mind. Today was Alan's birthday, and she was going to have to send a text message for Jasmine's sake. She pulled out her phone and quickly typed one out while Conrad booked them in.

Hi Jaz

Hope you are feeling okay. Wish your dad happy birthday for me. Have a lovely weekend. Speak soon.

Love E. x.

She really wanted to put, 'I hope your dad gets pissed, falls overboard, and is eaten by a shark.' But sharks didn't eat sharks, did they? Elena pressed send and turned the phone off in case Jasmine called and heard screams and shrieks. She was supposed to be spending the weekend with her poorly mother, not climbing trees with a real-life Tarzan in Scotland.

Now booked in, they were equipped with harnesses and helmets. Conrad expertly helped her with the safety harness and was mistaken for one of the guides more than once in his khaki hiking pants, red T-shirt, and black body warmer.

As usual, he delivered on his promise. Elena had a great time after overcoming her fears. He was very patient with her and was there every step of the way, encouraging and praising her bravery. She felt a real sense of achievement after navigating from tree to tree on a wire not much thicker than a piece of string and had really got into it.

'Can I have another go at the abseiling?'

'You can have a go on whatever you like, sweetheart.' He winked with a smile.

'Don't be rude, Mr Bailey. Will you watch me?'

'I could watch you all day.'

How does he always know exactly what to say?

Conrad stood at the bottom of the rock face, and she gave him a wave before bouncing down the wall in seconds, a vast improvement on her first attempt which had been a very slow walk down with lots of shrieks.

She removed the ropes and ran over to him like an excited little girl while he applauded her. 'You never cease to amaze me, Elena White. The way you came down that wall, you'd think you were ex-special forces.'

She made a gun shape with her finger and thumb and pressed it on his nose. 'I would tell you . . . but then I'd have to kill you.'

Conrad couldn't keep his face straight and burst out with laughter; his silly sense of humour had rubbed off on her. They spent the day like two kids playing in the forest, laughing and joking, even though she was nearing the end of their fantasy weekend and would soon have to face the cold reality of her problems. But right now, she didn't have a care in the world.

For all the brave treetop adventurers, there was the reward of a barbecue at the log cabin. Elena sat opposite Conrad on a rickety old picnic bench under the canopy of the trees, their changing colour indicating the arrival of autumn. She was tired, dirty, and had terrible hat hair from the safety helmet but sat in the soul-soothing setting of nature's city, holding a hot dog smothered in mustard and ketchup and with a polystyrene cup full of hot tea. She couldn't have been happier.

Elena watched contentedly as Conrad chatted to an American family who sat on the opposite bench. She loved the way he smiled when he talked, and his eyes sparkled with enthusiasm. There wasn't one thing she didn't like about this man. It crossed her mind that today could have been a compatibility test. She hoped for ten out of ten.

Elena managed to climb into the car happily exhausted. 'That was fantastic, thank you.' The soft leather seat was pure luxury to her taxed body.

'I'm glad you enjoyed it.'

'I feel like a real action girl, albeit a very knackered one.'

'Do you now?' he said suggestively.

'I think you've seen enough action for one day, Mr

Bailey, don't you?'

'Don't worry, there'll be no physical exertion tomorrow. Well, not on your part. So you can relax and spend the day being pampered.'

Bliss.

Darkness had taken hold when they pulled up on the hotel car park. They left the balmy warmth of the car, and the sharp air stung her nose and prickled her skin. An eerie mist had crept over the loch. Intrigued, they went down to take a closer look at the ghostlike apparition hovering above the water. The brightest star had left the great stage in the sky to give its smaller brothers a chance to shine. Elena looked up at the infinite matte black sky. She had never seen so many stars before. The more she looked, the more were revealed as the black dome silently gave away its secrets. Conrad shared the same quality; the more she looked, the more she saw and the more he sparkled. Her cheeks had a rosy glow from the crisp evening air, and she cuddled into him under his body warmer. He was like a hot water bottle. Conrad wrapped his arms around her and squeezed her into him. Everything was still and perfectly quiet like they were the only two people on the planet. Elena brimmed with contentment and couldn't wait for tomorrow.

She had tried to dismiss it, but her feelings where undeniable; she was falling, falling big time. That would explain her insane jealousy towards every living female under sixty. Yes, he was handsome—he was bloody gorgeous—but it was more than that. He had a way about him. It was something that she couldn't explain, but it was there, an aura. He was a real person who treated everyone on an even level, and she loved that about him. In fact, she loved everything about him.

Conrad's phone pierced the moment. 'Sorry, sweetheart, not great timing.'

She reluctantly peeled herself from his warm body and

noticed his brows knitted as he viewed the screen. He took a few steps forward, leaving her watching his back.

'What do you want?' He was very abrupt. It obviously wasn't a friend he was talking to. 'Oh no, no, shit! When did this happen?' There was a long pause. His head dropped and shook from side to side as he listened. 'I'm on my way. I'll be there as soon as possible.' His arm dropped lifeless at his side, holding the phone.

She could see his breathing was hard from the clouds of steam that rose above his head.

'Conrad, is everything okay?'

He turned to face her but didn't make eye contact, his shoulders hunched, eyes wide, his face ashen. She was startled by his dramatic change.

'Jesus, Conrad, are you all right? What's happened?'

He was in a trance and didn't answer. Suddenly, his whole body snapped upright as if it was coming back to life.

'I've got to go.' His tone hadn't altered from the phone call.

'What? Now?' Elena started to panic. 'What's happened?'

'I'm sorry. I'll arrange a flight and a car to take you home tomorrow.' He still hadn't made eye contact. It was like he was on another planet.

'On my own?' She was baffled and now frightened. 'Conrad, aren't you a least going to tell me what's happened?' He had his hand over his eyes and rubbed his temples. 'Can't I come with you?' She looked into his face, but the Conrad she knew wasn't there.

'No!' he snapped.

It was as good as a slap in the face. She felt physically hurt by his harsh reply. Her lip trembled as she fought back the tears.

He sighed wearily. 'That was my brother on the phone. My wife attempted suicide last night. They're not sure if she'll pull through.' His voice was low and calm.

Elena tried to speak, but the words wouldn't come out. The emotion had formed a dam in her throat. What could she say? Don't go?

He glance at his watch. 'I'm sorry, I've got to go. I'll be in touch.'

She stood like a lost child, alone, frozen to the spot in shock, and she watched as he raced back to the car. Five minutes ago, everything had been perfect, she couldn't have asked for more, and now it had all come crashing down. The bright lights from the Mercedes were unsympathetic and glared painfully into her eyes. She tried not to shut them, hoping it was just a joke and he would come running back to spend the day with her as promised. But it wasn't a joke. The exhaust roared with laughter as the four-by-four ripped him away from her. She watched the red lights disappear into the darkness.

A flood of emotion burst from her. Elena turned back to face the loch with her broken heart, she was utterly torn apart, her hot tears flowed down her face and cooled on her cheeks.

She sobbed uncontrollably. The realisation had hit her: She loved him completely. She had never wanted anyone the way she wanted him. Maybe she should have told him. Maybe he would have stayed. Deep down, she knew her hopes were like bubbles in the sky, floating aimlessly.

She held her fingers to her eyes in a fruitless attempt to stem the flow. The image of Conrad's face the moment he had turned around kept coming back to her. She fought against her own thoughts, but it was useless. Of all the things that worried her, this was the biggest. He still loved his wife. Olivia's extreme cry for help had worked. It was the wake-up call he'd needed. She'd seen it in his eyes. It was over.

It seemed Elena had been a good time, not a long time. She shivered from the cold; her emotions had drained her to the point of exhaustion. She didn't want to think anymore.

The dew on the grass left her feet damp as she limped back towards the warm lights of the hotel like a wounded animal. Elena entered the room. It felt desolate. All his stuff was there like he'd just popped out. The simple sight of the two chocolates on the crisp white pillows waiting for the lovers' return made her tearful. She scooped them up and threw them in the small wire bin next to the desk.

Elena stood at the end of the bed and looked around. She wished she could stay in another room. This was their room; it didn't feel the same on her own.

She showered and climbed onto his side of the bed, wearing one of his T-shirts, and curled up with his scarf, trying to keep apart of him there with her. She stared at the shadows on the ceiling for what seemed like hours as her head whirred around in confusion until, eventually, her body's need for sleep overruled her mind's need for answers, and Elena drifted into a restless sleep on a damp tearstained pillow.

The annoyingly loud hotel phone shrieked in her ears until her hand fumbled its way to it and lifted the receiver.

'Hello?' She really wanted to say 'Why are you fucking waking me up?' but settled for plain 'hello.'

'Good morning, Ms White. Mr Bailey has arranged for a car to pick you up at one and take you to the airport.' The warm female voice was far too cheery for this time in the morning.

'Right, okay.' She checked her watch. Nine thirty. Not so early after all.

'Meanwhile, if you need anything, please don't hesitate to ask.'

'There is one thing. Did Mr Bailey leave any message?' She knew the answer but had to ask.

'No, I'm afraid not. Is there anything else I can help you with, Ms White?'

'No, thank you.' She heard the lady on the end of the line wishing her a good day as she dropped the receiver back into its place.

There didn't seem any chance of a good day for the foreseeable future. Her head throbbed as she gazed at the bathroom door wishing he would strut in with a witty one-liner, wearing just his briefs. He could light up the room with that perfect smile, energizing her. He was like the sun to her solar panel, her power supply, essential.

Elena sat up and reached for her phone. No calls, no messages. She wanted to go back to sleep. At least she was free from her own thoughts while unconscious. Breakfast finished at ten. She wasn't hungry anyway.

She packed Conrad's case, determined not to get upset, but only got as far as a pair of jeans and T-shirt before the tears made an appearance. The blue bandage dress that he'd never got to see went in too. She couldn't even look at it, never mind wear it. If she took his case home with her, he'd have to come and pick it up. And although she didn't want to hear it, she needed closure.

Elena sat in the window for the rest of the morning while the cases stood by the door like two dogs waiting to be walked. She contemplated her return to reality: no job, no money, Alan, Jasmine, but worst of all, no Conrad. It wouldn't have mattered what life threw at her so long as he was by her side. He was her hope, her strength. She felt selfish for only thinking of her own problems and wondered how his wife was. A text or a phone call was out of the question and would probably enflame things even more.

There was a knock at the door. Five to one. It was time to go. The young porter took the bags and told her that they would be put straight into the waiting car. She thanked him and said she would be a few minutes. Elena took a last look around the room. It had been a weekend she would never forget, for good and bad reasons.

She stopped at the reception to hand in the key, wearing a pair of oversized sunglasses to cover her puffy red eyes. An elderly white-haired lady stood behind the desk, her head barely above the counter.

'Can I help you, miss?' Her face creased into a smile.

'I'm going home today. Do I need to sign anything? I was staying with Mr Bailey.'

The old lady's forehead rippled as her eyebrows rose. 'You must be Elena. I heard all about you the other day. I managed to get five minutes with him before he went for his run. That boy never stops, does he? Where is Con . . . er, Mr Bailey?'

Elena didn't want questions, she just wanted to go, but the old lady had made her curious about what he'd said. 'He had to leave early, some important business to take care of.' She fiddled with her sunglasses and felt ridiculous wearing them inside.

'He's so excited. I bet you are too?' The old lady screwed up her eyes like she was trying to see past the reflective barrier concealing Elena's eyes.

She hadn't got a clue what she was talking about but decided to go along with the conversation. 'Yes, I'm very excited.'

'He's been going on about his big plan, as he calls it, for a while, and now it's all happening for him.'

This is something I've been kept in the dark about. What big plan?

'Yes, it is, isn't it?'

'Mind you, nobody deserves to be happy more than he does.' The old lady had leaned in closer and glanced around her to see if anyone was about.

'Some of the guests we have here are stuck up their own arse, if you'll excuse my French.' She was now talking to Elena like a nosey neighbour gossiping over the hedge. 'But not Conrad. He treats us all the same, from the manager to the wee boy who picks up the leaves.'

The last thing she needed was a lecture on how great he was, but the old lady was sweet. Elena peered over the desk and caught a glimpse of her name tag: Maggie.

'If I was twenty years—well, maybe thirty or more like

forty years—younger, I'd give you a run for your money, lass.' She cackled and tapped the desk with her hand. 'Listen to me going on, will you give him a message from me?'

'Of course, I will.' That would be another excuse to ring him, and then maybe she could ask him what the hell this big plan is.

'Tell him Maggie said I hope all goes well. And once you're settled in, let me know how you're getting on.'

Settled in? What the fuck was going on? Elena was glad she'd decided to wear the sunglasses because if Maggie could have seen her eyes, she would have known Elena hadn't got a clue what she was talking about.

'Anyways, I'll not keep you any longer. Look after him, darlin'. He's one in a million.'

'Thanks, I will.' The phone rang and took Maggie's attention.

Elena left the hotel and got into the car, oblivious to the scenery that had made such an impact when she had first come. Her eyes were wide open, but she couldn't see a thing. She kept going over and over her conversation with Maggie.

After their chat in the department store café, she had really thought he was beginning to open up, but in fact, he was a million miles away. The thought that she couldn't have him was bad enough, but to think he had been making plans all this time that didn't include her made it worse. One way or another, she had to find out what was going on.

CHAPTER TWENTY-TWO

Elena stood on the pavement with her suitcase by her side and looked at the house. She dreaded going in because once she had crossed the threshold, it really was back to reality.

The driver had scuppered her plans to keep Conrad's case. He had been instructed to take it with him and deliver it to Mr Bailey.

Maybe she should text him. It wouldn't be unreasonable to ask how his wife was and if he was okay, would it? She didn't know what to do. Elena took out her phone, but the battery was flashing red.

She decided to go in, have a cup of tea, charge her phone, and then text him. She walked up the path. Her case followed up behind her, seemingly not wanting to go in either. With a sorrowful sigh, Elena turned the key and opened the door to the cold empty house. She stepped over the scattering of letters that lay on the hall floor and went straight to the kitchen.

Kettle on, she rummaged through her case to find her phone charger entangled with a pair of knickers. She plugged in her phone and hung the red G-string on the back of the kitchen chair.

He didn't get to see that pair.

There were so many things she should be thinking about: job, money, paying the rent; but Elena brushed it all to one side with the word that promised so much but usually delivered so little, 'tomorrow.'

Once again, everywhere she looked there he was: the suitcase, her phone, the kitchen he had tidied before they left. Elena sat at the table and cradled her aching head.

There was a rhythmical knock at the door. The sound sprang Elena to her feet like a jack-in-the-box.

Conrad.

She should have known he wouldn't leave her like this. She told herself not to get too excited. He may have come to end it properly.

Elena ruffled her hair and had a quick glance over herself before she hurried to the door. Taking a deep breath, she opened it with expectant eyes.

Of all the sights she longed to see, Alan was the last. To see him standing at her front door was like a punch to the ribs. It knocked the wind out of her. Elena threw the door back to close it, but he had anticipated her reaction and stopped it with the palm of his hand.

'Elena, please, I need to talk to you.' He didn't shove the door back in her face. He just stopped it from closing.

'I've got nothing to say to you. How the hell did you find out where I live?' The adrenalin coursed through her shaking body as she tried to close the door.

'Jasmine told me. I've come to apologise. I've behaved horrendously. I don't expect you to forgive me. I just want the chance to explain myself.'

What possible explanation could there be? 'You've cost me my job and ruined my reputation with the bank. I think you've got a little more than explaining to do, and I don't want to hear it.'

Elena now had something else to worry about. Every time the door knocked, she would be a bag of nerves in her own home.

'I've got a meeting at ten o'clock tomorrow with Simon Baker. I'm going to explain everything, get your job back and clear your name.' That had to be bullshit.

'And why would you do that? You seem to get a kick out of making life difficult for me.' She stopped pushing the door but kept a firm grip of it.

'Jasmine's been telling me what a good friend you've been and how much you mean to her. I don't want to jeopardise that, so I need to put things right.'

Anything for Daddy's girl, eh?

'I have a medical condition that makes me behave irrationally sometimes.'

He removed his hand from the door. Here was her chance, but the promise of a hassle-free friendship with Jasmine was tempting.

'I would rather not talk about it on the doorstep.' He looked embarrassed as he glanced around him. 'Just give me half an hour and you'll never see me again.'

Elena would have loved to have slammed the door in his face, but she desperately needed her job back. She had to try and salvage something from this mess.

'Half an hour and that's it!'

Alan gave a humble smile, and she stood to the side to let him in. Elena hoped she wouldn't live to regret it. If he got out of hand, she'd call the police. He wasn't going to mess her about.

'Go straight ahead to the kitchen.'

'Thank you.'

He was carrying a small gift bag and smelt of cigars mixed with a sweet perfume-like smell. She watched him walk into the kitchen as she closed the door. Had she just let in a wolf in sheep's clothing? Too late now.

Right, let's get this over with.

Elena strode confidently into the kitchen, trying to give the impression that she wasn't intimidated by him, although she was.

'I'm making tea, do you want one?' Her tone was borderline offensive.

'Yes, please,' he said meekly as he pulled out a chair and sat at the table.

She could feel his eyes burning into her back as she made the hot drinks. The silence was painfully uncomfortable.

Shit, the knickers. Elena placed his cup on the table. *Where are they?*

'Thank you. I've brought you this from Jasmine's. You left it there on the night of her party.' Alan held up the gold bag that contained the beret and perfume Jasmine had brought from Paris.

'Just leave it on the table.'

That's what the sweet smell was. Had he sprayed himself with her perfume?

Her eyes darted under the table, looking for the G-string. Maybe he was sitting on it.

Alan slurped his tea and gave a satisfied sigh. 'Just right.' Elena was feeling more anxious by the minute. 'Have you lived here long?'

'No.' She didn't want to get into chitchat with him. They were never going to be friends. 'What are you going to say to Simon tomorrow?' She stood with her back against the worktop and gripped her cup, her whole body tense.

'Thanks for the birthday text. It was a very nice surprise.' His face transformed from repentant to the smug egotistical arsehole he really was.

Oh god, what have I done. The echo of her heartbeat deafened her as it banged like a drum in her chest.

'I will tell Mr Baker that . . .' He stood and closed the kitchen door that led to the hallway.

'What are you doing?' she snapped, panic rising.

He turned his head, eyebrows raised innocently. 'There was a draught coming from your hallway. Couldn't you feel it?' He walked around the kitchen table towards Elena.

'I will tell him that you are a friend of my daughter's and that one of my employees had an unhealthy interest in you. And when you spurned their advances, they started a hate campaign against you.' His voice had a melodic ring to it like he was reading a children's story. But this was more of a horror story. He stopped a few feet away from her and placed his cup next to Elena's phone.

Be strong, don't let him terrorize you. 'So you're going to tell more lies then.'

Alan gave a snigger of superiority. 'Elena, do you really think an educated man is going to see me as a monster?' He paused and had the audacity to expect a reply. 'No, so I will save your neck, but everything comes at a price, doesn't it?'

Alarm bells rang. The bastard had tricked his way in. How could she have been so stupid?

'I think it's time you left.' Elena was doing her best not to show the fear or panic which clawed at her.

'That's not half an hour, is it? Silly girl.'

'If you don't get out right now, I'm going to call the police.' She spoke with a confident, determined tone.

Alan tipped his head back and emptied the teacup. He gently placed it down. His eyes punctured her veneer and diverted her stare to the floor. Elena knew she had just given him all the power. He unplugged her phone from the charger and dangled it by his finger and thumb.

'Call them on this? But it's broken.' He let it fall to the floor and stepped on the screen. If she'd been uneasy before, she was terrified now.

She glanced towards the door, and he followed her eyes. '*Don't* run for the door. We haven't finished negotiations yet, have we?'

He walked back around the table and sat in his chair, which blocked her way to the door. He crossed his legs and placed an elbow on the table, very calm and composed, like he was sitting in a street café on a sunny day. The bastard was enjoying every second of this.

'I'll keep my side of the bargain and even throw in a new phone. All you have to do is wear this.'

He dipped his hand into the gift bag, pulled out the beret, and threw it at her. Elena's hand instinctively shot up to catch it. She looked at the hat confused. Alan sat and watched her every move. His index finger ran across his lips backwards and forward like a cricket player running between wickets.

'You want me to wear this?'

'And this.' He pulled out her missing red thong from his jacket pocket and dangled it from his finger. 'Nothing else.'

She felt sick. Her whole body felt drained of all its strength. His stare was like an invisible force preventing her from moving. He had an ominous look in his eyes as he threw the underwear at her.

This was her home, the place she was meant to feel safe and secure, but his vile presence had spread like poison throughout the house, and it was the last place she wanted to be.

Elena frantically ran through her options. The home phone was in the hall, behind Alan, so was the front door. The back door was locked, and the key was in the kitchen drawer amongst the general junk. Her only hope was to talk her way out or do what he asked. The latter wasn't an option, but she didn't want to be the headline on tomorrow's paper. Although it was furthest from the truth, she had to show she wasn't intimidated by him.

'In your dreams maybe. Now get out!' She tried to control her heaving chest, but after she blurted that out, her stress levels were off the scale.

'Wrong answer.' He wasn't going to make it easy.

'If you don't fuck off, I'm going to call the police.' It didn't work the first time, but she didn't know what else to say.

'The phone's in the hall, I believe? Go on then. See how close you get to it.' This was beyond scare tactics.

'Conrad will be here any minute.' The idle threat was unconvincing even to her own ears.

'Nice try, but I think you'd have mentioned that first. Besides, I happen to know he is being the devoted husband at his wife's bedside at the moment.'

How the hell did he know that?

He reached into his inside pocket and pulled out a long thick cigar and a folding knife. 'You don't mind, do you?' he said conceitedly as he opened the knife which had a hole in the handle for the end of the cigar to slot into. He made sure she was watching as he folded the blade back and sliced off the end of the cigar. 'Besides, he'll be joining her soon once a couple of my friends have paid him a visit.'

Was he just trying to scare her, or was this real? Either way, it was working.

'You'll need more than a couple.' She was on eggshells, not wanting to give in but also not wanting to aggravate him.

Alan smirked as he sucked the flame from the lighter into the cigar. 'I know he thinks he's a tough guy, but I don't think he's bulletproof, is he?'

Just when she thought it couldn't get any worse, it increased tenfold.

'Christ, Alan, what have we done to deserve this? Does Jasmine know what you're really like?'

He snatched the cigar from his mouth. 'Don't you fucking dare mention her name!'

His fist came crashing down on the table, his face as red as the cigar tip. Elena jumped. Her feet almost left the floor.

'You are not fit to be in the same room as her, let alone be classed as her friend, you fucking tramp!' His red cheeks shook with rage. She'd touched a nerve.

'You don't realise who you're dealing with. Nobody, fucking nobody, makes a fool of me.'

My god, he really is deluded. 'If you go now and leave me

alone, I promise I won't call the police.'

He held his cigar next to his face and looked at her in astonishment. The heavy grey smoke slowly reached out its choking hands towards her.

'If there's one thing I've learned over the years, it's that money can get you out of anything. I could cut your throat right now and, with one phone call, have this place as clean as a whistle and several alibis while you'd be lying at the bottom of the river, you dumb bitch! It's rats like you that have to do as you're told, and while we're on the subject, get your fucking clothes off and put those on.' He stabbed the cigar towards the hat and underwear she was still clutching.

Was he bluffing about Conrad? Had he shown her the knife to scare her? She wanted to beg him to leave but was sure he'd get a kick out of that.

'I know why you're stalling, you filthy slut. I'll write you a cheque for two grand. That's got to be a lot more than you charge for a fuck. I've got condoms because god knows where you've been.'

From out of the blue, a voice screamed in her head, RUN, RUN!

In sheer desperation, she threw the beret in his face and darted towards the door. Elena didn't even get it open before she was yanked back violently by the hair. She fell flat on her back and banged her head. He leant over her shouting, but she couldn't make out what he was saying. Her senses were in shock from the blow.

Elena's eyes focused, and the double image of him merged into one. Her hearing sharpened to his insults.

'That was very silly, wasn't it? My money not good enough?'

'I don't want your money!' she screamed through her tears.

'Oh, I'm going to get a freebie am I? Well, if you're any good, next time, I'll pay. Now get your clothes off before I lose my patience.' He stood straight and ran his fingers through his hair.

Elena lifted herself up and knelt on her knees. He certainly wasn't bluffing. This was as real as it got.

Alan went to the sink, snuffed his cigar under the tap, and put it back in his pocket. He wasn't going to leave any trace that he'd been there. That was probably why he had bought condoms.

Elena was struggling to keep her composure. He was clearly enjoying watching her fall apart bit by bit. She was out of options and out of time. All that mattered now was getting out of there alive. Alan pulled his chair out, completely blocking the way to the hall.

'Strip and hurry up! I've got a dinner date with my wife. You're going to make me late.'

He really was the most abhorrent, despicable man. No, 'man' wasn't a word he was worthy of, a grotesque monster so warped and twisted it was impossible for a sane person to comprehend his behaviour.

'You can start with your blouse.' His voice was low and full of lust. He obviously sensed victory over her will. 'Get on with it then.'

Elena's fingers trembled and fumbled as she undid the top button hesitantly.

'Keep going.' His impatience and arousal were beginning to show.

Her hands were traitors and went against her every thought and undid every last button. The flimsy white blouse was parted, showing him her cleavage. She kept her eyes to the floor. She didn't want to see his smug face gloating, knowing he had beaten her down.

Alan leaned back in his chair and spread his legs. 'Let me see those tits then,' he demanded.

Elena removed the protective cloth from her body, which left him a clear view.

'That's more like it.' He unzipped his fly, and his hand delved inside.

'Put the beret on.' His voice was completely normal

like he'd asked her what time it was.

Elena hesitated. She was already humiliated beyond words.

'Get it on, slag!' From calm to maniac in a split second, Alan kicked it over to her. He was extremely volatile. She placed it on her head. He had succeeded. Elena felt like a cheap dirty tart. Degraded and ashamed, her head was bowed to the floor.

'Look at me!'

She raised her head.

'Oh yes,' he mumbled. He pulled out his erect penis and began to masturbate.

Elena screwed her eyes tight shut and desperately wished she could go back in time, to slam the front door in his face when she had the chance, but the hands on the clock only turned one way.

'Jeans.' His command almost caused her to vomit.

There was no point fighting. The sooner she did what he asked, the sooner it would be over, or would it? He was a man without limits. Was she going to live to see the day out? Fear had taken hold of her body. She barely had the strength to stand.

'Open your fucking eyes!'

Elena forced her eyes open. Beads of sweat had formed on his brow, and he was panting as he tugged away at himself.

'Come on then, jeans! Get them off, bitch!'

Each insult weakened her a little more and took away another piece of self-respect. Although he was the one in the wrong, she couldn't help feeling incredibly guilty like it was her fault somehow.

Her hands worked on their own and slid down the zipper.

'Turn around,' he hissed.

At least, this way, she wouldn't have to watch at him. She focused on a missing piece of grout in the tiles as she wiggled her tight jeans over her hips. She heard him groan as the denim slipped over her cheeks, exposing her flesh.

'I like black thongs, but I prefer red.' She could hear the repeated slap of his hand. The cigar smoke had stayed to watch the show.

'Put the red one on, and make sure you bend right over when you take those off. Show me the goods and don't make me ask twice, bitch. I'm going to fuck you raw.'

This was unbelievable. She was lower than low. Her whole body was trembling. Palpitations fluttered in her chest as she stood there with her jeans around her ankles and the beret perched on top of her head, like she was in some sort of freak show.

'I said don't make me fucking ask twice, didn't I? Take your bra off so I can suck on those big tits, you dirty slut.'

He wouldn't stop until he had taken every last drop of her self-respect. He wanted her broken beyond repair.

'Do it!' He stamped his foot petulantly.

Elena slipped her thumbs under her thong and began to slide them down when a knock at the door stopped her and sent her heart rate and hopes soaring. She spun around.

Alan jumped up off the stool and stuffed his erection back into his trousers.

'Fucking stay there and don't say a word.' They both stood frozen. Elena prayed whoever it was would keep knocking.

Please, God, let it be Conrad.

Unease was now sitting where smugness once had as Alan flinched at another knock at the door.

'Remember, you're locked in here with me,' he warned her as he opened the door a crack and peered down the hall to the front door.

The door banged louder this time. His frantic face turned to Elena, and he pointed his finger at her warningly.

He was showing his true colours. Anxiety crawled all over his face and riddled his body. He licked his lips like a naughty dog waiting to be punished. Elena held her breath and strained her ears as she listened for the slightest sound. She leaned over and pulled up her jeans. Alan's head shot around to her. He took out his folding knife and waggled it in front of her.

'I'll cut you in half if you make a sound. Got it?'

She could risk calling out for help, but what if they didn't hear her? She'd only get one chance. Elena decided to play it safe and do as she was told.

Conrad wasn't surprised Elena wouldn't answer the door to him. He had treated her badly, but when he'd taken the call about Olivia, he hadn't given himself time to let the shock settle, and after all they'd been through, he owed it to his wife to be there for her when she needed him most.

He banged on the door one last time. There were no lights on. She was probably out. He wandered back to his motorbike and decided to try her mobile.

Conrad stared at the windows as he listened to the dial tone, half expecting to see her shadow trying not to be seen. It went straight to answer phone. He hung up. What he had to say needed to be said face to face. He climbed onto his bike, disappointed he hadn't been able to get things off his chest.

Maybe she was at Jasmine's. He could try there. Conrad put on his helmet and started the bike. Jasmine's was the only other option he'd got, and he wanted to speak to her tonight.

He took the weight of the bike and kicked off the stand. Conrad glanced around to check the road was clear and then looked back towards the house. Something caught his eye and stopped him from pulling away. He removed his helmet to take a proper look.

Was it? He got off the bike and took a step closer. There it was on the brick pillar, a stubbed-out cigar.

Conrad's eyes went from the spent cigar straight to her front door. He strode back up the path and hammered hard with his fist.

'Elena, it's Conrad!' he shouted. Not a sound.

He knelt down and opened the letter box. Through the brushes, he could just see a bead of light from under the kitchen door.

He shot up, took a step back, and looked over his shoulder at the cigar stub. With one mighty kick, the door surrendered and flew open with a great crack. The kitchen door shut too. Conrad marched down the hall with white knuckles. Fists clenched tight, teeth gritted, he threw the kitchen door open.

Elena dropped to her knees, sobbing the moment she saw him, crying 'thank God.' She was visibly shaking. He was wounded at the sight of her like that, and why was she half-naked? Conrad's face hardened as he turned to Alan, who casually had both hands in his jacket pockets.

'What the fuck is going on?'

Alan was quick to answer. 'She called me and invited me over. She said for two grand, I could do whatever I liked. I did try to warn you about this one, Conrad.' Alan chuckled nervously.

Conrad walked over to him and looked at Elena. Black streaks of mascara marked the route of her tears. She was trying to cover her breasts with her shaking hands and was sobbing uncontrollably.

Conrad didn't say a word. He turned back to face Alan, and in the blink of an eye, his head came crashing down onto the bridge of Alan's nose, which burst like a ripe tomato. He crumpled to the ground, wailing in agony. Conrad grabbed the lapels of Alan's jacket and lifted him to his feet.

'You're making a mistake. That slag asked me over.'

Conrad glared into his face as blood pumped from his open wound down into his mouth. 'I warned you about talking like that.' Conrad snorted down his nose like a raging bull. He threw Alan like a rag doll. He crashed against the base units and yelled out in pain as he landed.

Conrad turned to Elena who was screaming in panic. 'Elena, Elena, has he hurt you? Has he touched you?'

She shook her head.

Alan had clambered to his feet. 'You're fucking dead, Conrad. You've gone too far this time. I know people, and you are finished.'

His threats only fuelled Conrad's anger. His rock-hard left fist crashed into Alan's face and threw him across the room. His blood splattered over the floor. Elena screamed for Conrad to stop, but he hadn't finished yet. He would deal with the consequences of his actions later. Right now, this arsehole was going to get what he deserved.

'Get up!'

Alan clawed at the kitchen drawers and managed to get to his feet. He swayed like a Saturday-night drunk, his brain bruised from the colossal force of Conrad's power. He made a desperate grab for some coffee cups that sat on the worktop and threw them at Conrad, who simply turned his back and dropped his head. The porcelain weapons were no match for the wall of muscle and had the same effect as a tennis ball, bouncing off his wide leather-clad back to smash at his feet.

Conrad turned back to Alan, who panted like an old man. He wiped the blood from his face, only to be replaced with a fresh gush.

'Finished? Good. My turn.'

Conrad stepped over to him, and a right fist to the gut folded Alan in half. He coughed and spluttered as he fought for breath.

'Conrad, please, no more. You're going to get into trouble. Call the police, please. Please.'

Elena was scared out of her wits. He felt physical pain at the sight of her like that.

Conrad wiped Alan's blood from his hands onto his jeans, removed his leather jacket, wrapped it around Elena, and held her tight while Alan was on all fours, wheezing like an old dog.

'Thank you,' she chanted between sobs, her head buried in his chest.

'Shh, it's alright now, sweetheart, it's over.' He rocked her gently from side to side.

The kitchen looked like a bomb site: doors hanging off, smashed cups everywhere, and a blood-splattered floor.

Conrad heard the crunch of broken porcelain. He looked over his shoulder to see Alan making a run for it. Before he could turn, Alan rammed into him and managed to get past. Conrad chased after him, but his legs buckled, and he fell to his knees in the hallway, and Alan escaped through the open front door.

He stood up feeling light headed as a warm sensation spread down his right side. He reached his hand around to find a wet patch.

'Oh my god! Conrad, no!' Elena screamed.

He suddenly felt exhausted and dropped back down to his knees.

'He stabbed you! You're bleeding!'

He lay down and knew he was about to pass out. Elena ran back into the kitchen and grabbed her blouse, holding it to his side.

'Conrad, stay with me.'

In a matter of seconds, the white material had turned red.

'Elena,' he whispered, 'call an ambulance, sweetheart.' His eyes closed.

As the red perimeter around him spread, his colour faded. She snatched the home phone from its cradle.

'Conrad, please stay with me.'

She dialled 999, her hands sticky with his blood. This time it was her turn to save him

.

CHAPTER TWENTY-THREE

The blue flashing lights lit up the street and reached into the hall as the ambulance pulled up outside. Elena knelt next to Conrad. She had covered him in a blanket to keep the cool night air at bay. The few minutes it took for the two paramedics to get their kit and enter the house were unbearably slow. She reluctantly stood and moved away from Conrad to let the medics get to work; the knees of her jeans were wet with his blood.

'How long has it been since he was wounded?' asked the older of the two men while the younger man removed the blanket and began to cut away Conrad's T-shirt.

'Ten minutes maybe. I'm not sure. Will he be okay?' She couldn't stop her teeth from chattering, not from the cold, from shock.

'What's his name?'

'Conrad. Conrad Bailey. He is going to be all right, isn't he?'

Worryingly, he ignored her question and joined his partner. Elena was encased in his leather jacket and watched through her fingers as the two men worked on Conrad.

The terror that Alan had put her through was nothing compared to what she now faced, and the sight of this big strong man lying defenceless in a red silhouette was heartbreaking.

He's going to be all right, she repeated over and over to drown out the question that kept trying to butt in: *What if he dies?*

Once again, the hall was filled with a flashing blue glow, and two police officers headed up the path. The middle-aged one acknowledged the paramedics and went straight to Elena, while the other officer remained outside and spoke into the radio attached to his shoulder.

'Hello, miss. I'm Sergeant Jeavons. Is this your property?'

'Er, yes.'

'And was it you who made the 999 call?'

The two paramedics mumbled to each other. She was trying to listen in, but the officers' questions were making it impossible to hear.

'Yes, I did. He is going to be all right, isn't he?' Again, the question fell on deaf ears.

'And your name is?' The officer was a large overweight man and blocked Elena's view.

She tried to go around him, but he held out his arm. 'He's in good hands. Now can you tell me your name, please?'

'Do we really have to do this now?' She was becoming increasingly agitated.

'Let's give them some space, shall we?'

'What?'

The officer ushered her back into the kitchen and closed the door.

'But I want to stay with him.'

'Let them do their work, miss.' He took out a small black notebook and pen.

'White. Elena White,' she snapped as she paced around in circles, her bloodstained hands pressed together against her lips.

'And the injured gentleman's name?'

'Conrad Bailey.'

The officer took a good look around the room. 'There's quite a mess in here. Can you tell me what happened?'

The agitation had turned into anger. Conrad was lying the other side of that door and could be dying for all she knew.

'I understand from your call that there's been a stabbing.'

'What? Fucking hell!' Elena's hands clutched at her hair in desperation. 'Yes, there's been a stabbing! The man I love is lying in my hall bleeding to death while I answer stupid questions that you can ask me anytime. Didn't you fucking notice him as you walked through, Sherlock?'

The officer's deadpan expression remained unchanged, and his eyes, which looked too small for his swollen face, were firmly fixed on Elena.

'I know this is a stressful situation, but please don't swear at me, okay?'

He spoke without emotion or feeling as if this were a training exercise and Elena was the new rookie.

'Now can you tell me what happened here tonight?'

She could hear the clanking and rattling of metal. It was a stretcher. They were taking him away.

'I've got to go with him.' She made a sudden lunge for the door, but he stepped to the side and covered the handle.

'You'll only hinder them, Ms White. I need to ask you a few questions, and then you can go to the hospital.'

The voices in the hallway became distant. Her anguish was unbearable, and the frustration of being held captive in her own home by yet another man was bringing out the worst of her temper.

'No, I'm going now. Get out of the way!'

'Just calm down. Calm down!' His words had the exact

opposite effect.

Her head spun as a complication of emotions ran through her: fear, anger, confusion, panic, all mixed together and each one vying for the domination of her thoughts.

'Did you stab, Mr Bailey?'

'Yes. I mean, no! Of course not. Can't we do this on the way to the hospital for Christ's sake?'

'I'm afraid not. Who stabbed Mr Bailey this evening?' His incessant questions under the circumstances were torturous.

She heard the sound of the ambulance driving away. 'Oh god, I don't believe this. Alan Windsor.'

The officer's pen waggled as it recorded the details. 'And is Mr Windsor a friend of either of yours?'

What if he wakes up and I'm not there? Will he be scared?

'Ms White, is Mr Windsor known to either of you?'

'What? His name's Saunders.'

'But you said it was Windsor?'

I don't even know which hospital they've taken him to.

'Ms White, is it Windsor or Saunders?' His tone was forceful, his body language hinted at his diminishing patience.

'It's Saunders, but he uses Windsor sometimes.'

'And is he a friend?' His eyes switched from his notepad to Elena who was nervously fidgeting with the zip of Conrad's jacket.

'He's my friend's father. Are we done now?'

Every second that ticked by, she thought about how he was. Was he awake? Was he in pain? She desperately wanted to be with him.

'And what was Mr Saunders doing here tonight?'

'Why don't you do your job and go and ask him instead of wasting time chatting to me?'

This was ridiculous. She was being questioned by the police while Alan was running around free as a bird.

'Calm down, Ms White.'

'Stop fucking saying that. What is there to be calm about?'

The other officer joined them. He was a much younger and slimmer man. He didn't introduce himself but glanced around the room.

'Anything?' asked Sergeant Jeavons. The younger officer leant into his superior and mumbled into his ear. Elena caught the word 'neighbour.'

'Is that Mr Bailey's red Ducati motorcycle parked outside?'

More pointless questions. 'Yes.'

'You were seen arguing with a man of Mr Bailey's description at this address a couple of weeks ago. That same man also rode a red motorcycle matching the one outside. Mr Bailey was also seen breaking into the property this evening.' The two men's unsympathetic eyes bore down on her.

'I've had enough. Get out of the way.'

'I'm afraid I haven't finished with my questions.'

'Well, I've finished answering them. Now get out of the bloody way.'

Elena reached around the sergeant to grab the door handle and got into a tussle with him. His partner repeated the two defunct words, 'calm down,' which acted like a red rag to a bull and sent Elena into a frustrated rage.

'Let me go to him, you bastards.'

She pulled at the arm of his jacket and pushed him, which had little effect. The other officer grabbed her around the waist as she hurled abuse at them.

'Elena White,' Sergeant Jeavons's voice boomed above the fracas, 'you are under arrest on suspicion of the attempted murder of Mr Conrad Bailey . . .'

His words pressed the pause button. She couldn't quite believe her ears. The rest of the caution went unheard as her brain struggled to comprehend the first sentence. As Elena stood in a state of shock, the sergeant's partner took the opportunity to handcuff her.

'You've got it all wrong. I haven't done anything.' It sounded like a line from a movie, but what else could she say? It was true.

Sergeant Jeavons led her through the hall, holding her upper arm tightly. The size of the bloodstain on the carpet was a shock to see as it was much larger than she had thought now they'd taken Conrad away.

Please, God, let him be all right.

'I've told you. Alan Windsor's the one you should be looking for.' Her words sounded pitiful. She was broken.

'I thought it was Saunders,' replied the sergeant dryly as he pulled her along.

Elena didn't bother to answer. She hadn't got any fight left.

He led her down the path. The street was littered with neighbours nodding and pointing. She dropped her head in shame and let her hair screen her face. There were two more police cars parked outside. An officer stood guard at the gate while three other officers addressed the audience that had gathered across the street. She was put into the back of one of the cars, and the sight of his bike brought back the tears. She had been terrified earlier that evening, degraded and humiliated, but it paled in comparison with this. Worst of all was not knowing how he was, not being there for him when he needed her most like he had once again. The car pulled away, and as she watched the bike at the side of the road all alone, it was like leaving him all over again.

Without doubt, Conrad had saved her life that night. Elena just prayed it hadn't cost him his.

Elena sat on the blue plastic-covered mattress.

They had taken all of her clothes and given her a one-size-clearly-doesn't-fit-all paper jumpsuit and black pumps to wear. Now she really did feel like a criminal.

She stared at the whitewashed wall. The room smelt of disinfectant and bleach but somehow still felt dirty. A tarnished stainless steel toilet sat in the corner and was the only focal point in the room.

She could hear the echo of the officers laughing and joking. It was just another working day for them, but for Elena, it was the most traumatic day of her life. They had ignored her pleas for news of Conrad's condition, which only added to her anxiety. She had waived her right to legal representation; it felt like an admission of guilt to take it. She was innocent.

All she could do was wait. They had taken her watch, so she had no idea how long she had been in there.

There were voices outside the grey metal door that penned her in. A small letter-box-sized hatch opened in the door and alerted her to the cold blue eyes that observed her. The hatch snapped shut, and a moment later, the welcome sound of the door being unlocked bounced off the walls. The door opened, and the dull echoes became fully formed words.

'Ms White, if you'd like to come with me, please,' stated the officer who stood at the door, his red face clashing with the white hair on his head.

Thank god, I'm finally getting out of here.

She sprang off the bed, eager to leave the oppressive room. 'Any news on Conrad Bailey?'

He ignored her question and held her arm, the same way Sergeant Jeavons had.

I don't think they're letting me go.

'This way, please.'

He led her silently down the corridor, past the row of cell doors and up a small flight of stairs. They entered another corridor through a set of double doors, and he stopped at a solid timber door marked 'Interview Room 3.' He knocked before he opened it and took her into a bare square room with a single window, which was blanked off with pale green vertical blinds.

Two men in their mid-forties sat at an oblong table against the wall under the window. The dark blue carpet and florescent strip light gave the room a depressing feeling, much like the cell. The only thing missing was the stainless steel toilet.

'Have a seat, Ms White. Jim, would you mind getting Ms White a cup of tea?' he asked her escort.

'No.' He sighed. His red face didn't mirror his answer. 'Sugar?' he asked begrudgingly.

'Two, please.' Her thankful smile was wasted on him.

'I'm Detective Summers, and this is Detective Cartwright.'

The two men looked more like office workers in their white and pale blue tieless shirts. Both men bore the signs of working long nights. Puffy red eyes, swollen faces, and bellies hinted at a diet of convenience food. Middle age had got a firm grip on the two men.

Detective Summers explained that it would be a recorded interview and asked her once again if she wanted legal representation, which she declined.

There was a knock at the door, and the red-faced officer entered with her tea. She thanked him as he placed it on the table and left without saying a word.

The interview began with Summers reading the police caution to her. Detective Cartwright had yet to speak and looked as though all his attention was being channelled into keeping himself awake. Summers asked her to tell them what had happened that night.

Elena wanted to get everything out in the open and started from when she had first bumped into Jasmine. The two men listened to the whole story like kids at story time. Elena left no detail out and was sure that once she had finished, they would let her go and take her straight to Conrad.

Satisfied that she had covered everything, she took a sip of her tea which was cold, had no sugar, and was almost the same colour as the polystyrene cup.

Both men sat in silence. Summers leaned back in his chair and folded his arms.

'I think you've been reading too many romantic novels, Ms White. It's all a bit far-fetched, isn't it?'

Elena held her head in her hands, she was weary with frustration. 'No, it's all true, every single word.'

'We've been in touch with Mrs Saunders. She said her husband has been with her all evening.'

'But that's not true. Was it Katherine Saunders you spoke to?'

'Yes, it was.'

Their tired eyes rested on her, and it felt like a whole theatre full of people was staring. Why would she say such a thing? Or were they playing games?

'So Alan was there when you spoke to her?'

'No, he wasn't.'

Elena felt like screaming. 'It's not his bloody wife you need to talk to, is it?' She hid her hands under the table, unable to stop them shaking.

Summers lent forward and rested his arms on the table. 'You were seen screaming at Mr Bailey outside your house only two weeks ago. You knew he was a married man, and he had called tonight to tell you to leave him alone. You slammed the door in his face—'

'No!'

'He lost his temper and kicked the door in, didn't he? He was seen kicking the door down.'

'Yes, but—'

'Then you argued, and he told you he never wanted to see you again. You felt used, hurt, and you wanted to hurt him, so you took a knife from the kitchen and stabbed him in the back as he walked away.'

'No, that's—'

'Mr Saunders was the first scapegoat you could think of.' He wasn't giving her chance to defend herself. 'You were probably jealous of his wealth. Maybe you even tried it on with him? You seem to have a thing for wealthy married men.'

Summers had his head cocked to one side and nibbled

on his thumb nail. Was he trying to provoke her?

Elena's throat was dry, and her head felt like it had been hit with a sledgehammer. It looked like she was going to need that solicitor after all.

'Mr Bailey has been seriously wounded. If he dies, you'll be facing a murder charge. Do you understand what that means?'

How could they be so incompetent? Or did Alan really have that sort of power? He'd said money could solve any problem. She held back her paranoia and tried to keep her composure.

'Can you please tell me how he is?'

'Now we've mentioned murder charge, you want to know how he is.'

Even the smallest weakest animal will attack when pushed to a certain point. He had just shoved Elena to hers.

'I've been asking about him constantly since I got here, dickhead.'

Cartwright perked up a little.

'I'm not saying another word to you, not because I'm worried about getting my story mixed up, because it's not a story, it's fact. Now take me back to my cell, and when you fuckwits have found that scum Alan Saunders, you can come and apologise to me. Interview terminated.'

The two men looked at each other with blank expressions. Elena wasn't taking any more shit. The only decent man she had met in years was fighting for his life somewhere, and she wanted to get out and be by his side. Fuck everyone and everything else. There was no point being polite, reasonable, or helpful. Where had that got her?

The red-faced white-haired officer returned to take her back to the cell. He reached for her arm.

'Don't touch me! Just show me the way. I'm not going to kick off.'

She marched out of the room, and Jim hurried behind

her, a little more red-faced than before. The cell door opened, and she marched in.

'Just a minute!' she called out before he could close the door. 'Could I have a proper cup of tea this time? Hot with two sugars. And if Dumb and Dumber want to question me again, I want a solicitor present. That's all, thanks.' It seemed that being obstinate worked, as she got her tea as requested.

Elena sat on the bed and waited for her apology. She waited and waited all night long until, exhausted with worry and stress, she fell asleep.

CHAPTER TWENTY FOUR

The mechanical clank of the lock woke her.

'Any news?' she mumbled as she came to her senses.

'Ms White, you're free to go.'

Elena peeled her face from the plastic bed. Her head throbbed like she'd been hanging upside down all night. Her eyes fluttered as they focused on the tall figure that had delivered the welcome news.

'If you'd like to follow me, you can collect your things from the desk.'

'Is there any news on Conrad Bailey?' She brushed her tangled hair from her face.

'I'm sorry I can't answer that question. I've only just started my shift. The desk sergeant should be able to help.'

Elena shot off the bed and hurried out. Despite his long legs, the tall officer walked at a very slow pace, and she could feel her patience wearing already.

The desk sergeant was a painfully thin man whose glasses where so thick they distorted his eyes. He placed a plastic bag that contained her things onto the desk and asked her to check and sign.

'Can you please tell me if there is any news on Conrad

Bailey? He was stabbed at my home last night.'

He pushed his heavy glasses back up his bony nose. 'One thing at a time.'

Her fury hadn't been doused overnight. 'I don't care about the bloody jacket and watch, for Christ's sake. Just tell me which hospital he's at. Can you do that?'

His tongue ran over his teeth like he was expecting a punch to be thrown while his eyebrows took cover behind his glasses. 'I'll go and ask.'

Elena tapped her fingers on the desk impatiently. After a short while, he returned.

'They took him to King's College Hospital.'

She grabbed the plastic bag and headed for the exit.

'You haven't signed for those,' he called out to her.

'Piss off,' she mumbled under her breath as she shoved the door open.

Elena walked clear of the police station and managed to find a public toilet. She ripped open the bag, took out her screwed-up £20, and was able to stomach the putrid smell long enough to change into her own clothes. She put on Conrad's jacket and headed back into the clean air. She tried to hail a cab, but unsurprisingly, no one would stop. She looked like a homeless junky: bloodstained jeans, huge man's leather jacket, wild matted hair, and a mascara-stained face. After several attempts, she managed to get a passer-by to stop and give her directions to the nearest bus that would take her to the hospital.

Elena ignored the rude stares and took her seat on the bus. The journey was painfully slow. The bus seemed to stop every two minutes, but a least she was on her way to him. She thought about Jasmine. This was going to be one hell of a bombshell. Elena wasn't looking forward to that conversation. She pushed it all to the back of her mind. Conrad was her main concern right now.

Finally, the bus arrived at the hospital. She followed the signs for Accident and Emergency and ran all the way. The receptionist was obviously used to seeing much worse sights and ignored Elena's dishevelled appearance. Before she got there, Elena was worried that the desk sergeant might have sent her to the wrong hospital, but they had got one thing right. He was on the Mary Ray ward, first floor, Cheyne Wing.

Elena took the lift and ran down the corridor. She arrived at the entrance doors to the ward and took several deep breaths to calm her nerves and her heart rate.

Please let him be okay.

She pressed the intercom. There was no answer, but a high-pitched beep indicated the lock had been released. She entered into the warm thick atmosphere. The smell reminded her of the dentist.

He's probably sitting up in bed with a couple of nurses fussing over him. Elena smiled to herself and hoped that's what she'd find.

The tears began to well at the anticipation of seeing him. Her head turned left to right as she moved along the ward with her eyes jumping from bed to bed. There was no one at the desk to ask.

There was a mixture of patients, from the very old and feeble to the young and woeful. She tried not to let her eyes linger on the distressing sights.

She got to the last bay: four of the six beds were occupied. The name 'John Marsh' was scrawled on the white board above the unmade bed. Elena's eyes shot over to the last bed in the right-hand corner. Conrad Bailey was written above it. Her heart stopped at the sight of the empty stripped bed.

Where was he?

Alarm bells rang, and she looked around for help. A young black nurse headed towards her with a concerned look on her face.

'Is everything all right? Can I help you?

'I'm looking for Conrad Bailey.'

Elena noticed that the concerned look remained firmly fixed to the nurse's face.

'I'm sorry. I'm afraid he's gone.'

Her words struck Elena with the impact of a bullet to the heart and took her breath. She turned her back to the nurse and gazed at the bed. The tears fell for him and for herself. She had missed the chance to say goodbye, to tell him she loved him. Guilt crept alongside sorrow. She felt like it was her fault. If only she had slammed the door in Alan's face, none of this would have happened. That thought was going to haunt her forever.

Had he been scared? Was he alone? He must have wondered where I was. Had he asked for me?

Elena closed her eyes and began to sway. She felt the nurse's arms around her.

'Come on, let's get you sat down.'

She sat Elena in the chair next to the empty bed and pulled the curtain around them.

'Are you okay? Do you need medical attention?'

Elena shook her head. Tears dripped from her jaw and trickled down the black leather.

'Is that blood on your jeans?'

She nodded.

'I think we need to get you looked at.'

'It's not my blood. I wish it were.'

'Are you taking any medication at the moment?'

'No, not yet.' She knew her appearance was making the nurse uneasy. 'I can't believe he's gone,' she whispered to herself.

'No, neither can I. We did try to tell him, but he wouldn't listen.'

Elena's eyes locked onto the nurse's. 'What do you mean he wouldn't listen?'

'Well, he's not in any fit state to be leaving the hospital, but once the police had finished speaking to him, he was adamant that he was going.'

Elena sprang out of the chair and grabbed her by the forearms, making her flinch nervously.

'He's not dead?'

'No, no! He signed himself out against—'

Before she could say any more, Elena had thrown her arms around her. 'Thank you!' she sobbed into her neck.

The grief had dragged her down and down like being underwater; the pressure had crushed every part of her body. Now she had risen back to the surface and could breathe again. The feeling was exhilarating, energising.

Elena released the poor nurse from her bear hug and wiped her eyes.

'Are you sure you're all right?'

'I've never felt better,' she beamed. 'I've looked better though.'

The nurse smiled.

'How is he?'

'He's okay, but he should still be in here resting.'

'Did he say where he was going?'

'No, he said he'd got something he needed to take care of, and it couldn't wait.'

Elena was buzzing with excitement and thanked the nurse profusely before she hurried back down to the ground floor. She got an elastic band from reception to tie her untamed hair back and went to the ladies to wash her face. She still looked a mess, but it was a slight improvement.

There was a good supply of taxis outside, and she got straight into the back of one and gave her address with an authoritative tone. Would she be allowed back into her home? She couldn't go to her mother's, not like this. Conrad's number was in her phone, which Alan had kindly stepped on, so she couldn't ring him, and he couldn't ring her.

Where was he going? What was so urgent? Elena was longed to see him, and she was jumping with nervous excitement.

The taxi dropped her off outside her house. The red Ducati was still there guard-like. It was a reassuring sight. A police officer was just leaving the house and attempting to close the broken front door. Elena explained who she was, and after a few questions and a private call on his radio, he said that they had all the evidence they needed, and she was allowed in. He kindly offered to stay with her for a while to make sure she was okay. Declining his offer, she asked if Alan had been arrested. The officer ran through their lines of inquiry and the various steps they would take, but the short answer was 'no.'

The police car drove away. Elena turned to face the hall. The red bloodstain on the carpet had turned brown, and from the span of it, she was amazed Conrad had survived. But he had, thank god, and that bastard's reign of terror was over. He was the one who was running scared now.

She walked into the kitchen and was shocked at the sight of it, even though she had been present at the time of its destruction. It was like a dream, well, a nightmare. It wasn't her home anymore, it was a crime scene. How could she stay here after all that had happened?

The problem was they couldn't call each other. He didn't know where her mother lived, and she didn't know his address, having only been there once. This was the only place he knew where to find her, and she was going to wait for him, no matter what.

CHAPTER TWENTY FIVE

It was almost dark when Conrad arrived at St Catherine's Docks. He knew that unless Alan's wife or daughter had told the police about his precious boat, they wouldn't have been there.

It was a long shot but worth a try. He hadn't told the police because he wanted to see him one last time, to watch him panic and squirm, because there was no way out of this one. Then he was going to pay Alan back for almost taking his life. Conrad intended to leave him semiconscious, so he could hear his rights being read to him once he had called the police.

He had never been on Alan's boat, but he knew where to find it. Just about everyone who came into contact with Alan got to see the selection of photos of his boat that he had on his phone. He was always boasting that he had pride of place at the docks and his was most powerful boat there.

Every step Conrad took hurt. His whole right side throbbed with pain. He was feeling tired now and a bit shaky. There was no way he could lie in a hospital bed, knowing this maniac was still out there. He reached under his shirt. The tips of his fingers were light red. His wound had bled through, and the dressing needed to be changed, but it would have to wait.

The water was perfectly calm like Conrad's appearance, but below the surface, the anger was swelling like a tidal wave that would destroy anything in its path. The image of Elena half-naked, trembling, and scared out of her wits played over and over in his mind. He had been calling her all day and went straight to her house once he had left the hospital, but the young officer guarding the front door didn't know anything. Conrad presumed she would have gone to her mother's.

There it was, a long sleek white shark-like boat with a cold black wrap around windscreen. Conrad headed down the ramp and onto the floating walkway. He came alongside the boat and listened. So long as Alan was on his own, Conrad would be okay, but if he had hired help with him, he'd be in trouble. Making his way to the rear of the boat, he could just about hear classical music. Conrad hesitated. He had no idea what he was walking into.

Fuck it.

He stepped onto the swim deck and could see a light on through the smoked glass doors of the main deck, which he moved up to quietly. He pulled the door. It wasn't locked and slid silently across. There was a strong smell of cigars and leather as he stepped into kitchen area. No sign of him. Maybe he was below deck.

Conrad walked towards the helm. To the left was a highly polished square table surrounded on three sides by an angular seating area. An empty bottle of whisky sat on the edge of the table. The entrance to the lower deck was next to the helm. He'd probably got pissed and fallen asleep on the bed.

Conrad made his way silently towards the front of the boat and stopped. He could see Alan's bare feet under the executive-style captain's chair. A half-empty glass of whisky sat in the cup holder of the high-tech dashboard.

Alan was slumped down in the chair fast asleep, with his head resting on his shoulder.

Conrad had made a real mess of his face. He was almost unrecognisable. His bottom lip was twice its normal size, a deep black gash ran across the bridge of his swollen nose, and both eyes bulged and displayed a combination of colours that any tropical fish would be proud of. Deep purple and several shades of red seeped into the mustard yellow around his eyes, which looked like a masquerade mask. Conrad had gone there with the intention of giving him another good beating, but as he looked at his battered face, he felt like he'd done a pretty good job first time around.

A sharp pain shot through his wound and made him wince, like his body was reminding him of what Alan had done to him.

How should I wake Sleeping Beauty? Whisky bottle smashed over the head?

That might have had the opposite effect from waking him up. Conrad picked it up anyway just in case Alan made a lunge for him.

'Wake up, shithead!' he roared in his ear.

No response. That must have been strong whisky.

Conrad kicked the side of the chair much to his body's disapproval. It spun around, and something bounced onto the floor. Alan faced him. His head sagged onto his chest.

Conrad picked up the small container, an empty medication bottle. He held his fingers against Alan's cold neck.

He was dead.

Conrad turned the chair back to its original position, put the whisky bottle back onto the table, and cleaned it with his shirt then did the same with the pill bottle and dropped it in Alan's lap.

He took one last look at him. 'You always were a bad loser, Alan.' He closed the sliding door and wiped the handle as he left.

Fatigue was taking its toll. He was weak and needed to rest. He took out his phone to call the police as he walked up the ramp back to street level. He was going to say he had just remembered that Alan had a boat moored at St Catherine's Docks. Conrad didn't want Alan's wife or daughter to find him like that, for their sakes.

An attractive dark-haired woman was heading towards him. She was on the phone and was walking briskly. He'd seen her before somewhere. He hung up before the call was answered.

Shit, Jasmine.

Conrad spun around, pulled up the collar on his jacket, ducked his head down, and walked casually in the opposite direction. He glanced over his shoulder and caught a glimpse of her heading down the ramp. He quickened his pace to get back to his car. There was no point calling the police now. Poor girl.

Elena sat in the lounge with the curtains closed; the front door had been crudely secured by a local emergency call-out company she had found on Google. She couldn't face the job of clearing the war zone that was her kitchen, so she had transported the essentials. The kettle was plugged in next to the DVD player; tea, sugar, and milk sat on the TV stand. She had placed a blanket over the bloodstain in the hall.

A shovel from the garden shed rested against the armchair where she sat. It was Elena's idea of protection. She wasn't sure what to do with it but felt better with it next to her, ready for action.

All the lights were on in the house like a beacon. She wanted to make sure that if Conrad came, he would know she was in. Every car or strange noise made her jump up and sneak a look between the curtains. The police were no doubt sick of her calls to ask if Alan had been arrested or if Conrad had spoken to them, as they had virtually told her 'Don't call us, we'll call you.'

The TV was on and played out its sitcom to an uninterested viewer. Elena sat and thought things over, and the problems started to stack up once again: no job; a reputation in tatters; no money, she certainly couldn't afford to pay tradesmen's rates to fix the house; worst of all, possibly no Conrad, as he had fled to his wife's aid. But he had come back, thank god. It was the thought of *why* he had come back that made her nervous.

Elena heard a car stop outside. She was beginning to tire of jumping, so she stayed in her chair. Then she heard footsteps up the path. She shot up and grabbed the shovel in a panic.

The owner of the footsteps knocked on the door. Her heart thumped. Poking her head into the hallway, she stared hard at the patched-up front door like she had X-ray vision. Another knock, this time more insistent.

'Who is it?' She couldn't hide the apprehension in her voice.

'It's Conrad.' Those were the two most wonderful words she had ever heard.

The shovel was tossed back into the lounge, and she ran to the door. Her hands shook as she unbolted it and turned the key in the padlock. Finally, Elena flung the door open, jumped at Conrad, holding on to him for all she was worth.

'I never thought I'd see you again.'

The pressure had built to a level even she was unaware of, and the emotion spilled over. His strong arms enveloped her, and once again, she felt safe. The stress and the worry faded away like condensation on a window.

'It's all right, sweetheart. Shh, I'm fine.'

She slid her arms around his waist, and he flinched with a hiss.

'I'm sorry, Conrad. I forgot.' Elena pulled back and looked up at his face. He was pale and drawn. 'Come on, let's get you sat down.'

'Yeah, sounds good.'

She led him by the hand to the lounge. He sat down in the armchair like a man twice his age. Conrad looked around the room and noticed the kettle and tea bags next to the TV, the duvet and pillow on the lounge suite, a half-eaten sandwich, and the shovel on the floor.

'Elena, what have you been doing?'

She knelt down next to him. Her big green eyes drank in his handsome face and satisfied her addiction.

'I've been waiting for you.' She spoke with the innocence of a child.

His lips squeezed tight against each other, and a heartfelt smile spanned his tired face. His eyes glistened with tears as he swallowed hard and paused for a moment.

'You're lovely, aren't you?'

Elena hadn't got the same control over her emotions. She was touched by his sincere words, and whatever he told her tonight, she was going to tell him that she loved him. Elena loved him in a way that she didn't think was possible.

'And why aren't you still in hospital, mister?' She did her best to stop the tears.

'Oh, you know. I had to get milk and stamps.'

She held his hand tightly with both of hers and shook her head with a smile. Elena loved his sense of humour, but he also used it to avoid serious conversation.

'Conrad, you don't look well. I think you need to go back to the hospital.'

His face was grey and his eyes dull. 'Can I get a coffee first? Wake me up a little.'

'Of course.' She didn't want to leave his side, not even to get the coffee from the kitchen.

'I thought you'd be at your mother's. I came straight here when I left the hospital, but the young copper on the door said he didn't know where you were.'

'Didn't they tell you?'

'Tell me what?' His brows knitted together.

She hesitated for a moment. 'They arrested me for

attempted murder.'

Elena wished she hadn't told him. His placid face hardened as he sat up from his relaxed position.

'Tell me that's a joke, please?'

'No, I'm afraid not.'

Elena didn't want him upset in his condition. She told him it was her fault for getting abusive when they didn't let her go in the ambulance with him, and once at the station, they gave her a slap on the wrist and let her go.

'Don't worry about it.' She flopped her hand dismissively. She knew he didn't believe the last part.

'I'll go and make you that coffee,' she chirped, trying to sound carefree. He seemed to let it go.

'Elena . . .'

She stopped in the doorway and turned to face him.

'It's going to be all right. You don't have to worry anymore.'

She nodded silently. Her eyes dropped to the floor in doubt. The trouble was there was so much to worry about. She wanted to say so many things, but he clearly wasn't well. Was it the right time?

'What's wrong?'

She shrugged, knowing the emotion would strangle the words.

'Come here, sweetheart.'

She knelt beside him once again. His eyes implored her to tell him what was on her mind.

'I was just thinking about all the mess, and when they catch Alan, he's going to drag my name through the mud. I won't be able to show my face around here.'

'Elena, that's not going to happen.'

'Oh, it will. He'll have great pleasure telling the police I'm a cheap whore, the bastard.'

Conrad took her hand away from her forehead and held it tenderly. 'It's over, sweetheart. Alan's dead.'

'What?' Her whole body jumped to attention. 'How do you know?'

'After I came here, I went home to clean myself up. Then I made a few phone calls, tried to find out where he might be hiding. It turns out Alan was a lot more unsavoury than I ever knew.'

That didn't surprise her after what she experienced.

'Anyway, I went to all the places I was told he may be: clubs, ex-mistresses. Nothing. The last place I went to was his boat, although I didn't think he would be there. But he was. He'd taken an overdose.'

'Oh my god!' Her hands sprang up to cover her mouth. Shock mixed with relief in almost equal measure, and then her thoughts turned to Jasmine. She would be absolutely devastated.

She didn't think it was possible to cry anymore, but the tears fell, for herself and for Jasmine too. Her father was dead, and surely, it was the death of their friendship also.

'Don't cry, sweetheart, you've got nothing to worry about now. It's over.'

She looked at his obscured face through the tears. 'Don't I? What about us? Are we over too?' Her thoughts had turned into words unintentionally and marched out bravely.

A slight flush of colour came to Conrad's face, his jaw clamped shut. The silence was unnerving, and she hoped it wasn't an answer.

'Your wife needs you now, I understand. It's fine, it's fine. I'm fine,' Elena blurted out.

The silence was suffocating. She tucked her hair behind her ear and picked fluff that wasn't there from the arm of the chair.

Conrad reached into his inside pocket and took out a tartan envelope and handed it to her. 'That's for you.'

She looked at it, totally confused.

'Open it.'

Elena tore open the paper to find a white card with an artist's impression of Loch Lomond. There was a message written on the card that said, *If you liked that, you'll love this.*

She glanced up at him. He looked anxious. She opened the card, and staring at her was a British Airways first-class ticket to New Zealand.

'Come with me, Elena. I've sold my business, everything.'

She had to reread the ticket to make sure it was her name on it.

'I've been planning this for a long time. I'd childishly called it my "big plan." It was all going well until you came along and threw a spanner in the works. I tried to keep away but couldn't, and I'm glad I didn't.'

Elena flicked through the images of their time together in her mind like pages in a book. It all started to make sense: Conrad's quiet mood when they'd left Jock's place and his secretive chat with the old man, he had gone there to say goodbye; at the gym with Sheldon also, when he'd said he would take him up on his offer, it was New Zealand, not London, they were talking about; the one-way conversation with Maggie at the hotel. She had finally got all the pieces of the jigsaw.

'I intended to give that to you after your spa day at the hotel, but it didn't go according to plan.'

Elena was overwhelmed by it all and hadn't said a word. She was trying to take in the sublime situation.

'I should never have left you at the loch, but when I heard about Olivia . . . I panicked. I didn't give myself a chance to think, and by the time I was on the plane home, it was too late.'

'And what if your wife does something like that again?' It's not what she wanted to say. Elena wanted to cover him with kisses, but it was a question she needed an answer to.

'A part of me will always care for Olivia.' He hesitated. The anxiety hadn't left his face. 'But my love died the day I found out about the affair she'd been having with my brother.'

She hadn't expected to hear that. He looked

embarrassed as his hand stroked his stubble. It had obviously taken a lot for him to confide in her.

'My brother was always competitive. I think he saw me more as a rival. As the business grew, so did the envy, and because he worked for me, he knew where I was, when I was in meetings, what time I'd be home.'

He looked vulnerable. It had left its mark on him. Even winners lost sometimes.

'The ironic thing was I thought he had turned over a new leaf, he made more of an effort and we were getting on better than ever. But all the time, he was revelling in the fact that he was making a fool of me, and they did so for at least six months.'

How could anybody be so cruel to such an honourable, decent man?

'I'm sorry, Conrad.'

He wasn't a man that sought pity. His head snapped back up to its usual proud position, and determination burned in his eyes.

'I'm not, not now. Everything happens for a reason, don't you think?'

Elena had always believed in fate, although the last few weeks had tested that belief to the limit. It had been a very bumpy journey, but she had finally reached her destination, and in that moment, she knew they were meant to be together.

'Elena, you haven't given me an answer.'

Her eyes rose to meet his. She couldn't believe there was a hint of doubt in his voice.

'Conrad, I would follow you to the end of the earth.' She leaned over and kissed his lips that felt so right on hers.

'You do know I'm never letting you out of my sight,' he said.

She nodded, her nose rubbing his.

'And you do know that . . . I love you, Elena White, like I have never loved anyone before.'

Could this really be happening? She held his face with both hands. God, she wanted to tell him so much.

'Conrad, I can't put into words what you mean to me. Love just doesn't cover it. I'd die without you.'

He pulled her close to him, their cheeks caressed. 'Well, you won't have to,' he whispered, his warm breath delivered the divine words. 'Me and you are going to live a long, happy life together, sweetheart.'

Love and honesty emanated from him, and all her dreams came true in that moment. He wanted her; he loved her. All the doubt and uncertainty that had plagued her had vanquished.

'What are you thinking?' he asked, their faces inches apart.

'A million things. I don't know where to begin. I love you, Conrad Bailey, that's number one. I'll start there.'

He gently ran his fingers over her soft lips. 'You're going to love New Zealand. It's one of the most beautiful countries I've ever been to: snowcapped mountains, breathtaking serene lakes, clear blue ocean, with white sandy beaches, waterfalls that dwarf most skyscrapers.' His face was full of excitement and enthusiasm. 'It's one great big playground, and the jewel in the crown is the people, so friendly and welcoming, down-to-earth.'

'If you love it, then I'm sure I will too.' She hadn't thought about it much. His *I love you was* still playing on repeat in her head.

'If you get homesick or you want to come back to England at any time, you can.'

'And what about you?'

'Me? I'll be right by your side, no matter what.'

Did he know the impact his words had on her? Just a few hours ago, she had been at her lowest point, and now she was deliriously happy, excited, nervous, and in love, all rolled into a ball that bounced around her body like a pinball machine, lighting her up.

'What more does a man have to do around here to get

a coffee?' He winked.

Elena shook her head. 'I'm sorry, I was daydreaming.' It wasn't a dream anymore.

She kissed him and got up. Conrad pulled himself out of the chair with a grunt.

'Don't get up, stay there and rest.'

'Don't worry, matron, I'm fine.' He gave her a cheeky smile.

Conrad followed her and glanced at the blanket covering his bloodstain as he entered the kitchen. Elena reached on tiptoes to the top cupboard and grabbed the coffee jar while Conrad surveyed the damage: blood splattered walls and floor, broken cups and plates strewn all over the place.

Wow, you really are a messy cook, aren't you?'

She smiled and noticed his light-hearted expression slip away as he looked around at the damage. 'I couldn't face clearing it yet. Sorry.'

'Don't apologise, it's not your mess, sweetheart.' He took out his phone. 'Do you have anything of sentimental value here?'

'Er, only the things you've brought me really.' *What a strange question.*

He dialled a number on his phone. 'Pack your clothes and whatever else you want to bring. You're not coming back here again. I'm taking you home.'

Elena was taken aback. He certainly knew how to bowl her over, but she couldn't deny the relief. The house had become a museum of horrors for her.

'I can't leave it like this.'

He held the phone to his ear. 'Yes, you can, sweetheart. You're not touching a thing—Isabelle, sorry to disturb you, I need a few urgent jobs taken care of tomorrow.'

Surely, he's not going to ask Mary Poppins to clean up this mess?

'Can you call Ian Duffey and tell him I need a new door and frame fitted at Elena's? Not a quote, I want it done straight away. Also, I need him to fix the kitchen unit doors. If they're beyond repair, he's to fit a new kitchen that matches the existing.' Conrad went into the hall and lifted the blanket with his foot. 'I need a new carpet fitted in the hallway and a team of cleaners to clear the kitchen. One last thing, can you get the Ducati picked up from Elena's?'

She stood in the middle of what looked like, and very nearly was, a murder scene while he took care of her once again.

'Oh, and, Isabelle, thank you . . . Yes, I do. The last twelve months, you've gone above and beyond, I really do appreciate it . . . Have a good evening . . . I will . . . I'll call you tomorrow . . . Bye.'

He put the phone back in his pocket and walked over to Elena who was holding the coffee jar, her eyes glazed with tears. He kissed her on the head, and his loving arms held her.

'You don't have to do that.'

He took the jar from her. 'I want to. The sight of you standing in this place makes my stomach churn. You deserve better, and I'm going to make sure you get it. I'll make the coffee while you go and pack.'

She ran her hand down his face. 'You're a good man, Conrad Bailey.'

He gently took her hand and kissed it. 'Come on. Let's get you out of here.'

Elena insisted on making his drink and sat him back in the lounge while she ran around upstairs like a tornado.

With Conrad's car full, Elena helped him into the passenger seat of his Range Rover. She had convinced him to let her drive as he was so tired. The first stop was the hospital. She wanted him to see a doctor to make sure he was okay. She ordered him to recline his seat and get some rest. Elena didn't even take a second glance at the house as she drove them away. Everything that mattered in her life was sitting right beside her.

CHAPTER TWENTY SIX

The next week was bliss. Elena fussed over him and made sure he was on the road to recovery. They spent lazy mornings in bed and had long late-night talks about their trip like two school kids going on their first holiday.

Conrad fired her excitement with his descriptions of all the wonderful places they would visit. The South Island would be their first port of call. He described in great detail places she had never heard of: Queenstown, Lake Wanaka, and the 'truly awesome,' as he described it, Milford Sound.

They would follow the rugged west coast and then cross over to the North Island and more names that painted magical images: Taupo, the Coromandel Peninsula, the Bay of Islands . . . The list went on. The passion and love he felt for the country were evident.

Elena was in awe of him and the whole situation. The first few mornings, she had woken in a panic, thinking it was all a dream. But it wasn't, and every morning, his strong arm held her close.

Everything was taken care of. Isabelle would be continuing to work for Conrad for another twelve months.

She was to oversee the finalities of the gym empire and was to arrange the storage of the contents of his home, along with the cars and bikes, until further notice. All they had to do was pack. Mary Poppins was on hand to take care of everything else.

Conrad had already rented a house for them in Auckland, which would be waiting for them once they had finished their three-month tour. If everything went well and they were both happy, he was considering launching a chain of fitness centres there as the 'Kiwis are fitness mad,' as he put it. He'd got it all mapped out.

Elena lay on Conrad's chest as they gazed at the night sky in the orangery. Soft music played, and they were too relaxed to refill their empty wine glasses. Conrad's fingers sailed through her hair. The pressure on her scalp rendered her limbs useless.

'Mmm, you know how to press all the right buttons, don't you?' she purred.

'I love to press your buttons . . . and lick them.' His voice was low and breathy.

'You are awful,' she mumbled, barely conscious. She was so relaxed. 'But I do like you.' Her head rocked as his chest shook with suppressed laughter.

'You make me laugh, don't you? You make me smile.'

Elena nodded dreamily and snuggled into his body.

'Tomorrow afternoon, we'll be on a big bird leaving the winter behind us. I can't wait for you to see it all.'

She lifted her head and looked up into his eyes. 'And I can't wait for you to show it to me.'

He screwed up his eyes suspiciously. 'And what about New Zealand?'

'You know what I mean, Mr Naughty.' She smiled to herself.

'Elena.'

'Mm?'

'Are you going to call Jasmine before we go?'

It had been bothering her all week. 'I don't know. What

do I say? I don't think she'll want to hear from me.'

'You've got nothing to feel guilty about.'

'I know. Maybe I'll write her a letter.' Elena didn't want to think about it. She pulled herself up and rubbed his chest. 'It's getting late. Shall we go to bed, my wounded soldier?'

'Yes. Carry me?' he whimpered with his arms held out.

'I'll get the stretcher, shall I?'

She grabbed his hands and helped pull him up. His injury was healing well, and he'd had the all-clear to fly.

'You do know what they do for wounded soldiers?' His hands slid over the contours of her hips.

'No, what do they do?' Her body reacted willingly to his lips on her neck.

'They raise the flagpole in honour of them.'

Her nose rested on his chin as she tried to conceal her silly grin. 'Do they really? Well, we'd better go and raise your flag pole then, hadn't we?' She arched her back to look at him with her eyebrows held high.

'Yes, I concur. I think it's only right that we do. The higher, the better.' He had taken on a serious frown and nodded like a back bencher.

Elena took him by the hand. 'Follow me then, soldier.'

He was her hero. Conrad had saved her in more ways than he knew. The darkness followed them as the lights went off, allowing the night to occupy the house once more.

Elena didn't have an appetite for breakfast. She was full of nervous excitement. Conrad munched on his toast as he paraded around the kitchen in tight white briefs and a clingy blue T-shirt. His hair was out-of-bed ruffled, and the shadow of his stubble highlighted his strong jawline.

How does he look so damn gorgeous first thing in the morning?

He shuffled through the morning's post like a pack of cards. 'There's one here for you, Elena.'

Mary Poppins had thought of everything as usual and

had arranged for Elena's post to be sent to Conrad's house. He placed the letter onto the breakfast bar where she sat. The bank's logo was printed in the right-hand corner, and Elena's first thought was to bin it. Today was the beginning of a new life. She didn't want anything to spoil it.

'Aren't you going to open it?' he asked as he poured himself another coffee from the cafetière.

'I don't really care what they want.'

She sipped her tea petulantly and fiddled with the back of her hair. As was usually the case, curiosity was the victor, and Elena tore open the envelope. She sat quiet as a mouse and read the letter to herself.

Conrad leaned over the breakfast bar on his forearms. 'What's it about?'

She lay the letter down with a self-satisfied look on her face. 'Well, apparently, there's been a full investigation into the reasons for my suspension, and I have been fully cleared of any wrongdoing.'

'Good.' He nodded.

'It then goes on to say that my job is available for me whenever I wish to return, at the same branch, which now has a new manager as Mr Baker has sought employment elsewhere.'

Elena's head tilted to one side, and her eyebrows floated high above her suspecting eyes, which were firmly fixed on Conrad.

'What?' There was a slight curve to his lips as he spoke.

'You didn't have anything to do with this, did you, Mr Bailey?'

'You were innocent of any wrongdoing, weren't you?'

'Well, yes.'

Now his face carried the self-satisfied look. 'There you go then.' He shrugged with a wink.

Everything had fallen into place nicely. Elena had informed the police that they were absconding. She had been asked to delay their travel plans until the investigation was over, to which she had replied, 'You can call me,' and had given her mobile number. Alan Saunders wasn't taking up any more of her life.

They had also been to see her mother to tell her of their immediate plans. Elena was worried about what sort of reception they may get, but within five minutes of meeting Conrad, her mother disappeared upstairs and came down in full makeup and was utterly charming to him the whole time they were there, which in turn earned her an invitation from Conrad to visit them once they were settled. And with Olivia agreeing to sign divorce papers, things couldn't have been better.

Elena checked her watch. It was almost time to go. She went upstairs to find Conrad.

The nursery door was open. He stood with his back to her and was gazing upon the lifeless room.

'Conrad?'

He turned to face her and was holding the cream floppy-eared rabbit.

'Is everything all right?'

He sat the cuddly toy back on the chair next to the window. As he walked over to her, his hand brushed lovingly along the cot. He kissed her on the lips.

'Everything's just fine, sweetheart.'

'No more tears, eh?' The tips of her fingers skimmed his neck.

'No.' He smiled unconvincingly. 'You go on down. I'm coming now.'

Elena respected his wishes. As she got to the top of the staircase, she heard his voice break as he said, 'Love you, son,' and closed the nursery door. The affinity between them was so strong, and his sorrow rolled down her cheeks as she descended the stairs.

Elena tidied the kitchen side, and Conrad bounced in, back to his usual self with a big clap of his hands. 'Ready?'

'Yes,' she beamed.

'Excited?'

'Yes, yes, yes!'

'Well, madam,' he said in a silly French accent, 'let me take you away from all of dis.'

She giggled away like a love-sick teenager. God she loved him.

Conrad wanted to drive them to the airport. Isabelle had been instructed to pick up the Range Rover personally, where, to her surprise, she would find the registration documents in her name. It was his thank-you to her for all her hard work and loyalty.

Elena stood arm in arm with him outside as they admired the noble structure.

'I love this house.' His head moved left to right as he took it all in. His gaze dropped down to Elena. 'But I love you more. Come on, let's go.'

Elena had been worried about the move, and now she felt silly. Conrad was walking away from such a lot: a very successful business that he had spent years building, a beautiful home, good friends. She could see why he called it his big plan. It certainly was a big gamble.

She sat in silence and watched the trees fly past in a blur as they drove to the airport. Everything had turned out perfectly, but there was one thing that had been bothering her.

'Conrad?'

'Yeah?' He glanced over to her. 'What's wrong, sweetheart?'

'I'm sorry, have we got time for me to go and see Jasmine?'

His eyes left the road to read the clock on the dashboard. 'Yeah, of course, we have.'

Elena's mouth dried at the thought of seeing Jasmine, but she had to. Otherwise, it would haunt her.

CHAPTER TWENTY SEVEN

They pulled up at the gates, and Conrad pressed the intercom to Jasmine's apartment block. No answer. He tried again. Still no reply.

'Maybe she's out.'

As soon as he spoke, Jasmine answered, not with 'hello' or 'who is it?' but a simple 'Elena?' Had she been waiting for her all this time?

They decided it would be better if Conrad waited in the car. He told her to take her time, but Elena knew she hadn't got long.

The short ride in the elevator was awful. Her breathing lost its rhythm, and she was huffing and puffing like she'd been for a run. The doors retreated into the walls, and Elena stepped out and tried to gain control of her mini-panic attack; Jasmine had left the door open for her.

Her head thumped, along with her heartbeat, as she entered the apartment.

'Hello? Jasmine?'

'I'm in the lounge.' Her voice was flat.

I don't want to do this.

Elena entered the open-plan lounge. Jasmine sat with

her legs tucked under her, holding a glass of wine. She was wearing black leggings and a baggy purple jumper, her hair was tied up, and she had no makeup on. There wasn't a hint of glamour. The place was bare, apart from the lounge suite Jasmine sat on.

'I've been waiting for you all week. Where have you been?

She had the expression of a worried parent, and Elena didn't quite know how to take the question. 'Er, I've . . .' She didn't know what to say. What could she say—I've been helping my boyfriend recover from your fucked-up father's attempt to kill him?

'What's going on, Jaz?' Elena gestured to the empty room. It was a temporary delay of the impending topic of conversation.

'I'm moving out, well, to be more precise, I'm being kicked out.'

'Why?' Elena stood as she hadn't been invited to sit down.

'Because . . .' Jasmine bit her bottom lip. 'I told Marcus about the baby.' Each word rose an octave as she struggled to finish the sentence. 'And he offered me £200,000 to get rid of it and never see him again.' She cleared her throat and wiped away the tears with the back of her hand. Elena sat next to her and rubbed her thigh.

'How fucking dare he? All this time, I thought I was special, like I mattered.' Anger and tears exposed themselves. 'How wrong was I? It turns out I was just a rich man's plaything after all. Bastard!'

The more Elena tried to think of something to say, the more she drew a blank.

'In case you hadn't guessed, I told him to go fuck himself and stick the money up his arse. What must he have thought of me? To think that I would kill my baby for money!'

Elena had never seen her like this. She was totally devastated.

'And now Dad's gone. He would have been so excited about being a granddad.'

She wasn't responsible for any of this, but Elena couldn't help feeling guilty somehow.

'I'm sorry, Jaz.' She wondered if it was the right thing to say. Sorry was something you said when you stepped on someone's foot. It didn't really meet the criteria.

Jasmine turned and looked her in the face for the first time. Her usually perfect dark olive skin was pasty and blotchy, the big brown eyes inflamed from constant crying.

'Shouldn't it be me saying sorry?'

Elena broke their gaze. She felt awkward, especially as she was dressed for a first-class plane trip halfway around the world. They sat in uncomfortable silence. Jasmine hung her head low.

'Did he really do all those things?' Her stare was fixed on the floor.

'Yes . . . he did.'

Jasmine got up and placed her half-empty wine glass on the fireplace. 'This is all my fault.'

'It's nobody's fault, Jaz.'

'Of course, it is. If I hadn't persuaded you to join that fucking website, none of this would have happened, none of it. And Dad would still be alive now.' Her head tipped right back, and her shoulders bounced up and down as she sobbed.

Elena hated seeing her like this. She stood and held her arms out. The invitation was accepted, and they held on to each other like it was the end of the world. Just for a moment, the close connection they once had was there, briefly allowing them both to say their silent apologies to each other. Elena broke their clinch and held her by the shoulders.

'Your dad loved you very much. You were everything to him.'

Jasmine's chin trembled. 'Did he know about me—what I do . . . did?'

'No, he didn't.'

'You never told him?' She seemed to search Elena's face for an honest answer.

Elena made sure she looked her in the eyes as she answered, 'Of course not.'

'Thank you,' she whispered. Her demeanour was a mixture of embarrassment and humbleness.

'What's next, Jaz?'

'I'm moving in with Mum. She's not good at the moment. I haven't told her about the baby yet. I think I'll wait awhile. I'm also taking over Dad's business, not sure exactly how it's going to work out, but there's no way I'm letting the scavengers pick away at all the contracts Dad worked so hard for.' Jasmine reached for her glass of wine and drank it all in one go. She seemed agitated. 'He left it at the top, and that's where it's fucking staying.'

Elena had never seen Alan in her before. Yes, there was a resemblance with the dark hair and eyes, but she had just seen a glimpse of his obsessiveness.

Jasmine would probably do what a lot of people seemed to when a parent died: they took on the personality traits that once annoyed them as a way of keeping them alive in some way.

'I think you've made the right choice.'

'Yes, so do I.'

Jasmine hadn't asked how Elena or Conrad were, not because she was selfish. Elena thought it was more to do with having to face what her father was responsible for. Elena tried to sneak a look at her watch. She couldn't stay much longer.

'Jaz, I've got to go.'

'So soon?'

'I'm going away. My flight's this afternoon.'

'Oh, you deserve a break. Maybe . . . we could meet up for a coffee when you get back?' Elena broke eye contact and played with her fingers anxiously. 'I'll understand if you're busy. It's fine.' Jasmine was quick to offer an excuse.

'No, it's not that. Conrad's moving to New Zealand, and he's asked me to go with him.'

'Oh.' Jasmine's face went blank, and she held her head perfectly still like she was in a trance. Her long black lashes desperately clung on to a single tear, which was set free with the blink of her eyes. She lowered her head and nodded. There was no way they could remain friends as much as they both wanted to. The ghost of Alan would always be there. It was there right now.

'It's a bit far to go for a coffee, isn't it?' Jasmine tried to lighten the mood.

Elena nodded with a faint smile.

'You know, when I first bumped into you, I felt sorry for you. I thought I had everything just right and you needed my help.' She shook her head. 'How wrong could I be?'

Jasmine had helped. Even though the last few weeks had been a living nightmare at times, it had led her to Conrad and, tragically for Jasmine, her father's death.

'I'd better go.'

Unnerving as it was walking into Jasmine's apartment, it was worse having to leave.

'Yeah, you go. I don't want you missing your flight. I'll walk you out.'

They headed to the door in silence. Elena stepped into the lobby and turned to face Jasmine who wiped her eyes with her fingers. They didn't speak but threw their arms around each other. They both sighed at the same time.

As they separated, the uneasy atmosphere wasted no time and jumped straight back in between them.

'Good luck,' croaked Jasmine.

'Take care, Jaz.'

Elena called the lift which was mercifully quick. She stepped inside the mirrored box and took one last look at Jasmine.

'Elena,' she called, 'be happy.' Elena nodded as she

squeezed her lips together, unable to speak.

The doors quietly closed on a girl she used to know.

Elena spent a moment in the entrance lobby and blotted her face with tissue before going back to the car.

She climbed back into her elevated seat next to Conrad. He turned down the music he was listening to.

'How did it go?'

Emotion still obstructed her throat, and she nodded to him as she clicked her safety belt in. Conrad gave her thigh a gentle squeeze and drove them away, respectfully silent as he let Elena mourn her lost friendship.

Finishing her spritzer, they left the first-class departure lounge, which was more like a Mayfair wine bar than airport hospitality. She buzzed with excitement as they walked hand in hand through the passenger loading bridge. The low powerful hum of the engines increased as they approached the entrance.

This is it!

They stepped inside the plane and a statuesque blond lady, with lips as red as her British Airways scarf, greeted them warmly. Conrad handed over the tickets. She addressed them both by name and directed them to the neon-lit staircase. Elena couldn't believe she was flying first class; she didn't even send her post by first class. At the top of the stairs, another goddess in uniform escorted them to their seats in an island in the centre of the cabin, which looked like an open-topped cocoon.

Elena sank into the luxurious navy-and-cream leather chair. Conrad sat next to her. A low dividing screen sat between them, everything was impeccable, and the smell of coffee and expensive perfume filled the compact space.

'Will this do, madam?'

'Oh yes, Conrad.'

He adjusted his seat and looked across at her. Was this too good to be true? He looked so handsome in his crisp white shirt and light grey V-neck sweater. He was every bit first class.

'Thank you.'

She didn't mean the air travel. It was so hard to find someone decent and honest in this world. People were unreliable and often went back on their word, not just men but friends, people you worked with, even parents. Elena had found the anomaly. He valued loyalty, and in return, he would give his.

'Elena, you don't have to thank me. I intend to spend however long it takes erasing all the bad memories you've been left with.'

She would never forget. She didn't want to. Sometimes from the greatest pain was born the greatest pleasure.

Elena got up and knelt on her chair. She leaned over the small divider and kissed his lips, a kiss of pure, unbreakable, unconditional love.

'Thank *you,* sweetheart,' he whispered sincerely.

An elegantly dressed grey-haired lady in the seat opposite gave Elena a knowing smile and returned to her book. She slipped back into her chair, and Conrad ordered champagne for them.

'Ladies and gentlemen, this is your captain speaking. On behalf of the flight crew, I'd like to welcome you on board British Airways' flight BA 0207 to Los Angeles . . .'

She jumped up in her chair. 'Conrad!' He was thumbing through the in-flight magazine. 'We're on the wrong flight. This one's going to Los Angeles.'

The air hostess came back with their champagne. He handed a glass to Elena.

'It's a long way to New Zealand, so I thought we could have a stopover for a week, do some shopping, see the sights.'

She had no control over her face whatsoever as it burst into a mad grin, and she clapped her hands quickly. 'Any more surprises I should be aware of?'

'There'll be plenty of surprises, sweetheart.'

He held up the bubbly golden glass. 'To new

beginnings.'

Elena sipped her champagne, blown away by it all.

'You do know these seats turn into a bed?' He had a mischievous glint in his eye.

'Mr Bailey, whatever are you suggesting?'

'I've always wanted to join the Mile High Club.'

Elena turned her body to face him. 'Well, maybe I can surprise you for a change.' She winked.

As the plane left UK soil, Elena felt complete contentment. She didn't know what lay ahead, but so long as the man she loved was by her side, she was ready to take on any adventure.

ACKNOWLEDGEMENTS

This book has been a real labour of love for me. It has consumed my every thought and taken on an importance I can't quite explain.

I would like to thank a few people who have helped me along the way.

First, to the team at dictate2us, for their editorial advice.

To Veronika Fabisiak of FAB Design + Marketing for creating the wonderful cover, and for much, much more. You have truly gone above and beyond.

To Bethan Blackwell, Emma Whitehouse, and Dawn Blower, three lovely ladies who read the book as I wrote it. Thank you for your encouragement and constant demands for more!

Special thanks also to all the gorgeous ladies on Facebook, especially those who test-read for me. Your kind, enthusiastic words are like petrol to my writing engine!

Jo, the writing goddess, thanks for your golden nuggets of advice!

I couldn't have done this without the unwavering support of my family. Thank you all for never doubting me.

And finally, a huge thank-you to you, the reader, for your precious time. I sincerely hope I have succeeded in entertaining you for a few hours . . . Maybe we could lose ourselves in another adventure sometime?

GET IN TOUCH WITH G.G. CARVER
Facebook: G. G. Carver – facebook.com/ggcarver
Twitter: @ggcarver

Printed in Great Britain
by Amazon.co.uk, Ltd.,
Marston Gate.